R. Barri Flowers is an award-winning author of crime, thriller, mystery and romance fiction featuring three-dimensional protagonists, riveting plots, unexpected twists and turns and heart-pounding climaxes. With an expertise in true crime, serial killers and characterising dangerous offenders, he is perfectly suited for the Mills & Boon Heroes line. Chemistry and conflict between the hero and heroine, attention to detail and incorporating the very latest advances in criminal investigations are the cornerstones of his romantic suspense fiction. Discover more on popular social networks and Wikipedia.

Lara Lacombe earned a PhD in mi_____ and immunology and worked i_____ the country before mov_____ job as a college scienc_____ue her other love—wr_____e with smart, nerdy h_____ve heroes. She loves to _____ ner on the web or contact her at _____ewriter@gmail.com

CHASING THE VIOLET KILLER

R. BARRI FLOWERS

PROVING COLTON'S INNOCENCE

LARA LACOMBE

MILLS & BOON

First Published in Great Britain 2021
by Mills & Boon, an imprint of HarperCollins*Publishers* Ltd
1 London Bridge Street, London, SE1 9GF

www.harpercollins.co.uk

HarperCollins*Publishers*
1st Floor, Watermarque Building,
Ringsend Road, Dublin 4, Ireland

Chasing the Violet Killer © 2021 R. Barri Flowers
Proving Colton's Innocence © 2021 Harlequin Books S.A.

Special thanks and acknowledgement are given to Lara Lacombe for her contribution to *The Coltons of Grave Gulch* series.

ISBN: 978-0-263-28367-9

1221

CHASING THE
VIOLET KILLER

R. BARRI FLOWERS

In memory of my beloved mom, Marjah Aljean, who inspired me to be my best and was a longtime fan of Mills & Boon romances. To Loraine, the love of my life, who has never allowed me to stop believing in myself, and to the many fans of my romance, mystery and thriller fiction over the years. Lastly, a nod goes out to editors Allison Lyons and Denise Zaza for the opportunity to lend my voice and creative spirit to the Intrigue line.

Prologue

They had become far too predictable. The nice-looking, shapely young women would leave themselves open to whatever—or whoever—came their way, as if they had not a care or concern in the world. Whether it was jogging for no good reason, walking by their lonesome in the dead, dark of night, being utterly lackadaisical in an unattended parking garage, stupidly leaving a car unlocked, a window open or other avoidable means of vulnerability, they were ripe for the picking, like a perfect and delicious red apple. Or even a green one—that worked for him, too. It made his mission almost too easy for someone who liked challenges. Not that he had anything against hardly having to work to satisfy his cravings, per se. Why should he care if the pretty, sexy ones fell right into his trap like enticing lambs to the slaughter? Wasn't that what every sensible and eager serial killer dreamed of?

He broke free of his admittedly dark reverie, recognizing that the moment at hand was quickly approaching. It wouldn't be very smart if his own overconfidence and, frankly, lack of scruples cost him another victim to add to his lovely collection of violets. There she was. Just like clockwork. Ticktock. Ticktock. He remained hidden and motionless in the shadows, watching excitedly as she tied her long and curly raven hair in a ponytail, adjusted her earbuds and set off running in colorful designer jogging attire. On the surface, the wooded area full of Douglas firs and Western white pines seemed safe enough, even during twilight hours, with lamps giving off just enough light and other runners to pass by for a sense of security. He assumed that was the runner's calculus, false as it was. Perhaps she planned to meet her husband or boyfriend afterward for dinner and sex or whatever. Or maybe she would settle for a nice hot shower and good night's sleep, before starting the boring work grind all over again tomorrow.

Unfortunately, she would never live to see another day. Or even an hour. She had seen to that herself. She was like a cornered and helpless rat, and it was time to take out of its misery by going in for the kill. Anticipating her every move like a champion chess player who had an aversion to losing, he was faster and smarter, enabling him to beat her to the point where she would normally have veered off to the left and another, more active jogging trail.

Instead, he was waiting for her there, flexing an expensive silk scarf as a prelude to what was coming. The terrified look on her pretty face and in those big, brown eyes was almost worth the satisfaction welling within him like a furnace ready to erupt. Almost. It wasn't till she tried halfheartedly in a moment of desperation to escape the trap that he had set that he cut her off and made sure her attempt fell like a flattened tire. Before any screams could erupt from her full mouth, he had already wrapped the scarf around her neck, twisting and tightening with pleasure in silencing her till her last breath was expended. Only then could he breathe a sigh of relief that he had succeeded in killing once again.

As the victim sank down to the ground, he pulled out

a single blue violet and stuck it between her lips that had remained parted even in death, as if welcoming his going-away-from-life present.

Chapter One

"We just got a report of a man being shot at an office building on Seventeenth and Bedford," the 911 dispatcher said tensely. "The victim has been identified as Roger Lincoln…"

Detective Dylan Hester's heart sank into his stomach as the name smacked him like a solid punch in the gut. Roger Lincoln was a former homicide detective for the Pebble Creek Police Department in the quaint Oregon town eighty-five miles south of Portland. Dylan canceled plans to stop by Lesley's Restaurant on Crome Street for a slice of homemade apple pie in lieu of lunch, and immediately headed straight to the scene—unsure if it was a crime, accident, suicide or attempted suicide. He hated to think any was the case, all things considered. A criminal act of violence would certainly be a hard pill to swallow. Especially at this stage of the game for the retiree. An accidental shooting of himself, as someone experienced with firearms, was hard to fathom. But wanting to check out on his own terms was no less painful to contemplate. Yet, for one reason or another, the man had shockingly been a victim of gunfire…

"I'm just two blocks away, Lily," Dylan told the dispatcher, ill at ease, hoping against hope that they weren't dealing with a fatality here.

Roger Lincoln had been his partner, mentor and good friend. He'd been someone Dylan had continued to rely on for advice even after Roger's sudden retirement last year at the relatively young age of fifty-eight. When his bad back made it impossible to do his job effectively, rather than take a desk job stacking papers, as someone who loved being out in the field as an investigator, Roger chose to walk away with his pension and pride intact after nearly thirty years on the force. He had remained connected to the department as a consultant on the Violet Killer case. A serial killer was strangling attractive young women, disturbingly leaving a single blue violet in their mouths as his calling card.

The case had been laid squarely on Dylan's lap as the youngest but most accomplished member of the homicide unit, at thirty-three years of age. A decorated veteran and former member of the US Army Special Operations force, he'd served in Afghanistan and Iraq, and had a bachelor's degree in criminal justice and master's in criminology. Not that professional and educational achievement or persistence had done him much good as yet in tracking down the cunning killer. Thus far, he had murdered seven local women over two short years—the latest victim just two days ago—in various locations and remained elusive as ever, in spite of the painstaking efforts of the Pebble Creek PD, working in conjunction with the Federal Bureau of Investigation, Oregon State Police and Blane County Sheriff's Department to identity the perpetrator and bring him to justice for his crimes. Could Roger, who had made no secret of his desire to get the Violet Killer as his going-away present to the department and doing right by the victims and the loved ones they left behind, have homed in on the killer's identity, thereby making him a threat that needed to be neutralized?

Dylan swallowed that chilling thought and asked Lily, "Who reported the incident?"

"The caller identified herself as the victim's niece, Naomi Lincoln. Apparently, she was having a video chat on the computer with him when the shooting occurred—"

That unexpected revelation threw Dylan for a loop, leaving him even more unsettled and causing the car to jerk toward oncoming traffic before he managed to regain control. Naomi Lincoln. He could only imagine the horror of what she must have witnessed before her very eyes. The name rang in his head as though surrounded by flashing lights, spurring a wave of emotions in Dylan, as someone he had tried hard to forget, failing miserably in that impossible endeavor. Naomi Rachel Lincoln happened to be his ex-girlfriend and almost fiancée, who had stunningly and inexplicably tossed aside what he'd thought was a love match made in Pebble Creek, if not heaven and earth, in favor of joining the US Secret Service two years ago. It broke his heart in more places than one, not to mention his spirit, when she told him the opportunity was simply too much to pass up. Even if it meant ending their relationship then and there. She did just that, without apparently much hesitation or looking back once she was fast out the door, leaving him high and dry.

Rather than try to talk her out of it—not sure he could have, even with what he considered pretty damned good powers of persuasion, given her own stubbornness and strong determination—Dylan did what he thought was the honorable thing, if not the most foolish, as a man who'd fallen in love with the biracial and shapely beauty who had him tied up in knots. He took a step back, maybe a few steps, wished her well and tried to get on with his life, hard as it would be without her in it. But pretending she didn't exist at all—a herculean task—was never in the cards. Through Roger, he'd kept tabs on Naomi and her burgeoning career in Miami. By all accounts, she was truly in her element as a Secret Service special agent, assigned to the investigation detail in building upon her previous career with the county as a crime victims service coordinator. But Roger had been quick to point out, whether Dylan wanted to hear it or not, that she wasn't seeing anyone seriously as far as he knew, as if to leave that window open for them to someday get back together.

Even if a small part of him found much appeal in that possibility, Dylan didn't see that happening, as too much time had passed and neither seemed willing to give up the lives they had carefully constructed like a well-built fortress on opposite sides of the country. He wouldn't ask or expect her to do what he wasn't willing to do himself. Some things simply weren't meant to be. He was sure this was one of them.

He pulled his unmarked dark-colored vehicle into the parking lot on Bedford Avenue of the three-story brick building that housed Roger's office. A squad car, its lights flashing, and a detective's cruiser were already at the scene. Dylan could hear the siren of an ambulance approaching. He raced inside and ran up one flight of stairs and down a long hall, turning to the right at the end, with a shorter hall that led to the second-floor office he'd visited several times since Roger set up his private detective and consultant agency, Lincoln Investigations.

An officer was standing guard at the door, looking grim. Dylan showed his identification. His deep molten-gray eyes rose over the officer's wide shoulders and spotted the detective inside. Apparently, they weren't dealing with an active gunman still on the scene to prevent Roger from getting treatment. But there may have been more than one victim.

"How many people are injured?" Dylan asked the officer just to be sure.

"Just one," he said tonelessly.

"Still one too many," Dylan grumbled, as knots churned in his stomach, which often happened when he had a bad feeling about something.

He stepped inside the midsized office, cluttered with folders on top of folders Dylan knew were files on national cold cases Roger consulted on or hoped to. There was a double-hung window overlooking the street. Careful not to contaminate what may be a crime scene as he walked across vinyl composite tile flooring, Dylan sidestepped potential evidence and was met halfway by his friend and colleague Detective Gregory Hwang.

"Hey," he said, his voice level. "Just beat you here."

"What have we got?" Dylan asked routinely, though knowing this was anything but routine. He glanced over at Roger Lincoln, who was sitting motionless in a highbacked ergonomic leather chair. His upper body was slumped over one side of an L-shaped wooden desk as if he had fallen asleep. Something told Dylan that he wasn't waking up anytime soon. If ever.

Hwang, a thinly built, seven-year veteran with short black hair and a heavy-stubble beard, was South Korea born, pushing forty and a single father of twin eight-year-old girls. He had been on the Violet Killer case from the start. Furrowing his forehead in three places presently, he confirmed Dylan's worst fears when he said, "There's no other way to say this, Dylan… Lincoln's gone…"

Dylan offered no response, though he was certain his dour expression said it all. How could this have happened? Did he really want to know? No, he needed to. He approached the desk and got a closer look. Roger's head lay in a pool of his own blood, soaking into thinning gray hair that was raggedly swept to one side. There was what looked to be a massive gunshot wound to his temple, marring the hardened, contorted features of his dark-skinned face. If he had to make a guess, based on his knowledge of firearms and their capabilities, Dylan would bet that the weapon used was a .45 ACP pistol. It appeared that a single shot was fired at point-blank range.

"Any sign of the firearm?" Dylan asked, while gazing at the blood-splattered floor around the desk.

"Not yet." Hwang flexed one of his hands covered by a nitrile glove. "I'm pretty sure we're not looking at a suicide here, if that's what you're thinking."

"I wasn't." Dylan knew for a fact that, since retiring, Roger favored a Ruger Blackhawk .44 Magnum revolver as his weapon of choice. This meant that the killer most likely used his or her own weapon to commit the crime. "Whoever did this was obviously smart enough not to leave the gun just lying around." Seeing no sign of Roger's weapon, Dylan figured the killer took it, too.

Even with the stark reality that this was murder, Dylan felt somewhat relieved that they weren't looking at a suicide, knowing Roger as he did. His differences with Naomi aside, Dylan wouldn't have wanted her to have to deal with such a crushing blow of Roger dying by his own hand. Not that the cold-blooded murder of Naomi's uncle would be any easier for her to deal with.

"Could we be looking at an attempted or completed robbery?" Hwang asked, not sounding as if he believed this.

"I doubt it. Robbers don't usually expect to find a pot of gold in a private detective's office." Dylan pinched his nose thoughtfully. "No, this was personal." Just how personal, he wasn't quite sure yet, but he had his suspicions.

Hwang cocked a brow. "You think it had something to do with a case he was working on?"

"That's what we need to find out," Dylan said, remaining noncommittal for the time being. "Better get the crime scene unit in here," he muttered bleakly.

"They're on their way, even as we speak," Hwang pointed out expectantly. "Whatever went down in this office and for whatever reason, Roger Lincoln didn't deserve to die this way. He was one of us and we'll do it by the book in solving this case as quickly as possible."

Dylan nodded, knowing the detective was just as up to the task as he was in dealing with a violent criminal act that needed to be properly investigated till its closure. Out of the corner of his eye, Dylan spotted something shiny beneath Roger's desk. Donning a pair of nitrile gloves, he bent down and grabbed it. It was a shell casing. Gazing at the manufacturer's marking, he saw that it corresponded with his estimate on the type of weapon used to shoot Roger. Holding up the spent casing, Dylan said, "Looks like the shooter left something behind after all."

"Sloppy," Hwang expressed, pleased, while presenting an evidence bag for Dylan to drop the casing into.

He did just that, while imagining the horrific moment of impact for Roger. "Either that, or the perp just didn't give a damn, figuring we wouldn't know what to do with it."

Hwang sneered. "Let him keep thinking that."

"We need to know who's come in and out of this building in the past hour," Dylan told the detective. "Hopefully, there are security cameras that can help us pinpoint Lincoln's killer, giving us the tools to fill in the blanks of identifying the perp."

Hwang concurred. "I spotted at least one surveillance camera when I came in. Apart from that, there seemed to be plenty of other people entering and exiting the building during the lunch hour, besides the killer. Chances are one or more saw something...or someone suspicious..."

"Maybe," Dylan said, having reservations about just how quickly they could solve this case. Most people simply weren't that observant when it came to paying attention to those around them. A clever perp could practically introduce him or herself to unsuspecting passersby and still not stand out. Dylan hoped that wasn't the case here, but he wasn't holding his breath on that front. He looked at an empty spot in the center of the desk where Roger's laptop had been, judging by the dust that formed a perfect rectangle. Had the killer stolen the computer? If so, why? Was something incriminating on it that might lead right to the perp's proverbial front door?

"Yeah, I noticed the laptop was missing, too," Hwang said, jutting his chin. "Looks like Roger's cell phone has also vanished. Pretty suspicious, huh?"

"It's much more than that," Dylan told him regrettably. "Roger was apparently video chatting on the laptop with Naomi when he was shot—"

"Seriously?" Hwang's jaw dropped with disbelief. "Sorry about that, man." He paused. "Have you talked to her about it?" Hwang was aware of his history with Roger's niece and that she was the adored child Roger never had, as well as someone who had worked with the police department in her former capacity.

"Not yet." Dylan drew a ragged breath. "I wanted to get more information before I called her." It wasn't a conversation he was particularly looking forward to, no matter the way things ended between them, but one that had to be done.

"Do what you need to do," Hwang said understandingly, "difficult as it will be. I can handle things here till the medical examiner and forensic team arrive."

"Thanks." Dylan shifted the weight of his tall, firm frame from one foot to the other, while pondering the possibility that Naomi may have critical information on the shooting, beyond the lethal act itself. Did Roger say anything to her that could have led to his death? Did she see or hear the shooter? Did the perp see her on the laptop screen? Whichever scenario Dylan played in his mind, it rattled him. The last thing he wanted was for Naomi to not only be a witness to murder but also be in potential danger herself. Though she was presumably still safely away in Miami, something told him that wouldn't be for long. Even if it was too late to save Roger, she would undoubtedly be returning to Pebble Creek to bury her uncle. Dylan was pretty sure there was nothing he could do or say to make Naomi stay put while the investigation into his death was underway, whether he wanted that or not.

He peered at Roger's disfigured face, or more specifically, at his lips that had turned wickedly purple. They were slightly open with blood spilling out of a corner. There seemed to be something inside the mouth. Still wearing the nitrile gloves, Dylan carefully parted Roger's lips and pulled out a saliva-moistened and bloodied violet.

"I'VE GOT A rock-solid lead on the so-called Violet Killer that has dogged me since retirement..." were the last words Secret Service Special Agent Naomi Lincoln's uncle, Roger Lincoln, uttered before she heard what sounded like a gunshot. Aghast, she watched him keel over as blood gushed from a gaping wound on the side of his head. A shadowy figure moved behind him, staying just out of view on the small screen of her laptop, before it went totally black.

In spite of being overwhelmed with emotion, while feeling utterly helpless to the moment at hand, Naomi had immediately called 911 to report the crime. Though she prayed that her uncle could somehow survive the atrocious and cowardly attack, she feared it was too late to save him. Before her very horror-struck, bold hazel eyes, someone—maybe this Violet Killer—had attacked the man who had raised her alone since she was ten years old after losing his brother, Milton, who was Naomi's father, and her mother, Paula, in a terrible head-on car collision. That was twenty years ago. Now, at thirty and an only child, Naomi was faced with the real possibility of having no more family she could lean on and give the same solid support in return.

It was this frightening prospect that weighed heavily on her mind as Naomi stood barefoot on the cold cherry micro-beveled hardwood flooring in the sunken living room of her downtown Miami, Florida, apartment. She shared the place with fellow Secret Service agent Sophia Menendez, currently on assignment out of state. Naomi turned her thoughts back to the serial killer who had terrorized Pebble Creek over the last two years. She hadn't kept up much with the case, other than knowing that a madman in the vein of the Boston or Hillside Stranglers was strangling to death local women and leaving a violet behind, while apparently taunting the authorities and daring them to stop him. When her uncle had retired, Dylan Hester had been assigned as lead investigator of the case. Last she knew, the killer was still very much at large. Had he changed his MO and gone after the man who was the closest thing she had to a father for two decades?

Naomi looked at the cell phone chiming in her hand.

The caller ID identified the person requesting a video chat as none other than Dylan himself. A quiver shot through her as thoughts about him flooded her head. He was once the love and lover of her life and someone she'd envisioned a real future with, where the commitment to each other stood the test of time and with it came children to cement their bond. But something happened that threw her fantasies entirely out of whack. Or at least those pertaining to Dylan. A remarkable opportunity arose two years ago to join the United States Secret Service. All things considered, professionally speaking, it was an opportunity she could not turn her back on, hard as it was on her personal and romantic life. It would enable her to take a few giant steps toward using her knowledge on crime victims to foster a career in which she was able to go after those who would seek to victimize others through money laundering, counterfeiting and financial institution fraud, among other serious crimes. Now she had to wonder if she could do it over, would she? Naomi closed her eyes for a moment while considering this, before opening them. The answer was yes, even though with a heavy heart. The truth was that while her uncle Roger took Dylan under his wing, allowing his life in law enforcement to take off, her own career choices were limited at best had she stayed in Pebble Creek. Her uncle wisely recognized this and—though he understood it would likely mean an end to her involvement with Dylan, given the long-distance relationship neither she nor Dylan wanted—encouraged Naomi to pursue other paths to the success she deserved and her parents would have approved of, which she did. The painful trade-off was that it meant sacrificing her love life, not knowing if she would ever meet the likes of a Dylan Hester again. Or if she would even try.

Naomi hesitated to answer the phone, knowing what came next would rock her world, one way or another. She wiped tears from her golden-complexioned high cheeks, courtesy of the genetics of a white mother and African American father. Accepting the call, she saw Dylan's face appear. "Hey…" she uttered nervously.

"Hey." The timbre of his voice was still as richly deep and soothing as Naomi remembered. Her ex-boyfriend's ruggedly handsome, well-defined features had also changed little since she last saw him. His raven hair was in a newer square cut bordering an oblong face that was clean-shaven, but the gray eyes with flecks of brown and gold were just as intense as before.

Naomi trained her eyes on him, eager for information, knowing the nature of the first direct communication between them in over a year. Her heart raced. "Is my uncle Roger—" Her voice broke, unable to complete the question.

Dylan's forehead furrowed. "Roger didn't make it," he voiced sadly, while being direct. "I'm so sorry, Naomi."

Even suspecting as much before hearing the words, the pain of confirming her worst fears wasn't any less throbbing. Her knees wobbled, but she resisted sitting down. "Did you get the person responsible?" The query made it clear that she knew this was cold-blooded murder and not a self-inflicted gunshot fatality. Her uncle—who had never married, choosing his career over being in a committed relationship—loved life as much as he could. Even in retirement, with a bad back and a little crankiness, he would never have considered taking such a terrible course of action, to leave her to remember him in that awful way.

Dylan's eyes lowered lamentably. "As yet, we have no one in custody in connection with Roger's death."

Naomi wrinkled her dainty nose with disappointment. "Why would someone kill Uncle Roger…?" She had her thoughts about the matter, but would hold on to those for now, till she got the official read on the investigation.

"I was hoping you could shed more light on that," Dylan said tentatively. "I realize that this is a bad time— the absolute worst—but the more we know and the quicker we know it, the more we have to work with in apprehending the killer as soon as possible." He paused. "I understand that you were video chatting with Roger when the incident occurred…?"

Incident? That almost made it sound like a slight disagreement between neighbors. Or perhaps a confrontation at school that went nowhere. This was no incident, but rather a horrid act of brutality.

Naomi nodded with a heavy sigh, then ran a small hand through her long brunette hair, styled in a shaggy fringe. "We talked mostly about me," she admitted, before the hard part came. "He was always checking up on me, seeing what I was up to. If I needed anything. It was our way of staying connected…" She swallowed and her lower lip shook. "Then he started to talk about the Violet Killer and a lead he'd developed on the person."

Devon pursed his lips. "Did he give you the name of a suspect?"

"Never got the chance before…" The words stuck in her throat like a chicken bone and Naomi forced herself to keep from crying again, needing to be strong to get through this.

"Did Roger happen to send you any information he'd gathered on the case?"

"No. He said he wanted to keep me out of it for the most part." Naomi now wished he had been more forthcoming and she had pressed for more—maybe it might have made a difference—before it was too late. She peered at Dylan's face on the small screen, sensing he was holding something back. What was he not saying? "Why do you ask?"

Dylan scratched his jaw. "Roger's laptop is missing. We think that whoever killed him took it, along with any possible damaging evidence it may have held."

She batted her curly lashes before narrowing her eyes at him. "So, you believe my uncle was the victim of the Violet Killer?"

"Too early to say," Dylan contended ambiguously. "At this point, we're keeping all options on the table as we investigate what happened."

Reading between the not-so-thick lines, Naomi concluded in her own mind that this serial killer was the key suspect—if not the only one. Especially when coupled with her uncle's cryptic final words. It sent a chill down her spine.

"So, I assume you're coming to the funeral?" Dylan asked, smoothing one of his thick brows.

"Do you even have to ask?" Her eyes grew hotly. "Uncle Roger was the only family I had left…"

"I know." Dylan's shoulders slumped. "Okay, it was a dumb question. Guess I just figured that maybe with your work schedule, it wouldn't permit you the time to break away."

"Seriously?" Her lower lip hung incredulously as he seemed to be digging himself an even deeper tunnel. Was this his way of knocking the Secret Service? Or her for leaving Pebble Creek and him behind? Neither set well with her at the moment. This wasn't about her or them. "I think I'm allowed to attend funerals of loved ones," she said tartly. "Of course I'm coming to Uncle Roger's funeral!"

"Understood." Dylan's voice dropped an apologetic octave. "Let me know when your flight is scheduled to arrive and I can pick you up at the airport."

"Don't do me any favors," she tossed at him sarcastically, still feeling insulted by his insinuation regarding her work and ability to get away. "I'll take an Uber, thank you."

He jutted his chin. "Have it your way."

"I have to go," Naomi said hurriedly, before either said anything else they might regret. Or had they already said pretty much all there was to say of consequence?

"Fine." He lowered a hard gaze, then looked up again, where it seemed to soften. "See you when you get here, unless we somehow manage to avoid each other until the funeral."

She refused to let him bait her into a cynical response. Or did he not want to see her during the trip, as if the memories of what they once had were too painful to separate the man from the detective? If that was the way he felt, far be it for her to object. "Goodbye, Dylan," she said curtly, and hung up.

Afterward, Naomi had second thoughts about the way the call had ended. It was unavoidable that they would cross paths, over and beyond his attendance at the funeral as her uncle's friend and former partner, apart from anything else. In spite of their history, that was then and this was now. Both she and Dylan needed to get past it and act like adults moving forward. At least she intended to, while throwing the ball back squarely into his court.

Naomi went into the peninsula kitchen and poured herself a calming glass of red wine, taking a sip. Admittedly, no matter how adult-like she wanted to handle things with Dylan, she was not looking forward to coming face-to-face again with the man whose heart she broke for all the right reasons. They were certainly right for her at the time, if not him, and she fully understood this. But she saw little chance of dodging Dylan Hester, since he was investigating her uncle's murder and she needed to pay her final respects to him. And there was more to it than that. She had to stick around long enough to make sure that her uncle Roger's killer was brought to justice. Even if that meant bumping heads with her ex. She would just have to deal with any—or all—awkward moments between them as best as possible. Even then, Naomi knew that, where it concerned Dylan, that was much easier said than done.

Chapter Two

Having taken a connecting flight from Portland, Oregon, to Pebble Creek's small but busy airport, Naomi sat in the rear of the Uber, where she took in the sights of the coastal town she grew up in. Not much had changed since her last visit. They passed by cottonwood tree-lined streets with clusters of condominiums, single-family dwellings, small businesses and parks situated throughout. Beyond that were log cabins and farmhouses on rolling hills and forested land. She remembered feeling trapped here, as if the bigger world would somehow pass her by had she not seized the moment when opportunity knocked. How might things have been had she failed to answer the call to improve her life? Would she have forever regretted it? Or gone on a different path where romance and a promising relationship were given a chance to flourish?

Naomi caught a glimpse of the lake where she and Dylan first made love on his friend's boat. The moment was forever etched in her mind, set in stone, and was probably when she realized she had fallen in love with him. It was an experience that shook her entire foundation and made all things seem possible. The truth was, she had never fallen out of love with Dylan. How could what they had have been so easily replaced with another?

Yes, she had tried to move on in the romance department, but hadn't had much luck there, not too surprisingly, as Dylan was a hard act to follow. Given the way things ended between them, Naomi was sure Dylan had found someone else to share his life with and couldn't blame him one bit—even if her uncle had suggested otherwise, giving her hope that there might still be a possibility for them to resume their relationship at some point. But she was a realist. After all, she had never given Dylan any indication that there was any hope of them getting back together. How could she and be fair to him? Or herself?

Maybe that was her mistake. Or maybe this was the way it was meant to be.

The car pulled up in front of the two-story Craftsman-style home on Maple Lane that Naomi had grown up in and always saw as a place to come back to. No matter how far away she went.

"Here we are," said the friendly male driver, peering through the rearview mirror.

She acknowledged as much, before getting out. As she stepped into the mid-August sunlight, the hot air hit Naomi in the face like a gentle slap, without the humidity she had grown used to in Miami. After the tall, sandy-haired driver unloaded her bags from the trunk, she thanked him, having tipped in advance.

"Enjoy your stay," he said routinely.

Naomi gave a slight smile, though recognizing that this was anything but a trip to enjoy in returning to her hometown. She carried her travel bags up the cobblestone walkway, almost expecting her beloved uncle Roger to come out and greet her with a big bear hug, as was his custom. The thought that this would never happen again tugged at her heart emotionally.

For an instant, Naomi froze in her tracks, feeling as

though someone were watching her through an upstairs ornamental window. Was she imagining things? Or had someone broken in, trying to take advantage of the tragedy, and was caught in the act? After peering at the window again and seeing no one, she quickly dismissed this as the jitters of coming to a now-empty house that sat on two acres of land and overlooked a creek. Stepping onto the front porch with its tapered columns, she took the key out of her hobo bag and unlocked the door.

Inside, Naomi set her bags down and took in the stucco walls, rustic log furniture and parquet flooring. There were a few framed photographs on a living room wall of her uncle standing tall and proud as a detective with the Pebble Creek Police Department and alongside other officers. She moved up to the stone fireplace mantel, where there were photographs of her, Naomi's parents and Roger in happier times. One picture, in particular, caught her eye. It was of Dylan and her, taken by Naomi's uncle while they were at a county fair three years ago. She was surprised he'd kept the photo on display. Or maybe not, considering how fond he was of Dylan, who was like a son to him in every sense of the word. Naomi knew the feeling was mutual, meaning Dylan was probably struggling just as much as she was with her uncle's untimely and violent death in spite of Dylan's loyalty to his job as a detective with the Pebble Creek PD, which needed to come first as he looked into the homicide. Naomi choked back tears as the image of her uncle being gunned down once again flashed in her head. Shaking it off, she walked through the house, soaking up more pleasant memories and reacquainting herself with the surroundings. In the kitchen, dirty dishes were still on the quartz countertop and in the farmhouse sink. Her uncle had never been the tidiest person. Now, sadly, it would be up to her to clean up for him, as though he would eventually come through the front door and thank.

Naomi grabbed her laptop shoulder bag and a garment bag and headed up the squeaky L-shaped stairs. Bypassing the master suite, she stepped inside the spacious bedroom that had once been hers and that Uncle Roger had insisted would always be there any time she wanted to visit. It was taupe colored with a platform bed and pine dresser. A glass computer desk and ergonomic stool sat in the corner. She set up her laptop there, unpacked a few things and took a long shower, feeling lethargic after the long plane ride.

After putting on a fresh set of clothes—a yellow, white-striped top with cuffed sleeves, black straight-legged slacks—she pulled back her thick hair and tied it into a ponytail, applied a tiny amount of makeup, for effect, then slid her feet into a pair of loafers. Naomi headed back downstairs while checking her cell phone for messages. She half expected one might be from Dylan, making sure she had arrived safely. Not that she needed a polite gesture for old times' sake from an ex-boyfriend who had likely moved on to someone else. As it was, there was no call or message from him. Probably just as well, she thought, even if a part of her felt just the slightest—or maybe more than that—disappointment, for whatever reason.

There was, however, a text from her boss, Jared Falcony, the hard-nosed US Secret Service special agent in charge of the Miami Field Office. Though she had taken a few personal days off, Naomi had learned since working for the Secret Service that everyone had to be ready at any time to assume an official capacity in the event of an emergency. But he only wanted to reiterate his condolences for her loss and allow her the time needed to do what she must to get her uncle's affairs in order. She texted back, thanking him.

There was a voice mail from her Secret Service colleague and roommate, Sophia, who specialized in computer and telecommunications fraud investigations. Naomi listened as Sophia offered any help she needed, then updated her on the latest in-house gossip. Nothing out of the ordinary or otherwise to be concerned about.

Naomi was just about to shut off the phone, when a text message appeared. It came from a caller identified as Blue Violet. The message read simply:

I see you.

Her heart skipped a beat. A Peeping Tom? Or worse, a serial killer? Naomi's heart skipped another beat and her eyes darted around the living area as if someone were actually standing there watching her. She saw no one. Could the person be hiding somewhere, waiting to spring out at her like a ravenous leopard? Feeling panicked, she swiftly moved toward the piece of luggage near the door that contained her department-issued firearm. Unzipping the bag, she removed a locked hard-sided container and managed to steady her trembling hands enough to unlock it. She pulled out a Glock 9-millimeter pistol and a loaded magazine, bringing them together to form a usable weapon of self-defense in this instance.

Crouching low, Naomi moved toward the clerestory windows and peeked through a sliver in the faux wood blinds. There was no indication of anyone surveying the house. Or her. Not that she could see the entire landscape and places one could be hiding atop one of several hills. Or amid the tall cottonwoods and cherry trees on the property. But there was still the possibility that an intruder was inside the house, though Naomi was certain she had locked the front door. Could a window have been left open by Uncle Roger to let fresh air in? And, unknowingly, a dangerous killer?

Determined to maintain her cool under fire, even while potentially in harm's way, Naomi methodically checked each room downstairs, keeping the gun aimed and ready to fire at a moment's notice. She made her way back upstairs and did the same thing, fearful that someone could come out of nowhere and attack. But again, she came up empty. Maybe it was a prankster who had somehow stumbled onto her cell number. Or even a wrong number that came at the wrong time.

While still keeping the firearm handy, Naomi slowly descended the stairs and, thinking she heard a sound, moved cautiously toward the front door. She sensed someone—perhaps her uncle Roger's shooter—was on the other side, hoping to catch her off guard. Not a chance. After sucking in a deep breath, she quietly unlocked and gripped the brass knob, before slowly turning it.

Yanking the door open, she stepped back and aimed the barrel straight at the tall and physically imposing killer's face, while yelling, "Don't move!" Or so she'd imagined the dark-haired, gray-eyed man standing there was the killer.

Naomi reconsidered this belief and gulped when she stared up at the good-looking, square-jawed face and dimpled chin of Dylan Robert Hester.

Though clearly startled, he didn't make a move. Broad shoulders were covered with a navy knit blazer worn over a solid-fitting light pink shirt, and the rest of his well-developed frame filled out nicely in dark blue twill pants.

He kept black apron-toe leather shoes firmly in place on the wooden porch.

With a straight look, in a crisp tone of voice, he said coolly, "Welcome back to Pebble Creek, Naomi."

HONESTLY, DYLAN HAD expected a less-than-enthusiastic greeting from the woman he had never quite been able to extricate from his mind, as if meant to forever haunt him with all she brought to the table. Indeed, had she told him to get lost or please don't try to re-create a past she had no interest in resuming, he would have completely understood. After all, her intentions had been pretty clear two years ago where they were concerned. What he hadn't expected was to be treated like an enemy combatant. Especially under the circumstances where they were on the same page, insofar as mourning Roger's death as a homicide. Dylan stared into the barrel of the gun she still had pointed at him, as though in a trance. What was that all about? Had the stress of what happened to her uncle been that much to stomach? "Hello to you, too," he said sardonically. He raised his hands in a mock surrender. "Okay, you've got me. Now would you mind putting that damned thing down, Secret Service Special Agent Lincoln, before someone—me—gets hurt...or worse...?"

Naomi's diamond-shaped face was even lovelier than before, if that was possible. And her tall and slender frame, with long and shapely legs, still left her about six inches shorter than his height of six-three. He liked the ponytail but hoped to get the chance to see her long hair flowing freely while in town, which in his mind enhanced her natural features. Her eyes, an enticing mixture of brown, gold and green hues, locked with his for a long moment as if still assessing her next move. Or target.

"Sorry." She finally lowered the gun while still clutching it tightly. "Thought you were someone else."

"For his sake, I hope the man keeps his distance," Dylan couldn't help but quip, though she had obviously been shaken by someone. Who?

Naomi regarded him suspiciously. "How did you know I was here?" He noticed she was less defensive in her tone, but no less cautious.

"I didn't," he admitted. "I dropped by hoping you would have arrived safe and sound." He grinned sidelong. "Looks like you were ready and waiting..."

"It's not what you think." She glanced at the gun and back. "Didn't want to shoot you." A soft smile played on her thin lips. "Not this time anyway—"

"So you say." He met her eyes dubiously. "Are you going to invite me in?" Naomi seemed to ponder the notion for a long moment, before finally nodding. She stepped aside as Dylan walked past her. When she closed the door and faced him, he had to ask, "What's with the gun? Who did you think was on the other side of the door?"

"I'm not sure..." She walked over to her bag and put the weapon away, replacing it with her cell phone. "Someone calling himself Blue Violet sent me a text." She showed it to Dylan.

"'I see you.'" He read the disturbing words aloud. Even more alarming to him was the sender's handle, Blue Violet. Though this wasn't generally known to the public, it was a moniker that had occasionally been used by the Violet Killer when taunting the police. The perp always used a disposable burner phone for cryptic messages, making it all but impossible for police to track and identify the caller. Was this their serial killer? And why did he send Naomi, of all people, a text?

"I wasn't sure if it was some creep's idea of a sick joke," she said warily. "A voyeur hiding in the woods. Someone who latched onto me randomly and is not watching at all, but getting a charge out of keeping me wondering." Her lower lip quivered. "Or something more sinister, such as this Violet Killer coming after me, like he must have come after Uncle Roger. Either way, it spooked me. Then I heard someone at the door…and, well, I thought I might need to defend myself—"

"I understand." Dylan was glad to know she was well equipped and clearly capable of protecting herself from a dangerous perpetrator. He was less comfortable with the notion that she may have unknowingly made herself a target by returning to Pebble Creek. "You did the right thing."

Naomi peered. "You don't think it was just a prank, do you?"

"No," Dylan told her candidly, not wanting her to let her guard down by sugarcoating it.

She arched an eyebrow. "What aren't you telling me…?"

Normally, he acted on a need-to-know basis during a criminal investigation. But in this case, with the victim being her beloved uncle and her own life at risk, Dylan didn't see any way around it other than being straight with Naomi. He looked at her worriedly. "The man we believe to be the Violet Killer has been known to use Blue Violet as his handle when harassing investigators. He typically tosses the phone after leaving an enigmatic or mocking message."

"But how would he have gotten my cell phone number that's unlisted?" she questioned, ill at ease.

"Roger's cell phone is missing. We think it was taken by the killer, along with his laptop. The unsub would've had access to your cell number and any other personal information stored on the two devices."

Naomi rolled her eyes but remained mute as if waiting for what came next.

Dylan drew a breath, wishing he didn't have to feed her hunger for pertinent information. But the circumstances left him no choice. "Afraid there's more to it than that…"

Her lashes fluttered nervously. "Such as?"

"A violet was found stuffed inside Roger's mouth," Dylan uttered painfully. He shifted his weight from his right foot to the left. "It's the perp's calling card. Meaning that your uncle was, in fact, targeted by this serial killer—most likely because Roger had made it his mission to bring him down and was zeroing in on a suspect."

Naomi sighed. "I believe Uncle Roger was about to tell me more about the killer when he was silenced…" she spoke bitterly.

"Looks that way." Dylan hated that she had been forced into this investigation, but there was no getting around it. The killer clearly knew who she was and apparently where.

"So, what does he want with me?" Naomi's eyes widened disquietingly. "Or do I even need to ask, given the young women of a similar profile he's gone after…?"

"Maybe nothing," Dylan suggested, even if he suspected otherwise. But tossing at her the worst-case scenario could do more harm than good. Better not to scare her to death for the time being. "Could be that this is just part of the unsub's sick games, meant to scare you and keep us guessing while we track down any leads in the investigation." In truth, Dylan instinctively was troubled by this unexpected twist in the case. Like it or not, so long as she was in town, Naomi had a giant target on her back. Which meant he had to do double duty in both protecting the former love of his life—whether she wanted this or not and in spite of essentially kicking him to the curb two years ago—and capturing a ruthless killer who seemed as confident in his scheming as he was reckless. Dylan hoped that it was the latter that would prove to be the unsub's undoing.

Chapter Three

"What do you think you're doing?" Naomi asked as Dylan moved his large hand toward her face. The last thing she wanted was to give him the idea that this more-than-a-little-awkward reunion between them was step one in getting back together. Not that the notion was unappealing to her on the whole, having thought about what they once had many times and how nice it would be if things had gone in a different direction in their lives. But why start something neither of them was prepared to finish? For better or worse, her life was in Miami now, even if she missed him much more than she cared to admit.

"Just doing you a little favor." He pushed away a tendril of hair that had found its way out of Naomi's gathered hair and fallen across her forehead. His deft finger burned against her tender skin, reminding Naomi of what it felt like when he touched her. "That better?"

"Yes, thank you," she confessed, resisting the urge to scratch where the hair had been.

"Good." He flashed her his trademark crooked grin that always seemed to win her over. "Now, where were we?"

Naomi found herself weak in the knees as she took in Dylan, who was every bit as nice on the eyes as the day she walked away from him and what they had. The slate-gray eyes were as deeply sexy and mesmerizing as ever. She zeroed in on the cleft in his chin that had always captivated her all by itself. She fought an urge to touch it, hoping he wasn't somehow able to read her mind.

Naomi forced herself to refocus on the moment at hand, freaked out at the thought that a killer had invaded her sense of security and was out there somewhere waiting to strike again. With her as a potential target, so long as she was in Pebble Creek. "Do you think the perp could have been in this house?" Her eyes went around the room, imagining that he had breached her uncle's property—perhaps right under his nose—before turning back to Dylan.

His brows twitched. "Was there any sign of forced entry?"

"No, not that I could detect." But had she been thorough in checking every possible point of access? Maybe she missed something. Wasn't a diabolical killer capable of almost anything, if he put his mind to it?

"I doubt the unsub has been that brazen as to break into Roger's house," Dylan said, rubbing his chin. "Not that I would put it past him, if he was desperate enough— such as believing Roger had kept incriminating information in the house."

"I haven't seen any sign that he brought his work home," she pointed out. Which wasn't exactly the same thing as saying that hadn't been the case.

Dylan chewed his lip. "I didn't get that impression. But still—"

Naomi watched as he scanned the place and could read his mind. "Though Uncle Roger talked about doing it, I see that he never got around to installing a security system, believing the property's location and surroundings to be safe enough to put it off."

"Yeah, I got on him about that." Dylan frowned. "Nowhere in Pebble Creek is safe enough these days, I'm afraid. That notwithstanding, chances are the killer got what and who he was after in Roger's office—and isn't gutsy enough to press his luck by breaking into an ex-cop's house as well, knowing we're in hot pursuit. But that doesn't make the threat any less serious. To be on the prudent side, I'll have a forensics team dust for prints and run a sweep for any hidden cameras or obvious gaps in security."

"Thanks." Naomi appreciated his help to ease her concern, even if Dylan was only doing his job and what came natural as a detective. She supposed it was more than that, given his loyalty toward her uncle. And, if honest about it, Naomi decided that with her past involvement with Dylan, he wouldn't want to see her hurt, in spite of the way things ended between them. Her mind turned to Uncle Roger. Growing up, Naomi had always believed him to be tough as nails, practically invulnerable. Now she knew he had proved to be all too vulnerable against a determined foe who wanted him dead and made it happen.

"In the meantime, I don't think it's a good idea for you to stay here," Dylan cut into her thoughts. He fixed his gaze upon her as if it was more than a mere suggestion.

"I'm sure I'll be fine," she said bravely, even if feeling less than confident on that front. "As you suggested, the killer isn't likely to show his face around here—regardless if I may have overreacted earlier. I just got here and am not about to let him or anyone else drive me away like a frightened little rabbit needing to run for cover."

Dylan, who had made himself comfortable by taking a seat in her uncle's favorite log rocking recliner, gave her a reproving look. "No one, least of all me, is doubting your capabilities and you're certainly much more than a frightened little rabbit. Be that as it may, I still think it's best to err on the side of caution."

Naomi put her resistance on hold for a moment. "How cautious are we talking about?"

"Maybe you could stay at a hotel or—" Dylan stopped on a dime, leaving Naomi to read between the lines.

"With you?" Her eyes widened at the implication, as though it was the worst possible thing he could suggest. She warmed in imagining them living together—even if only temporarily. It was something they had once talked about, when dating seriously as a prelude to getting married. But the proposal never came. Had he gotten cold feet, in spite of hinting at such? She wondered if it would have made a difference if he had asked her to marry him. Would she have said yes and dashed her plans to work for the Secret Service?

"Hadn't meant to suggest anything of the sort," he claimed smoothly. "It's not a half-hearted come-on, I promise. We've been over and done with for two years now. I get that. It is what it is. That said, I do have plenty of room and a guest bedroom at my house. It's by the lake, has a nice security system and isn't likely to attract unwanted visitors. I would be happy to play host during your stay in town. I just want you to be safe, Naomi. I owe that much to Roger."

Though she found his offer more than a little tempting, Naomi gave him a firm, "Thanks but no thanks, Dylan. I'm a member of the US Secret Service, more than capable of protecting myself from any threat that comes my way. If the person who killed my uncle wants to come after me, too, he is welcome to try. I have my gun and know how to use it. I'm also trained in hand-to-hand combat and jujitsu. So, I'm not going anywhere."

Naomi sighed, while trying hard not to show him that in spite of everything she just said, having a demented serial killer possibly set his sights on her was still very unsettling. To say the least.

"Well, you've made your case admirably," Dylan said, his voice spiced with sarcasm and resignation. "As you already seem to have your mind made up in the stubborn tradition of your uncle, I won't persist in trying to dissuade you from staying."

Naomi smiled thinly. "In following Uncle Roger's footsteps, I'll take that as a badge of honor," she said proudly.

"It is," he agreed and got to his feet. "Just be careful."

"I will be." She knew his concern for her welfare was genuine. As was hers for his health and well-being, the awkwardness of the moment to go with their estrangement as a couple notwithstanding.

Dylan stepped closer. "Do you need any help with the arrangements, now that Roger's body has been released to the funeral home?"

Truthfully, Naomi had barely wrapped her head around the idea that her uncle was dead and, as his only living relative, she would need to step up and see to it that he had a proper burial. But that wouldn't stop her from doing what needed to be done. "I think I can handle it," she responded placidly. "Uncle Roger purchased a burial plot right next to my parents' resting place in the cemetery. He wanted to be buried beside his brother, whom he was very close to."

"Okay." Dylan nodded thoughtfully. "I have to go. If you run into any problems along the way, you have my number."

"I'll keep that in mind," she promised, feeling the warmth from their close proximity. She took an involuntary step backward lest she allow a desire to touch him cloud her judgment that it was best to leave the past where it was. "Please keep me abreast on the investigation into Uncle Roger's death."

"I will." He put his hands together. "Roger's SUV should be released shortly, after forensics is finished combing it for possible evidence pertaining to the crime. I'm sure he'd want you to have it—so long as you need transportation while you're in town."

"Thank you." Naomi imagined it would feel weird driving her uncle's SUV, knowing he would never be behind the wheel himself again. It was just another adjustment she would need to make, difficult as it was.

Dylan glanced over at the bag where she had placed her firearm and grinned out of the side of his mouth. "I'm guessing you finished at the head of your class among Secret Service agents in firearms training?"

"Close enough," Naomi admitted, actually taking second place, just behind her friend Sophia. "It's an ongoing process throughout every agent's career with the Service."

"Figured as much, as it's the same for those of us in the Pebble Creek PD."

She gazed at him in earnest. "I really wouldn't have shot you, if that's what you're thinking." She hoped he knew deep down inside that she would always care for him enough to stay out of harm's way, including bullet wounds.

"Nice to know." He held her gaze with a straight look. "The last thing I need is to be mistaken for the bad guy where you're concerned."

"You were never the bad guy, Dylan." She wanted to make this clear to him. "My leaving wasn't about you."

She thought he understood that. Or had this just been wishful thinking on her part?

"I know—that's what you told me." Skepticism rang from his tenor.

"It was true." Her voice did not waver. The last thing Naomi ever wanted was for him to think that their breakup was a reflection of her no longer wanting them to be together. Couldn't have been further from the truth. In an ideal world, they both could have had it all, beginning with each other. But in this real world, she was forced to choose one path over another, painful as it was. So she did, knowing she would have to live with the consequences, for richer or poorer. Sickness or health. Love or loss.

"I just wish we had talked about it more," Dylan asserted, as if still carrying a mighty chip on his broad shoulder.

Naomi winced, wishing they didn't have to deal with this now. What more was there to say? Would it have made any difference had he asked her to stay? Had she needed to hear those powerful words come out of his mouth? No matter. It was too late now for what never happened. Wasn't it?

"There's no point in going there, Dylan," Naomi argued, fighting off the feelings of guilt that gnawed at her like a final exam she needed to pass or risk failure.

His jaw clenched. "I get it, you've moved on."

"Haven't you?" she assumed pensively in meeting his hard eyes.

Dylan shifted his gaze and took a deep breath before returning to her face. "Yeah, I guess I have."

Had she expected him to say otherwise when giving him no reason not to move on with his life? She wondered miserably what his current girlfriend looked like. Gorgeous, Naomi supposed. Probably sexy, too. She'd never asked her uncle specifically about Dylan's personal life, not sure she wanted to know.

The idea of another woman stealing Dylan's heart, soul and bed bothered Naomi more than she'd realized. Till now.

THROUGH HIGH-POWERED BINOCULARS, the Violet Killer watched inconspicuously from a safe distance atop an uneven hill, behind a cluster of large ferns. He saw the dark-haired, tall police detective step outside the house with the striking niece of Roger Lincoln. She looked even better than he remembered. And better than the images Lincoln had of her on his computer, which was now in the possession of the Violet Killer. Along with incriminating information that could have exposed him to the local authorities and FBI agents trying to track him down like a wild animal on the loose. He sensed the overprotectiveness of Detective Dylan Hester as though he was determined not to let her slip from his grasp and into the arms of a killer. But the detective's efforts would prove futile. As they had with the others the Violet Killer had set his sights on. Now that Lincoln's niece had become the latest object of his affections—and long overdue at that—the Violet Killer intended to settle for nothing less than to see to it that Naomi Lincoln joined his other violets in blissful death.

But all in good time. Fortunately, patience had been his virtue for the past two years, serving him well when he needed it most, against his worst instincts. He wasn't about to get too overeager or cocky to his own detriment. Not when half the fun was watching and waiting like a lion and its helpless prey, till the perfect time to strike. By then, it would be too late to do anything other than accept her fate. Until then, he would continue to hide in plain view, loving the attention he was getting and the satisfying fear he had brought upon the citizens of Pebble Creek. Especially the women, many of whom had become afraid of their own shadows.

The Violet Killer gazed through the binoculars as the pretty Secret Service agent headed back into the house and the police detective casually walked away and got into his vehicle. He sat in it for a while as though reluctant to leave, and the killer could only imagine what steps he was taking to try to keep Lincoln's niece out of harm's way. Try all he wished, but it would make no difference when all was said and done. Naomi Lincoln was living on borrowed time before she joined her uncle—who overplayed his hand and paid for it—in the grave.

The Violet Killer furtively stepped away from the bushes and coolly made his way down the other side of the hill and to his own car. Inside, he started it and was on his merry way, while making plans as he usually did in staying one step ahead of everyone else.

Chapter Four

Dylan sat in his car for a long moment outside Roger's house, regretting that he had let things get personal with Naomi. He had no right to act like a bitter ex, even if part of him felt that way. He hadn't exactly fought hard to keep her there in Pebble Creek, thinking it best not to stand in the way of a dream she worked hard to achieve. Never mind if it came at the expense of asking her to marry him and all that might have occurred afterward as husband and wife. Not to mention father and mother, had they decided to go in that direction. But that was two years ago and their beds had been made. Right now, he needed to stay focused and give Naomi what she really needed from him: capturing the man who murdered her uncle. This, of course, would achieve the added goal of stopping the Violet Killer in his tracks, hopefully before any more young women could be lost. Including Naomi herself, who Dylan believed was a potential target for the killer.

After starting the car, Dylan drove off. He got on the speaker of his cell phone and ordered investigators to come to Roger's house with Naomi's consent to dust for fingerprints that might not belong and other possible indicators that it was part of the homicide that took place at Roger's office—including running a sweep for any illegal surveillance or audio equipment. With that in motion, Dylan rang Detective Gregory Hwang.

"Is Naomi here?" he asked curiously.

"Yeah. Just left her at Roger's house," Dylan informed him, wishing they could have spent more time talking, against his better judgment.

"How's she holding up?"

"About as well as you might expect when you're a virtual eyewitness to your only living relative being gunned down."

"Yeah, figured as much," grumbled Hwang.

Dylan concurred, feeling helpless at the thought of losing his good friend. "What did you come up with on the security cameras inside or outside Roger's building?"

"Not much we can use, I'm afraid. A camera inside wasn't working and one outside showed movement around the time in question, but so far everyone we've been able to identify checked out as far as what they were doing there and when. We've extended the perimeter in checking out other surveillance cameras in the area that might have picked up something."

"Good." Dylan sighed, sensing that the killer was too clever to make himself easy to pick out of the crowd, much less identify, without some effort. Especially given his almost uncanny ability to go after young women with near impunity. "Naomi got a text message from Blue Violet, claiming he was watching her. Must have homed in on her after stealing Roger's cell phone."

"You think he's actually going after Naomi next...?" Hwang's voice dropped an unnerved octave.

"At this point, I wouldn't put anything past the unsub," admitted Dylan, wishing he could feel otherwise. "What better way to really get under our skin than targeting

Naomi as another way to show his total disregard for the law, while challenging us to stop him?"

"Are you planning to let Naomi stay with you while in town, to be on the safe side?" Hwang asked curiously.

It was a reasonable question that Dylan would have expected from the detective, who knew that his fondness for Naomi had never wavered, their differences aside. And that protecting her from a madman was a priority. Too bad she couldn't see it that way at the moment. "Right now, she wants to stay put," he said, acquiescing to this. "For the time being, I'd like to beef up patrols in the area and keep tabs on her."

"I'll put in the request," Hwang agreed. "Shouldn't be a problem."

"Hope not." Dylan knew that with the serial killer investigation underway, the department's manpower was being stretched thin. Maybe the perp was counting on this to terrorize Naomi right under their noses. Dylan wasn't about to allow that to happen. Not if he could help it.

After disconnecting, Dylan headed for the Pebble Creek Police Department crime laboratory, where the bullet removed from Roger's head had been analyzed, along with the shell casing found at the scene of the crime. Dylan saw this as an important step in trying to identify the unsub, who in an apparent act of desperation went away from his normal MO in shooting Roger to death.

Entering the modern lab, Dylan was greeted by George Suina, a forensic and firearms analyst and full-blooded Pueblo Indian, who had been with the department for nearly a decade. His jet-black hair, just grazing narrow shoulders, belied his midfifties age. "Hey, Dylan," he said in a friendly tone. "Bet I know why you're here."

Dylan grinned humorlessly. "You know me too well, George. What have you got for me?"

"Plenty." His sable eyes widened teasingly. "Come with me."

Dylan followed him to a workstation, where Suina had a monitor on, with a split screen overhead. "Looks like you were spot-on, Dylan, in linking the bullet casing you found with the bullet taken out of Roger Lincoln. On the right side of the screen is an image of the mangled bullet removed from Lincoln's head," explained Suina. "It was fired from a gun barrel with four lands and grooves and had a left-hand twist." He turned to the other side of the screen as Dylan observed attentively an image of a shell casing. "As you suspected, the ballistic markings on the .45 ACP casing you located are a perfect match with those from the bullet that killed Roger Lincoln. Or, in other words, both came from the same gun."

Dylan nodded sullenly. "Figured as much. Looks like our serial killer unsub is packing a .45 ACP handgun… and is more dangerous than ever." Not to mention likely being in possession of Roger's Ruger Blackhawk revolver as well. Meaning there was an even greater sense of urgency in bringing him down. "I don't suppose you were able to pull any prints off the bullet or shell casing?"

"No such luck, I'm afraid." Suina shook his head, frowning. "On the fingers-crossed side of things, though, with the good possibility that the shooter used the same weapon before, we've entered the bullet and shell casing evidence into the ATF's National Integrated Ballistic Information Network, with the aim of getting a hit on the firearm and triggerman."

"One can only hope," Dylan said and crossed the fingers on both hands theatrically in support of this effort. Having worked previously with the ATF or Bureau of Alcohol, Tobacco, Firearms and Explosives, he knew they were a great federal partner in the war on crime. Maybe this case would be no exception in achieving results. But he wasn't expecting miracles, either, knowing that the unsub was not going to make this easy for them to bring him down, having proved that after two years of serial murdering. But he had made a tactical error in going after Roger, and it just might be the first step to his undoing.

AFTER DYLAN LEFT, Naomi put aside her unease to finish unpacking. She wondered if it had been a mistake not to take up his offer of refuge. Was she letting her pride get in the way of common sense? On the other hand, wasn't that putting the cart ahead of the horse to allow paranoia to run her out of the house prematurely? Till proven otherwise, she had to assume that her uncle's house—soon to be hers if she read him correctly when alive—was safe enough to go about her business, knowing that she had self-protection, should it come to that.

Just as she was trying to decide what to have for dinner, with the pickings in the refrigerator rather slim, Naomi jumped when she heard the doorbell ring. Her first instinct was to go for her weapon. That thought quickly subsided as she looked out the peephole and recognized one of the three people standing there—one woman and two men—as being Tabitha McKinnon, a crime scene investigator for the Pebble Creek PD from when Naomi did some work for them as a crime victims service coordinator. Dylan had given her a heads-up that they were on their way to dust for prints and check for bugs, but she had spaced out on this with different things on her mind. She noted they were carrying equipment for their assignment.

Naomi opened the door and greeted them with a smile.

"Hey, Tabitha." She singled her out, having to look up at the tall, thirtysomething woman with butterscotch-blond hair cut short with curtain bangs.

"Hi, Naomi. Nice to see you again. Sorry it's under these circumstances."

"So am I." Naomi eyed the two men, also in their thirties. One was a tall Hispanic, his dark thick hair worn in a pompadour style. The other was African American, even taller, with a jet-black flat top. Tabitha introduced them as Detective Raymond Cruz and forensic science technician Vince Iverson, respectively.

"Detective Hester asked us to give the place a sweep for bugs and see if we can collect any forensic evidence that points toward an intruder entering the premises," Iverson said.

"Yes, I was expecting you." Naomi invited them in. "Thanks for coming."

"We'll try to be quick, if not thorough," Cruz told her, removing latex gloves from his blazer pocket.

Realizing her presence would only be in their way, possibly delaying doing their jobs, Naomi said, "Why don't I get out of your way. I could use some fresh air anyway. Just holler when you're done."

"Will do." Tabitha smiled at her. "Hopefully, we won't find anything unusual."

Naomi seconded that as she grabbed her cell phone and was out the door. Fortunately, she had put everything away that needed to be. With any luck, the coast would be cleared to make the most of her time there, while feeling relatively safe and secure. She took a deep breath and made her way to the wooded area on the property where she had spent much time when living there, hiking and running on a well-worn path, two of her favorite pastimes. She recalled being joined by Dylan once in a while, though they tended to use the isolation from the house more to make out than exercise. Admittedly, she missed the feel of his mouth upon hers and wondered if it could happen again.

Naomi's reverie was interrupted by the sound of crackling leaves. She nearly jumped out of her skin as she whipped around, thinking she might be attacked and preparing for battle, having left her firearm at the house. But instead of a deadly assailant, she witnessed a rather large brown squirrel with a long tail scurry across dirt and leaves, hop onto a cottonwood tree, climb up like its tail was on fire and leap from one precarious branch to another, till out of sight. Naomi couldn't help but smile, reminding her of what she loved about the Pacific Northwest and its varied inhabitants blending so well with nature.

With the scare behind her, she headed back to the house, figuring they must be nearly through with their work. No sooner had she reached the door than Tabitha stepped onto the porch. "I was just about to come looking for you."

Naomi sensed by her expression that something was up. But what? "Did you find something—?"

"Let's go back inside," Tabitha said evasively.

"Okay." Naomi followed her through the door, where Cruz and Iverson were standing over the rustic coffee table. Several items were spread across it. "What's this?" she asked.

Cruz turned to her with a sour look on his face. "We found a number of bugging devices throughout the house," he said, holding one of them up with a gloved hand. "They include tiny cameras and electronic listening devices. Seems as though someone's been keeping tabs on Roger and his activities, apparently without him being the wiser."

Naomi was shocked. The thought that her uncle's house had been bugged rattled her. Equally unnerving was the notion that someone might have been watching her while naked before and after her shower. "Who could have done such a thing?" she asked, but she already had her suspicions, when coupled with Uncle Roger's death purportedly at the hands of the Violet Killer. Could the two be unrelated?

"We're not sure," Cruz said with a catch to his voice. "Obviously one or more persons on a mission of some sort to monitor Roger—or anyone else coming and going to the house."

"Did you get all the bugs?" Naomi's eyes popped wide with pessimism.

"We think so," Iverson chipped in confidently. "We'll double-check, to be on the safe side."

"The bugs have been dusted for prints and we'll also see if we can pull any DNA off them," Tabitha said. "Maybe we'll get lucky. Same with the other data we've gathered."

Cruz frowned. "Given the circumstances surrounding Lincoln's death and no security system on the premises, my advice to you, Naomi, is to stay elsewhere till this is sorted out, for your own safety."

"I'll keep that in mind," she said tightly, recognizing how vulnerable she was at the house with a serial killer on the loose. She wondered if Dylan was still up for some company. Or would that cramp his style as a single man who had admitted to having one or more women take her place in his life?

DYLAN HAD ALREADY been on his way to Roger's house to see if they had found anything interesting when his cell phone rang. He grabbed it off the car seat and saw the caller was Naomi. A pang of excitement coursed through him to hear the sound of her voice, just as had been the case when they were seeing each other. That dampened somewhat as he came back to reality and the fact that he and she were no longer a couple, hard as this continued to be to come to terms with. He clicked on the speaker-phone. "Hey," he said to her equably. "What's up?"

"Does that offer to stay at your place for now still stand?" she asked. He could hear the tension in her tone.

"Of course." He could use the company—her company, in particular. But he wasn't about to say that. Or draw the wrong conclusions again. "Why the change of heart?"

"They found the place bugged!" Naomi snapped. "Someone had been watching and listening to Uncle Roger, for who knows how long…"

Dylan cursed under his breath. He was pretty sure that someone was the Violet Killer. Though this was not the modus operandi of the serial killer, per se, desperate times may have called for desperate measures. Perhaps he had been tracking Roger's movements for some time, as the former police detective had been tracking the unsub and homing in on his identity. With no security system in place and relatively easy access to the house, it wouldn't have been too difficult for someone to break in and plant the devices, unbeknownst to Roger. Or Naomi, for that matter.

"I'm sure your colleagues will fill you in on the details…" Naomi's bitter voice broke into his thoughts.

Dylan could only hope the installer had been careless and left behind prints, DNA or other evidence they could work with in identifying the perp. Meanwhile, Naomi needed to be protected from whoever might wish to come after her. "Repack your bags. I'm on my way," he said, his voice steadfast.

"I intend to have a security system installed," she pointed out defiantly. "Then I'll be out of your hair in no time."

"You can play in my hair anytime you want." Dylan remembered how much she loved running her hands through his thick hair. And vice versa. Now was probably not the right time to think about that, but he couldn't help himself. "Seriously," he amended, "you needn't be in any hurry to go back there. As I said, my place is more than large enough to accommodate you for as long as you're in town." He assumed that would be for only a few days. After the funeral, he imagined she would be eager to return to the new life she had established for herself. Dylan found himself strangely already starting to wish that weren't true. At the same time, so long as a killer was on the prowl, he believed that the farther away from Pebble Creek Naomi was, the better.

"See you when you get here," she told him without comment, and hung up.

Right after, his cell phone rang again. This time it was Tabitha. "Hey," he told her, while keeping an eye on the road. "Naomi just told me about the bugs found."

"Yeah, looks like someone was up to no good in planting surveillance equipment in Roger's house," she reiterated.

"Why don't you guys do a sweep of his office," Dylan ordered. "Maybe there's something there we missed."

"Sure thing."

"Let me know if you find anything." He had no doubt she would at that, even while Dylan wondered just what the unsub or someone else hoped to get out of such listening and video devices. It did no good to speculate but he would anyway. Information was valuable only when you had possession of it. He wouldn't put it past Roger's killer to use any means necessary to protect his identity, including trying to stay one step ahead. Or keep his opponent one or two steps behind. Whatever it took.

ADMITTEDLY, NAOMI HAD been curious about the house Dylan lived in. When they were together, he was staying in a condominium in the center of town. It was a bit small, but cozy in a manly type of way. Her uncle had mentioned casually last year that Dylan had purchased the lakefront home without giving many details, other than that he was living there alone at the time. Was he still? A flash of jealousy ripped through Naomi at the prospect of another woman stealing Dylan's heart, as if it would always belong to her. How silly was that, all things being equal?

Dylan drove his department-issued vehicle onto a circular drive till they came to a Western red cedar log cabin, two stories high. "Well, this is it," he said nonchalantly. "Home sweet home."

"I see…" was all Naomi could say, noting that aside from the Pebble Creek Lake frontage, the lush landscaping included mature aspen trees for privacy. She could only imagine what the inside looked like.

As though reading her mind, Dylan said with a half grin, "Shall we go in?"

She smiled. "Yes."

They got out of the car and unloaded her bags, before heading up a winding concrete paver walkway and onto a wraparound deck with reclaimed barn oak planks and two wooden Adirondack chairs. Inside the cabin, Naomi stepped on multicolored slate tile flooring. A quick scan showed her cedar wood walls with a vaulted ceiling and exposed beams. The floor-to-ceiling windows had open sheer drapes and looked out majestically onto the lake. Modern minimalist furnishings blended with contemporary accent pieces caught her eye.

"Shall I give you the grand tour?" The deep sound of Dylan's voice reached her as he was turning off the security system.

"I'd love that," she gushed, unable to help herself, as she had always been intrigued by architectural design in housing.

They set the bags down and proceeded to go through the downstairs, which included a two-story rusticated brickwork fireplace in the great room, a gourmet kitchen with black stainless steel appliances, butcher block countertops and island with wooden swivel stools.

"It's awesome," Naomi admitted.

"Yeah." Dylan seemed to take it in stride.

She gave him a curious look. "So why did you decide to sell your condo?"

"I always talked about wanting something on the lake—or have you forgotten?" He didn't give her a chance to respond, as if to rub it in. "When this place came on the market at a great price, I jumped on it, loving the idea to be right there at the water for swimming, fishing and boating."

Naomi realized that they had talked about living in such a place together. She couldn't help but wonder what might have been if she had stayed and moved in with him. Going up the flight of solid wood spiral stairs and seeing the second floor was no less impressive to Naomi, as each room was spacious with antique furnishings and large bay windows. They lingered just long enough in the master suite with its king sleigh bed that she couldn't help but consider whom he might be sharing the bed with these days. Was it really any of her business at this stage of the game?

Dylan didn't seem to notice her contemplation—or maybe decided to keep it to himself—as he guided her past a fully furnished room that had been turned into a home office, to the guest bedroom, which was as impressive as the others. It had a panel bed, rustic dresser and a comfortable-looking wingback chair.

"This is yours, for as long as you like," he said evenly. "There's a full bathroom right through that door." He pointed across the room.

"Thank you." Naomi gazed up at him. "Are you sure I'm not imposing?"

"I'm sure."

She should have left it at that, but did not. "I just don't want this to be weird."

"Weird?" He cocked a brow. "How so?"

"Not sure how your current girlfriend would feel having your ex staying at your cabin, even for a few days…"

"Wouldn't know about that, since I don't currently have a girlfriend. So you're safe." Dylan grinned with amusement. "I'll bring up your bags and then whip up something in the kitchen. You must be starving. I know I am."

With that, he left her there and Naomi wondered how she ever let him get away. Her reasons were certainly sound enough. She loved her job, her apartment and the fast-paced lifestyle of Miami. But was it enough in the absence of a meaningful relationship with a significant other? Especially after losing her uncle, the one man who seemed to get her. Other than Dylan.

Chapter Five

While making a fresh salad to go with leftover lemon baked chicken breasts and bran muffins, Dylan couldn't help but imagine him and Naomi cooking meals together in the gourmet kitchen. After all, that had been the plan, right? Till she bailed on him and any future they might have had. Including buying the dream log cabin he now occupied, as husband and wife. But he couldn't and shouldn't hold that against her. Not after two years of trying to put what they had behind him. No, he had to stay focused for the moment on keeping Naomi safe for as long as she let him. At least till they were able to get the jump on the Violet Killer before he could ever lay a hand on her. Or, for that matter, hopefully any other woman who fell into his crosshairs.

"There you are…" Dylan gave a halfhearted smile.

"What can I do?" Naomi asked. He noticed that she had let her hair down. He liked the shaggy fringe hairstyle. It suited her. Dylan imagined his hands could get lost in all that hair.

"You can grab the wine out of the fridge." He paused for effect. "I assume you still like red wine?"

She smiled to one side of her mouth self-consciously. "Yes."

"Good. The wineglasses are in there." He pointed

toward the glass-front cabinet, above the double-bowl, drop-in sink.

"Will do." He watched her open and pour the wine, while thinking how sexy she looked in the process, even if not the wiser.

They sat at the natural wood dining table in silence while watching each other eat, before Naomi batted her lashes and asked ill at ease, "You're going to get this guy, right?"

"Yeah, we will," Dylan promised. He could read the uncertainty in her eyes and the pain of loss she had been forced to endure at the hands of a serial killer. This made Dylan all the more determined to make his words hold up. "It's only a matter of time."

"But how many more people have to die before then?" she questioned, while slicing a knife into the chicken breast.

"Wish I could answer that," he spoke honestly, sitting back in his chair. To do otherwise would be disingenuous when dealing with a serial killer, who by his very nature killed more than two people to qualify as such. Meaning any indeterminate number would likely be followed till he could be stopped. "The good news is that we now know the caliber and model of the gun used to shoot Roger. It's an important piece of the puzzle in trying to nail the unsub."

"He probably ditched the weapon." Naomi brushed her nose. "Or stole it to make it harder to trace."

"Maybe—but my guess is that using the firearm was a spontaneous attack that came only after the killer found himself desperate to maintain his anonymity." Dylan wiped his mouth with a paper napkin. "That, along with his arrogance as a serial murderer, tells me that he likely still has the gun—believing he's safe to use it again, if necessary."

Naomi rolled her eyes. "You're probably right. Hope it leads to his downfall." She picked up a muffin and rotated as if inspecting it, then took a small bite and looked at him. "So, how's your mom these days?"

"She's good," he answered stoically, realizing Naomi was deliberately shifting the conversation to something a little more palatable. For his part, talking about his mother was less than ideal, though Naomi got along well with her when his mother chose to be around, which wasn't often. Abigail Sorenson, who used her second husband's surname, left his father when Dylan was just six years old. She had been ambiguous about the reasons why, but he suspected it had to do with his father's alcohol abuse and inability to hold down a job. Even with that knowledge, Dylan had a hard time dealing with the separation to this day, always wondering in the back of his mind if it was something he did or didn't do that was the final straw in the divorce. "My mother's on husband number three now," Dylan uttered with a shrug. "He's the lawyer who handled divorce number two. They're currently living in Vermont."

Naomi met his eyes with an unreadable look. "Do you get out there much to visit?"

"Not much. Too busy these days." He left it at that, while wondering if she would.

"And your sister?" Naomi probed, forking lettuce.

Dylan smiled, finding her a more welcoming topic. "Stefany's doing great." His sister was four years older and an anesthesiologist, working as an infectious disease specialist with Doctors Without Borders, along with her Argentine husband, Theodore Gonzalez. Stefany didn't seem to have the same hang-ups regarding their parents that he did, which Dylan believed was a good thing. "She's currently busy saving lives in Southern Africa," he said satisfyingly.

"That's wonderful." Naomi flashed her teeth. "You must be so proud of her, doing such a noble thing with her life."

"I am, definitely." Dylan sipped his wine, gazing at Naomi. He wondered if she thought any less of her own lot in life as a Secret Service agent. Did he think less of his own career? "Of course, all things are relative," he pointed out coolly. "We all make choices and as long as Stefany is happy with hers, so am I." Even as the words came out of his mouth, Dylan regretted saying them, so as to imply things he didn't necessarily wish to regarding Naomi's career choice.

She seemed to pick up on this. Lifting her glass, she took a quick drink and uttered, while getting to her feet, "Think I'll call it a night, if you don't mind…"

"Hope it wasn't something I said," Dylan voiced lamely.

"It wasn't." Naomi put on a brave face. "I've just had a long day and am exhausted."

"I understand." He kept his voice level and stood, not wanting to make things worse between them. When Naomi was about to remove her plates from the table, he said, "Leave it. You should get some rest. I'll clean up and…see you in the morning."

She nodded and forced a smile. "Good night, Dylan, and thanks again for letting me stay here."

"No problem," he assured her.

"By the way," she said, after taking a few steps, "I assume you can recommend a great security system I can have installed at Uncle Roger's house?"

"Yeah, I can do that."

"Good."

Dylan didn't go any further, watching as she walked away and up the stairs. As it was, he really didn't see the point in putting in a security system in a house that she would presumably be placing on the market with her return to Miami. Unless she planned to hold on to the property as an investment. Or do something to increase its value before selling. Whatever the case, he intended to delay making that recommendation for as long as possible. Or at least till they could get a better handle on the unsub as a legitimate threat to Naomi in Pebble Creek.

After clearing the table and putting the plates, silverware, and glasses into the dishwasher, Dylan grabbed his cell phone and got the latest update on the investigation from some members of the Violet Killer Task Force, while strategizing on where they went from here with a deadly perpetrator still on the hunt to add to his violets and victims.

By the time he had hit the sack an hour later, Dylan found himself unable to sleep. Indeed, sleep had been hard to come by ever since he had been working this case. Even harder since Roger Lincoln was murdered. Beyond that, sleep wasn't coming any easier knowing that Naomi was just down the hall, undoubtedly sleeping like a beautiful baby after her long flight and scary moments at her uncle's house. Dylan had once thought they would be sharing that bed the whole night through, night after night—making love with all the passion and promise that came from being together two years ago. But that dream had died a slow death, replaced by the reality that Naomi had moved on to a different part of the country. With possibly another man in her life.

When Dylan finally drifted off to sleep, that last thought played on his emotions more than he wanted to admit.

NAOMI'S HEART RACED as she watched her uncle Roger gunned down before her very eyes. He slumped over, a wound to his head bleeding profusely. The unsub was just out of sight. But then, his twisted face suddenly appeared, filling the laptop screen. She didn't recognize him. His dark, foreboding eyes stared back at her; then he broke out into maniacal laughter that boomed in her ears. She shrieked, drowning him out and, in the frightful moment, forcing her awake, having broken out in a cold sweat.

It was just a nightmare, Naomi realized, once she had come to terms with the fact that she was in bed, alone, safe from the bad man who murdered her uncle. But whose bed? It took her another moment to regain her equilibrium and remember that she was staying in Dylan's guest room. She half expected him to come rushing in like a good looking knight in shining armor, having heard her cries, as she had when opening her eyes. What would she tell him? It was so embarrassing, even if he understood on some level, given the horror of what she had witnessed two days ago. She could only hope this was a one-off. The last thing she needed was to be haunted by this creep.

Dylan never came in. With the light of day streaming in through the bamboo blinds, she knew that it was daytime. Grabbing her cell phone from beneath the plush pillow, Naomi saw that it was just after 7:00 a.m. She had been so tired that she slept through the night. Before that, she recalled feeling the sting in Dylan's unfavorably comparing her career choice with his sister, Stefany's. Or had she only imagined something that was totally off base? Either way, it hadn't set well with Naomi. She didn't need to be reminded of what—or who—she gave up. There was no pushing a rewind button. Surely he knew that. So why insinuate what might have been had she chosen to stay in Pebble Creek? With him?

Dragging herself up, Naomi pushed aside the thoughts, wanting only to get through the funeral and back to the life she had created in Miami. But could it possibly be that easy to leave and forget everything and everyone who had brought her back home? Including, on at least some level, Dylan Hester?

After washing up and putting on clothes, Naomi went downstairs, expecting that Dylan may have made her breakfast, in playing the role of host. Instead, she found a note he'd left on the kitchen counter and started reading it:

Morning, Sleepyhead—hope you slept well. Had to go to work. There's coffee made. The fridge is stocked and a couple of cereals are in the cabinet. Help yourself to whatever you like. I had someone drive Roger's SUV over, which I'm guessing you'll need. Keys are inside. If you need anything else, let me know. See you later. Dylan.

He added the four-digit master code to the alarm system for turning it off and on as needed.

Naomi smiled. Looked as if he'd thought of everything. Though part of her felt she could get used to this—including his comfortable cabin and the man himself—the other part of her felt that might be a big mistake that neither of them needed. Right now, she only wanted to get some coffee into her system and a bite to eat, and then continue the difficult task of funeral preparations for her uncle Roger.

Forty-five minutes later, Naomi was inside his red

Ford Explorer. She picked up the familiar scent of her uncle, making it all the more difficult to know that he was gone and wasn't coming back, no matter how much she wanted to convince herself otherwise. She could only hope that his killer was made to pay for what he'd done, sooner than later, through arrest, conviction, and incarceration.

Naomi drove down the winding road away from Dylan's cabin, wondering how long she would stay there. Would he really be okay with them temporarily sharing the same space and separate bedrooms? Would she? Thoughts of when they were red-hot lovers crossed her mind, causing a bodily reaction. She managed to still the heated waters of desire that had never gone away for the man, even with thousands of miles separating them. Was it as difficult for him as well, putting aside the bitter feelings that were likely still permeating on his part? Just because he wasn't currently involved with anyone didn't mean he was a monk, either. Even if that thought irritated her, Naomi had to draw the line on natural jealousy and being reasonable, given their situations as they were. Not like she had any other choice in the matter.

Gazing up at the rearview mirror, she noticed a dark SUV on her tail, seemingly coming out of nowhere. She couldn't see the face of the driver through tinted glass. Was he or she doing that deliberately? Naomi pressed down on the accelerator, increasing her speed, putting some distance between her and the other vehicle. Just as she thought she was safe, it came upon her again, so close that she feared the driver might ram into her and try to force her off the road. What was their problem? Naomi's pulse raced as she envisioned the driver being none other than the Violet Killer—the man Dylan believed was responsible for her uncle's death. Was he coming after her now? But how would he have known her whereabouts? Unless he had followed them from her uncle's house yesterday and waited patiently for a chance to strike.

Again, Naomi sped up, her heart beating wildly. Just as she was prepared to dart into an upcoming strip mall parking lot, believing it might be her best chance to survive, having left her gun packed away, the SUV mysteriously stopped the aggressive tactics. It actually had slowed down and turned onto a side street and quickly disappeared from view, making Naomi wonder if she had imagined the whole thing. Maybe this serial killer thing was getting to her in ways that had her questioning her judgment when she needed to remain in control. Or might that have been the unsub's plan all along, to keep her guessing and off balance?

She drove into the strip mall parking lot and, after pulling into an open slot, sucked in a deep, calming breath. Taking out her cell phone, Naomi rang her best friend with the Secret Service, Sophia Menendez, for a video chat, needing to hear a familiar voice. She accepted the request, her gorgeous face appearing on the screen, surrounded by a brown ombre hairstyle with bangs. Bold, dark eyes stared at Naomi.

"You look like you've seen a ghost!" Sophia said, never one to mince words.

"Not quite, but something just as unsettling." Naomi made a face. "Or at least in my, at times, vivid imagination."

"Tell me…" her friend pressed.

"I could've sworn that a dark-colored SUV was trying to run me off the road—or worse." Naomi gasped.

"What would give you that idea?"

"It started with a text message I got when I arrived at

my uncle's house," she told her, "from someone calling himself Blue Violet."

"As in the Violet Killer?" Sophia's full lower lip hung down. As a true crime addict, she was fascinated with the case before Naomi ever mentioned her uncle Roger's involvement.

"It would seem so," Naomi muttered. "I believe he got my number from my uncle's cell phone that's missing. The demented killer apparently wants to taunt me as the next of kin."

"That's scary." Sophia's voice cracked as her brow creased.

"It gets worse... My uncle's house was bugged." Naomi sighed. "Someone's been watching, listening to him...and apparently me, before the devices were discovered by the police."

"Seriously?" Sophia's head snapped back. "That's too creepy."

"Tell me about it," Naomi groaned. "I'm afraid it might have been the work of the unsub." She wondered if this could be only the tip of the iceberg into just how far this person might be willing to go in terrorizing her.

"Please tell me you're not still staying at that house."

"I'm not." She paused thoughtfully. "Actually, I'm staying at Dylan's cabin—"

Sophia's eyes flashed. "You mean Detective Dylan Hester, the same guy you dumped two years ago?"

"Yes, that Dylan," Naomi almost hesitated to say. She didn't exactly consider what she did as dumping Dylan. They had never officially broken off their relationship. It was more of an unspoken reality, given that they lived so far apart, it was impractical to stay together and somehow make it work. "He offered me temporary shelter and, well, I took it, rather than stay at a hotel…and possibly be an open target for a serial killer—"

"You don't have to explain," Sophia said understandingly. "The most important thing is to keep you safe till you can come back home—that is, Miami," she made clear.

"That was what I was thinking," Naomi told her, pushing aside other implications in so doing. While the idea of remaining in Pebble Creek and falling back into Dylan's muscular arms had its appeal, she understood that the career she had worked hard for was elsewhere. She hoped he could respect that.

Sophia seemed to think otherwise. "Of course, that doesn't mean you can't take a trip down memory lane in the bedroom, for old times' sake, if both parties agree."

"I'll keep that in mind." Naomi laughed, finding she needed that at this moment. "Right now, I just want to get through the funeral without crying my eyes out." She jutted her chin. "And not allow my imagination to get carried away in believing that a serial killer is around every bend in the road, waiting to get me."

"Maybe it was your imagination," allowed Sophia, "and maybe not. Just be careful. Serial killers can be pretty calculating, if nothing else. Finding weak spots to keep potential targets on their heels is how they roll in playing a demented game of hiding-in-plain-view-and-seek."

"I know." Naomi twisted her lips, welcoming Sophia's coolheaded and knowledgeable perspective. "I'll be fine. Better let you go."

Sophia nodded. "Keep me informed on anything else that comes up."

"I will." Naomi gave her a smile and signed off. Afterward, she started the car again and drove back onto the street. She cautiously glanced at the rearview mirror, as if expecting the other SUV to reemerge ominously. It did not, thank goodness. She debated whether to burden Dylan with this or not, given that he already had his plate full with the Violet Killer case and the investigation into her uncle's murder, with the two apparently joined at the hip. Shelving the musings, Naomi turned her attention to paying a visit to the funeral home and the eventual burial of her uncle Roger.

Chapter Six

The Violet Killer Task Force gathered for its weekly meeting in a conference room at the Pebble Creek PD— the stakes getting higher by the day for bringing the case to a close with the capture of the unsub, whose adeptness at avoiding identification and apprehension caused tempers to flare. No one wanted to be held responsible for another strangulation death of a victim, with the serial killer seemingly laughing in their collective faces. At least this was how Dylan saw it as he waited his turn to speak while sitting at the rectangular meeting room table.

Standing at the podium was FBI Special Agent Patricia Stabler. The attractive criminal profiler and member of the Bureau's National Center for Analysis of Violent Crime was in her late thirties, tall and slender with crimson hair styled in a long, textured pixie cut that flattered her round face and green eyes. Wearing a sleek tan mélange pantsuit and black leather mules, she was all business when it came to doing her job. Even if it meant at the expense of her marriage, which had reportedly ended largely due to Special Agent Stabler's dedication to the job, believing her personal sacrifice was worthwhile when it meant pursuing dangerous criminals and bringing them to justice. Dylan couldn't decide whether to admire or reject her position. Yes, putting everything you had into your work was indeed admirable. But not if it had a detrimental effect on your love life, which was more important to him at the end of the day.

He wondered if choosing between career and a serious relationship could ever be so simple. Would he really be prepared to walk away from the job for love, as opposed to fighting like hell to preserve both? Dylan thought about Naomi. She, too, had chosen career over a relationship and possible family down the line—never putting herself in the position Patricia Stabler had. Was this by design, so as not to have the hard choices?

Dylan kicked himself for thinking that. Was it selfish of him to have wanted Naomi all to himself, never mind what she wanted? Whatever his regrets where it concerned their previous involvement, he was certain that she was more than capable of balancing a love life and whatever it entailed, including children, with any professional pursuits. He respected her too much to think otherwise. She simply had to want it bad enough someday. He wouldn't fault her for pursuing a dream, any more than he would fault himself for following his own dream of joining the military and police force. If he and Naomi were meant to be, it could still happen. If not, she would forever remain in his heart. Even if he had to fight hard to keep her and these feelings at arm's length.

He turned his attention to Special Agent Stabler as she methodically went through the ins and outs of their unsub in a deep, throaty voice, and the sense of urgency in tracking him down.

"The man we're dealing with here almost certainly suffers from narcissistic personality disorder—or an exaggerated sense of self-importance, while at the same time, possessing a pretty low self-esteem—and can definitely be characterized as having antisocial personality disorder. Not unlike other serial murderers—Ted Bundy, Gary Ridgway, John Wayne Gacy, Gerald Gallego or even Jack the Ripper himself, the consummate unsub serial killer. While he's not the typical sexual predator or child molester murderer such as these, our unsub is every bit as cold and calculating and a true psychopath, if there ever was one." Patricia slid a hand through her hair and pursed thin lips. "He handpicks his victims the same way people study and select the perfect peaches or tomatoes from the grocery store. Whether or not he had a rough childhood, an overbearing mother or some other psychological hang-ups is immaterial, per se, to the fact that he is fully in control of the situation. Or at least he thinks he is. Till we can prove him wrong." She took a deep breath and her eyes blinked. "In his head, the unsub is on a mission in his attacks on the women in this town. He won't quit on his own. He can't, even if he wanted to. That's not how it works with serial homicidal maniacs. The fact that he has chosen to divert from killing only women is only by necessity in his warped and pompous mind. It's not likely to stick. Nevertheless, he's effectively challenging everyone in this room to step up and figure it all out, before he strikes again—or after…"

Dylan took that as his cue and, as the lead detective on the case, went to the podium, alongside Detective Gregory Hwang.

"You ready for this?" Hwang whispered in his ear.

Dylan understood that he was asking due to the delicate nature of a serial killer crime case involving not only his mentor, Roger, but ex-girlfriend, Naomi, who had become part of the investigation, like it or not. "Yeah, I can handle it," he assured Hwang as much as himself. Turning to his fellow Task Force members, with a nod to Patricia Stabler and Police Chief Vernon Frazier, Dylan spoke coolly. "Let's bring everyone up to date on where things stand at the moment."

He walked over to one of the side-by-side large bulletin boards. On it were oversize headshots of seven women and one man. Dylan began with the women. "These are the known victims of the so-called Violet Killer." He stretched out his long arm and, pointing a long finger, named them one by one as if for the first time in respecting their unfortunate and untimely demise. "Conchita Kaplan, twenty-four, a schoolteacher. Linda Allen, thirty-one, a lawyer. Yancy Herrera, twenty-six, a hairstylist. Odette Wolfe, twenty-nine, a waitress. Rosa Vasquez, thirty-three, a dancer. Madison Cherish, thirty, a novelist. And Vera Bartlett, twenty-two, a senior at Pebble Creek College, became the latest female victim four days ago. In each case, the victim died from ligature strangulation, with the killer's calling card being a single blue violet placed strategically between the lips of each woman as if a work of art. The location of death varied from the victim's own residence to a parking garage to the woods—basically wherever the unsub found most opportune to strike."

Dylan sucked in a deep breath, knowing the newest victim would be the most difficult to talk about. He looked up at the smiling face of the man who had taught him so much about being a police detective, for whom he would never be able to thank enough, and that opportunity had been forever taken away from him. "Two days ago, a former member of our detective team, Roger Lincoln, was found shot to death in his office, where he worked as a private investigator. Roger continued to be connected to the department as a consultant on the Violet Killer case." Dylan paused, closing his eyes and opening them again to gaze at the photograph of the man.

"We have reason to believe that Roger was a victim of our serial killer. A violet was left in his mouth by the unsub. Apparently, Roger had managed to crack the case in identifying the perp and was on the verge of blowing this thing wide open when he was killed in a desperate effort to keep him forever silent. But there was a witness.

"Roger was having a video chat on his laptop when he was gunned down." Again, Dylan needed to take a moment as he turned away from the board as Naomi's beautiful face filled his head. He hated that she had to see what she did and live with it for the rest of her life, but this was where things were because of the unsub's actions. "He was speaking to his niece, Naomi Lincoln, a Secret Service agent based in Miami. Some of you may remember that, two years ago, Naomi worked with the department as a crime victims service coordinator for Blane County before moving on. According to her, Roger was on the verge of revealing who the Violet Killer was, before someone crept up behind him and executed him in front of Naomi's very eyes. She never saw or heard the unsub, but he doesn't know that for certain, putting her at risk. Naomi is back in town for Roger's funeral and staying with me." He squared his shoulders, not ducking from where he stood in wanting to protect her. "We have history. Besides that, the perp took Roger's laptop and cell phone, giving him vital information, including Naomi's cell phone number, which he has used to harass her in text messages. If that isn't enough, we've learned that Roger's house and office have been bugged, maybe by the unsub, hoping to gather more damaging info. Or worse, further target Naomi. Until we know for sure one way or the other, or we have someone in custody to that effect, I'll do what I can to keep her safe."

"I wouldn't expect anything less," Police Chief Frazier

spoke approvingly. At sixty-two and African American, he was a twenty-five-year veteran of the force, having transferred there from the Portland Police Bureau as a young detective and worked his way up. "I think everyone in this room has the greatest respect for Roger Lincoln, one of the finest detectives we've had. Making sure nothing happens to his niece, Naomi, is something he would expect from us."

Dylan nodded appreciatively at the baldheaded and brawny chief, who wore tortoiseshell glasses over crusty black eyes and had a graying chevron mustache. He was a stand-up guy who allowed his detectives to do their job with minimal interference, adding meaningful input when necessary. "As yet, we have no DNA, fingerprints or other workable evidence to point to anyone in particular as the Violet Killer. That hasn't stopped him from taunting us seemingly every chance he gets, as if we haven't a clue as to how to stop him. With respect to tracking down the violets themselves, or their source, the flower happens to be one of the most popular in Oregon and is widely grown, in addition to being carried by an abundance of nurseries—making it all but impossible to connect the dots to one individual." Dylan sucked in a deep breath and frowned with growing frustration. "This notwithstanding, there have been—and still are, in some cases—viable suspects…" He turned toward Hwang, who took it from there as he walked toward the other bulletin board, where there were enlarged pictures of several men.

"As of now, we've interviewed a number of persons of interest," Hwang said, scratching through the hair on his chin. He then raised his finger to home in on the first one. "Neil Murray, thirty-four, teaches at Pebble Creek College. He was seen leaving the scene of one of the murders. Trent Oliver, twenty-six, is an unemployed mechanic who showed a hostility toward women. Blade Canfield, twenty-nine, is a trust fund baby who likes to throw money around like it's going out of style, and had a relationship with one of the women that ended badly. Alfonso Mendoza, forty-two, who's been in and out of prison and has a history of stalking pretty women." Hwang gazed at the final photo. "Last but not least there's Zachary Jamieson, a thirty-five-year-old florist employee with a passion for violets, who was found lurking around an area in which one of the victims was killed.

"Murray and Canfield have rock-solid alibis, while Oliver, Mendoza and Jamieson remain persons of interest," Hwang said, returning to the podium. "So far, we haven't been able to place any of them near the crime scene around the time Lincoln was killed. Doesn't mean one wasn't there and perpetrated the act, in addition to strangling the women. We do, however, have a bead on the type and caliber of weapon used to kill Roger Lincoln. A .45 ACP handgun. If we find the murder weapon, everything else may fall into place in taking down the Violet Killer."

Dylan added a few more thoughts, as did Special Agent Stabler and Chief Frazier, before other members of the Task Force weighed in on where they were in the investigation, with everyone on the same page in their determination to achieve the goal of bringing this case to a close with the arrest of the perp before anyone else had to die.

As the meeting broke up, Patricia Stabler caught up to Dylan in the hall. "Hope everything works out for you and Roger Lincoln's niece in terms of having her back while she's in town and in harm's way."

"Thanks." Dylan's eyes flashed at the FBI profiler and wondered if she was alluding to anything beyond his being Naomi's protector, which was probably the most he could hope for at this stage of their lives. "I'll always have her back," he said firmly.

"The FBI often works very closely with the Secret Service, so I applaud her in pursuing that path," Patricia said.

"Naomi loves what she does for a living," he almost hated to admit, but did so anyhow.

"Good for her." Patricia showed her teeth and Dylan wondered if this was one of those career-before-love-life moments. Or was he misreading her?

"The sooner she can get back to it, the better for everyone." Dylan hoped he wasn't giving away his mixed feelings in losing Naomi again to her career. He would do nothing to interfere with it. Especially given the stakes a serial killer had raised in a game of life and death.

"The FBI will continue to use all its tools, Hester, to help bring down the Violet Killer," the profiler contended. "It's one of those make-or-break cases that beg to be cracked and dissected."

Dylan grinned. "Spoken like a true NCAVC professional."

"Just telling it as I see it," she insisted.

"Well, we'll gladly accept all the help we can get from the FBI," he told her, not willing to kick a gift horse in the mouth. Even if it meant jockeying for position in the investigation and sometimes competing strategies for being most effective in solving the case.

Chief Frazier came up to them and stood eye to eye with Dylan, while giving him a vague expression. "Got a sec…?"

"Sure." Dylan watched as Frazier and Patricia shared a few words, before he followed the chief to his office.

It was in a corner on the main floor of the building and spacious with a picture window. The wood blinds were open a crack. On a U-shaped executive desk was a framed photograph of Vernon Frazier and his wife of forty years, Evelyn. It reminded Dylan of what he could still have in a long and lasting romance and marriage, should this opportunity present itself with the right woman. Naomi immediately came to mind, whether he tried to block this thought or not.

"Have a seat," Frazier voiced tonelessly.

Dylan sat in one of two office chairs while watching his boss plop down onto his own massage desk chair, wondering what this was all about. He guessed it pertained to the investigation.

"How's Naomi doing?" Frazier peered at him through coal eyes.

"She's coping," Dylan answered as best he could. "Like us, she wants answers as to why this had to happen to her uncle as well as the other victims of the Violet Killer."

"Yeah, I understand. Roger and I go back a long way. I never wanted him to retire, but… Well, you know the man. His pride wouldn't allow him to take a step back." Deep furrows lined Frazier's forehead. "Maybe if he had stayed on the force, it might have been a different outcome."

Dylan agreed, but as nature had already taken its course, said, "We'll never know."

"What has Naomi, whom I've heard good things about as a member of the Secret Service, told you about what she witnessed on the laptop?"

"Only what I already mentioned. She saw Roger get shot, but not who shot him."

"Maybe she remembers more than she thinks," Frazier suggested, leaning forward.

Dylan sat back. "Not sure I follow you."

"In times of great stress, people often block out the hardest things to remember. That may or may not be the case here, but as she's staying with you, it doesn't hurt to press Naomi for any useful information you can derive from her that might be pertinent to solving this case."

"I'll see what I can do." Even then, Dylan was concerned that pressing her too hard might be counterproductive. And even resentful on Naomi's part. But at the same time, if she could fill in a blank or two, wouldn't she want to do that, if it meant identifying a serial killer on the loose?

Frazier shifted his body. "Good. At this point, we can use all the help we can get." His cell phone rang and he answered. Dylan watched the chief's face darken before he hung up.

"What is it?" Dylan asked.

"A young woman has been reported missing," Frazier spoke, sounding ill at ease. "She could be yet another victim of the Violet Killer."

DYLAN WAS GLUM when he passed the unsettling news on to Naomi later that afternoon by the lake, where he found her standing on the grass outside his house. "Her name is Sandra Neville. The twenty-nine-year-old orthodontist was supposed to meet her parents for dinner last night. When she didn't show up or call, both uncharacteristic according to them, they naturally became worried, given the current state of affairs, and filed a missing person report."

Naomi cringed. "Do you think she's dead…?"

Without saying it, Dylan knew she was asking specifically if the orthodontist may have fallen into the clutches of the Violet Killer. Though he feared this might well be true, he didn't want to immediately jump to the worst-case scenario. "Hopefully, she simply lost track of time," he threw out unevenly.

"But what if she didn't?" Naomi questioned. "What if he has her…and she's still alive and needs to be rescued before it's too late…?"

"We're doing everything we can to try to find Ms. Neville," he sought to assure her. "The fact that she was reported missing in less than twenty-four hours gives us more time to work with." His voice dropped an octave when carrying on. "Unfortunately, if she has encountered the Violet Killer unsub, it could be too late to save her. From what we know, the perp has typically stalked his victims and when ready to attack, has done so in rather quick fashion. But again, we're not there yet, so let's just take a wait-and-see approach."

Naomi tucked a loose hair behind her ear and he sensed she had something on her mind. She looked up at him and said with a catch to her voice, "This may or may not be anything, but something happened earlier today…"

"What?" Dylan tensed.

"Well, I could've sworn that someone tried to run me off the road." She waited a beat. "Or at least intended to frighten me half to death."

Dylan didn't like the sound of that, all things considered. He glanced around them warily, feeling pretty secure in his surroundings. But even with that, the idea of Naomi being a target to a killer shook him. "Let's go back inside and you can tell me more about this—"

Minutes later, they were seated on the modern chenille sofa, where Naomi wrung her hands. "The car just seemed to come out of nowhere and was on my tail," she contended nervously. "When I put some distance between us, it followed. Finally, it turned onto a side street and that was that. Not sure what to make of it."

"What type of car was it?" Dylan asked.

"It was a dark SUV," she told him. "Not sure what model."

"Could you make out anything on the driver?"

"No, the glass was tinted." Naomi batted her lashes. "Maybe I freaked out for no reason."

"Or maybe for all the right reasons." Dylan jutted his chin. He hated to think that the unsub was privy to Naomi's whereabouts at any given moment. Especially now that she was essentially under his protection and, Dylan wanted to believe, safe from harm.

She frowned. "So, you think that could've been the Violet Killer sending me an unnerving message?"

"Too soon to say," he spoke honestly. "Has he sent you any other text messages?"

"No." She sighed. "That's a relief."

Dylan agreed, believing that if it had been the unsub, he likely would have found it hard to resist taunting her as part of his psychological games. Still, nothing said that the perp couldn't still be toying with them both, keeping him and Naomi guessing as to what he might try next. "I'll check if the vehicle you described matches any owned by our current list of suspects," Dylan said. "In the meantime, if anything like that happens again, let me know pronto."

"I will," she promised and gave him a deadpan look. "Hopefully, the missing woman will show up soon and everyone can breathe a little easier."

He seconded that, but his instincts told Dylan that this might not end well for Sandra Neville, even if the cause for her disappearance was something—or someone—other than the Violet Killer.

Chapter Seven

Saturday was overcast, matching the somber mood of Naomi as she stood beside Dylan at the Pebble Creek Cemetery for the funeral of her uncle, Roger Lincoln. She was wearing a dark gray dress suit and low-heeled black pumps, and she'd put her hair in an updo style for the sad occasion. As difficult as it had been when attending her parents' funeral two decades ago, this may have been even more painful, if that was possible. Aside from being old enough to truly appreciate the loss, Naomi couldn't imagine anything worse than losing a loved one to violence and witnessing it all at once. Her only solace was that her uncle Roger had found his way to a place alongside his brother, Milton Lincoln, where they and Naomi's mother, Paula, could be at peace.

Eyeing Dylan in a black suit that fit well on his frame and made him look even more handsome than usual, Naomi felt grateful for his support and friendship through this trying time. She knew it was just as difficult for him, mourning the loss and trying to find Roger's killer. Last night, she'd been sure another nightmare of the shooting would happen. Especially after Dylan had told her about a missing woman who was possibly another victim of the madman on the prowl. But to Naomi's surprise, she had slept without any bad dreams she could remember.

Perhaps it was due to feeling Dylan's powerful presence, even if in another room; knowing he was just a shout away should the bogeyman come after her in nightmares or reality. And what about when it was time to return to her real world? Would the specter of her uncle's tragic death continue to haunt her like a woman possessed?

Naomi gazed at the mourners, recognizing some and not others. She couldn't help but wonder if her uncle's murderer had actually dared to show his face while hiding in plain view, for some kind of sick gratification. She'd heard that this was the maniacal manner in which some killers got their kicks right under the noses of law enforcement—which, in this case, was on guard and sprinkled throughout the cemetery should trouble arise—even while the unsub gave the guise of being present for the right reasons. She sensed by his intense demeanor and shifting eyes that Dylan was thinking the same thing. Had they always been on the same wavelength when it counted most? Or was she mixing apples and oranges when sizing him up and regretting the way things ended between them two years ago?

Naomi turned her attention to Pastor Krista Gilliam as the attractive and slender thirtysomething woman picked up on where she left off in the church, focusing on Roger's career and love of the community. Caught up in the emotion, Naomi wept and found herself holding on to Dylan for support. He seemed comfortable with it and placed a long arm around her waist.

"You okay?" he whispered sympathetically.

"I will be," she promised him, knowing it was what her uncle would have wanted, in spite of his untimely demise.

After the gravesite eulogies, Naomi greeted mourners, thanking them for coming. Police Chief Vernon Frazier took her hand in his while offering his condolences.

"I'm so sorry about this, Naomi," he voiced from the heart. "Roger was a fine man who always spoke very highly of you."

Naomi's eyes crinkled. "I felt the same way about him."

"If you need anything, let me know," the chief said.

"I will."

Detective Gregory Hwang expressed his sympathies, followed by other members of the Pebble Creek PD. Naomi was then approached by a tall, slim red-haired woman in a dark gray striped two-piece skirt suit and matching heels. "FBI Special Agent Patricia Stabler," she identified herself. "I never got to meet your uncle, but from what I've heard, he was a highly regarded member of the police force." She reached into the pocket of her suit jacket and pulled out a card. "If you ever need to talk about what happened, I'm a criminal profiler and investigative psychologist, ready to help."

Naomi took the card and nodded. "Thank you." She watched as Agent Stabler moved on to Dylan and the two exchanged a few words. Obviously, they were working together on the case. Still, Naomi couldn't help but wonder if the pretty FBI profiler was his type. Or if he was in any way interested in her. Naomi quickly dismissed the thought from her head, realizing that she had no claim on Dylan to feel jealousy. To suggest otherwise would be to give in to feelings that both had apparently put behind them, to one degree or another. No matter how difficult it was to bear.

The last person to pay respects was a petite, well-dressed African American woman in her early fifties with brunette hair in a buzz cut. "Hi," she said nervously, taking Naomi's hand and squeezing it. "My name's Brenda Quinlan. I was dating your uncle when he passed."

"Really?" Naomi raised a brow at her, taken aback by the news. Not that her uncle Roger had talked much about his love life, as he was a very private man when it came to his own romance. Having never married, he seemed fairly content to spend his life alone for the most part. When had that changed?

"We'd only been out on a few dates," she explained as if reading Naomi's mind. "He was a good man and talked about you all the time. I'm so sorry for your loss."

"Yours, as well," Naomi had to say graciously. She wished they had gotten to know one another when Uncle Roger was still alive. He deserved to have someone special in his life. Naomi felt the same way about herself. But was it too late for that? She turned to Dylan, who was now speaking to Brenda, as if they were old friends. Naomi wondered if he was as lonely as she felt at times. Or had they each made their own beds to lie in by themselves?

"DID YOU KNOW Uncle Roger was seeing someone?" Naomi asked from the passenger seat of Dylan's official vehicle.

"He never mentioned that to me," Dylan responded levelly as he drove them to the lawyer's office, where Roger's will would be divulged. It had surprised him that Roger had included him in the will. As far as Dylan was concerned, he didn't want anything that Naomi should have. "I'm sure if things had gotten serious, Roger would've let both of us in on it."

"I suppose." Her voice cracked. "Brenda seems like a nice person."

"I agree." Dylan felt that Naomi was nice, too. But that wasn't enough to seal the deal in giving them the type of relationship he had dreamed of. Maybe things wouldn't have worked out for Roger, either, once they got past the get-along-with-each-other stage. No one would ever know for sure now. He couldn't help but think that the same was true with him and Naomi. They were both alive and well, but still not on the same page in their pursuits in life, which no longer included each other.

"Do you think the unsub was at the cemetery?" Naomi broke into Dylan's musings.

"It's possible, but probably not," he responded confidently. To Dylan, the funeral was somber enough without the person responsible for Roger's death rearing his ugly head. That didn't mean the perp wasn't brazen enough to try to show his face. But with the grounds blanketed by cops and the FBI, it didn't seem to be in the cards for the Violet Killer to press his luck by overplaying his hand. "My guess is the unsub is lying low for the time being, waiting for the right time and place to make his next move."

"Maybe he's already made it," Naomi spoke glumly and Dylan read between the lines. "Any more news on the missing woman?"

"She's still unaccounted for," Dylan hated to say, staring through the windshield as he approached a red light. Sandra Neville had been missing for more than thirty-six hours, a troubling sign if ever there was one. But he, for one, wasn't about to give up hope that she might still be alive. "Search and rescue teams are out in force throughout the county, trying to find her. We won't give up till we know her whereabouts and condition, one way or the other."

"I can't imagine what her family must be going through at the moment." Naomi took a breath. "Then again, I guess I have some idea. I just buried my uncle, and no amount of hoping will ever bring him back."

"True." Dylan could hardly counter that reality. He could try, though, to look at it another way. "However, Roger left behind something precious that he would want to stay strong in his absence, and that's you."

"I know," she said emotionally and faced him. "Uncle Roger would want that for both of us."

Dylan glanced at her with a smooth grin. "So why don't we try our best to adhere to his wishes, even under the cloud of his killer still at large."

Naomi's shoulders squared acceptingly. "Okay, I'm with you and Uncle Roger. I'll try to abide by his wishes."

"Deal," Dylan seconded, and wondered if he, too, was up to the task, with the unsub continuing to cause headaches and a woman still missing to be concerned about.

NAOMI AND DYLAN entered the law office of Benjamin Gardner, Roger's attorney. The seventysomething, white-haired man was tall and on the frail side, wearing a skinny-fit dark blue suit. They shook his hand and sat on brown tweed visitor chairs, while Benjamin took a seat on a midback black leather chair behind a sprawling vintage wood desk.

"Thanks for coming," he said, adjusting silver wire-rimmed glasses. "My condolences for your loss. Roger was a good friend and will be missed in that regard and as a client of longstanding." He paused and fiddled with some papers on his desk, as if to find something to do with his hands. "Anyway, let's get down to business."

Naomi was admittedly a bit nervous as she waited to see what her uncle had decided upon in what turned out to be his final act, without his being the wiser. She wasn't really surprised to see that he had left Dylan something in his will. After all, the two remained close even after her uncle quit the force. Whatever the case, she was totally fine with it, wanting only to settle his estate and see where she went from there. She glanced at Dylan and he glanced back with a comforting grin before gazing at the lawyer with what she believed was largely curiosity.

When he spoke again, Benjamin said simply, in giving Naomi a direct look, "Roger left his property, including the house and land, to you, Ms. Lincoln, along with his car, savings, stocks and bonds, and proceeds from his life insurance and place of business, once liquidated." He took a breath as Naomi considered her uncle's generosity and the attorney turned Dylan's way. "As for you, Mr. Hester, Roger left money for you to buy that powerboat you've always dreamed of, wanting to make sure you had no more excuses for putting it off." Dylan looked clearly taken aback and humbled as he gave a chuckle. "He also bequeathed to you a photograph Roger took of you and Ms. Lincoln, which he considered his favorite. I believe it is sitting on the mantel in the living room of your house, Naomi."

She smiled thoughtfully. "I'll make sure he gets it," she said, regarding Dylan and remembering the occasion when the photo was taken.

"Oh, and uh, Roger also wanted me to pass along that you should keep an eye on his niece," the attorney told Dylan, "no matter where she hangs her hat."

Dylan seemed to contemplate the somewhat unusual wish, before breaking into a half grin and peering at Naomi. "I can do that," he promised in a determined voice, causing her heart to skip a beat in the moment. Was this her uncle speaking from the grave in doing his part to see to it that they stayed connected, even if apart?

"Well, that's it," Benjamin said, as if glad to be done. "Any questions?"

Twenty minutes later, Naomi and Dylan sat at a booth

in Lesley's Restaurant for lunch. It was a popular hangout for law enforcement, specializing in seafood and desserts. It also happened to be where they had their first official date, bringing back memories, mostly pleasant, for Naomi. She wondered if Dylan was feeling it, too. Asking, though, was not an option, in case he had gotten too far past that time in their lives to want to go back, even in thought.

"If I'm not mistaken," Dylan said, as if reading her mind while studying the menu, "on our first date here, you ordered the crispy shrimp and buttered noodles. Correct me if I'm wrong…"

Naomi couldn't help but blush and be impressed at the same time. "You're not wrong," she admitted. "You're spot-on."

He flashed his teeth smugly. "Shall we try it again?" he challenged her.

She accepted. "Sure, why not."

Dylan ordered the same lunch and both also ordered lemonade to down it. "Just like old times, huh?"

Naomi wasn't sure she was prepared to go quite that far, but liked the notion anyhow. She forked a shrimp. "I suppose it is."

"I guess Roger wanted to do his part to make sure we didn't forget the good times," Dylan said, his voice lingering.

"I think you're right." She went for the noodles. "So, when do you plan to buy the boat?" Naomi imagined being on it with him for a day on the lake.

"As soon as I get this business with the unsub behind me." Dylan ate shrimp and Naomi found she enjoyed watching him eat. "How about you? What are your plans for the house you now own?"

Her eyes flashed. "Haven't really thought about it,"

she confessed. Not with everything else that had gone on. "I'll probably put it on the market." Would it make any sense to hold on to the property if she lived elsewhere? Wouldn't keeping the house only bring up sad memories?

"Maybe a good idea," Dylan said flatly. "I'm sure you could fetch a pretty good price in a hot market these days—even more with a first-rate security system installed ahead of time for the next owner."

Naomi dabbed a napkin to her mouth. She agreed she should have it installed, whether living there or not, if only to add to the property's value. "You're right," she said, then listened as he suggested a home security company to get in touch with.

"So, I suppose you'll be heading back to Miami now that the funeral is over…?"

Her lashes fluttered. "Are you trying to get rid of me?" Maybe she had overstayed her welcome at his cabin.

"Believe me, that's the last thing on my mind." His earnest look was convincing.

"Then what?"

He sat back and sighed. "I just thought that as long as the Violet Killer unsub was seemingly targeting you, it might be a good thing if you left town, if only for the time being. Of course, if you wanted to come back after he's been brought down, you'd be more than welcome to do so."

Naomi waited a long beat, trying to gauge his words. Was he inviting her to return after the dust settled, to maybe try to pick up where they left off two years ago? Or was she overthinking, as usual? Did they really have a chance to make things work when her life was now elsewhere? As it was, she had been giving the timing of her departure some thought. She wondered if he would agree with her plans, while looking him in the eye. "Actually, I think I'd like to stay here for a while longer."

"Really?" Dylan cocked a brow in surprise while holding his glass of lemonade.

"Yes. With Uncle Roger's killer still on the loose, I feel as if I need to do something to help."

"Such as...?" He peered at her uncomfortably.

"I don't know," she said, moving food around her plate. "Maybe join in on the search for Sandra Neville."

Dylan frowned. "Are you sure that's a good idea?"

"Why not?" Naomi remained resolute in her decision. "She's missing and her family is worried sick from what I've heard, and understandably so. Every second that goes by where she's not found is like sticking a dagger into the hearts of those praying that Sandra's still alive. I wouldn't want anyone to have to deal with what I've just gone through, if there's any way possible to prevent it. If I can help to locate her, one way or the other, I want to do that."

He continued to eye her skeptically. "Don't you have an assignment to get back to?"

"My boss has given me some space to deal with Uncle Roger's death," she reported. "I'm sure he would be okay with a few more days to that effect." Nevertheless, Naomi intended to convey this to him, to be sure it met with his approval.

"We could always use extra volunteers in the search," Dylan conceded, shifting to one side. "You have my support, but only if you continue staying at my house for as long as you're in Pebble Creek. It's still safer there for you while the Violet Killer is terrorizing women—and possibly targeting you—and would allow me to keep an eye on you more successfully, in honoring Roger's wishes."

Naomi couldn't help but smile, feeling comforted at

the idea of him being her handsome protector, even if she was more than capable of protecting herself from a serial killer. One could never be capable enough, she knew. "You drive a hard bargain, Detective."

The lines around Dylan's mouth remained inflexible. "So, is it a deal?" he pressed.

She laughed. "Yes, it's a deal."

"Good." He finally softened his protective stance and gulped down the rest of his lemonade. "Why don't we swing by your new house and pick up the photograph Roger so generously passed on to me."

"Great idea," she said, while conjuring up poignant memories that would probably be best if remained buried in the photo.

AFTER CHECKING THE house for any signs of an intruder, they ended up in front of the fireplace mantel, where Dylan lifted the photograph that Roger had left him in his will. Studying it, Dylan was struck at just how handsome they looked as a couple. Naomi, dressed in a wine-red printed sports bra and white denim shorts, was every bit as shapely and sexy as she was today.

"Nice, huh?" he remarked openly, holding it at an angle so they could share the visual.

"Yes," she said, smiling. "We had fun that day."

"Yeah." Dylan gazed at the picture again. What he wouldn't give to go back in time and relive being a couple at the county fair and well on their way to being in love. How could he have known that a year later, they would unexpectedly go their separate ways and his heart would end up broken? But life always threw you curves. It was how one responded to this that defined the person. Training his eyes upon Naomi's gorgeous face, Dylan drifted his gaze down to her generous mouth. It was open just a tad and seemed inviting him to kiss. The overwhelming urge to capitulate was more than he was able or willing to pass up. Lifting her chin, he kissed those lips and braced himself for a flat-out rejection of the advance. Instead, she allowed the kiss to linger, seemingly as into it as he was. Though the surge of desire rolled through him like a tsunami, he forced himself to pull back.

Naomi, batting her eyes, touched her mouth. "What was that all about?"

Dylan asked himself the same question. He wanted it to be about possibilities for the future with a pinch hit from the past. But he knew better than to get his hopes up for something that was likely out of reach. Grinning crookedly, he responded, "Just a kiss for old times' sake. Sorry if I overstepped."

"It's fine," she said tonelessly. "Maybe we both needed that for closure."

He frowned, not liking the sound of that, but not surprised, considering where they were at this stage of their lives. Which was definitely not together. The sooner he reconciled with that, the better he could be happy for her living in Miami as a Secret Service agent. With possibly some other guy waiting in the wings.

"Whatever you say," Dylan voiced thickly. "Let's get out of here."

She nodded stiffly, seemingly content to leave it at that.

Chapter Eight

Later that afternoon, Naomi threw on cuffed boyfriend jeans and a knit top to go with her slip-on sneakers and put her hair into a ponytail while wearing a black running cap, before joining other volunteers in the search for Sandra Neville. They were in a wooded area not far from her house that had already apparently been searched to no avail. But the belief among authorities was that, in many instances, it was the second or third try that yielded results, for better or worse. Naomi hoped it was for the better in finding the missing woman alive. She was in a group of four people—two women and two men— between the ages of early twenties and midseventies. They were all on a first-name basis and everyone seemed friendly enough and fully vested in the mission set forth. Though Naomi felt at ease with them, it occurred to her that some kidnappers and killers got a perverse thrill in blending in with searchers, while putting on a perfectly innocent front. Could whoever was responsible for Sandra's disappearance be hiding in clear view?

Breaking away from that unsettling thought, Naomi went back to the unexpected kiss earlier that reverberated throughout her bones. Still reeling from it, she had almost forgotten the impact Dylan's potent kisses had on her mind and body. It came back loud and clear like a romance movie in living color. He was the lover who took her up into the clouds, higher and higher, wanting more. But circumstances had brought her back down to earth. No matter how much she still felt for him, Naomi doubted the same was true in reverse. Asking Dylan for a second chance at a long-distance relationship was likely a path he wasn't interested in. Could she really blame him? Was it not a recipe for disaster?

Her focus again shifted as she found herself slightly ahead of the others, having gone farther than the perimeter established by the law enforcement coordinating the search. Naomi was just about to turn around after plowing through some dense shrubbery beneath the trees, when her eyes landed on a frail and dirty human arm sticking out like a sore thumb from the undergrowth. Naomi's heart skipped a beat. Even without seeing the rest of the body, she sensed that the search for Sandra Neville had come to a tragic end.

DYLAN ARRIVED AT the scene with a heavy heart. He knew it was a long shot—and longer with each passing hour that she remained missing—that Sandra Neville would be found alive. Now it appeared as if the worst-case scenario had occurred. At least this was what had been conveyed to him, as he approached the crime scene tape. Along with the fact that it was Naomi who first discovered the corpse. Spotting her now, being comforted by other search volunteers, outside the perimeters of where the investigation was underway, Dylan had to put aside an urge to go over and take her into his arms. That would come later. And any second thoughts on her insistence upon staying in town and being part of the investigation unofficially and indirectly into the killing of Roger. Right now, it was important, for both their sakes, that he put first his role as the lead investigator of the Violet Killer case.

Climbing over the yellow tape with his long legs, Dylan met up with Detective Hwang and Agent Patricia Stabler, who were standing just feet from the deceased woman.

"Is it her?" Dylan asked to confirm, shifting his gaze from one to the other.

"Yeah, afraid so," Hwang uttered bleakly.

"Her ID makes that clear," Patricia added, holding it up in front of him with a nitrile-gloved hand. "It was on her person. Sandra Adrienne Neville, age twenty-nine."

Dylan frowned and gazed down at the fully clothed decedent. Even with the sun's rays starting to weaken, filtering down through the trees at this time of day, and her body partly obscured by the scrubs, he could see that she was slender and African American, with black hair styled in a side-swept undercut. She almost appeared to be sleeping, with her head lying slanted on a pillow of underbrush.

"Any signs of foul play?" he asked.

"There's bruising on her neck and wrists," Patricia pointed out. "She definitely put up a struggle with someone…"

"Looks like that someone is our unsub," Hwang said. "A cursory gloved check in her mouth indicated that stuck inside is a blue violet, courtesy of the Violet Killer. We left it there for forensics and the medical examiner to duke it out over."

Dylan's brow furrowed. This was the first African American victim of the unsub, illustrating his willingness to go after any women who fit the general description of those he targeted as young, attractive and available to put down. More concerning to Dylan was how this was af-

fecting Naomi. Already considered a potential target of
the serial killer and biracial, did this freak her out? Put
her in any greater danger?

Hwang, seemingly reading into that, wrinkled his
nose. "If Naomi hadn't spotted the decedent outside the
boundaries, we might never have found her—"

"I know," Dylan conceded musingly. "Still, after witnessing Roger's murder and now this—I just wonder how
much more she can take…" It was a question he wasn't
sure he wanted to know the answer to.

"Maybe more than you think." Patricia gave him a
knowing look. "If they thought she couldn't cut it, the Secret Service would never have brought her on board, trust
me." She put a hand on his arm. "Go talk to her." Patricia sighed, removing her hand. "Anything might help—"

"I will." He nodded in agreement, while acknowledging in his head that Naomi was more than capable of dealing with adversity, even if his natural instincts were to
want to shield her from uncomfortable circumstances.
Right now, his best bet was to be there to support her for
at least as long as she was in town. How long that would
be was anyone's guess. After her latest traumatic epi-
sode, maybe now she would decide it was best to head
back to Miami, as far away from the perp and his homicidal urges as possible. If that happened, they would go
from there on the nature of their continuing involvement.

Before Dylan could make his way to Naomi, the medical examiner arrived. Dr. Martha Donahue was in her
early forties and small with short caramel balayage hair
in feathery curls. She touched her white-framed glasses
as she approached the three. "Came as soon as I could,"
she said, sounding exhausted as though having just run
a marathon. "What are we looking at?"

"A deceased African American female," Dylan said

reluctantly. "Appears as though she's the victim of foul play in a manner consistent with other young women who have recently fallen prey to a serial killer."

"Looks like she put up a fight," Patricia said, "and, hopefully, took some DNA from her attacker."

"We'll see." Martha narrowed her small blue eyes and slid on a pair of white cotton gloves, before crouching and beginning a visual and physical inspection of the victim. Dylan never felt particularly comfortable with this aspect of criminal investigations, where decedents were no longer able to call the shots in terms of privacy and dignity. He wished Sandra could open her mouth and tell them as much as she could in helping to find her killer. Forensic examination and an autopsy would have to suffice. He watched the medical examiner delicately manipulating the victim's neck. "Judging by the condition of the neck area, my preliminary assessment is that the decedent died from strangulation caused by some kind of ligature." She turned her attention to one of the victim's hands. "Looks like there may be some blood under the fingernails, indicating the killer may have left behind some DNA, if not her own."

"How long has she been dead, Doc?" Hwang asked.

Martha examined more of the corpse. "If I had to make a preliminary guess, I'd say it's been less than forty-eight hours."

Dylan winced. This would indicate that Sandra Neville was likely murdered close to the time she went missing and at the location where the body was found. He suspected that she may have gone for a short hike, where she ran into her killer, who in accordance with his pattern of behavior, lay in wait, catching her off guard. At that point, she was pretty much the perp's for the taking.

He watched as the medical examiner removed the unsub's calling card from the victim's mouth, holding up the wet and discolored violet, as if it was a trophy. "Looks as though your Violet Killer has struck again," Martha stated grimly.

"Yeah, I was afraid of that," Dylan muttered with resignation. With another person added to the unsub's list of victims, Dylan could think only that he would be damned if Naomi were to be next. He made his way over to her as she was still huddled around the group of volunteers who shared the grisly discovery with Naomi. She reacted when seeing him and he wasn't quite sure what she may have been thinking. He pulled her away to a spot where they could speak alone. "Hey," he said evenly. "How are you doing?"

"Not too good." Naomi pursed her lips. "This is quickly becoming a nightmare."

Those sentiments were perfectly understandable to Dylan. How could they not be? He had come to the same conclusion—only drawn out over the last two years plus. But gazing at her face and lowered eyes, he sensed that there was something more going on. "What is it?"

She gazed up at him and pulled her cell phone out of a pocket. "I just received this text message…"

Dylan looked at the small screen and read:

She reminded me of you. Still, a poor substitute for the real Naomi Lincoln. See you soon…

Alarmed that the unsub had again threatened Naomi and was possibly watching them at that moment, Dylan guided her back to the other volunteers. He sized each one up in assessing their innocence. After some questions and feeling reasonably certain that none were behind the ominous text message, he told Naomi fixedly,

"Wait here till I get back. And under no circumstances do you go into the woods on your own."

She batted her lashes. "Don't worry, I'm not going to make myself easy prey for this killer," she insisted. "If it's his intent to come after me, it won't be on his own terms."

Dylan nodded, feeling that she got it. Since she was a federal law enforcement officer herself, he wouldn't have expected anything less. Still, he hated to have to leave her for others to protect. But with the unsub once again snubbing his nose at the entire Task Force for his own sick gratification, catching him had to be a top priority. Especially with another victim already in the books.

THAT NIGHT, NAOMI lay in bed, tossing and turning, while trying hard not to feel guilty about the death of Sandra Neville. Though, rationally speaking, she knew it wasn't her fault that a psycho serial slayer targeted the orthodontist. But in an irrational way, she couldn't help herself. After all, didn't the unsub practically confess that he chose Sandra because she reminded him of her?

Still, a poor substitute for the real Naomi Lincoln. See you soon...

The mere thought gave Naomi a chill. He was telling her she was to be his next victim. Apparently, the Violet Killer was not only stalking her, but had managed to blend in with the volunteers in the search for Sandra Neville. No doubt, he was laughing his head off at being so close to capture, yet so far. Dylan, FBI Agent Stabler and other law enforcement had immediately fanned out in trying to locate the perp. Alas, with no success. He had apparently come and gone like a thief in the night. Leaving everyone more than a little unnerved and frustrated.

But Naomi refused to allow him to take away her courage as a Secret Service agent and as a woman who knew an intimidator when she saw one. The Violet Killer was not going to send her packing while leaving behind the tortured memory of her uncle, who was ever so close to identifying and helping to put away the unsub, before he himself was taken out instead. She owed Uncle Roger that much to hang around and do what she could to see justice done, even if uncertain how best to achieve that goal while limited in her official capacity. Something told her that Dylan would prefer that she stay out of it, as though her presence would somehow hinder the investigation. Or was it more his need to be her protector in keeping her out of harm's way at all costs?

Either way, Naomi had to be there and could only hope that Dylan could respect that. She was giving him no choice, with them both wanting the same thing at the end of the day. To stop the Violet Killer from terrorizing the community. That notwithstanding, the thought of Dylan holding her in his arms, making love to her, somehow comforted her, even if he and she were no longer together. She still felt the pleasant sting of his kiss from earlier in the day. Was it truly a mere one-off to nostalgia and nothing more? Or a strong indicator that something was still there between them that needed to be explored?

Shutting her eyes, Naomi drifted off to sleep, fully expecting another nightmare to surface involving perhaps the murders of Uncle Roger and Sandra Neville in a frightful convergence. Instead, she got hot and passionate lovemaking with Dylan that seemed so real that she became lost in it to the exclusion of anything else.

IN THE MORNING, Dylan made breakfast while waiting for Naomi to get up. He'd listened in at her door before calling it a night himself and thought he heard some soft sounds he couldn't decipher. Resisting the urge to go in and see if she would welcome his company, he instead retreated to his own room. It would be foolish to complicate their lives any more than they already were. With a multiple-murder investigation well underway and Naomi being in the perp's crosshairs, the last thing either of them needed was to go down memory lane, clouding their judgment in the present. Whether she headed back to Miami now or later, it would happen soon enough. Allowing one kiss to give him hope that they could turn back the hands of time would not be a smart move on his part. Been there, done that. No thank you. He shouldn't go there, if he knew what was best for him. Or was he prepared to truly say what was best for him and what was not?

His thoughts turned to Sandra Neville, the latest female victim of the Violet Killer. Number eight and counting. But this one came with even more unsettling connotations. She had apparently been targeted with Naomi in mind, if the unsub was to be believed. He had directly threatened her life. This was raising the stakes dangerously and far too close to home for Dylan. Not only was Naomi his one true love who got away, but now she was back and staying with him, if only for a while longer. He was not about to allow a serial killer to take this little time they had together away from them.

Before he could chew more on that thought and get back to work on the griddle, Dylan looked up and saw Naomi walk into the kitchen. She was still in her sleepwear of a purplish chemise and black pajamas shorts, with her hair down and uncombed, and barefoot—all of which turned him on more than he wanted.

"Good morning," she said, rubbing her eyes.

"Good morning." He took a chill pill, trying not to

think of just how sexy and inviting she looked at the moment. "Sleep well?"

Naomi blushed thoughtfully. "It was a bit restless, as you might imagine."

"Yeah." How could he not relate? What she had been put through yesterday from sunup to sundown would have made sleep hard to come by for anyone. Or might her erratic sleep pattern have been caused by something more of a carnal nature, like his own restless sleep? "Hungry?"

She nodded. "My stomach is growling." She ran her hand over her flat stomach as if to stifle it.

He wasn't surprised. After picking up a pizza when they got home last night, neither of them ate very much before she went to bed. He, in turn, stayed up longer, making some calls and trying to keep up with the many layers in the Violet Killer investigation. Progress was painfully slow. Yet with each passing day and another victim, they were still putting together clues that would ultimately take down the unsub, one way or the other.

"Good." Dylan grinned at her. "Hope you like blueberry pancakes and bacon." He seemed to recall this was one of her favorite breakfasts once upon a time.

"Yes." Naomi flashed her teeth and seemed to applaud him for remembering. In truth, there wasn't much that he didn't remember when it came to their time together. But he didn't need to tell her that.

"Have a seat and breakfast will be served shortly."

"Thanks." She sat on a stool and tasted the orange juice he had already poured into two glasses. "Anything new on the investigation since last night?"

"Not really," Dylan reported. "The perp got away, but we're still interviewing people and checking out any surveillance cameras leading into and out of the woods."

"Do you think that he actually killed Sandra Neville to get to me?" Naomi's eyes were wide with incredulity.

"I think he'd like for you—frankly, all of us on the Task Force—to believe that to mess with our heads." Dylan set the plate of steaming pancakes and bacon before her on the island. "More likely," he suggested as a good possibility, "Ms. Neville may have been a target for the unsub before you even returned to town and he was simply waiting for the right opportunity to strike. The fact that she happened to be African American was perfect for his mind games. And to keep up with his preying upon women of any color, so as to terrorize all women in Pebble Creek." This sounded plausible to Dylan, even if his gut instincts felt that picking on Naomi as Roger's niece had played some role in the latest victim's death.

"Well, it's definitely working," she commented and bit into a piece of bacon. "What woman in town wouldn't be shaken to the core with what's been happening with seemingly no end in sight?"

"The end will come," Dylan tried to assure her as he set his plate down and plopped onto the stool beside her. "Whether it's Harold Shipman, David Berkowitz, Edmund Kemper, Aileen Wuornos, you name it, they've all run out of steam sooner or later. This won't be any different. The Violet Killer will slip up or otherwise be brought down by good old-fashioned police work." Dylan firmly believed this as he sliced up his pancakes. Never mind the few serial killers, such as Jack the Ripper, who may have successfully eluded authorities before modern technology and forensic science took away their natural advantages. The Violet Killer serial madman would not have a long shelf life. They would see to it.

"So, what's with you and Special Agent Stabler?"

Naomi tossed out casually, as she sipped coffee from her mug.

Dylan lifted a brow. "Excuse me?"

"You two seem to have hit it off."

"Yeah, I guess we have, if you're referring to a solid working relationship." He stared at her, sensing that she was implying something of a sexual nature. Was she actually jealous of the FBI profiler? "Other than that, I can assure you that it's strictly professional. Word has it that she's involved with another agent. Besides that, Agent Stabler is not my type."

"Oh." Naomi sipped her coffee and looked embarrassed that she had chosen to go down that road, indicating that she was still interested in him, romantically speaking. This gave Dylan the opening to satisfy his own curiosity on that theme, once and for all.

"What about you?" He forked a stack of pancakes. "Have you left some Secret Service agent or other lucky guy hanging while you're away?"

She batted her lashes. "If you're asking if I'm seeing someone, the answer is no. I've probably gone out on maybe two dates since arriving in Miami—and both proved to be disastrous, truthfully." Naomi met his eyes soulfully. "Guess it's not as easy to move on as I'd imagined."

Dylan's brows lowered. "Did you really think it would be?"

"I don't know what I thought." She ran a hand through her hair edgily. "I just didn't want things to be any harder than they were in leaving. I know I made sacrifices and have to live with that." Naomi picked up her mug and tasted the coffee thoughtfully.

"We've both made sacrifices," Dylan acknowledged considerately. "That's part of life. We deal with it and try not to look back at the what-ifs too much." He only wished he had practiced more what he was now preaching. It was hard not to imagine the life they could have had. But seeing how well Naomi had done in her life after relocating, wishing she had stayed in Pebble Creek was being unfair to her. And him.

They ate in silence for a few minutes, as though weighing whether or not to say anything that might shatter the tentative truce in their understanding.

Finally, after wiping her mouth with a napkin, Naomi said coolly, "I plan to meet with Agent Stabler."

"Oh…" Dylan looked at her, wondering if this was still about something going on between him and the FBI agent that Naomi needed to ascertain for herself, before considering any possibility of repairing their own fractured relationship.

"Yes, she invited me at Uncle Roger's funeral to reach out to her, if I wanted to talk." Naomi took a hesitant breath. "Guess I would like to pick her brain in trying to gain more insight into this Violet Killer. Might help me to better come to terms with the type of perp he is and what my uncle may have been able to pick up in identifying him."

Dylan weighed whether or not he thought that was a good idea for Naomi to get more deeply vested in the case. Wouldn't that make it tougher to deal with Roger's loss? Or would it make it easier to digest while, at the same time, enabling her to tap into Patricia's expertise in characterizing the unsub as a big step in ultimately bringing him to justice? Maybe it could also be a way for him and Naomi to reactivate what they once meant to each other.

"Go for it," he told her with a straight look. "Agent Stabler definitely knows her stuff and has been a real asset in this investigation. Hope she can give you what you need."

Naomi smiled. "Thanks for your support, Dylan."

"No matter what, that's something you can always count on," he told her, grinning back, and meaning every word.

Chapter Nine

That afternoon, Naomi arranged to meet Patricia Stabler for coffee at the Java & Tea Corner on Willow Road. She wasn't sure if the FBI profiler would agree to a Sunday get-together, but it proved to be no problem. Indeed, for some reason, the special agent seemed just as eager to talk as Naomi. She rose from the side table to greet the gorgeous redhead, whom Naomi felt relieved that Dylan had no romantic interest in, in spite of the undetermined nature of their own relationship at the moment. "Hi," Naomi said awkwardly, noting that her pixie hair had even more volume as if freshly styled. Naomi's had put her own hair into a high ponytail.

"Hey." Patricia, who was casually dressed and wearing flats, smiled. She held out a thin-fingered hand in a professional motion, which Naomi shook. "Good to hear from you, Ms. Lincoln."

"Please, call me Naomi," she insisted, "Agent Stabler."

"Only if you'll call me Patricia."

"You're on." Naomi smiled sideways. "Shall we sit?"

"Sure." Patricia tossed her handbag on a corner of the table and sat across from her. Naomi was sure the FBI agent was packing. What one wasn't? Though, at times, feeling naked without her own weapon—especially in the tense environment she found herself in—Naomi had chosen to keep her firearm under lock and key at Dylan's place for this occasion, knowing that Patricia would have her back, should trouble arise.

They ordered espressos and pecan scones, after which Patricia nibbled on a scone and, peering at her, asked directly, "How are you doing, Naomi?"

She thought of giving the pat answer of good or fine, but given that she had taken the profiler up on her offer to talk about what was going on, that would obviously not hold up very well. So, instead, Naomi looked her in the eye and spoke truthfully. "I'm having trouble dealing with the fact that Sandra Neville's murder may have been meant as a warning to me by the Violet Killer that my turn is coming…"

Patricia's eyes grew wide. "What makes you think that?"

Naomi took out her cell phone, brought up the alarming text message and showed it to her.

"Seems like he wanted to get my attention." Naomi sucked in a deep breath. "And it worked."

"Hmm…" Patricia said musingly, gazing at the small screen. "I'd heard that he had texted you previously. But this is definitely taking it to another level."

Naomi concurred. "Since my uncle was murdered, I get the impression that the unsub has somehow latched onto me for some sick game—or worse—in the aftermath. Not sure if he's just getting some perverse thrill out of toying with the niece of the private investigator he gunned down, or what." She paused again, tasting the coffee. "Maybe you can shed some light on this—"

"I can try," the profiler indicated, sipping her own drink ponderingly. "From what I understand, you were never able to get any type of visual of the unsub on your laptop when he shot Roger, correct?"

"Correct. Just his shadow." Naomi shuddered at the thought. "If I'd only had some sort of inkling of what was about to happen, I could've at least warned my uncle, to give him a fighting chance."

"There was nothing you could have done." Patricia's tone rang with sympathy. "The unsub has become skilled in his modus operandi over the course of his killings. He wasn't about to break that pattern by revealing himself to you through a computer screen. That close call notwithstanding, you apparently got his attention in moving forward."

"How so?" Naomi tried to get into the unsub's head while grabbing a scone off the plate and taking a generous bite of it.

"My assessment of the man we're dealing with here is that he sees you as a sort of extension of Roger Lincoln, whom he viewed as a serious threat to exposing him. Being privy to info he took off your uncle's laptop—including perhaps that you're a Secret Service agent—the unsub, with his arrogance and proclivity for pushing the envelope, simply couldn't resist taunting you as a way to get under not only your skin, but that of the entire Task Force hunting for him." Patricia tilted her face. "Does that make sense?"

"Yes," Naomi answered, even as she tried to comprehend it in her head.

"As for Sandra Neville's death," Patricia pointed out, "she may or may not have been targeted because of her race, but it's more likely that she was targeted because of her routine and the unsub's risk assessment. Being African American was probably more happenstance, though certainly something that was apropos in his evil mind." She reached across the table and touched Naomi's hand. "So don't beat yourself up about Ms. Neville's misfortune. It is no more on you than the Violet Killer's other female victims."

Naomi nodded, feeling some comfort in her words as a criminal profiler. Still, she needed to get a better read on the serial killer if she was to more properly come to grips with his actions—and maybe what was yet to come. She took another bite of the scone, then asked, "What else can you tell me about the perp, aside from the fact that he goes after young, attractive women? What makes him tick?"

"I'm actually asked that a lot." Patricia sat back, contemplating the questions calmly. "Where do I start?" She sipped the espresso. "Most serial killers we hear about are sexually motivated in their actions, be it rape, torture, mutilation, cannibalism or some combo before death, or afterward. Fred West, Jeffrey Dahmer, Richard Ramirez and Dean Corll come to mind. Well, not the unsub. He does not sexually assault his victims—an important distinction from the aforementioned—but does strangle them to death, while leaving no DNA that can be traced back to him. This is not to say that he doesn't receive some type of gratification akin to sexual from his killings. And whether or not he was the victim of child sexual abuse is another question that can only be answered once he's identified."

Patricia grabbed another scone, holding it as if a prop. "As to what makes him tick, I would say it's the thrill of the kill. It turns him on to know he has the power of life and death over his chosen victims, and is not afraid to use it whenever the opportunity presents itself." She bit into the scone. "There's a predatory nature to the unsub, in which the killings have become somewhat of a sport for him in hunting for females who fit the characteristics that capture his fancy. So, that pretty much sums up the Violet Killer, other than the fact that, like other serial murderers, he aims to continue his work while avoiding capture at all costs."

"Interesting…" Naomi swallowed thickly as she contemplated the lengths the unsub was willing to go to in order to avoid capture, such as taking the life of her uncle Roger along with anyone else who stood in his way. Including her, Dylan and the criminal profiler sitting across from her. "Is there any significance to leaving the violet as his calling card?" she wondered curiously.

Patricia licked her lips. "In my experience, there is no significance in criminals' calling cards, per se, other than to keep law enforcement guessing and off balance." She wrinkled her nose. "If I were to stretch it here to try to make some sense of it, I'd say that the sweet aroma of the violets may emulate the tantalizing scent of a woman in the unsub's head, that fades with the victim's dying breath. But I wouldn't take that to the bank."

She chuckled humorlessly and Naomi pondered the notion, realizing she had been given a chilling crash course on the serial killer and like minds, making her uncomfortable. Still, at the same time, it made her feel better in having more to work with in sizing up the unsub who murdered eight women and her uncle. "Guess we both better stay away from violets," she said drily.

"You think?" Patricia rolled her eyes. She put the coffee mug to her mouth and gazed at Naomi thoughtfully. "I've heard some good things about you as a member of the US Secret Service."

"Did Dylan tell you that?" Naomi asked out of curiosity. Or was it more an assumption? Did their shoptalk include her as the subject matter?

"No," the FBI agent insisted. "I have my sources within the Secret Service. I wasn't prying. As you know, our agencies often work closely together in federal law enforcement. Your name came up when talking about the Violet Killer case that's made national headlines, including your uncle's involvement in the investigation."

"I see." Naomi wished she hadn't jumped the gun in practically feeling as though Dylan had crossed the line in his professional association and their personal relationship. Of course it had become common knowledge, even in Secret Service circles, that a serial killer was active in Pebble Creek, as would be the case for similar investigations around the country in the age of cable television and social media. The fact that it may not have risen to the level of a national security concern did not make it any less serious for law enforcement. "I do my best in carrying out the duties I've been assigned to do," she uttered humbly.

Patricia smiled. "So, when will you be heading back to Miami…?"

Naomi hedged over her mug. "I plan to stick around here for a little while," she confessed. "I've got some extra personal time, so…"

"Figured as much." The profiler gave her a perceptive look. "If I'm reading you correctly, in honor of your uncle, you would love to be on hand when we take the unsub down."

"Yes, ideally," Naomi acknowledged. In her heart of hearts, that would be the best way to give herself peace of mind. And allow her uncle Roger to rest in peace in his grave. But she also knew she couldn't put off returning to work forever. Especially since it had been more than two years since the killings began and the perp was still at large. Who was to say that he might not be continuing to murder women in Pebble Creek two years from now? "I'm not getting my hopes up that this will happen," she told her.

"Well, so long as you are in town and, undoubtedly, wanting to stay close to the investigation, you might as well make it official…"

Naomi cocked a brow. "Meaning…?"

Patricia leaned forward. "In representing the FBI as a key element of the Violet Killer Task Force, we'd love to have you on board as a sanctioned witness consultant in the case, just as Roger was. If you like, I can make this official request to the Secret Service. It may be a bit outside the norm, but given that you're an important witness to one of the Violet Killer's crimes, the first person on the scene of another murder attributed to him, and you're being taunted by the killer, it seems quite appropriate, under the circumstances."

"Yes, it does, doesn't it?" Naomi found herself in total agreement. She should be part of this criminal investigation into her uncle's murder, as well as those poor women who fell prey to this psychopath serial killer. Especially since the unsub seemed determined for some reason to draw her in like a spider in his web of strangulation deaths. But would her boss go for it? And would Dylan be on board?

Reading her thoughts, Patricia said, "If you need to run it by Dylan first or…"

"Let's do it!" Naomi practically shouted in a defensive manner, while wondering if Patricia thought they were a couple again. Had Dylan indicated anything of that nature? Either way, she didn't need his permission, even if Dylan was the lead detective on the local level in the investigation. Moreover, they had worked together in an official capacity before. Why should this be any dif-

ferent? "Put in the request and I'll clear it with my boss,
Jared Falcony, who runs the Miami Field Office."

"Wonderful." Patricia flashed her teeth and raised her
mug to toast. "With any luck, we'll catch the perp before
you have to leave."

"I hope so." Naomi lifted her coffee and the two mugs
clinked. Even then, the thought of going back to Miami
and leaving Dylan behind again weighed on her. This,
in spite of the fact that their relationship had ended two
years ago and there was no real indication on Dylan's part
that he wanted to start it back up. Well, there was that
nostalgic kiss, that did more than stir up old memories.
At least for her. Was this true for him also, his words to
the contrary? Even so, she wondered as well if fantasies
could go only so far as she recalled the dream last night
in which they made love like it still meant something to
them in the real world. Maybe it did.

STANDING ON HIS DECK, a beer in hand, Dylan was admittedly curious as to how the coffee meeting between
Naomi and Patricia went. He imagined the two women,
both strong and independent, got along well and could
even become friends once this case was over and they
went back to their respective jobs with the foremost federal law enforcement agencies. There was also reason to
believe that in her expertise as a criminal profiler, Patricia could certainly be helpful in giving Naomi some
real perspective on the Violet Killer, in characterizing
him and trying to anticipate his next move. On the other
hand, Naomi, as an eyewitness to Roger's murder and
the one who discovered Sandra Neville's body, was just
as valuable in what she brought to the table. That, along
with her being an equal in her role with the Secret Ser-

vice, had to appeal to the FBI agent in her determination to bring the unsub to his knees before long.

As far as he was concerned, Dylan had no problem with Naomi reaching out to a key member of the Task Force, if it meant helping her to get through this ordeal as best she could. They were all dealing with it in their own ways, and he was no exception. Watching young women in the community die so senselessly, with their whole lives ahead of them, put a definite strain on his ability to separate the daily grind of police work from the harsh realities of life and death. It played with his psyche and he didn't like it one bit. The only true way to return to some sense of normalcy was to put an end to this reign of terror.

When he saw Naomi drive up, Dylan's heart skipped a beat for some reason. He wasn't sure if it was in anticipation for what she had to say or the sheer joy of knowing she had made it back safe and sound, with a serial killer out there seeking an opportunity to isolate her. Whatever the case, Dylan couldn't help but feel relief as Naomi got out of the SUV and headed toward the deck.

"Hey," he said evenly, greeting her.

"Hey." Her tone was unreadable, but she offered him a smile, as if for what came next.

"How did it go?"

She took the beer bottle from him and took a generous drink, before handing it back. "Why don't we talk about it inside?"

"Okay." Dylan followed her through the door, his interest piqued.

Chapter Ten

"So, here's the thing," Naomi began, pacing the room as though she had lost something. "Special Agent Stabler and I—actually, it was her suggestion—thought it might be a good idea for me to become a temporary member of the Violet Killer Task Force, as an official Secret Service agent consultant."

"Oh, really?" Dylan's eyes danced with amusement, feeling somewhat relieved that Patricia hadn't tried to practically recruit her as an FBI agent. "Makes perfect sense to me."

She stopped pacing, staring at him. "Seriously?"

"Of course. Did you think I would try to pull rank on the special agent, as if I could, and shoot down her idea?" He lowered his chin. "Well…?"

Naomi fluttered her lashes. "Truthfully, I assumed—and even Agent Stabler—that you might balk at the idea, not to pull rank, but as your way of pushing back on my greater involvement in order to protect me from the unsub."

Dylan stepped closer to her. It was true that he would do anything to keep her safe. Roger would expect no less of him. But it was just as true that he knew from first-hand experience that when Naomi put her mind to something, there was little he could do to stop her. So why try? Especially when her unique position in the scheme of things made her continued presence helpful in the investigation. He understood her need, under the circumstances, to hang around for as long as she could to try to help nab the perp, if at all possible. "So, your boss is on board with this?" Dylan didn't imagine that she could have an open-ended sabbatical from her official duties with the Secret Service, no matter how many strings Patricia managed to pull in that regard.

"Haven't run it by him yet," admitted Naomi, wringing her hands. "But, since Patricia, er, Agent Stabler, will be making the request as a key FBI point person in the investigation, I don't imagine it will be a problem."

Dylan grinned. "Then it won't be with me," he assured her and took a sip from his beer bottle. Part of him loved the idea of working with her in an official capacity again. Another part welcomed the idea of her staying in Pebble Creek for as long as possible, as he couldn't help but enjoy being around his onetime love. Still, the longer she was in town, the more at risk Naomi was for being in the Violet Killer's realm. Meaning, she would need to remain vigilant at all times. He delivered that wisdom to her in a caring tone.

"Yes, I'll keep eyes in the back of my head for any signs of the unsub approaching." Naomi regarded Dylan with a straight face. "Seriously, I won't knowingly put myself in danger. Or give him an easy way to attack. But I won't run and hide like a mouse from an alley cat, either."

"Never thought you would," he made clear. After all, it was the fighter in Naomi that had attracted him in the first place. Once he got past her hot looks and sexy body. And her totally appealing personality.

"Glad to hear that." She moved right up to him and, once again, took the beer and drank some. He had never known her to be much of a beer drinker, but he didn't mind sharing the bottle. "Oh, there is one other thing..." she teased him.

"What might that be?" he was almost afraid to ask, and eager to hear at the same time.

"This..." Naomi cupped his cheeks, lowered his face and planted a firm kiss on Dylan's mouth. He was happy to kiss her back, tasting the beer off her mouth. The kiss continued for at least a full minute with neither making a move to pull away. Every part of Dylan's body was aflame with desire to carry this further, maybe all the way to his bed. Or hers. Did she feel the same way?

Using all the strength he had, Dylan broke away and peered into her eyes. "Is this another for-old-times'-sake moment between us?"

"Maybe." Naomi put a finger to her moist lips and blushed. "Or maybe it can be a for-new-times'-sake moment, if you're open to that possibility."

Those were words Dylan had dreamed of hearing from her inviting mouth for a long time. The possibility of resurrecting their love life was enticing beyond words. How could it not be? She was everything to him, and that had not changed over time. Or had it? But what exactly did she mean with the possibility for new times in a relationship? And were any such possibilities practical, given their circumstances in life after the Violet Killer case had long passed?

Now seemed like as good a time as any to say what had long been on his mind, sticking to it like glue as to what might have been. "I was going to ask you to marry me two years ago," he confessed.

Naomi's mouth opened to an imperfect O. "Why didn't you?" she asked, a catch to her voice.

"You know why." His lips pursed, believing it should

have been obvious, even if unspoken at the time. "You told me about your plans with the Secret Service and relocating to the other side of the country. I wasn't about to make you choose between a dream job and me."

Her brows twitched. "Sounds like a copout to me, Dylan," she spoke bluntly. "If you weren't man enough to say what was on your mind, don't blame me for moving ahead with my own life. If you wanted to marry me, you should have asked!"

"Would it have made a difference?" He held her gaze, feeling his heart beating rapidly while wondering if he had indeed blown it, big-time, for all the wrong reasons.

Naomi sighed and turned away from him. "I have no idea," she indicated candidly. "Things were clicking between us then. I wanted more from you. I also wanted more for myself." She refaced him. "Had you proposed, it could have changed everything. Or not. I guess we'll never know."

"Yeah, guess not," he snorted, angry more at himself than anything. Why hadn't he been more courageous, instead of trying to do right by her and her ambitions, and just let the chips fall where they may? Had he done so, they might be husband and wife today, with a child on the way. Instead of two single people who had missed their moment in the sun. Or was it not too late to turn the ship around and recapture what they lost?

"I'm going to go take a shower," Naomi cut into his reverie with a sharp tone. "And, no, it's not an invitation to join me, Dylan. I think a kiss is enough for today. Maybe that's as far as this was meant to go. After all, throwing caution to the wind doesn't seem to be in your DNA in matters of the heart."

Dylan stood there flatfooted and speechless as she sashayed away, feeling as though he had let the best thing to ever happen to him slip from his grasp. Again.

HAD SHE OVERREACTED? Cast blame where there was none? Or maybe made him the heavy to make herself feel better in going to work for the Secret Service when she could have been Mrs. Dylan Hester. This weighed heavily on Naomi's mind the next day as she went out for a morning swim in the warm waters of Pebble Creek Lake all by her lonesome. Last night, she and Dylan barely said two words to one another while eating leftover pizza from the night before. It was as if each was afraid of saying something that might put the other off. For her part, she was still trying to come to grips with the missed opportunity of the proposal that never happened. Had Dylan confided in Uncle Roger about it? Had he encouraged him to step aside and allow her career to blossom? Or had Dylan decided all on his own that he would use her news as a convenient excuse to back down from a legal future together? All the more frustrating to Naomi was that she loved her job with the Secret Service and couldn't imagine being deprived of the opportunity. As such, could she really blame Dylan for not standing in the way of such an achievement and the personal growth to accompany it?

Casting aside the self-pity, confusion and second thoughts, Naomi swam the freestyle stroke, something she had been doing since childhood. She had perfected it and become just as proficient with the backstroke and breaststroke while swimming often in the alluring waters of Miami Beach. It was no less enjoyable in Pebble Creek Lake, even if she was in a crappy mood. Dylan had left early for work without them seeing each other, having retired to their separate rooms for bed. She would give him his space and he was willing to give Naomi hers.

But that could last for only so long, since she was still living in his cabin. While she was in town, they would need to work together to some degree toward a common goal of solving her uncle's murder and other homicides attributed to the Violet Killer. Whether she and Dylan could remain on friendly terms or more than friends beyond that was another matter altogether.

As she homed in on her surroundings, Naomi realized that she had swum farther away from the waters close to Dylan's cabin than she had intended. She scanned the shoreline, where there were other lakefront houses and condos, reflecting the popularity of the area and boom in construction. For whatever reason, Naomi had the feeling she was being watched. But by whom? She noted a speedboat from a distance. There was a man on board who seemed to be looking in her direction. Was she just being paranoid? She turned back to the coast. Only now did she notice the tall man, wearing a dark cap and dark clothing. He was standing on grass, looking through binoculars—at her! Was he merely checking out the gorgeous scenery, with her as an added attraction? Or were his motives more sinister?

Naomi felt a chill at the thought that the man might be the Violet Killer, sizing her up for the strangulation kill. Were that the case, he was also making it clear that he knew her whereabouts and was coming for her. Her heart racing, she started to swim away from the man and toward the cabin. She almost expected him to jump into the water and come after her. With powerful legs and sheer determination, perhaps he could catch up to her and drown her, even if she put up a good fight. Using her own skills in the water, Naomi picked up the pace, determined not to let her life end at the hands of a demented killer. When she approached the shoreline, she darted her eyes in the direction where the man had been standing, fearful that he had already kept up with her and would be waiting for her to come ashore. But she saw no one. He had vanished practically into thin air. Or had he been there at all? Had she only seen what she wanted to?

Doubting her own eyes, Naomi climbed out of the water, her one-piece floral bathing suit clinging to her like a second skin. She grabbed a microfiber beach towel from the grass and ran across it in a hurry as if her life depended on it. Once inside, she made sure the doors and windows were locked and reactivated the outdoor motion detectors to alert her to any possible intruder approaching the cabin. A gaze through the window wall gave no indication that someone was out there. Still, her instincts were going crazy with concern. She scaled the stairs and went into Dylan's office. Cutting on his laptop, she pulled up the quad split screen to check out the multiple security cameras on the property, catching every point of entry. There were no signs of activity. Could the unsub have somehow outsmarted the surveillance system, waiting to strike once she let her guard down?

Not taking any chances, Naomi ran into her room, where she opened a bottom dresser drawer and removed the locked container holding her loaded Glock. She took it out and readied herself, should she need to use it in self-defense. It was suddenly as quiet as a mouse in there. She moved stealthily out of the room, down the hall and back to the first floor, eyes darting for anything that moved. Nothing.

Lowering her weapon, Naomi breathed in a sigh of relief, while wishing that Dylan would walk through that front door as an added means of reassurance. No one was after her. At least not this day. She wondered when it was that she became so easily spooked. Had witnessing the execution of her uncle and finding a dead woman been enough to cause her to lose confidence in herself? If so, how did she get it back even while feeling vulnerable? These troubling thoughts were interrupted as Naomi heard her cell phone ring. Was it another threatening text message from the unsub? Once again, her heart skipped a beat. She walked to the kitchen island, where she had left the phone, and lifted it in expectation. There was a text. Only it was from her boss, Jared Falcony. He had approved the request for her to be on temporary loan to the Violet Killer Task Force for anything she could bring to the table in solving the murder of Roger Lincoln and related homicides.

DYLAN RODE WITH Gregory Hwang to the crime lab, where there was news on DNA and other forensic evidence collected in connection with the murder of Sandra Neville. Both detectives hoped this might be the break they were waiting for in identifying a suspect in her murder.

"As yet, we have no new leads on anyone who may have been at the scene of the crime at the time it occurred," Hwang muttered from behind the wheel. "Surveillance cameras around the wooded area have not turned up anything we can put a finger on in the investigation."

"What about the search volunteers?" questioned Dylan from the passenger seat. "Anyone stand out as suspicious?"

"Not really. Some were wishy-washy on why they were there at all, as if it was just to hang out with people. So far, everyone we've interviewed has an alibi for at least one of the killings attributed to the Violet Killer."

This didn't surprise Dylan. His own assessment of those in Naomi's circle of volunteers was that they were truly dedicated to finding the missing woman alive and seemed genuinely shaken up that it didn't turn out that way. He suspected that the unsub was spying on Naomi from a safe distance to allow for a quick getaway. Speaking of getaway vehicles, it made Dylan think about the dark-colored SUV Naomi thought had an aggressive driver in it—possibly the Violet Killer—in putting the fear in her. "Anything on that SUV we're looking for?" Dylan asked Hwang, knowing they had already eliminated it as being owned by one of their current suspects.

"We're still trying to track it down," he answered woefully. "Turns out, we have more than our fair share of dark SUVs registered in the county. It's a long shot, but we may be able to break it down to a few that were possibly on that street at that time."

Dylan nodded to that effect. He was still not entirely convinced that the SUV incident was actually connected to their serial killer investigation. But if Naomi felt threatened enough to make it an issue, they were going to take it seriously. While this definitely commanded his attention, he found himself drifting back to the spat, if it could be called that, with Naomi yesterday after her get-together with Patricia Stabler. Dylan had known from the moment he did it that he had put his large foot in his mouth when he brought up the marriage proposal that he never gave Naomi. Why couldn't he have just left well enough alone and not said anything? Didn't they have enough on their plate without complicating things further between them? If he had wanted to drive her out of his cabin and back to the house she had inherited from Roger, Dylan couldn't have made it any easier. All he could do now was hope he hadn't blown things altogether and they could get past this and keep her safe till the unsub was caught. Or Naomi had decided it was taking too long and headed back to Miami. Admittedly, the idea that he could still sweep her off her feet was something he was happy to entertain. Could he really let her go again when the kisses they shared told him that the old magic and chemistry between them was still alive and well? Or was he deluding himself in thinking he could repair something that may well be unfixable at this stage?

"You've gone quiet on me over there, Hester," Hwang commented from behind the wheel of his department-issued sedan. "What's up?"

Dylan bared his soul to him, feeling the need to unload. "Naomi and I have shared a couple of kisses since she's been back in Pebble Creek," he confessed. "I told her I wanted to propose two years ago, but didn't want to step on the toes of her new career with the Secret Service. That went well." He made a sarcastic groan. "She somehow turned it around on me and accused me of essentially not stepping up to the plate when I had my chance. I could hardly push back against that. Maybe I did blow it and will have to live with the decision I made for what I thought were the right reasons." Dylan sighed and gazed out the window. "The last thing I wanted to do was make things uncomfortable for her while she's staying with me. Especially when a serial killer is still on the prowl around town."

"Wow!" Hwang expressed in an empathetic tone. "Looks like you've really put yourself in a jam."

"You think?" Dylan rolled his eyes sarcastically.

"Doesn't mean it's a box you can't climb out of, Dylan. Talk to her, man."

"I've tried that and it didn't get me very far."

"So, try again until it does," Hwang pressed. "If you still love her, and I'm sensing that you do, then you need to find out if she feels the same way. Then try to fix things. If what you had is still meant to be, don't let distance, figuratively and literally, stand in your way. Once this case is over, maybe you need to consider relocation, if that's what it takes. I hear that the Miami Police Department is always looking for great detectives. That way, you'd be within shouting distance of the Secret Service field office there. I'm just saying."

"I hear you," Dylan said, shocked at the suggestion that he quit the force. He tried to imagine giving up his job as a senior detective to start over elsewhere. If Naomi did it, why couldn't he? But would that even be enough to prove his love and win her back? Or had he burned his bridges to her heart?

"Second chances, if this is one of them, don't come around every day," Hwang pointed out with an edge to his voice. "I should know."

Dylan took in his honest words. He knew that Hwang had lost his wife to divorce three years ago, leaving him to care for their twin daughters. A good father, Hwang still pined for his ex, hoping she might someday walk back into his life. Dylan wanted the same thing with Naomi, when he got right down to it. But wanting something and being able to make it happen were two entirely different things.

Chapter Eleven

"I've got some positive news for you guys," George Suina said almost jubilantly as the forensic science technician greeted Dylan and Hwang at his workstation in the crime lab.

"We could sure use some," Hwang moaned dramatically.

"Yeah," agreed Dylan, while withholding judgment.

"All right." Suina pinched his nose. "Why don't we get on with it, then. We removed DNA from under the nails of Sandra Neville that wasn't her own. It almost certainly came from the person who attacked Ms. Neville in her struggle for survival, which unfortunately came up short. But she gave us something to work with in developing a forensic profile of the suspected perp. We're using the FBI's Combined DNA Index System, or CODIS, to see if there is a DNA match within its Convicted Offender and Arrestee Indices that can be linked to other serial violent offenses and/or known offenders. If our unsub is anywhere in the system, this will flush him out."

"That is huge," Dylan admitted with optimism. Having what would amount to their first potential DNA profile of the unsub might be just what they needed to break this case wide open. Assuming he had left behind other DNA during the commission of crimes.

"Yeah, I agree," said Hwang. "So, how long are you going to keep us hanging before we have some results?"

"Never soon enough, right?" Suina grinned glibly. "The labs are pretty busy these days, as you know. But serial killer cases, such as the Violet Killer, get priority. You'll know as soon as I do if there is a hit."

Dylan wrinkled his nose, sharing in Hwang's impatience. Still, this was a step in the right direction, so best to take it for what it was worth. "Anything else?" he asked the analyst.

"As a matter of fact, there is," Suina voiced teasingly. He turned on his monitor and they saw a digital image of a footprint. "Crime scene technicians came across a shoeprint beneath the undergrowth where Sandra Neville's remains were discovered. We believe the footwear outsole impression of a size-ten right shoe may have come from the unsub during the process of subduing and killing the victim. Of course, someone else could have left the footprint some other time. We can rule out it belonging to Ms. Neville, whose feet were measured at size eight."

"Was it an athletic shoe, dress shoe or what?" Hwang asked.

"That's still a work in progress," Suina bemoaned. "We'll work as hard as we can to try to come up with the manufacturer, brand name and any distinctive pattern that you can work with as possible forensic footwear evidence in trying to nail the perp."

"Let us know when, and if, you come up with anything pertinent," Dylan told him.

Suina patted him on the shoulder. "You bet."

Outside, Hwang faced Dylan. "Think the DNA belongs to our unsub?"

"You have a better answer?" Dylan challenged him.

"Not really."

"Neither do I. Let's just wait and see if we have a match and go from there."

"Yeah." Hwang bobbed his head.

Dylan's cell phone buzzed. He took it out of his pocket and saw it was a text from Naomi. She believed it was a distinct possibility that someone had been watching her while she was swimming in the lake.

HAVING REPLACED HER swimsuit with a blouse and slim ankle pants, while putting her feet into some espadrille slip-ons, Naomi waited anxiously for Dylan to return to the cabin. When he did, she nearly ran into his arms, knowing they would protect her. But she held back, not wanting to mix the emotions of their past relationship with the confusion about where things stood right now. Besides that, there were more pertinent things to focus on that required some degree of professionalism, with a killer possibly stalking her.

"Are you all right?" Dylan's deep voice illustrated the strain in his features.

"Yes," Naomi told him, having shut off the motion sensor alarm for outdoors when she saw him coming.

He stepped closer, inspecting her, as if to be sure. "Tell me what you saw and where while swimming."

She gathered herself, running a hand through hair still wet from the water. "Well, I had gone out and drifted south, away from the lake frontage of your cabin," she explained. "I suddenly had a sense that someone was watching me. That's when I saw a man standing on the grass with binoculars aimed straight at me."

"You're sure he wasn't just checking out the lake?" Dylan flashed her a questioning look.

Naomi batted her lashes. "If you're asking me if I could swear that he was homed in on me, I would say no.

But given there was no one else in sight, other than a boat that was too far out, it seemed like a reasonable conclusion." Even if one she herself questioned. "In any event, I didn't want to stick around and see what happened next. So, I swam back to shore as fast as I could and went into the cabin. I checked the security video cameras on your laptop around the perimeter of the property and saw nothing unusual. Still, it was something I thought you should know." She neglected to mention that she also grabbed her firearm to be on the safe side.

"What did the man look like?" Dylan asked evenly.

"He was tall and wore a dark cap to go with dark clothing. I was afraid when I got back on land that he would be there waiting for me. But there was no sign of him, including where I first spotted him." She smoothed an eyebrow. "Maybe he was just binocular gazing and I happened to come into his view," she speculated, wondering if it was a good idea to scare Dylan into thinking she was in trouble.

"Or maybe you were on to something in that you were being watched," he said thoughtfully. "Care to take a walk with me so you can show me where you first saw this man?"

"Yes." She gave him a tiny smile, belying the tension between them that was thick as fog.

Outside, they walked across the grass toward the lake and then followed the bends and curves of the shoreline that took them in the direction where Naomi knew the man had been standing. At one point, her shoulder brushed against Dylan's hard body and the sensations echoed through her. Had he sensed this? Or even felt the same?

"Look, about yesterday—" Dylan gazed at her, as if to break the spell he had over her bodily reaction to him.

"I was out of line in bringing up something that was best left in the past where it belonged."

"I'm the one who should be apologizing," Naomi said sincerely, in owning up to her own role in their confrontation. "You had every right to say what was on your mind."

"Really?" He made a humming sound of disagreement. "I never intended to make you uncomfortable."

"You didn't." She saw no reason to guilt-trip him. But she did think it appropriate to be honest at the same time. "You should have said what was on your mind two years ago, Dylan. After what we had, you owed me that much, regardless of how I might have responded."

"You're absolutely right," he said. "I was boneheaded when thinking that by proposing, I would only be putting you on the spot and possibly standing in your way. I should have manned up and just put it out there, giving you the option to make your own fully informed choice, one way or the other, and let the chips fall where they may…"

Naomi was happy to hear him say that. Even if saddened that she never got the chance to say she would marry him, probably on the spot in the way she felt about him. Whether that meant she would have still wanted to go to Miami or not, she honestly couldn't say one way or the other. At least now they had cleared the air and could be friends, if nothing else. Or so she hoped. "Can we just start over?" she asked tentatively, unsure what that meant exactly. Or if he was ready to do that, beyond a working relationship.

Dylan's eyes crinkled when he smiled. "I'd like that very much."

"Me, too." She smiled back at him, wondering if there was still a chance that romance might blossom between them. When they reached a certain area, Naomi stopped and studied the lake and distance from where she believed she was swimming. "I think he was standing around here."

Dylan peered at the water for a long moment. Then he began looking at the grass and took a few hesitant steps, as if trying to avoid a land mine. He halted, staring at what looked to Naomi to be an impression that could come only from a shoe. He knelt and studied it further.

"What is it?" she asked curiously. "You think he left that…?"

"Maybe." Dylan stood up and favored her with an indistinct expression. "Seems like it could be a size ten…"

She lifted a brow. "I don't follow."

"There was a size-ten shoeprint found near the spot where you discovered Sandra Neville's body," Dylan explained. "It was obscured by the underbrush. Forensic specialists believe it may have been left there unintentionally by her killer. If the man you saw is one and the same, he could have been wearing the same pair of shoes and, unbeknownst to him, provided us an important clue— make that two clues—in identifying him."

"Wow." Naomi was excited at the possibility, but this quickly lessened as reality hit like running into a door. "It's a long shot that this footprint belongs to the man who was watching me."

"Yeah, it is," Dylan admitted, careful not to step on the print that was so close to the water it was almost as though the person standing there was itching to jump in. Possibly to come after her. "But it could also be a rare slipup by the unsub that can only work to our advantage." Dylan pulled out his cell and took a few pictures of the shoeprint from various angles and lengths. Afterward, he made a call. "Hey, George, I'm sending you some photos of a shoeprint left by the lake, not far from my cabin. I'd like you to compare it to the digital footprint taken from the Sandra Neville crime scene and see if they could possibly have come from the same shoe. Make it ASAP. Oh, and let's get someone over here to collect any potential forensic evidence, doing it by the book, in case it belongs to our unsub."

Naomi watched Dylan taking charge in not wanting to provide any loopholes that any good lawyer could exploit, should it come to that. It was one reason that she had become attracted to the detective initially, in working for and alongside her uncle Roger. It led to other reasons for that attraction that would turn into love. A love, she knew deep down in her soul, that had never died and was alive and well, in spite of them moving in different directions. Or was she actually the only one guilty of turning her back on what they had?

"A CELL PHONE and laptop were found in a dumpster. We think they may belong to Roger," Dylan informed Naomi the next day, after getting off the phone. They had just finished eating breakfast and seemed to be getting along again, having gotten past a few hiccups in their relationship. Or whatever he wanted to call what was going on between them. He was curious as to where she stood on the subject, but now was not the time to get into that.

"Who found them?" Naomi asked curiously as they stood on the deck.

"Apparently, a homeless man was digging around in it for food or who knows what. A uniformed officer, Carol Newton, spotted him holding a garbage bag and checked it out. Seeing the items inside, she immediately became suspicious and turned them over to forensics. Could be a false lead." Dylan sighed. "Or it may be the break we needed to uncover important information in your uncle's death and break the case wide open." He wasn't getting his hopes up and Dylan certainly didn't want Naomi to get too excited, either. But it was a possible development that needed to be investigated, along with other leads they were pursuing. "I'm on my way to the crime lab to see if they've come up with anything."

"I'd like to come, too." Naomi looked at him intently. "Now that I'm part of the Violet Killer Task Force for the time being, I'd like to be kept in the loop on any serious movement in the case."

Dylan had no real reason to deny her this request. Especially as the Secret Service, FBI and even the Pebble Creek PD were all on board, believing that Naomi could be a real asset as the only living witness to at least one of the homicides attributed to the unsub. "Understood," Dylan said in an agreeable tone. "Let's go."

She gave a satisfied smile. "I'm ready."

Fifteen minutes later, they were in the crime laboratory, where digital forensic analyst Tabitha McKinnon was with Agent Patricia Stabler.

"Hey, you two," Patricia hummed, making Dylan wonder if she thought they were a couple again. Or was that more wishful thinking on his part?

"Hey," he said to the profiler.

"Agent Stabler," Naomi spoke formally to her. "Hi, Tabitha."

"Naomi," the analyst greeted her unemotionally from her workstation.

"Looks like we're all here for the same reason," remarked Patricia. "Tabitha was just about to enlighten me on where things stood."

Dylan faced Tabitha. "I understand you have a cell phone and laptop," he said tonelessly.

"Yeah, we have them," Tabitha confirmed. "Both

items appear to have been worked over pretty good by someone who obviously didn't want what was on them to be recovered."

"Have you determined if they belong to my uncle Roger?" Naomi asked eagerly.

"We were able to remove partial prints from the phone and laptop that matched Roger's prints on file," Tabitha announced triumphantly. She pulled open a drawer and slid out a shelf. On it were a bagged cell phone and laptop. "Apparently, the unsub had no problem with the possibility that we might retrieve the items and link them to Roger. It was as though the perp wanted to rub it in our faces as something he could get away with, as if untouchable."

Dylan noted that Naomi looked to be unstable on her feet. For an instant, he feared he may have to catch her before her legs collapsed. Patricia picked up on it, too, grabbing her arm, then asking: "Are you okay?"

Naomi steadied herself. "I'm fine. Just seeing the laptop that my uncle was using when we…" She paused. "Anyway, I hope it provides some answers."

"Don't we all," seconded Patricia.

Dylan followed up on that. "Were you able to get any information from the cell or laptop?" he asked the forensic examiner.

"The cell phone, yes," Tabitha answered and frowned. "No such luck with the laptop, I'm afraid."

"Tell us what you have from the phone," pressed Patricia, peering at her.

"All right." Tabitha turned on her monitor, where they saw a digital image of a cell phone. "Since Roger's cell phone was locked and has a fingerprint scanner, in order to get inside with no password option, we had to use specialized software to mimic what turned out to be his thumbprint. We were able to take a high-resolution image of the print in our system to create a 3D-printed mold. Worked like a charm to unlock it!" A series of phone numbers appeared on the monitor. "We're still going through it, but these were the calls Roger made in the days leading up to his death. Do any of them ring a bell, Naomi?"

Staring at the screen, she responded thoughtfully, "Yes, my own number is there. Not sure about the rest. Probably client contacts and…leads…" She choked back the words. "At least one number was probably a woman my uncle had been seeing. Her name's Brenda Quinlan."

"We'll check it out," Tabitha promised evenly.

Dylan doubted that Roger's girlfriend played any role in his death, but they would not rule out anyone. Or leave any stones unturned in getting to the truth and the culprit. "What about his laptop?" he asked, recalling her disillusion there. "Anything at all?" He imagined that the unsub destroyed any info it contained before discarding the laptop.

"Zilch." Tabitha's lips twisted. She walked to the shelf with Roger's damaged computer. "Whoever dumped the laptop scrubbed it of all files, making recovery all but impossible. Still, there are ways in which we may be able to retrieve at least some of the so-called lost information. But that will take time."

"Time we don't have," groaned Dylan, knowing every second counted in solving this case.

"Might I make a suggestion?" Naomi put forth, studying the laptop.

"Be our guest," Patricia responded interestedly.

"My colleague in the Secret Service, Agent Sophia Menendez, happens to be a whiz when it comes to computer and telecommunications fraud. Retrieving lost files, and quickly, is right up her alley." Naomi gazed at Dylan and Patricia. "Given the sense of urgency, if you like, I can give Sophia a call and have her take a look at the laptop."

"The FBI would certainly have no problem with that," Patricia said. "We know the Secret Service is on par with our agency in investigating computer crimes. If Agent Menendez is able and willing to take a crack at it, why not?"

"You'll get no argument from me there," Tabitha agreed. "This isn't about fighting over who should get the first dibs in outwitting the system cleaner. We all just want to solve this case by any means necessary."

Dylan was inclined to concur with all of them. He trusted Naomi. If she trusted her colleague to handle this in an expedited manner and with positive results, he certainly wouldn't stand in the way. "I'll need to clear it with Chief Frazier," he pointed out, "but as far as I'm concerned, it's a go." He nodded at Naomi. "Give her a call and let's get the ball rolling."

"Thank you." Naomi showed her teeth. "I'll call Agent Menendez right away."

Dylan smiled back, knowing this was something Naomi needed in contributing to the investigation into Roger's death. Any relevant info he left behind on the laptop couldn't come soon enough, especially since Roger hadn't bothered to back up any files online. Probably never thinking it would need to come down to that as a possible means in solving his death.

Chapter Twelve

Feeling empowered and a bit more settled after seeing her uncle Roger's laptop that represented the last conversation they ever had, Naomi went outside, where she could gather her thoughts before speaking to Sophia in private. It had been more difficult than she had expected to keep it together, after witnessing a murder and having the evidence of it practically stare back at her. Now the hope was that the unidentified person responsible would be exposed and brought to justice. This was her way of playing an important role in making that happen, thanks to Dylan, Patricia and Chief Frazier allowing Naomi to step outside the box in pursuit of findings that might still exist within a laptop, as if her uncle's final message from the grave.

She took out her cell phone and speed-dialed Sophia's number, practicing in her mind what Naomi wanted to say to her. When she appeared on the screen, Sophia was all smiles. "Well, hello, stranger…"

"Hey." Naomi smiled thinly. It hadn't been that long since they last talked, had it? "Do you have a sec?"

"Of course. Just got back to Miami and I'm already bored to death. Don't tell that to Jared Falcony, though. Otherwise, I might be sent for an assignment in Timbuktu."

"Speaking of Jared…" Naomi mentioned that he had

approved her sticking around Pebble Creek for a bit longer in a consultant capacity. "Anything I can do to help find the Violet Killer."

"That perp gives me the creeps—in a Samuel Little kind of way," Sophia said, making a face in reference to the serial killer who was believed to have murdered dozens of women during his lifetime. "I'm glad to hear that you're helping out there. After what you witnessed, it's understandable you'd want to try to do right by your uncle and those poor women the unsub targeted."

On that note of support, Naomi cut right to the chase. "I need a big favor."

"Okay, sure. What's up?"

"They found Uncle Roger's laptop," explained Naomi. "It's been wiped clean. Meaning anything that he may have had in his files that could lead to the unsub has been erased. I was hoping that you could take a look at the laptop and see if anything can be recovered. I'll okay it with Jared, of course."

"I'd be happy to check it out." Sophia's eyes lit. "And Jared won't object," she spoke confidently. "He wants to see justice served in this case as much as I do. Can't make any promises, but this is in my repertoire. If there's a will—and there always is—I will do my best to find a way, no pun intended."

"Thank you." Naomi grinned, knowing she could count on her friend at crunch time. And vice versa.

"I'm guessing you need this like yesterday, instead of tomorrow?"

"You guessed right. The sooner we can see if there's anything there, the better."

"Got it," said Sophia. "Overnight the laptop to me and I'll get started right away."

"Will do." Knowing her friend, Naomi waited for Sophia to say what else was surely on her mind.

"So, what's happening with you and Detective Hester?"

"We're working our way through some issues," she said pensively. "Other than that, everything's fine."

"When you say *fine*, do you mean you're not tearing each other's hair out? Or are the embers starting to burn again?"

Naomi laughed. "You do have a way with words. No embers burning exactly, but we have had our moments," she had to admit.

"So, you're starting to have feelings for the man again?" persisted Sophia.

Naomi thought about it. Feelings? It went much deeper than that. Those kisses made that abundantly clear to her. "Not sure the feelings ever went away," she responded truthfully. "I'm just not sure what to do with them. Or if I should even try to make waves that he may not be ready for, bumpy waters and all."

"Do whatever you need to resolve unsettled issues, Naomi. Just be sure you don't get in over your head and end up hurt—or coming away with new regrets."

"I hear you, Sophia." Naomi colored. "I'll be careful," she promised her, not wishing to take a leap of faith only to fall overboard. On the other hand, romance was always a risky proposition. Was it not? Maybe seeing where things could go with Dylan wasn't such a bad idea. Till that proved to be the case.

When she hung up, Naomi saw Dylan standing there. He offered her a slow grin, making her wonder just how much of the conversation he had heard. She froze at the thought of trying to explain her words and meanings. "Hey," she uttered hesitantly.

"Hey." His expression was now unreadable, as if by design. "How did it go with your friend?"

"She's in." Naomi's cheeks rose gleefully. "Sophia's ready to see if she can reclaim Uncle Roger's deleted files. Or as many as possible."

"Good, because the chief is on board, too. Let's see if she can work some magic."

Naomi chuckled. "No pressure, right?"

Dylan grinned sidelong. "There's always pressure," he voiced thickly. "That's the nature of the beast called law enforcement that we're both sworn to. That can only be lessened when we can bring the Violet Killer case to a close."

This was something for which she could not offer a sarcastic comeback. The unsub had made sure of that. So long as her uncle's killer remained at large, there could be no letting up. Not till he was under lock and key. Or otherwise no longer a threat to society. Or her. "Agreed," Naomi told Dylan without a catch to her voice.

"THERE'S NEWS," DYLAN informed Naomi an hour later over the phone in video chat, knowing it was something pertinent to the investigation into Roger's death. "An arrest has been made of the man we believe planted the surveillance devices at your uncle's house."

She perked up at the announcement. "How did you find him?"

"We were able to trace the serial numbers of some of the equipment back to the store where they were purchased—and ultimately to the person who bought the devices."

Her eyes widened. "Do you think he's the Violet Killer...?"

"That's yet to be determined," Dylan spoke frankly.

"I'm about to interrogate him. We'll see how it goes." He practically expected her to ask if she could sit in on the interview, knowing the unsub had invaded not only Roger's privacy but Naomi's as well, not to mention may have been responsible for her uncle's death. But, at the moment, she seemed content to take a wait-and-see approach.

"I'll be waiting to hear what you find out," she told him equally.

"I'll let you know what happens," he spoke simply, and disconnected. For an instant, Dylan thought back to Naomi's cryptic words to her colleague Sophia he'd overheard from their phone call earlier. *I'll be careful.* By the look on Naomi's face, he'd gotten the distinct impression that she wasn't referring to the investigation into Roger's death. Or the serial killer case, in general. Dylan had a feeling it was more about being careful as it pertained to matters of the heart. As if to say she was fearful about moving into dangerous territory in rekindling their relationship. In fact, he would never hurt her willingly. Could she say the same about hurting him? Or was that the point—repeating history with the same result?

Casting these thoughts aside, Dylan gazed through the one-way glass into the interrogation room, where they had let the suspect sit by himself for a while, a common tactic in law enforcement designed to both frustrate and unnerve the person. His name was Tony Ketchum. The forty-four-year-old was an ex-employee of a security firm. He had been let go six months ago after being accused of illegally planting hidden cameras in a shopping mall women's restroom. Police investigated, but no charges were ever filed.

"What do you think?" Patricia asked, standing alongside Dylan in observing the chunky suspect with a slicked-back, salt-and-pepper-colored hairstyle. He was dressed in casual clothing. "Could this be our unsub?"

Hesitant to speculate on appearance alone, much less draw conclusions that may not pan out pending a thorough search of the suspect's residence and vehicle, Dylan answered coolly, "We're about to find out." Sure that the profiler was eager to take her own crack at the suspect, should this prove to be warranted, Dylan left her and Chief Frazier, with an equal interest in the outcome, to step into the room.

It was big enough to fit three or four people comfortably, but not so big as to waste space and make it less intimidating. There was a wooden rectangular table and two metal chairs. Dylan sat in the one unoccupied across from the suspect. He had been advised of his rights and gave no indication as yet of wanting a lawyer before speaking. Studying the man who at the very least was a voyeur and could well be a cunning serial killer, Dylan waited a beat before speaking. "I'm Detective Hester. Do you know why you're here, Mr. Ketchum…?"

The suspect, who was handcuffed, snorted. "They just told me it had to do with some illegal surveillance equipment. I thought this was already settled?"

"It was, if you're referring to the mall restroom investigation," Dylan said. "That's not why we're here."

Ketchum lowered thick brows over blue-gray eyes. "Then suppose you clue me in…"

"I'd be happy to." Dylan glanced at the one-way mirror. "Some hidden surveillance devices were found at the office and home of a private investigator named Roger Lincoln. Know anything about that?"

Ketchum reacted, clearly shaken. "Why would I?" he claimed.

"Because you were the one who planted them." Dylan

peered at the suspect, fighting to maintain control at the prospect that he might have seen Naomi in the nude and enjoyed it. But he didn't believe that was necessarily the perp's primary objective.

"That's crazy," he insisted. "I don't know what you're talking about."

"Cut the crap, Ketchum." Dylan realized playing the nice guy was getting him nowhere. "We were able to trace the bugs back to you—including video surveillance of you purchasing them. There's DNA as well that I'm betting will link you even further to the crime. No sense in denying it, if you know what's good for you. Or not as bad as it's going to get. The bigger issue is what your motivation was for planting the devices. Care to tell me?"

Ketchum bottled up, as if weighing his options, which were few to none that could get him out of this trap. Dylan decided it was time to increase the pressure. "What do you know about the Violet Killer?"

The suspect cocked a brow ill at ease. "He's that serial killer, right?"

"Right." Dylan wondered if playing dumb was a half-hearted, last-ditch effort to save himself from a fate of his own making. "Besides strangling local women, the killer is also suspected of murdering Roger Lincoln. The same private eye whose house you bugged. Am I starting to connect the dots here easily enough for you to understand, Ketchum? Did you shoot to death Lincoln, who it just so happens was investigating the Violet Killer and about to close in on him?"

"Whoa!" Ketchum's voice shook. "I didn't kill anyone. And I'm not this Violet Killer."

"If you want to convince me of that, you'd best start talking—and fast!" Dylan regarded him with an intentional menacing look.

"Okay, okay," the suspect muttered, sighing. "Yeah, I planted the bugs in Lincoln's house. But it had nothing to do with murder or a serial killer's vendetta…" Ketchum wrinkled his bulbous nose. "My ex-wife hired Lincoln to dig up dirt on me in a custody battle. I only planted the devices to learn what I could about what he knew, so I could be better equipped to fight her in court. That's it!"

Not entirely convinced, Dylan pressed him on some details they knew about the serial killer unsub and also Ketchum's whereabouts during the last three murders attributed to the Violet Killer. Ketchum seemed genuinely thrown by the questions and was able to account for his whereabouts during the days and times in question, subject to verification. "Would you be willing to take a lie detector test?" Dylan asked, using another name for a polygraph, which was routinely used by law enforcement agencies to try to rule in or out suspects in crimes. Though inadmissible in criminal court, it gave authorities a mostly reliable sense of whether the suspect was being truthful or not.

"Yeah, I'll take it," a rattled Ketchum agreed without preconditions.

Half an hour later, Gail Takamura, a forty-year-old licensed, professional polygraph examiner for the Pebble Creek PD and state of Oregon, administered the test. "The suspect passed it," she reported unceremoniously to Dylan, Patricia and Chief Frazier, after leaving the interrogation room. The thin, dark-haired examiner flashed amber eyes hotly. "He's not your Violet Killer."

Though disappointed, Dylan had already decided that Tony Ketchum was not their unsub. Aside from the polygraph results, honestly, he didn't see the out-of-shape former security firm worker as being athletic enough to chase down women as a serial killer and vanish quickly while leaving no evidence behind. Dylan was sure that the search of Ketchum's property would back him up.

Patricia was on the same page. "The real unsub would like nothing better than for us to nab someone like Ketchum to pay for his crimes, leaving him to possibly go elsewhere and pick up where the Violet Killer left off in Pebble Creek."

"So we're back to square one, more or less," Frazier grumbled.

"Not exactly," Dylan begged to differ. "We can eliminate at least one concern that the unsub had been spying on Naomi as an offshoot of his targeting of Roger. That said, Tony Ketchum is still guilty of planting surveillance devices illegally and will have to answer for that."

Everyone was in agreement. Unfortunately, this did little to ease Dylan's concern that the unsub was still a threat to Naomi and had to be taken seriously in this regard. As well as the danger posed to females throughout the town. Until they could put an end to his serial strangulation homicides and make the community safe again.

Chapter Thirteen

"The Violet Killer unsub wasn't the one responsible for planting the bugs in Roger's house and office," Dylan told Naomi as they stood in the great room.

Her eyes rolled with shock. "Seriously?"

"Wish I could say otherwise." He pursed his lips. "We would've loved to have been able to kill two birds with one stone, so to speak. But as it turns out, a man named Tony Ketchum put the devices in as part of a custody battle. His wife had hired Roger to investigate him and this was Ketchum's ill-advised attempt to gain the upper hand. In any event, he passed a polygraph and his alibis checked out for the latest Violet Killer murders." Dylan jutted his chin. "As such, he's been eliminated as a feasible unsub."

Naomi tried to hide her disappointment. The idea that the one who had spied on her uncle and was likely a voyeur on her movements around the house was a different creep altogether than the serial killer terrorizing the community was unsettling. To say the least. Moreover, it meant that the man who murdered her uncle Roger was still running free, snubbing his nose at all of them seeking his capture. "I suppose it was too much to expect that a homicidal perp who had successfully evaded the law for more than two years would trip himself up so easily," she moaned begrudgingly.

"Perhaps," Dylan agreed. He ran a hand through his thick hair. "All is not lost, though. The Violet Killer investigation is still ongoing, including ballistics assessments in trying to identify the gun used to kill Roger, and other leads we're pursuing. Even an effort to establish a link between shoeprints taken from the Sandra Neville crime scene and near the lake where you believe someone was watching you may yield some results in connecting dots."

Naomi nodded, feeling renewed sureness that the unsub would be brought to justice, one way or the other. "We'll get him," she spoke confidently. "In the meantime, it's good to know that the man who chose to invade my privacy has been apprehended."

"Yeah, there is that." Dylan's tone afforded the protective nature of their association she had come to expect and depend upon to a certain extent. "Thank goodness for not-so-small favors."

"Yes." She moved up to him as they stood by the rustic maple mantel. Sitting on it by its lonesome was the framed photograph of the two of them that her uncle had left to Dylan, almost as if for safekeeping. Naomi wasn't irked in the slightest that he had chosen not to give it to her, believing that the picture somehow belonged to Dylan as a reminder of everything that was once great about them. Something her uncle Roger was confident she would never lose sight of at the end of the day. Raising her eyes to Dylan's face, she asked impulsively, "Will you dance with me?"

Seemingly taken aback, he gave her an up-and-down look. "There's no music."

"Wait right here." Naomi dashed over to her cell phone

she'd left on the coffee table. Grabbing it, she turned it on and went to her downloaded music, picked out a slow song and played it. Heading back over to Dylan, who hadn't budged from his spot, eyeing her with amusement, she challenged him. "Now what's your excuse?"

He gave her his trademark grin, putting his hands to her waist. "Can't think of one."

"Don't even try." She put her arms around his neck boldly. "Let's dance."

Dylan laughed. "It would be my pleasure."

They moved even closer together, bodies pressing and molding sensuously to configure to one another as they danced slowly, but surely. Naomi, drowning in his intoxicating manly scent, lost in Dylan's strong arms, felt that, indeed, the pleasure was all hers. Or at least as much as his, if not more. Being with him like this felt right. It would feel even better if she kissed him. Lifting her chin, she watched him lower his, clearly on the same wavelength, before their mouths met. And began to have a life of their own. Parting her lips ever so slightly, Naomi dived in for more smooching and tasting, prying Dylan's lips open to better accommodate her own. He acted accordingly, kissing her with the passion of two lovers, causing Naomi to feel as though she were floating on air. Held down only by his sturdy grip and hungry kiss.

Her senses heightened, breathing erratic and arousal off the charts, it was all she could muster to break free of the lip-lock. "Maybe we should pick this up in your bedroom."

Dylan gave her the benefit of his lustful but hesitant gaze. "You really think that's a good idea?"

Without trying to overthink things or, for that matter, underthink them, she responded desirously, "I can't think of a better one." She met his eyes daringly. "Can you...?"

He licked his lips as though ready to dive into a pan-fried T-bone steak. "Now that you mention it, I think it's an excellent idea. In fact, I believe you said something about picking this up... Think I'll get the ball rolling in that regard." Before Naomi could react, Dylan had hoisted her up and into his arms and started carrying her through the great room and up the stairs, where they would take an uncertain but needed journey down memory lane. Only with a very current approach to their sexual desires.

IT WAS ALL Dylan could do not to jump Naomi's bones right on the spot when they were dancing and tasting each other's mouths. But he had shown some restraint, hard as it was, and managed to get them to the master suite. Though they had left the soulful music downstairs, he was quite confident that they would be able to make their own music, with all the notes humming lyrically.

Setting Naomi on her feet, Dylan began removing her clothes, eager to see her naked again. He had little doubt she would present the same picture of perfection that drove him nuts with wanton desire two years ago. As though eager to please, Naomi pitched in to hurriedly undress and display her nudity for his eyes only. She did not disappoint. All the curves and bends in the right package of taut slenderness. Her breasts were not too small, not too large, but just right—waiting to be caressed, the erect nipples tasted like sweet wine.

"You still like what you see?" Naomi's eyes widened teasingly.

"What's not to like?" Dylan licked his lips appetizingly. "You're a meal fit for a king."

"I'm happy to be your queen, Dylan." She gave him

a toothy smile, while fumbling with the buttons on his shirt. "Do you have protection?"

"Yes." He was happy to see that, like him, she didn't confuse wanton desire with recklessness. If children were ever to become part of the picture for them, there would be a time and place for that. Right now, it was all about them and satisfying pent-up needs.

He removed his pants, underwear, shoes and socks, tossing them aside, till he was totally nude. His firm erection left little doubt where he stood in wanting to be with her. Naomi studied it in wonder while taking in the whole of his body. "You haven't changed a bit, I see," she gushed.

"Thanks, but I think I have," he corrected, and it had nothing to do with his workout regimen. Or healthy living to make for a healthy body. "You see, I'm two years wiser. And, as such, two years hungrier for a meal that only you can provide for the ultimate nourishment."

"I want you, too," she promised, a catch to her tone. "Like now!"

As she lay invitingly on the chenille bedspread, he got a condom out of the drawer of a weathered oak nightstand, tearing it open and swiftly putting it on. Without further delay, Dylan slid onto the bed and halfway into Naomi's waiting arms. There, they picked up where they left off, exchanging fiery kisses, moving from their mouths to cheeks and chins and back again to each other's lips. She was driving him crazy and he loved it. The need to be inside her building up like steam in a freight train, he nevertheless held back, wanting Naomi to need him even more than she did. Using the tips of his fingers, Dylan brought them down to her sweet spot and adroitly massaged till she was wet and wanting. She quivered mightily to his touch and left no doubt that he was succeeding in his endeavor.

"Make love to me, Dylan," begged Naomi. "I'm ready!"

"That's all I needed to hear," he told her in a deep tone of voice. Lifting up, Dylan sandwiched himself between her splayed legs. Entering her hot body, he drove in hard and often, with Naomi encouraging with each thrust. Her moans and movement were intoxicating to his libido, playing with his mind as well, with lust drowning out everything else. As she gripped his buttocks, he felt Naomi's powerful orgasm, her body shaking like an earthquake of satisfaction.

They had sex for as long as Dylan could stand it, before his need to explode took over. As his orgasm broke free, practically paralyzing him with the potent release, he sucked in a ragged breath and allowed nature to take its course. Naomi followed suit, as a second wave of climax manifested itself, allowing them to ride the wave of carnal delight in tandem, their slickened bodies moving harmoniously till reaching the end of the line.

Afterward, both lay still for a long moment, catching their breaths and sharing a few kisses for good luck, before uncoupling. "Was it as good for you as before?" Naomi asked, putting her mouth to his shoulder.

"I might have thought that was an impossible mountain to climb," Dylan said honestly, playing footsies with her. "But after what we just went through, I think it's obvious that the sex between us is better now than ever."

She blushed. "I can't argue with that."

"Neither can I." He touched one of her nipples, getting an immediate reaction. "Guess some things never die, but only strengthen with time." What that meant exactly in the scheme of their separate lives, Dylan wasn't sure. Were they meant to be only fantastic lovers but not soul mates? Why not both? Or was this laying the groundwork for some necessary give-and-take, especially on his part?

Naomi chuckled. "Maybe we're vampires that only needed to be reawakened," she quipped.

He laughed. "You can bite me anytime you like."

She nibbled playfully on his neck. "Don't give me any ideas."

Their easy banter and sheer sexual compatibility reminded Dylan of how good they were together. As if he could ever have forgotten. It was a welcome respite from working the Violet Killer case and stressing over it and keeping Naomi and other women out of harm's way. Suddenly, feeling reenergized, he found Naomi's mouth and conquered it again with hard kisses, for which she reciprocated in kind. He became aroused, as did she. One thing led to another, with him grabbing a condom, for a repeat performance. Only this time, having appeased their primordial urges, they were able to take it nice and slow. When it was finally over, Naomi rolled off Dylan and both started giggling like little children. But with decidedly adult sexual appetites.

As they lay there for a long, silent moment, Naomi propped on an elbow and asked pointedly, "So, where do you see this going…?" Her eyes sharpened at him. "Or was what just happened more about a roll in the hay for a fun trip down memory lane?"

Dylan cocked a brow in surprise. "Is that what you really think?" As Naomi mulled that over, considering it was she who initiated the sex, he couldn't resist throwing it back at her. "I could ask you the same thing."

Her mouth furrowed. "So why don't you?"

He knew why. Because Dylan didn't believe for one minute that all she wanted from him was to be taken to bed. Any more than merely sex, no matter how fantastic, was all he wanted from her. Indeed, he wanted so much more. The entire package. He just wasn't certain she felt the same way. At least as it pertained to living in the same place at the same time in pursuing a romance. "Long-distance relationships never work," he uttered pessimistically.

"That's because the parties involved fail to make a concerted effort to at least try to make it work," Naomi offered reasonably.

Dylan met her eyes. "Is that what you want, a long-distance relationship?" He noted that this had never been an option presented to him two years ago.

Thinking about the question, as though she had never zeroed in on it full-fledged till now, Naomi lowered her gaze and admitted waveringly, "I don't know…"

Just as they both contemplated their past and future, a cell phone rang. Dylan could tell from the peppy ringtone that it came from Naomi's phone. He actually welcomed the distraction to give them more time to assess what they wanted from each other and whether it was even possible to attain. "Better get that," he told her.

Unenthusiastically, Naomi rolled off the bed and Dylan enjoyed the view of her firm backside as she walked toward her clothes in a pile on the floor. Picking up cropped pants, she fished around for her cell phone before studying it. He watched her cringe, as though being the bearer of bad news. "What is it?" Dylan asked, sitting up.

"It's from him…" Her voice broke. Dylan climbed off the bed and met Naomi halfway. With a trembling hand, she held up the cell phone so he could read the text message with his own eyes:

Such a pretty violet. Too bad she had to die. You're next…

Dylan wrapped Naomi within his protective arms, fully understanding why she was shaken up. He cursed within at the thought that the unsub continued to harass her. To what end? Would he actually try to come after Naomi when they were ready and waiting for him to even try? Just as ominous was the implication that another young woman had been murdered by the Violet Killer. "Don't let this creep get to you," Dylan cautioned Naomi as best he could offer reassurance.

"How can I not?" she shot back. "I know it's just words. But they have meanings and since the unsub's already proven what he's capable of, I have to wonder when the frightening texts will turn into something more sinister."

As if on cue, Dylan's own cell phone rang. He reluctantly released Naomi from his grip and took a few steps to his floored trousers, lifting the phone from the back pocket. The caller was FBI Agent Patricia Stabler.

"Hey," he said tentatively. "What's up?"

"A woman was found dead this evening in her apartment." Patricia sucked in a deep breath. "Looks like the Violet Killer has struck again."

NAOMI ARRIVED AT the crime scene with Dylan. Though he would've preferred to spare her witnessing yet another murder, she believed it was incumbent upon her to see if the latest victim was another person of color. The fact that the unsub had chosen to make her part of his sick games made Naomi feel vulnerable. It also steeled her, making her more determined than ever to see him brought down. If she played any role in the woman's death, she needed to face it head-on and do her part to support the Task Force put together to halt the unsub in his tracks.

The three-story apartment complex was located on

Camden Lane, not too far from Dylan's cabin, but far enough away that Naomi still felt safe there. In spite of the unsub's chilling texts and an unnerving sense that he was watching her every move, there was no solid proof that he had encroached upon Dylan's property. Much less, actually entered the cabin. Still, neither she nor Dylan were taking any chances, staying armed and ready, should the need arise to defend themselves.

Keeping up with Dylan as he worked his way through the usual barriers around and within the scene of a homicide, Naomi felt the loaded 9-millimeter Glock in a leather holster inside the waistband of her wide-leg slacks, worn with an oversize cardigan, reflecting a chill in the evening air. "I'm sure it's nothing you haven't seen before," Dylan advised her, "but be prepared anyway. Death is never a pretty sight."

"Tell me about it." Naomi rolled her eyes. Yes, apart from seeing enough of Sandra Neville's remains to stay with her, she had encountered corpses as a member of the Secret Service. Though unpleasant, it came with the territory. That included being thrown into the mix of a serial killer case. "I'll be fine," she assured him, even if still feeling a bit jittery after receiving the purported perp's text message.

"Okay." Dylan nodded before they approached Detective Hwang, Agent Stabler and other law enforcement personnel. Onlookers were being questioned and kept at bay. "What's the latest?" Dylan asked casually to no one in particular, having been filled in on some of the details before they arrived.

"The medical examiner has arrived to transport the body to the morgue," Hwang said. "Forensics is going through the apartment for evidence." He took a notepad out of his pocket and flipped through the pages. "The victim is a white female who has been identified by her roommate, Julia Bridges, as twenty-six-year-old Sylvie Maguire, a graduate student at Pebble Creek College and part-time bartender at the Owl Club on Bogue and Tenth Street. According to the roommate, when she got back home at approximately seven from class at Pebble Creek College, she found Maguire, fully clothed and lifeless on the floor in her bedroom. A violet was sticking out of her mouth."

Oddly, sad as it was to see another young woman lose her life, Naomi found some comfort in the fact that the latest murder did not appear to be race based. In spite of the texts that were clearly intended to intimidate her, as though it was personal. She chose to believe, as the profiler had indicated, the unsub's targets were less about physical characteristics and more about the often random nature of serial homicides and the opportunistic targeting, even when scoping out the victim's habits and locations prior to an attack.

Dylan cringed. "Is there a boyfriend or...?" Naomi immediately understood that Dylan was automatically going for the standard process of elimination. Female victims of homicide were much more likely to be murdered by current or ex intimates than any other type of offender. Exploiting a high-profile serial killer's MO by being a copycat murderer to throw the authorities off was not unheard of.

"She's been single for a while, says the roommate," Hwang responded, seemingly putting that angle to rest. "Still, we're checking her relationship status out, and also going door-to-door to assess the landscape and see if anyone saw anything."

"At least one person saw everything," Patricia said dreadfully, running a hand through her hair. "The perp who snuffed out the victim's life like a candle. With her fair skin and long, thick red locks, Sylvie Maguire could well have been my little sister. Instead, she has been denied the ability to carve out a long future with all its benefits."

Dylan bristled. "Yeah, it's probably the worst part of this for all the victims and their families."

Naomi felt the same, having experienced it firsthand with the loss of her uncle, whom she would never get to have long conversations with on the ups and downs of life. Not to mention, he would never have the opportunity to walk her down the aisle, assuming that were to ever happen. She considered briefly the amazing and all-consuming sex with Dylan earlier, reminding her of just how good things were between them before she left two years ago. Now they seemed to be at a crossroads in determining where they went in their relationship. Would she call making love one time—make that twice—as intense and unforgettable as it was, a relationship? Would he? Was there enough there to bridge the gap that still seemed as wide as Pebble Creek Lake itself?

"I understand you received another text message, Naomi," Patricia said, breaking through her reverie.

Snapping out of it, Naomi saw that Dylan and Hwang were now bringing Chief Frazier up to speed. "Yes," she told the profiler. "It came just before we learned about the latest victim." Naomi warmed at the thought of making love to Dylan mere minutes before they were brought back to reality in stark and distressed fashion.

"Can I see it?"

"Sure." Naomi took out her cell phone and brought up the text, which still left her on edge.

Such a pretty violet. Too bad she had to die. You're next...

"Hmm..." Patricia frowned. "So, he's continuing to harass you, even while murdering others..."

"I think he may be stalking me in person, as well." Naomi squirmed as she thought about the man watching her in the lake.

Patricia acknowledged as much. "Dylan mentioned it."

"What do you suppose it means, if anything?" Naomi questioned, ill at ease. "Is it a warning of more intimidation to come? Or does the perp have something much worse in his demented mind where it concerns me?" She shuddered to think of what he could be planning, if orchestrated successfully.

"Let me work on that in the unsub's psychological profile," Patricia responded willingly. "Could be that I'm missing something here. If so, I'll find it. In the meantime, I suggest you not let your guard down, for even a minute. The worst thing you could do would be to underestimate the threat, which could only embolden the person who's doing this into further, more decisive actions."

"I get the picture." Naomi felt her firearm and wondered if she would be called upon to use it to defend herself. "I'll keep my eyes open." She knew Dylan would as well, along with the extra patrols he had ordered for the neighborhood. Perhaps that would be enough to do the trick. Either that or give the unsub greater determination to succeed in what he had in mind.

Naomi turned as the medical examiner came out, identified by Patricia. Dr. Martha Donahue looked tired, but made a beeline for Chief Frazier and Dylan. "The victim was definitely strangled to death," she told them dolefully. "As to a more definitive analysis, I should have the completed autopsy report in the morning."

After she answered a couple of routine questions, the body bag containing the corpse of Sylvie Maguire, the Violet Killer's newest victim, was carted away.

Chapter Fourteen

The next day, Dylan headed to the medical examiner's office to get the official word on Sylvie Maguire's death. Though this was more or less routine, it was never as simple as that to him. Each victim who died at the hands of the unsub was a human being—or had been prior to her murder—and deserved to be respected in that regard and given a decent burial. Knowing precisely how they died and connecting it with a single perpetrator would keep the focus on apprehending the killer and giving the victims the ability to rest in peace, accordingly. More than that, Dylan wanted to do his best to keep Naomi from a similar fate. With the unsub feeling brazen enough to send her frightening text messages and possibly stalking her, Dylan would move heaven and earth to protect Naomi. Whether they were on the path toward a reawakening of their romance or had mind-blowing sex to release pent-up passions with no expectations for more remained to be seen. Neither of them had talked about it after getting back to the cabin last night—each retreating to their separate bedrooms to sleep alone—as if to do so would only lead to more harm than good. For his part, Dylan knew he wanted Naomi for much more than a one-night stand. He sensed she felt the same. So why was it so hard for them to own up to this and do something about it? Would they really allow themselves to miss the mark again, knowing that second chances rarely turned into third ones?

Arriving at his destination, Dylan let the thoughts rest for now, as he refocused on his detective side and a serial killer case that continued to dog him and the Pebble Creek PD. And would not let up for them and the Task Force, till they could wrap up the investigation. This wouldn't happen unless the unsub was brought to his knees.

Martha Donahue was all business upon his arrival to her spacious office with a nice view out of a square pivot window. "Since I have a couple more autopsies to perform and we're both pretty busy these days," she said, "I'll cut to the chase, Detective Hester. Sit." She proffered him a black task chair in front of the desk, where she was seated.

He sat down, leaning back. "How did she die?" he asked with anticipation.

Martha touched her glasses, then glanced at the monitor on her desk. "Ms. Maguire's official cause of death was due to asphyxiation, as a result of ligature strangulation. I estimate that the time of death was anywhere from around five to seven yesterday evening."

Dylan's brows knitted. He imagined how torturous it had to have been to be suffocated to death. "You think it was the same killer as the other women?" he asked straightforwardly, for the record.

Martha wrinkled her nose. "As I always like to point out, I'm a medical examiner, not a detective, Dylan. That being said, having followed the Violet Killer case closely, based on the autopsies done on the victims, the similarities are too striking to believe they were committed by different individuals. Right down to the violet left behind that never varies in size, shape and color. So, there you have it, Detective, in a nutshell."

Dylan nodded, having already reached the same conclusion in looking at the signs pointing entirely in one direction. "Any indication of sexual assault?" He had to ask, even if the victim was fully dressed when discovered. Or that it went against the grain of the unsub's modus operandi. But MOs could change. And it also wouldn't be the first time a perp had forced sex upon a victim with her clothes on.

"There's no evidence that the decedent was sexually assaulted," the medical examiner stated. "Nor, for that matter, was there evidence that the victim had engaged in consensual sex on the day she died."

"Just checking, for the record."

"Understood." Martha sat back. "Any more questions?"

"That's it for now." Dylan rose, pushing aside the possibility that someone other than their unsub was responsible for Sylvie Maguire's murder. That meant they could officially, more or less, make her female victim number nine of the Violet Killer, with Roger, a male casualty, increasing the total to at least ten known victims to date.

WHEN NAOMI GOT a call from Patricia Stabler asking her to come into the police department for a chat, she readily agreed, anxious to see what the profiler had come up with in trying to get into the unsub's head. Just as he was trying to get into Naomi's own head, and succeeding, to some degree. On the whole, though, she refused to buckle under to his lunatic tricks, knowing this would give him all the power in a tug-of-war she had to win. For herself, the other women targeted and her uncle.

Naomi saw Patricia seated at a desk in the back of a

rather large room with cubicles for the various detectives and FBI agents. Most were empty at the moment, as nearly all hands were on deck in the Violet Killer investigation. She passed by a metal desk that used to belong to her Uncle Roger but, seeing the nameplate, was now occupied by Dylan. Naomi had mixed feelings. She was certainly happy for Dylan that he had rightfully been promoted to his current position and held it with pride. But she felt saddened at the thought that her uncle had retired too soon, which, through no fault of his own other than doing his new job in private investigation, paved the way for someone to take his life.

"Good morning," Patricia said cheerfully, having stood up to greet her.

"Good morning," Naomi returned and ran a hand through her hair.

"Welcome to my little neck of the woods. With any good fortune, it'll be short-lived and I can go wherever they tell me to next—"

"It's a tough life." Naomi admittedly could relate. Working for the Secret Service, she had often traveled far and wide from home, leaving little time for a social life. Was she really okay with that? Or had spending time with Dylan given her cause to reassess what her priorities in life should be? And what they should not be.

"It can be," Patricia spoke musingly. "It can certainly wreak havoc on one's love life." She took a breath. "But hey, we all make choices, professionally and personally, and have to live with the consequences, for better or worse."

"True," Naomi agreed, but didn't necessarily feel good about it for the FBI agent or herself. Maybe they both needed to make some better choices in their lives. Or possibly end up alone and wondering what went wrong to put them there.

"Have a seat," Patricia said, sitting back at the desk.

Naomi took the faux leather side chair and adjusted herself.

Patricia clasped her hands. "Based on what you've been going through with the text messages and apparent stalking by presumably the same person believed to be responsible for the Violet Killer murders, I've reworked my psychological profile of the unsub, as it relates to you."

"Tell me..." Naomi leaned forward, hanging on the profiler's every word with more than a little interest.

"All right." Patricia took a breath. "Having evaluated the texts and the killer's overall tendencies as a serial stalker and murderer, I believe that his infatuation with you goes well beyond the fact that you and he are indirectly connected through Roger. My sense is that the unsub may have come into contact with you directly in some way."

Naomi's eyes widened with shock. "You mean face-to-face?"

"Not necessarily, but it is certainly a possibility."

"When? Where? Are we talking about since I've returned to Pebble Creek?" The notion unnerved her.

Patricia stiffened. "Perhaps. But more likely, you and he may have met or known each other even before your return," she suggested. "The unsub could have discovered this inadvertently when stealing your uncle's laptop, thereby triggering in the recognition an unnatural fascination, which the unsub may have seen as somehow meant to be in his warped state of mind."

"Are you saying the Violet Killer could be someone I knew at any time in my life?" Naomi's lower lip hung down. "Like from high school? College? Even before then? What?"

"More likely, it's much more recent than that," Patricia said coolly. "You could have met him while shopping, socializing, exercising or through some other means. Could be that it was only in passing or happenstance, possibly without your even being aware of it. But through his eyes, it is a connection that he cannot resist acknowledging in his own way through the text messages and stalking from a safe distance. If this is the case, that will likely escalate into attempting to reach you in a face-to-face way, to fulfill whatever fantasies he may have conjured up during the progression."

Naomi felt sick as she digested all that had been said. The thought that this psychopath could have been within feet of her before he began killing women was unsettling, to say the least. What if he had gone after her before she left Pebble Creek—ending her career with the Secret Service before it began? Then she would never have been given the opportunity to work her way back to Dylan, no matter what the future may hold for them. "How does this supposed scenario factor into the unsub's serial killer cravings?" she dreaded to ask. "Or are the two somehow unrelated in his damaged mind?"

"Oh, they are definitely related," the profiler responded. "I believe the unsub suffers from some level of attachment disorder. In needling you through the texts and stalking, he sees it as merely a means to the same ending he had inflicted upon the other victims of his obsession—death."

Naomi mused uncomfortably. "Could I have somehow encouraged this lunatic without realizing it?" She hated to think that he had become obsessed through her own unintended actions.

"I seriously doubt that." Patricia jutted her chin. "This has nothing to do with your behavior and everything to do with his."

"Is there any way to get him to lay off?" Naomi asked with desperation. "Such as telling the perp I'm not interested in a reply text? Or would that only embolden him and freak me out even more?"

"You definitely do not want to provoke him by contacting him in any form," stressed Patricia. "I'm only telling you this for informational purposes to better understand what we're dealing with here as it relates to what you're experiencing. I intend to run this by the team, but wanted to talk to you first. Let us do the heavy lifting in pursuing and stopping the unsub."

"I will," Naomi promised, knowing deep down inside that playing with fire could only get her burned. She wasn't going to go Lone Ranger in pursuing her stalker outside the investigators, including Dylan, tasked with bringing him down. "Sorry I asked."

"Nothing to apologize for, Naomi." Patricia reached out and touched her hand. "This has all of us a little freaked out. We're on top of it and beyond till the end."

Naomi nodded and gave a comforted smile. She appreciated being given a new perspective in characterizing the unsub, even if it left her wondering who it might be. And if there was any way to jar her memory in producing an image the Task Force could work with in identifying the killer.

"WE'VE GOT A hit on the gun used to shoot Roger," Hwang told Dylan as they walked and talked on the first floor of the police department. "Or not so much the actual weapon, but important info about the firearm."

"Go on…" Dylan pressed, taking anything they could get in advancing their objectives in this case.

"According to the National Integrated Ballistic Information Network, based on data entered into the system on the bullet that killed Roger and the ballistic markings on the shell casing, they were able to link it to bullets that came from the same weapon that has a gun barrel with a left-hand twist and four lands and grooves. The .45 ACP handgun was used earlier this year in an armed robbery at a party store in nearby Stafford Heights that left one man dead and a woman critically injured. The robber-shooter, identified as forty-seven-year-old Aidan Powell, was killed three weeks later when his car spun out of control on Route 18. The murder weapon was never found."

"Hmm…" Dylan mused aloud. "So, someone else—the unsub—ended up with this same firearm and used it on Roger?"

Hwang nodded. "My guess is that Powell dumped the murder weapon into the black market and the unsub snatched it up, not wanting to use a registered gun to do his dirty work."

"Makes sense in a homicidal perp's way of thinking," conceded Dylan, feeling frustrated that the killer seemed to somehow continue to stay a step or two ahead of them. But that calculating could go only so far before he could no longer press his luck and come out ahead. "We need to find that gun—and the triggerman himself," Dylan declared. "I think there's no doubt that if strangling his victims won't do the trick or he's otherwise backed into a corner, the unsub's more than willing to shoot anyone who gets in his way."

"Yeah, that's the scary part," Hwang muttered. "Not that the citizens of Pebble Creek could be any more frightened these days, so long as the Violet Killer remains at large. On that front, I've got some more news you need to hear."

"What is it?" Dylan stopped midway as they scaled the stairs for the second floor, where their desks were located. He gazed at Hwang's unreadable eyes.

"Forensics matched the size-ten shoeprint found near Sandra Neville's remains with the footprint you located at the spot by the lake near your cabin," the detective told him.

"Really?" Dylan's voice rose. "Are they sure about that?"

"They're pretty confident that the prints are the same size, same manufacturer, same impressions left on the grass. Could be entirely coincidental or circumstantial evidence that the same man was wearing the shoes at both scenes—your call..." Hwang started moving up the steps again with Dylan. "If you ask me, I think Naomi is on to something that our unsub has been tracking her, while at the same time going after other women. Unless we stop him, it's only a matter of time before she becomes his main focus—"

"Yes, that's what I'm afraid of," Dylan said worriedly, sensing all along that the unsub had some kind of fixation on Naomi and could try to raise the stakes at any time. He wasn't about to let that happen. Not so long as Dylan was still breathing. Once they reached the second floor, he told Hwang, "For the record, I don't believe in coincidences any more than you do." That included the dark SUV that Naomi believed was following her, which they had yet to track down.

Hwang gave a half smile and patted him on the shoulder. "Never thought for a moment that you did."

Dylan acknowledged this and headed toward his desk, when he spotted Patricia and Naomi moving toward him.

Both had serious looks on their faces and he felt a twinge in the pit of his stomach in wondering what was on their minds.

"Ladies," he said in a gentlemanly tone, belying his curiosity. "What's up?"

"We've got a new angle on the unsub…" Naomi spoke ambiguously. He saw the unease in her eyes, almost as though she were about to cry. But she blinked this away and extended her chin resistantly.

"I believe the Violet Killer's fixation on Naomi may go deeper than we ever thought." Patricia batted her lashes. "Let's assemble the Task Force now and talk about it."

"TAKE A GOOD look at the suspects' faces," Dylan told Naomi, as she strode up to the bulletin board and studied the large photographs. Patricia had laid out to the Task Force her revised criminal profile on the unsub, with the belief that his fixation on Naomi, in particular, was most likely developed from a past connection, real or imagined. And that it would probably progress to a deadly obsession, if allowed to go unchecked. As she grappled with this terrifying prospect, Dylan and Hwang had shown a correlation between footprints found at the scene of Sandra Neville's dead body and the area where Naomi believed a man had been checking her out through binoculars. The detectives also pointed out the fatal path of the gun used to kill her uncle Roger. All of which sent a chill up and down Naomi's spine. She examined each photograph carefully, knowing she would be given all the time she needed, especially if she were able to positively identify someone she recognized. But she drew a blank. None of the men—some more intriguing than others in facial structure, hairstyle or eye color—particularly stood out as someone who looked familiar. Was that because she simply couldn't remember? Or had never pinned it down to memory? Naomi sucked in a deep breath. The more likely answer, as Patricia had suggested, was that the connection, if one could call it that, was one-sided. It was all in the head of a psychopath. Making him all the more disturbing and dangerous.

She turned away from the bulletin board and gazed right into the intense gray eyes of Dylan. "I'm sorry," she uttered sincerely, "but I don't recognize any of these men."

Instead of expressing disappointment, he seemed to take it in stride. "Not a problem. The unsub is most likely someone you have no knowledge of, while concealed in open view. It was worth a shot." The hard lines in Dylan's face softened. "Don't worry, I won't let him get anywhere near you."

"I know." Naomi didn't doubt for one second his commitment to her as the lead detective on the case. She wasn't as certain about his commitment to her as a man and lover. Or vice versa. That was something they would have to address at a later time. When they weren't in a room full of law enforcement personnel whose sole mission was to capture a serial murderer before anyone else could be strangled or shot to death. "If the unsub should try," she spoke bravely, "I'll do whatever I need to protect myself. Or anyone he might go after."

Dylan's eyes crinkled satisfyingly. "Wouldn't expect anything less from you, Secret Service Agent Lincoln."

Naomi offered him a smile and took a seat in the front, while Chief Frazier took to the podium and gave what amounted to a pep talk in encouraging the Task Force members not to let up even in the slightest, till they had the Violet Killer in custody. Or he was taken out of commission, should it come to that. No one went against the grain in their shared determination to see this endeavor through successfully.

Chapter Fifteen

Later that afternoon, Naomi invited Brenda Quinlan, the woman her uncle Roger had been seeing before his death, for tea. She had gotten Brenda's number from his cell phone, feeling compelled to make contact with someone he had obviously cared for. Also, Naomi had hoped her uncle might have said something to her, even inadvertently, that could provide a clue about the killer. Dylan's cabin seemed the safest place to meet in protecting herself, with no reason to believe the unsub would go after the woman her uncle had been romantically involved with and was otherwise no threat to him.

"Thanks for reaching out to me," Brenda said with a smile, wearing a cream-colored, wide-brimmed floppy hat as they sat on the Adirondack chairs on the deck.

"Thanks for coming." Naomi smiled back and lifted her teacup, filled with chai tea. "Since you were in my uncle's life toward the end of it, I thought it might be nice to talk."

"I agree. Roger would've loved for us to get to know one another. He couldn't wait for you to return home to put that into motion."

"I wish I had come before it was too late," Naomi expressed, sensing the sadness and regret from her, which she too felt. "But life always seemed to get in the way, whether an adequate excuse or not." Knowing her uncle, Naomi was sure he would be admonishing her for going down that road, as one who always believed that she was doing what she was supposed to and he encouraged such to the very end of his life.

"That's normal," Brenda said, sipping her tea. "Roger knew that and couldn't have been prouder of you."

Naomi blushed. "I felt the same about him."

"The man was never dull and definitely a good catch." Brenda showed her teeth. "We had plans to go to the jazz festival in Seattle next year."

"I know he would have enjoyed that," Naomi said, remembering his appreciation for such great jazz vocalists as Ella Fitzgerald and Sarah Vaughan. It just wasn't meant to be. Or, if it was, the unsub had disrupted any such plans. On that thought, Naomi gazed at Brenda and, after tasting the tea, asked causally, "Did my uncle happen to mention anything to you about any of the cases he was working on?"

Thinking about the question for a moment or two, she responded, "Not that I can recall. He didn't seem all that interested in talking much about his work, focusing mostly on light subjects, hobbies and getting what he could out of life." Brenda eyed her curiously. "I've been keeping track of the murder investigation. Are you working now with the police in the investigation?"

"Yes, I'm offering consultation, as a witness to the crime," admitted Naomi, hoping this might spur something in her. "My uncle's laptop and all his files were taken by his killer. The laptop's been found and we're trying to retrieve any pertinent info from it, but that could take a while. I just thought that maybe Uncle Roger, talkative as he could be, might have confided in you anything that could be helpful in the investigation."

Brenda tasted more tea thoughtfully. "Come to think of it, the last time I spoke with him, Roger did mention something about finally finding the missing pieces of a mystery that he couldn't shake. He didn't elaborate on it, but seemed confident that it was something he was about to solve."

"Only he never got the chance to," Naomi said, wrinkling her nose, wondering what those missing pieces were that might lead them to his killer.

"Maybe he did solve it," suggested Brenda. "I know he spent a lot of time on his laptop, sometimes even when we were together. If you're ever able to get those missing files, you could have the answer you're looking for."

Naomi believed that to be true, as well. But could Sophia recover what the unsub had intentionally destroyed? And, if so, would it come too late to save more lives at the hands of the serial killer?

"Good idea to speak with Brenda," Dylan told Naomi, as they ate the Italian sausage lasagna she made that evening, along with red kale and sweet corn bread. Not used to cooking for anyone other than herself these days, Naomi liked the idea of making meals for Dylan. Didn't they say that good food was the way to a man's heart? Or would it take more than that to win him over again in full? "I believe that those missing pieces of a mystery are within our reach, one way or the other."

"Hope so." She forked a slice of lasagna, gazing at him. "That time can't come soon enough, with a creepy, unstable unsub seemingly lurking around every corner just waiting to strike when we least expect it."

"But that's perhaps his Achilles' heel," Dylan said sharply. "We are expecting him to make a move toward you—at least it seems like that's part of his illogical thought process. If that's the case, we'll be ready."

Naomi's lashes batted at him. "You mean use me to set a trap?"

"Not a chance!" Dylan's voice snapped. "I would never put your life on the line as bait, trust me." He wiped his mouth with a napkin. "What I meant was after what Patricia laid out, we won't take any chances that the unsub might try to up the ante. Until we get him, I've got an officer outside 24/7 and regular patrols that should deter even the most determined foe, when I'm not around myself."

"I see." Admittedly, she was content to have him so concerned for her welfare, in spite of the fact that Naomi had grown used to protecting herself. But she had never dealt with someone so diabolical and unbalanced as the Violet Killer. While he might not pursue her back to Miami, as long as she remained in Pebble Creek, he posed a clear and present danger. Dylan understood that and had her back. She wouldn't have wanted it any other way. Except perhaps if what he felt was more romantic affection than he'd let on.

"Glad you do," Dylan said easily, eating more food. "Whatever else may have ended things between us before, we're in this together."

Naomi smiled, feeling reassured, maybe in more ways than one. "Yes, I believe we are."

That night, they slept in the same bed. Rather than try to psychoanalyze each other's intentions or overthink things as far as the future was concerned, they mutually agreed to put such thoughts aside, as well as the ins and outs of the Violet Killer investigation, in favor of the powerful sexual chemistry between them here and now. Naomi excitedly gave in to desire, feeding off Dylan's erotic cravings, as they made love well into the wee hours of the morning. Each gave as much as they took in the battle for physical appeasement, reaching time and time again, till spent.

Before she fell asleep, her head comfy on Dylan's hard chest, Naomi knew what her rapidly beating heart was telling her in no uncertain terms. She was still very much in love with Dylan. Whether he wanted to hear this or not or if it would make any difference in how they moved forward was still very much in question.

THE NEXT MORNING, Dylan slipped from bed, with Naomi still sound asleep like an angel. He could watch her beautiful face at peace all day, if only there weren't more pressing concerns to deal with. Namely, catching a serial killer. One who would like nothing better than to add Naomi to his list of deadly conquests, if given the opportunity. Dylan watched her for a bit longer, feeling aroused at the thought of the incredible sex that once again took his breath away last night, leaving him wanting more and more of her sexy body and gentle soul. Not to mention her intelligence, humor and drive, all presenting the complete picture of perfection as a remarkable woman. What was there not to love? When had he ever stopped loving her, whether he tried to convince himself otherwise? It was what to do with this love that threw Dylan for a loop. Was there still a chance they could have a go at a relationship? He still wanted it all from her. But was he willing to do whatever it took to make that happen in a way that was equally agreeable to Naomi?

Dylan chewed on those thoughts as he got dressed, had a quick bite to eat and headed off to work. He checked in with the officer on duty named Ed Palmer, a US Navy veteran, age thirty-three, who sat alert in his vehicle, before Dylan got into his own car. He started the ignition and drove away from his property with Naomi still occupying the better part of his mind.

No sooner had he pulled onto the highway, when Dylan's cell phone rang. He was surprised to see that the caller was his sister, Stefany Gonzalez. His first thought was that there was something wrong. Though they were close—or as close as siblings could be who lived on different continents—busy lives kept them from having frequent contact. Okay, he admitted to himself that was a lame excuse for not communicating regularly in today's times of cell phones, the internet and social media.

Dylan accepted the video chat as he glanced at the phone in the dashboard mount. "Hey, sis."

Stefany's beautiful oval face appeared on the screen. It was surrounded by sun-drenched, short flaxen hair in an asymmetric style. "Hey, little brother." Her bluish-green eyes, inherited from their mother, twinkled. "I had a little time to kill and thought I'd check in on you to see how you're doing."

"Good to hear from you, Stefany." He grinned, noting she was wearing her medical scrubs, working with Doctors Without Borders in Southern Africa. "How's Theodore?"

"Busy like me, trying to keep up with our patients and their many needs."

"If anyone can do it, you can," Dylan stressed, proud of her for her dedication to the job and marriage at the same time. He wanted to experience that combo, too, but needed the right partner to complete his life. She was within reach, yet still just outside his grasp. Or so it seemed.

"I do my best." Stefany chuckled and then turned serious. "So, what's going on in your world?"

"Same old, same old," he said, wanting to spare her the mundane and uncomfortable aspects of his daily life.

She frowned. "I heard that you're still dealing with a serial killer run amok there."

Dylan winced. "Yeah, it's been an aggravating problem we're working overtime to solve," he groaned.

"And you will, Dylan," she encouraged him. "Stopping bad guys is what you were meant to do."

"Sometimes I wonder about that," he admitted, feeling the burden of the profession in dealing with a persistent unsub who didn't know when to quit. Dylan watched the road, then glanced back at her.

Stefany pursed her lips. "I can't imagine you doing anything else."

He felt the same way, as he loved police work; but Dylan couldn't help but wonder if he might be better suited to a new line of work. One in which stress and strain were less of an issue. And he had more time to do the things he truly loved like boating and, more than that, being in a committed relationship, where he could spoil the love of his life with affection, attention and anything else she wanted. Was it time for a change? Could he make it happen? Dylan looked at his sister. "I do have news."

"What?" Stefany asked anxiously.

"You'll never guess who's back in town."

"In that case, just tell me," she insisted.

"Naomi." Dylan waited for a reaction. He knew that Stefany had accused him of letting her get away, placing the blame for their relationship coming to a screeching halt squarely on his shoulders. For a while, he had resented the charge, believing he had done the right thing by allowing Naomi to chart her own course without his interference in putting undue pressure on her. Now he agreed with his sister and took full ownership of blowing his chance with Naomi. Had he asked her to marry him two years ago, it would have at the very least put everything on the table, for better or worse.

Shock registered across Stefany's face. "Oh, really?"

"Yeah. Naomi's uncle, Roger Lincoln, was killed and she came for the funeral."

"So sorry to hear about that," Stefany expressed.

"Yeah, it hit her hard." Dylan glanced at the small screen. "Now she's part of the Violet Killer Task Force." He explained the connection between Roger and the unsub, including Naomi witnessing her uncle's execution.

"Wow." Stefany's voice dropped a sorrowful octave. "I can't imagine what Naomi must be going through."

"She's dealing with it," Dylan spoke levelly, nearing his destination.

"And how are you dealing with seeing Naomi again?" Stefany put out bluntly. "Or shouldn't I ask?"

"She's staying with me," he said tonelessly, "for safety purposes." At least it started out that way. He thought about how far they had come in such a short time. "We're working through our issues."

Stefany smoothed a thin eyebrow. "Are you saying you might get back together?"

Dylan considered that the sex between him and Naomi was hotter than ever, proving that the sexual chemistry had never disappeared. And they seemed just as compatible intellectually. Even on a professional level, they had no problem being in sync. To him, this was an opening he was determined not to let close again. If he had any real say in it. But he thought it best not to get his sister's hopes—or even his own—up. Just in case his best efforts to keep Naomi in his life proved all for naught. "Let's just say anything's possible," he responded, leaving it at that.

Stefany seemed content with the response and didn't pry further. "Well, I have patients to get back to, so..."

"So, I'll let you go," Dylan said smilingly, reaching the police department. "Talk to you soon, sis." He meant it this time, recognizing that they needed each other, even from a great distance. Just as he needed Naomi, with the distance part yet to be determined.

"You better." Stefany peered at him and gave a little wave before hanging up.

Dylan parked in his spot. He grinned when thinking about his wise big sister. The notion of her and Naomi being sisters-in-law appealed to him. He imagined they could learn a lot from each other. But he still needed to put a ring on Naomi's finger. Would she accept it as his future wife two years after he failed to propose the first time around? Or could he be setting himself up for another big disappointment?

Before he could go there, Dylan knew they had to deal with the Violet Killer, once and for all. If Patricia's assessment of the unsub was accurate, then Naomi was at even greater risk of his psychopathic obsession. Making it all the more imperative that they nail the perp without delay.

Dylan exited the car and headed toward the building.

Chapter Sixteen

"I think we have something…" forensic print analyst Vince Iverson told Dylan, Chief Frazier, Hwang and other law enforcement members of the Task Force in the conference room.

"Go on," Dylan urged him, noting the enthusiasm in his voice.

"All right." Iverson scratched his flat top. "From the latest identified victim of the Violet Killer, Sylvie Maguire, we were able to pull a latent palm print from a tennis bracelet she was wearing when killed. We ran it through the FBI's Next Generation Identification biometrics and criminal history system of digital and automated information and got a hit." He took a breath and turned to the bulletin board. "The print matched one on file for a DWI for Zachary Jamieson."

"The florist worker?" Dylan said, as the name registered immediately. The thirty-five-year-old was one of their primary suspects as the Violet Killer. The fact that Jamieson had a predilection for violets, in particular, and had been caught hanging around the crime scene where schoolteacher Conchita Kaplan's body was discovered made him an obvious early suspect. But they had not been able to make anything stick. Till now.

"Yeah," Iverson confirmed, "it's him."

"I want Jamieson picked up immediately," Frazier ordered. "If this is our unsub, we don't want to give him an opportunity to escape our dragnet."

"We're on it!" Hwang declared.

"While we're all on the same page here," Dylan said, "we need to get a search warrant ASAP for Jamieson's residence and vehicle for evidence of his criminality. That includes the firearm used to kill Roger Lincoln. The unsub may have also chosen to hang on to Roger's own handgun, as a keepsake, which would be further evidence tying the serial murderer to Roger's death."

Frazier's brows twitched. "Get a judge to sign the order and let's get the evidence we need to put this guy away and take back our community!"

Dylan felt his blood pressure rise with the possibility that they could be one step closer to ending this nightmare in Pebble Creek. But before he told Naomi the news, only to give her false hope, Dylan wanted more concrete evidence that they had their unsub and he wasn't getting away to hurt her or any other woman ever again.

THE OLD FOURSQUARE stucco house was located on Ashford Street at the end of the tree-lined block. Dylan, Hwang and Agent Stabler, along with other police and FBI agents, approached the last known residence of Zachary Jamieson cautiously and with guns drawn, along with a search warrant. Though there was no sign of the red Jeep Renegade registered to Jamieson, Dylan went with the assumption that the suspect may still be inside the house, armed and very dangerous. The plan was to take him in alive, if at all possible. It was the only way to delve into the mindset of a purported serial killer for future reference. But that would be up to Jamieson, should it come to that.

Once they had ascended the house's porch steps, Dylan directed others to take their positions and be ready for whatever went down. He then gave the door a hard knock and yelled, "This is the police. Open up!" When there was no response, Dylan repeated the order sharply. Again, nothing from inside. Fearful that the suspect might try something dangerous, Dylan eyed two burly officers and nodded permission to break open the front door. They used a metal ram for the door breaching, bursting through.

With a Smith & Wesson M&P40 pistol in hand, Dylan led the others inside the two-and-a-half story residence. The first thing he noticed was the flowery-sweet scent of violets. Patricia noted it, too. "You can tell he's a florist," she quipped humorlessly, while holding her .38 Special revolver straight up.

Dylan sneered, eyes darting left and right for any signs of movement and seeing none. "That's not the half of it."

"Tell me about it," she agreed, as they walked across the mosaic-tiled entryway and onto the engineered hardwood floor.

Traditional furnishings were accented with vases filled with violets. The welcoming facade aside, as if leading the unsuspecting down a dark hole, Dylan signaled for the investigators to fan out. He took the lead in heading up the straight staircase to the second floor. After going from room to room, it was clear that no one was present. It appeared as though someone had left in a hurry. Could Jamieson have somehow been tipped off?

Once he was able to lower his guard, Dylan put the firearm back in his shoulder holster. The team's mission for the moment turned to a search for hard evidence. Donning nitrile gloves, he started with the master bedroom, digging through drawers and looking under the bed. Nothing of note, beyond a plastic bag of what appeared to be crystal methamphetamine. Dylan ignored the illicit drug possession for the time being, as he turned to the closet. Rifling through clothes and pushing aside shoes, he spotted a box on the shelf. Removing it, he looked inside and saw what Dylan was certain was a .45 ACP pistol. Much like the one used to take out Roger.

"What do we have here?" Patricia's eyes grew when Dylan held up the weapon downstairs.

"Is that what I think it is?" Hwang asked attentively.

"One can only hope." Dylan flashed them a deadpan look, not willing to get ahead of himself till ballistics was able to confirm that this was indeed the Roger Lincoln murder weapon.

An hour later, the verdict was in. At the crime lab, George Suina was practically giddy and subdued at the same time, when he announced, "The .45 ACP handgun you discovered was the one used to shoot to death Roger Lincoln."

"Are you sure?" Dylan asked, more for effect than anything. He knew that the firearms and forensic investigator wasn't one for putting out speculation over facts. Especially when it came to solving a homicide as part of a broader investigation into a serial murderer. But it didn't hurt to hear him say it again as it related to this case.

"As sure as we're standing here," Suina declared, turning from Dylan to Hwang to Patricia, and back again at his workstation. He turned to his monitor, which showed a split screen. "We test-fired a bullet still in the chamber of the .45 ACP firearm from a gun barrel with four lands and grooves with a left-hand twist and matched it to the bullet used to shoot Roger. The ballistic markings on the shell casings were identical—meaning they could only have come from the same weapon."

"The murder weapon," Patricia said with an edge to her husky voice.

"When we couple that with the fingerprint linking Zachary Jamieson to Sylvie Maguire's murder, looks like we've finally put the solid pieces together to nail Roger's murderer and the Violet Killer," Hwang stated with satisfaction.

Dylan nodded, feeling uplifted that they knew who the unsub was. "Now we just need to locate Jamieson before he can hurt someone else."

A BOLO, short for "be on the lookout," alert was issued for the suspect, believed to be on the run, and the vehicle he drove. In the meantime, forensics was called in to do a more thorough search of Jamieson's house. Though more crystal meth and drug paraphernalia were discovered, along with some rope that could have been used as the ligature in the strangulations, there was no sign of Roger's stolen firearm that Dylan had hoped to recover in bolstering the case against the suspect. But he was obviously smart enough to get rid of the weapon. That notwithstanding, the evidence pointed squarely toward Jamieson as Roger's killer and Dylan knew that every second counted in the search for him.

NAOMI HAD A sense that something was up, even if she couldn't put a finger on it. Call it women's intuition. Or the strange yet satisfying look on Dylan's handsome face. She suspected it went beyond the lovemaking that kept them going for much of last night. Or the powerful vibes of deep affection that seemed to resonate between them in the process that could no longer be denied. So what then?

"We've got him..." Dylan clutched her shoulders and grinned as they stood in the great room. "The man who killed your uncle is now in custody."

Naomi's face lit with shock. "When? How? Who is he?"

"His name is Zachary Jamieson," explained Dylan. "He's a florist employee and one of our original suspects. Hidden inside his house, where he lived alone, we found the .45 ACP handgun used to shoot Roger." Dylan let that sink in as she contemplated the enormity of the news. "There's more irrefutable evidence tying Jamieson to the Violet Killer case. A latent palm print found on a tennis bracelet worn by Sylvie Maguire, the latest murder victim, when she was killed, belonged to Jamieson. He must have sensed that the walls were closing in on him. When we went to arrest him, he was already on the run."

"And how did you manage to capture him?" Naomi gazed at Dylan curiously, knowing how elusive the man had been for two years and counting.

"Once we were able to identify the unsub, Jamieson lost his uncanny ability to operate in plain view. We put out an all-points bulletin for his arrest. It didn't take long for the car Jamieson was driving to be spotted. After a short chase, he was forced to come to a stop in the parking lot of a convenience store. Once he stepped outside the vehicle, heavily armed police and FBI agents were waiting and swarmed him like bees on honey. Wisely, Jamieson surrendered without incident."

Naomi sucked in a deep breath. "So, it's over?" she dared ask.

"Actually, it's only just begun," Dylan corrected her, though she was sure he got her meaning. "We need to interrogate the suspect and see what he's willing to give us. Then he'll face justice and be punished accordingly for his crimes. Long process, but we're loaded and ready to go."

"Good." The knowledge that the perp who murdered her uncle was off the streets was slightly overwhelming to Naomi, but still a big relief. Not only for her, but the loved ones of the other victims of the serial killer.

"If you'd like to sit this one out, in terms of seeing the suspect in person, I'll understand," Dylan voiced sympathetically.

"I wouldn't." She batted her lashes boldly. "I need to get a look at him to be able to put this behind me, to the extent that's possible."

"All right." He held her gaze intently and Naomi wondered what else was on his mind. Maybe he was considering where things stood between them as they moved forward. This weighed on her, as well. Only time would tell, but she believed they had turned a corner in their relationship and, for her part, there was no turning back.

Without prelude, Naomi lifted her mouth and kissed him. "Shall we go?"

DYLAN STOOD BETWEEN Naomi and Patricia, watching through the one-way glass as the suspect sat in the interrogation room. Zachary Jamieson was medium sized and about six feet tall in leisurewear. The bushy-browed, blue-eyed florist worker had beige-blond hair in a taper faded on the sides, short quiff style. Dylan tried to picture him as the elusive serial homicidal psychopath they had been after for two years. Though at a glance, Jamieson may not have seemed like the prototype for their killer, Dylan realized that serial killers came in all shapes, shades and sizes. Anyone could fit the bill if motivated enough to become a killing machine. Detective Hwang sat across from the suspect, nibbling at the edges in seeing what he could derive from him, before Dylan and Patricia took their turn at bat grilling him. Jamieson had yet to be formally charged, which would likely necessitate lawyering up, limiting what he might say.

"Does he look familiar at all?" Dylan asked Naomi, noting Patricia's theory that they had probably crossed paths before.

Naomi studied the suspect carefully before turning away, as if too painful to look at further, and responded honestly. "Not really. Nothing's clicking. I mean, I suppose I could have passed him by here or there, but to say, yes, I know him—I can't…"

"It's fine." Dylan put his hand on hers, enjoying the touch of Naomi's soft skin. Just as he liked when their lips brushed before leaving his cabin. It told him that she was just as serious about seeing where things went with them as he was. This excited him as something to very much look forward to. But, right now, there was still unfinished business. "We have Jamieson dead to rights and can spare you needing to connect dots in any way."

"I agree," Patricia told her. "It looks like the perp has dug his own grave, so to speak, and he won't be able to climb out of it. Not this time."

To that end, Dylan felt relieved that without the benefit of Roger's deleted files, they were able to get Jamieson to uncharacteristically trip himself up with amateur missteps. Now they only needed to run with this and put the case to rest.

"I'm glad." Naomi faced him with a relaxed expression. "Now that the threat the serial killer posed to me and other women has been neutralized, I think I'll swing by my uncle's house for a bit."

"Really?" Dylan wondered if she had begun to tire of staying at his place. Was he reading her wrong in believing they were rebuilding something special?

"I need to go through his things," she explained, "and see what can be kept or donated or needs to be thrown away, before the house is put on the market."

So, she did plan to sell. He bristled at the thought. Did that mean her return to Miami was now imminent? Had he expected otherwise? Should he be surprised, even with the heated passions and more that they had enjoyed since she got back to town? Dylan realized that it didn't matter, as he was prepared to do whatever it took to be with her, if she wanted to be with him. "Sounds like a smart move on your part," he told her, feeling it should be safe enough for Naomi to go there on her own. "I'll come by and help as soon as I'm done here."

"That would be great." She smiled and glanced at Patricia, before gazing at Jamieson. "Good luck with him in there."

Patricia grinned. "Thanks. It's his luck that's run out."

Naomi nodded. "Hope so."

Dylan walked her out and returned, ready to go at the suspect in securing a confession on all fronts.

Chapter Seventeen

Dylan walked into the room, carrying two evidence bags. He placed them on the table and sat across from the hand-cuffed suspect in the same chair Hwang had occupied, before leaving the interrogation room on cue. It was left to Dylan to turn up the heat on Zachary Jamieson. He wasted no time in this regard. "I'm Detective Hester. You've been a busy man these past two years, Zach," he spoke curtly, following Hwang's lead. "Or would you prefer I call you Blue Violet?" He never gave the perp a chance to answer. "It's over now. Your best bet is to co-operate with us and maybe you can escape death row." In truth, Dylan knew that in Oregon, crimes qualifying for the death penalty in recent years generally did not include serial murders, such as those attributed to the suspect. If Jamieson didn't know that, it wouldn't hurt to use as leverage for now.

Jamieson snarled. "As I told the other detective, I have no idea what you're talking about. I didn't kill anyone, least of all Sylvie Maguire."

Dylan was undeterred. He slid a plastic evidence bag containing a tennis bracelet toward the suspect. "This belonged to Sylvie Maguire. Your palm print was found on the murdered woman's bracelet. Can you explain that?"

"Yeah, I can," he said nonchalantly.

"This ought to be good." Dylan was barely able to suppress a sarcastic snicker.

Jamieson shifted in the chair, ill at ease. "I gave Sylvie that bracelet. It was a gift to a friend, nothing more."

Dylan rolled his eyes skeptically. "A gift?"

"Yeah. I knew she liked jewelry, so I bought it for her."

"Where did you buy it?" pressed Dylan.

"A jewelry store near the florist shop where I work. I paid for it with my credit card."

Dylan remained unconvinced but knew this could easily be checked out. Even if he and the victim were acquainted, the suspect could have had a beef with her and murdered her. Or strangled her, in spite of their supposed friendship, as a serial killer. "You say you were friends. Where did you meet Sylvie Maguire?"

"At the Owl Club. She tended bar there," Jamieson replied swiftly.

That much made sense to Dylan, believing that the Violet Killer likely had gotten to know at least some of his victims, luring them into a false sense of complacently, till ready to kill. He peered at the suspect. "Why did you run?"

"I panicked." Jamieson lowered his head. "When I heard that Sylvie had been murdered the same day we were hanging out together, I figured I'd be blamed for her death." He took a deep, uneven breath. "Looks like I was right."

Dylan wasn't easily swayed by good actors—or even bad ones, for that matter. Serial killers were, by their very nature, cunning and good with denial. But he wasn't ready yet to throw the hammer at the suspect as the Violet Killer. Dylan grabbed the other evidence bag that held a .45 ACP handgun and put it in front of Jamieson. "Do you recognize this?"

He stared at the weapon, then glared at Dylan. "No. Why should I?"

"Because it was found in a box in your bedroom." Dylan waited a beat. "This gun was used to murder a private investigator named Roger Lincoln. Know anything about that?"

"I've never seen that gun before." Jamieson's face reddened. "No idea where it came from."

Dylan considered that the weapon had been cleaned of all prints, making it impossible to prove definitively that he was the shooter. That was hardly enough to let him off the hook. He glared at the man. "You've got to do better than that," Dylan said, repeating an at-times effective cliché.

"It's the truth," Jamieson maintained, setting his jaw. "Someone must be trying to set me up," he claimed in a panicked voice.

Dylan mulled over that possibility, small as it might be, as he glanced at the one-way mirror and wondered what his colleagues' take was on this. Was the suspect feeding him a bunch of lies? Or was there something to his story? "What size shoe do you wear?" he thought to ask, homing in on the stalking and text messages Naomi had endured.

"Eleven and a half." Jamieson cocked a brow. "Why?"

If this was true, it left Dylan contemplating if he could be working with someone else in perpetrating the murders. Though most serial killers worked alone, it wasn't unheard of that two or more persons had joined forces in committing homicidal acts of violence. The so-called Hillside Stranglers, Kenneth Bianchi and Angelo Buono Jr., and serial killer tandems Leonard Lake and Charles Ng, and Charlene and Gerald Gallego, came to mind.

Could that be the case here? Or was Jamieson as their unsub climbing up the wrong tree?

NAOMI DROPPED BY Dylan's log cabin to grab her laptop, bottle of water and firearm. She didn't expect she would need the 9mm Glock on this occasion, but tucked it in her waistband holster to be on the safe side. She noted that the officer on duty on the grounds had been reassigned. That was quick, but not too surprising, she supposed, with a suspect in police custody and other assignments to take on. Naomi drove to the house she grew up in. Walking around inside, it almost felt like the first time since returning to Pebble Creek, having spent most of it tucked away at Dylan's place. She had mixed feelings being back there, remembering happier times, while also coming to terms with the fact that her uncle Roger was gone. Selling the house would be difficult, but also the right thing to do, given that she would not be living there and could not afford to maintain two places at once. Exactly where she would call home was still up in the air.

When her cell phone rang, Naomi took it out of the back pocket of her gabardine pants. She saw the caller was Sophia for a video chat and wondered if her Secret Service colleague had made any headway in retrieving the files from Uncle Roger's laptop. Since they had already identified the Violet Killer, Naomi doubted it mattered anymore what her uncle had uncovered.

"Hey," Naomi said, and immediately noticed the earnest look on Sophia's face. "What is it?"

"Sorry it took longer than I thought to get back to you," she said. "Fortunately, I was able to recover enough of the deleted files to give you what you wanted. I'm sending them to you now. Take a look on your laptop…"

"Okay." Heading up to her room with it, Naomi asked with interest, "Can you give me a hint?"

"I can do better than that." Sophia licked her lips. "Your uncle was able to find a major hole in the alibis of one of the suspects."

"Really?" Naomi set the laptop on the computer desk and positioned herself on the solid wood stool. "I assume you're referring to Zachary Jamieson, who was arrested today for Uncle Roger's murder and the deaths of nine women as the Violet Killer."

"I hadn't gotten the word." Sophia frowned. "Actually, the unsub your uncle fingered as the likely serial killer was a man named Blade Canfield."

Before Naomi could wrap her mind around this revelation and pull up the files, she heard a noise from inside the room. Looking up, she saw standing there in denim jeans, a knit hoodie jacket and dark sneakers a tall, lean man in his late twenties with a short black side-swept messy hairstyle and sinister-looking dark hooded eyes. In one gloved hand, he was holding a gun pointed at her. The other hand held a silk blue scarf—the kind Naomi imagined might be used to strangle someone.

"Good to see you again, Naomi…" the man said in an eerie tone of voice.

"CAN I HAVE a word?" Chief Frazier stuck his head into the interrogation room with an unreadable expression.

Dylan nodded, and stood. He grabbed the bags of evidence. "Be right back," he told the suspect. Not that Zachary Jamieson was going anywhere for the time being, as Dylan weighed whether or not he was their unsub. Outside the room, in addition to the chief, standing there were Agent Stabler, Detective Hwang and George Suina. All looked tense, prompting Dylan to ask, "What's up?"

"There's been a new development," Frazier said stiffly. "Actually, more than one." He scratched the tip of his nose. "The Secret Service uncovered evidence in the Violet Killer case." He glanced at Patricia, deferring to her.

"Secret Service Agent Sophia Menendez, at Naomi's request, was able to recover relevant information in the death of Roger Lincoln and the serial homicides investigation," Patricia announced, a catch to her voice.

Dylan was happy to hear that Naomi's friend and coworker came through with something to help their case. "I'm listening…"

"It moves us away from Zachary Jamieson as our main suspect," she said, "and directly toward trust fund baby Blade Canfield. Roger was able to trip up Canfield's supposedly airtight alibis for his whereabouts during many of the murders. Using both legal and otherwise means, Roger gained access to bank accounts and money that went straight from Canfield to so-called witnesses who lied for him. This corresponded to some of the phone numbers we took from Roger's cell phone. At least one of the witnesses came clean to Roger and was prepared to testify against Canfield to that effect, before the man mysteriously vanished and can be presumed dead, if Canfield had his way of self-protection at all costs."

"Turns out Canfield recently sold a dark-colored SUV that matches the one Naomi reported was trying to run her off the road—or worse," Hwang stated. "The perp's been running rings around us for two years."

Dylan reacted to the shocking info. "No denying the strong circumstantial evidence here for Canfield's guilt as the Violet Killer," he said musingly. "It certainly appears to let Jamieson off the hook—for these crimes anyway." While seemingly pointing at Blade Canfield as the unsub. "But we need more concrete evidence to tie Canfield directly to the murders, if we're to put him away for good…" Dylan cautioned, not wanting the suspect to use his wealth to try to circumvent justice.

"We've got it," Suina chipped in. "Just received notification from CODIS that they found a match for the crime scene DNA taken from beneath the nails of murder victim Sandra Neville. It matched Blade Canfield's DNA that was collected after an arrest eight years ago, following a brawl at a bar that left the other person with a broken jaw. Charges were ultimately dropped, as the victim apparently refused to testify. It was believed that Canfield bought his way out of trouble."

"Not this time," Dylan snorted; the DNA match was just what they needed to beat the perp at his own deadly game. "It's time he's finally held accountable for his crimes." It suddenly occurred to Dylan that Naomi was still in danger. "Naomi's at Roger's house, which she now owns," he clarified. "If Blade Canfield sees this as an opening to go after her—"

"Then he will likely act on his dark impulses and anomalous fixation on Naomi," Patricia argued.

"We've already put out a warrant for Canfield's immediate arrest," Frazier declared. "My guess is that he's probably already figured out the walls are starting to close in. If he's smart—and Canfield seems to think he is—he'll be more interested in saving his own neck than anything else, by skipping town."

"That's an assumption I'm not willing to gamble Naomi's life on," Dylan stated flatly, his heart skipping a beat at the mere thought of Canfield catching her off guard. He took out his cell phone and called her. *Answer*, he pleaded after several rings, before it went to voice mail. Dylan cursed within and left her a message, updating her on the investigation and Blade Canfield as a serious person of interest, warning her to be on the lookout for the extremely dangerous suspect. "I need a SWAT team to go to Naomi's address posthaste," Dylan ordered, thinking Canfield could try to take her as a hostage, if cornered. "I'm heading over there myself," he said, praying it wasn't too late to tell Naomi everything he felt for her and was willing to do to make them a couple for a lifetime.

"I'm going with you," Patricia told him. The sharp look in her determined eyes told him there was no room for argument.

"Let's go," Dylan said succinctly.

"What about him?" Hwang asked, pointing through the one-way window at Zachary Jamieson.

Dylan glanced at the suspect. "Let him sit there till we can check and recheck any and everything about him and any possible role he may have played in the Violet Killer case." They were not about to let a guilty man slip through their fingertips. Even if the number one suspect as the Violet Killer was now Blade Canfield, who could be targeting Naomi as his next violet to snuff out like a delicate flower.

Chapter Eighteen

Naomi's first instinct was to go for her weapon. She figured that she had a decent chance to get off one round, maybe two, that could stop the intruder in his tracks before he ever knew what hit him. But she also knew that even with him pointing a gun at her haphazardly while also dangling a scarf, he would likely still be able to fire it and hit her at least once. That one time could prove fatal. Then she would never get the opportunity to make things right with Dylan, in professing her love and strong desire to build a life together. It was with that fervent hope in mind that Naomi decided it best not to throw caution to the wind. Not yet. She figured if the perp had intended to kill her immediately, he would already have done so.

"I'll take that," he said tersely, snatching the cell phone from her grasp. It was just as Dylan was phoning, before it went to voice mail. "You won't be needing this anymore."

Naomi watched the intruder shut the phone off and hurl it at the wall as if to see how far it could bounce off. Would Dylan sense that something was wrong? Had Sophia reported the interruption of their phone call? Regardless, Naomi feared she was on her own at present in dealing with the dire situation she was in. "Do we know each other?" she asked the man inquisitively, in considering his own words to that effect, *"Good to see you again, Naomi..."* Naomi studied him as she continued to sit on the stool, as if stuck like adhesive, while he hovered like a portentous shadow. Sophia said his name was Blade Canfield. Naomi recalled that he was one of the Violet Killer suspects the Task Force had put together. Was he friends or even partners in crime with Zachary Jamieson?

"Guess you don't remember." The man frowned, as if disappointed. "Why am I not surprised? Two years ago, at a club, I tried to strike up a conversation, but you just blew me off."

She peered at him, trying to put the face into her memory. Not normally one to blow off someone who was respectful in initiating a chat, Naomi suspected that he was not. Then there was the fact that she was dating Dylan at the time and would not have been interested in giving any other man false encouragement. "I'm sorry," she told him, trying to sound as sincere as possible. As if this might somehow get him to back off. Or give her a better opportunity to go on the attack.

"Yeah, I'll bet." He rolled his eyes. "Actually, you did yourself a favor. You were supposed to be my first victim. Practice makes perfect and all that. But you left town before I could put my plan into action. Another unfortunate violet had to take your place. And another and another—till I really got into a groove. Imagine how shocked I was when I stole Roger Lincoln's laptop after killing him—and discovered that the very person he was talking to just before his death was you, the violet of my dreams." He laughed whimsically. "Seemed like the stars found a way to line up again much to my liking. All I needed to do was be patient. Looks like it paid off big-time, as you came back to this house with no security system in place and without backup, as if to sign your own death warrant—"

Naomi was stunned beyond belief. He had planned to murder her before she moved to Miami? How had she been so fortunate to escape his deadly desires? Had she stuck around, could she have been able to somehow stop him before he could kill other women? Her uncle Roger? And had she now come full circle so this lunatic ended up murdering her anyway, as if her fate had been sealed two years in the making?

"I know it's a lot to take in," he said wryly. "But it is what it is. Anyway, for the record, my name's Blade Canfield. But I guess you already know that, thanks to your friend." He cursed and contorted his features. "Should have done a better job making sure those files from your uncle's laptop could never be recovered. Now that the cat's out of the bag, it's forced me to have a change of plans. Oh well, what's done is done."

"That's true." Naomi's voice shook disconcertingly. She could only imagine what his previous or current plans were for her. Neither had to be good, considering the outcome for the other women he'd targeted. She hoped against hope that she might be able to reason with him somehow to buy needed time. "So, maybe you should just quit while you're ahead and go somewhere else in the world, where no one can ever find you. After all, you have the resources, right?" Having money to burn, by all accounts, gave him some leeway in planning an escape.

"You'd like that, wouldn't you?" Canfield chuckled derisively. "Sorry, no can do." He waved the gun precariously. "By the way, in case you didn't recognize it, this happens to be your uncle's Blackhawk .44 Magnum revolver. I thought it would be appropriate to use to finish you off." He raised the silk scarf. "Unless, I decide to strangle you with this instead, like I did the other hapless women who fell into my trap with no means to escape. Haven't decided yet. Fortunately, I'm in no hurry." He held up the weapon again that belonged to Naomi's uncle—another hard pill to swallow—making her weak in the knees and wondering if he would use it to kill her as well in a strange irony. "I needed to ditch my own firearm—planting it in the bedroom of a patsy named Zachary Jamieson I set up to take the fall for the death of Lincoln and my last violet victim, Sylvie Maguire. Ingenious, truly. Jamieson made it almost too easy to befriend, only to strangle the unsuspecting Sylvie after he left her place, knowing the cops would pin the blame on him. Which they did and, by extension, the other murders perpetrated by the infamous Violet Killer."

Canfield laughed, obviously pleased with himself. Then, just as quickly, his countenance darkened bitterly. "But, no thanks to you, it appears as though your boyfriend, Detective Hester, and his fellow police, FBI and Secret Service counterparts are on to me. Too little, too late, I'm afraid. At least for you…" He pointed the gun straight at her face. "Get up!" She hesitated to do so, fearing he might shoot her on the spot. "Now!" His voice echoed throughout the room.

Naomi got to her feet slowly while weighing her options. Did she go for broke now and reach for her weapon? Or at a later opportunity, assuming there was one? Had Dylan figured it all out and was planning a countermove to thwart the serial killer's plans before he was able to kick them into gear? "Oh, and I assume you're packing," Canfield said, as though reading her mind. "I would be, if I were you. Turn around," he ordered. "And don't try anything stupid, if you value your life."

Naomi very much valued her life and any future she

might have with Dylan. As such, she did as Canfield demanded, believing that he was too full of himself and obsessed with her to simply shoot her in the back of the head and call it a day. Still, she closed her eyes, the life Naomi still wanted flashing before her like a motion picture in vivid color, as he came up behind her, placing the cold barrel of the gun to her cheek. He removed the firearm from her holster, tucking it away in his jacket pocket. "Good girl," he said succinctly. "Now move…"

Naomi felt the gun poke her in the back as she headed out of the room and down the hall and stairs, with Canfield right there every step of the way. "Where are you taking me?" she hesitated to ask, as they reached the first floor. Would he try to use her as a bargaining chip to get out of town? Or did the killer have something more sinister in mind?

"Not very far," Canfield said, shoving her out the door. "We're just going to take a little walk out into the woods."

"And then what?" Naomi challenged him, reading between the thin lines.

"Then I'll let you live, once I no longer need you as an insurance policy, and I'll escape to my car waiting for me at the top of the hill—and you'll never see me again…"

She wasn't buying it. He planned to kill her, to feed his ego and add to his murderous conquests. Then flee, to leave Dylan to find her body and be broken for what might have been and frustrated that he had once again been outfoxed by the Violet Killer. She couldn't allow that to happen. "You won't get away with this," she spat, if only to throw him off his game a bit.

"When have I heard that before?" he mocked her, pushing her forward again. "I think I will, as always, and there's no one to stop me. At least, not this day."

Naomi hated his confidence, stemming from being

able to successfully terrorize the town for two years. This would backfire on him, she was sure. But would it be too late for her to escape his lunacy? "It was you watching me in the lake, wasn't it?" she asked to be sure, as they headed toward the trees.

"Yeah, I confess," Canfield conceded. "Couldn't resist checking you out, while keeping you on edge at the same time. Same was true with the text messages and when I stayed on your tail one day with my SUV after you drove from Hester's cabin, before allowing you to escape unharmed. Half the fun has been playing with your head. Guess the two-year delay has been well worth the wait."

Naomi cringed as he validated her beliefs and further connected the dots in tying him to the murders. She looked over her shoulder and asked, in an effort to keep him talking, "So, what's with the violets anyway? Are they just something you dreamed up to leave in the victims' mouths for the shock factor? Or is there another deep-seated reason for that?"

"I admire your curiosity, Secret Service Agent Lincoln." Canfield chuckled. "Doesn't hurt to indulge you. No, there is no abused-as-a child or rejected-as-an-adult or some psychological mumbo-jumbo explanation. The truth of the matter is that I happen to appreciate the delicacies of violets, which is akin to the ladies I chose to put out to pasture. The violet as a going-away present seemed most apropos, while at the same time giving the cops fits in trying to figure it out." He chortled wickedly. "I see it's catching."

"Don't flatter yourself," Naomi shot back, hoping to catch him off guard. "I'm not a big fan of violets, no matter the use. What you choose to do with them is your business."

"Glad to see we're on the same page," he quipped, shoving her ahead roughly.

When they were deep enough into the woods, Naomi was certain that he would strangle her, in keeping in line with the other victims' fate, shooting her only as a last resort. She needed to make her move to prevent either occurrence. Or die trying.

AS HE SPED through traffic, Dylan wanted to kick himself for jumping the gun in assuming they had the unsub in Zachary Jamieson. Even if the pieces fit at the time, they may have fit too perfectly. All the more reason Dylan felt he should have, at the very least, questioned the assumptions. Had he left the door open, he would not have essentially given Naomi a coast-is-clear message, putting her own life in jeopardy.

"How did we not see Blade Canfield for who he truly was?" Dylan faced Patricia in the passenger seat.

"Because he worked overtime to keep that from happening," the profiler responded, having just tried to call Naomi, to no avail. "That's classic among smart serial killers. Canfield weaved an elaborate labyrinth that kept us going around in circles. Fortunately, Roger Lincoln was able to figure things out. Some of his methods may have been questionable, but no one can argue with the results, thanks to the Secret Service computer whiz finding a way to crack his computer files."

"I agree," Dylan said, giving a mental thumbs-up to Sophia Menendez. She definitely did right by Naomi in giving them what she promised, and then some, including an alert that she had been cut off in a phone chat with Naomi and feared she was in danger. He pressed down on the accelerator to move faster, knowing that every second was one second less needed to reach his destination before it was too late. "Can you try calling Naomi again?" he asked Patricia, hoping that she still had access to her phone and could help them help her.

"Will do," she said. Again, no response, frustrating them both.

As he approached a blue BMW X6 parked off the side of the road on the hill, Dylan's first thought was that it might have been abandoned. But, given the high cost of the luxury vehicle, that seemed unlikely. It then occurred to him that the car was simply left there as a temporary measure, till the driver returned and could then leave in a hurry without much attention. Blade Canfield came to mind. On an uneasy hunch, Dylan pulled up behind the car. He called into the Pebble Creek PD and requested they run the plate number.

"The vehicle is registered to a Blade Nicholas Canfield," the dispatcher said momentarily.

Dylan's heart skipped a beat as they got out of the car, with their weapons drawn. Both wore bullet-resistant vests as they moved toward the vehicle. No one was inside. "Canfield's gone after Naomi at her house," he said knowingly.

"And this is to be his escape route," the FBI profiler uttered.

"If anything happens to Naomi…" Dylan found himself unable to finish the thought, as losing her just when he had found her again, only this time with no more tomorrow, was more than he could bear.

"Don't give up hope," insisted Patricia. "We can still get to her before Canfield can carry out his homicidal urges against the object of his fixation."

Dylan had to believe that, as he was determined to stay optimistic that everything would work out and Naomi would be unharmed when this was over. "I won't," he promised. "We'll proceed on foot, so as not to alert Canfield, and head to the house through the woods."

"I was thinking the same thing," she told him.

They started down the hill, when Dylan spotted some movement in the trees. It was Naomi and Canfield. He was forcing her to walk at gunpoint. Patricia saw it, too. She took out her firearm. "It's better that we split up and hit him from two angles, if need be."

"I agree," Dylan said, lifting the pistol from his holster. He motioned for her to move in one direction, while he went in another. All one of them needed was a clear shot and they could take down the serial killer before he could lay a finger on Naomi.

Moving stealthily down the knoll, Dylan was determined to make sure the love of his life lived to see another day. Make that many more days, weeks, months and years. They had come too far in rebuilding a relationship to see it end prematurely. He made his way into the woods, careful not to tip his hand, sure the same was true for Patricia. The preferred thing would be to keep Canfield alive to answer for his crimes. But if it came to saving him or Naomi, Dylan never flinched in knowing which was the only real choice.

He watched from behind a tall cottonwood tree, gun aimed and prepared to shoot, as Canfield and Naomi stopped walking. She turned to face the serial killer, who put his own firearm in his jacket pocket, replacing it with a scarf. "Sorry, I lied," Canfield told Naomi coldly, as he flexed the scarf between his hands. "I can't let you live. It'll be too much fun watching you die and then getting away once again."

Naomi sneered defiantly and retorted, "I lied, too, when I told you I wouldn't put up a fight. Bring it on."

Just as Dylan was ready to intervene, spotting Patricia

coming up fast, both watched with amazement as Naomi used a mixture of old-fashioned hand-to-hand combat and jujitsu to take down her opponent. When Canfield tried to go for his gun, she kicked it away effortlessly. He reached inside his jacket pocket for a second gun, which Dylan suspected was Naomi's own confiscated firearm. She easily dislodged it from his hand and used her attacker's desperate and futile attempts to regain the upper hand against him, till he was fully subdued.

Taking no chances, Dylan announced his and Agent Stabler's presence and rushed toward them. Seeing him, Naomi's eyes lit and she fell into his arms. "What took you so long?" she cried lightheartedly.

He laughed a little as Patricia made sure her abductor and a killer stayed down, if not out. "Got here as soon as I could," Dylan told Naomi. "But looking at the way you manhandled the perp, it seems like you had things well in hand."

"Desperate times called for desperate measures," she quipped, still clinging to him as if being apart was unbearable. He felt the same way. "There's Uncle Roger's firearm," Naomi indicated, nodding her head at the weapon the assailant had been carrying, resting comfortable in the dirt. "It was apparently going to be his ace in the hole if he was unable to strangle me to death."

Dylan eyed the second firearm on the ground. "I take it the other gun belongs to you?"

"Yes, he took it from me under threat of death," she moaned. "Can't wait to reclaim, once it's been processed as part of a crime scene."

"Shouldn't take long." Dylan furrowed his brow at the mere thought of Canfield succeeding in his deadly endeavor. Using Roger's .44 Magnum revolver as a weapon against Naomi would have made it even worse, after having murdered her uncle before Naomi's very eyes. "Thank goodness Canfield fell short on both counts."

"Tell me about it," she stated without humor.

Patricia handcuffed the serial killer. "We've got him!" the FBI agent declared victoriously. She chuckled while helping a dazed and bruised Canfield to his feet. "Or should I say, you did, Secret Service Special Agent Lincoln."

"Only did what I had to," Naomi said modestly. "Thanks for having my back."

"It's my job and honor." Patricia showed her teeth. "We all had each other's backs in bringing down this vile creature."

"Couldn't agree more," Dylan seconded, before reading Canfield his rights as the SWAT unit and other law enforcement converged on the scene and took the scowling prisoner away.

"DID HE HURT you at all?" Dylan asked once they were back at the house alone.

"No, not really," Naomi responded, ignoring the soreness in her back from some poking and prodding by the serial killer. "But not from lack of trying."

"I'm sorry it had to come to that."

"It could've been much worse." She frowned thoughtfully. "Canfield gleefully admitted that he had actually targeted me for his first kill two years ago."

Dylan's expression hardened with shock. "You can't be serious?"

"He claimed we met at a club, but I balked at his advances—which apparently were little more than a ruse to get me alone to practice the sick art of murder. I left for Miami before Canfield could take another crack at me."

Dylan cursed beneath a deep breath. "The mere

thought that he could've killed you back then, depriving you of a future you deserved…"

"He didn't, though," Naomi pointed out gratefully.

"We dropped the ball in prematurely putting it all on Zachary Jamieson," Dylan muttered with annoyance.

"Don't beat yourself up over it," she stressed sympathetically, against his inclination to blame himself for not catching the killer sooner. "Canfield had us all fooled. He confessed to setting Jamieson up with the weapon used to kill Uncle Roger, along with killing Sylvie Maguire and the other women. Canfield also admitted to being the one who sent the text messages, was stalking me by the lake and was the driver of the dark SUV."

"Just as we'd ascertained through the clues he left behind." Dylan shook his head, clearly still annoyed with the revelations nevertheless. "The perp knew no boundaries in his criminal behavior and wicked mind."

"True enough," concurred Naomi, having lived through it and coming out on top. "But he overplayed his hand and finally ran out of luck."

Dylan nodded. "We owe you for that, Naomi. I don't think the perp ever saw what was coming when he attempted to strangle you."

She chuckled. "Given that I feared for my life, he gave me no other option but to put my training to good use." That notwithstanding, Naomi felt comforted in knowing that Dylan and Patricia were prepared to take Canfield out, had she been unable to bring him down herself.

"We'll need you to come downtown to make an official statement," Dylan said gingerly. "If you want to wait till tomorrow—"

"I don't," she told him emphatically. "No time like the present. The sooner you have whatever you need to make sure Blade Canfield rots away behind bars, the better."

"Thought you might say that." Dylan pulled her into his arms, giving her a quick peck on the mouth. "Between the serial murders, kidnapping and attempted murder, and maybe stalking thrown in for good measure, I'm pretty sure that Canfield's days of wreaking havoc on our community are over!"

Naomi found comfort in those words as she kissed him this time, even as her thoughts turned to other matters of the heart that still needed to be fully addressed and responded to by Dylan, accordingly.

BY THAT EVENING, when things had settled down and they were alone at Dylan's log cabin, safe and sound, Naomi felt it incumbent upon herself to put all her cards on the table, knowing just how easily this moment in time could have slipped away forever without Dylan realizing exactly where she stood in her strong feelings for him. She wasn't about to allow anything—or anyone—else to come between them.

"I have something I need to tell you, Dylan..." she began eagerly as they stood in the living room.

"Me first." He held up a hand while regarding her in earnest.

"Uh, okay." She met his gaze intently.

"Here goes..." Dylan gave a deep sigh. "Two years ago, I foolishly let you get away without conveying what I should have. Now I'd like a redo, and hope it's not too late." He took a box out of his pocket, opened it and, to Naomi's surprise, removed a pear-shaped diamond ring. "I've been saving this for the past two years, hoping I might someday be able to give it to you. That day has come." He calmly placed the ring on her trembling finger. "I'm asking you to marry me, Naomi. But before you respond, I wanted you to know that I'm prepared to move to Miami, in support of your career with the Secret Service. I love my job, but not nearly as much as I love you. I can catch on with the Miami PD. Or find some other line of work, I don't care. I only want to spend the rest of my life with you as my wife and mother to any children we wish to bring into this world." Dylan gave an anxious grin. "You can tell me what you're thinking now."

Naomi could barely hold back tears in digesting his heartfelt words and what he was willing to sacrifice to make her his wife. It told her all she needed to know about the man, making her own decision only that much more satisfying. She stared mesmerizingly at the engagement ring, set in 14K rose gold. It was a perfect fit and was right where the ring belonged. Gazing up into Dylan's eyes, Naomi uttered, "What I'm thinking is that while I love working for the Secret Service, it falls short of what I really need in my life to be happy—and that's you."

He cocked a brow nervously. "So, what are you saying?"

She flashed her teeth. "I'm saying that I love you, Dylan Hester, and yes, yes, yes, I'll marry you a thousand times, wherever we chose to call home!"

"Seriously?" He broke into a big grin.

"As serious as I've ever been in my life," she promised him.

"You've made me the happiest man." Dylan gave her a mouthwatering kiss, which Naomi returned in full, before he pulled back. He eyed her curiously. "But how do you want this to go with the job situation?"

Holding his gaze, she responded, having given it some long consideration. "I plan to retire from the Secret Service and reopen Uncle Roger's private investigation agency. I can put my skills to good use, with some worthwhile investigations and consultancy work." She put her ring hand in his. "I was hoping we could go into business together. I'm sure my uncle would've approved had he been given the opportunity to show his support. But if you prefer to keep working with the Pebble Creek Police Department, that's fine by me. Having you as my husband is more than I could ask for at this stage of my life. Anything else would be a bonus."

"Then it's a bonus you shall have." Dylan took her into his arms. "It would be my pleasure to partner up with you in keeping Roger's private investigation firm alive. Working with the Pebble Creek PD had its rewards, but they can't compare with taking on this exciting new venture, side by side with my wife. So, yes, count me in, Naomi."

He kissed her again with even more yearning that packed a spine-tingling punch, and she reciprocated in kind, before telling him again just how much she cherished his love and gave as much or more back to him. And would do so for the rest of her life.

Epilogue

The sixty-foot power cruiser sat still on the lake on a sunny Saturday afternoon on a day in late June. It was a dream come true for Dylan Hester, courtesy of his mentor, Roger Lincoln, who left funds in his will to help make it happen. Sharing the boat and all its comforts and joys was Dylan's wife, Naomi, who was two months' pregnant with their first child. The co-owners of Lincoln and Hester Investigations were taking a break from their day-to-day married and professional lives to spend some time on the water with family and friends. It was a welcome respite after dealing with the long trial and conviction of serial killer Blade Canfield, who due in part to the testimony of Naomi, the state's star witness, would be spending the rest of his life behind bars at Oregon State Penitentiary. His high-powered defense proved to be no match for the strong case presented by the prosecution for his guilt. Once his fate had been sealed, Canfield began to sing like a canary, practically bragging about his road to homicidal tendencies. This prompted FBI profiler Patricia Stabler to write a true-crime book on the perp, swept up in the desire to add to the annals of serial killer psychopaths. Cleared in the Violet Killer investigation was onetime suspect Zachary Jamieson, but he was still contending with drug possession charges.

Dylan stood on the deck, taking in the magnificent view while counting his blessings. First and foremost was having the love of his life, Naomi, as his wife, lover and best friend, to experience the highs and lows of life, wherever they took them. They had survived a two-year separation and a crazed killer to find their way back to one another, and were the better for it. He couldn't imagine a life without her and, thankfully, wouldn't have to.

"I'm glad you didn't let Naomi get away this time, little brother," Dylan's sister, Stefany, whispered in his ear from behind, as though reading his mind. She and her husband, Theodore, had flown in from Africa to spend a little time with Dylan and his bride, for some relaxation and fishing.

Grinning, he turned Stefany's way and replied, "Hey, I learned from the best. With you and yours as a guide to a happy marriage, it was only a matter of time before I got smart enough to follow suit."

Stefany laughed. "Better late than never."

It was a philosophy Dylan agreed with wholeheartedly, as Naomi and the little bundle she was carrying meant everything to him and so much more.

"You look positively glowing!" Sophia Menendez uttered to Naomi, as they sat on the sectional sofa in the air-conditioned console below deck.

"Oh, really?" Naomi batted her eyes, flattered. She was thrilled that her former roommate and fellow agent with the Secret Service had decided to pay her a visit, accompanied by Sophia's drop-dead gorgeous, tall, dark and handsome boyfriend, Lucas Etheridge. Moreover, Naomi enjoyed the feeling of being a wife to a terrific, hardworking guy in Dylan, as well as impending motherhood, now that their first child was on the way. They had spoken about having a couple of more children down the line but, for now, being in the company of each other was more than she could have asked for in a partner. "I'll take that as a compliment," she teased Sophia.

"It definitely is," her friend made clear. "Between that brilliant complexion, your cute new ginger-curls hairstyle, glow of pregnancy and power of love, what's not to compliment."

"Can't argue with you there." Naomi laughed, resisting the urge to feel her belly, something that Dylan had perfected of late. She had no doubt he would make a great dad, just as he made a marvelous husband. In the post Blade Canfield/Violet Killer era, both had been able to successfully transition from their respective jobs with the Secret Service and the Pebble Creek Police Department to carry on with her uncle Roger's detective agency. They brought it to a new level by expanding the types of investigations and using social media to build their brand. As a result, they were able to work on starting a family and building bridges with others they were close to, while making Dylan's lakefront log cabin their home as a couple with Naomi adding her own touches to truly belong.

"Doesn't mean we don't miss you like crazy at the Secret Service," Sophia said, making a somber face to express such. "Even Jared has recognized what an asset you were to the agency. If you ever want to get back in, we'd love to have you."

Naomi beamed, a good feeling to know she was appreciated by her former employer. Especially her old boss and Sophia herself. "Thanks, but no thanks," she told her in a heartfelt tone of voice. "As much as I enjoyed performing my duties for the agency and miss working with you, in particular, I'm so much happier in my new life as Mrs. Dylan Hester and soon to be a doting mom."

"Figured as much." Sophia chuckled. "Just thought I'd put it out there."

"And I love you for it, girlfriend." Naomi gave her a toothy smile. "As for the Secret Service, I'll settle for being able to tap into your expertise from time to time when working a case." She was mindful of Sophia's amazing efforts, along with Naomi's uncle Roger, in helping to make the case against Blade Canfield.

"Anytime!" Sophia promised, grinning back.

"Well, let's not keep our men waiting any longer," Naomi said, eager to wrap herself in Dylan's welcoming arms.

Sophia agreed. "Yes, let's not."

They both stood and went back up to the main deck, where Naomi wasted no time going to the man of her dreams come true. Dylan did not disappoint, laying a solid kiss on her that left little doubt that she belonged to him and only him for the rest of their lives.

* * * * *

PROVING COLTON'S INNOCENCE

LARA LACOMBE

This one is for A and A. To be fair, they're all for you two, but let's make this one official.

Chapter One

Jillian Colton had just stepped out of the shower when the doorbell rang.

She frowned as she reached for her towel. It was after ten at night—not exactly the usual time for a social call. Probably just a neighbor dropping off a misdelivered package, she decided, wrapping a second towel around her wet hair. Certainly nothing to get excited about.

But as she continued to dry off, the doorbell rang again, followed a few seconds later by a loud pounding on her door.

Maybe not a package after all, she mused.

"Coming!" she yelled as she slipped into her bedroom and hastily dressed in a pair of sweatpants and a long-sleeved T-shirt that had seen better days. She unwound the towel from her hair and finger-combed through the long strands. Then she grabbed the baseball bat that was leaning against the wall by her bed and headed down the hall.

The odds that someone hostile was standing outside her door were slim, but as a crime-scene investigator with the Grave Gulch Police Department, Jillian knew all too well what could happen to someone who let down their guard. And though her brother had recently killed Len Davison, the serial killer who had been terrorizing Grave Gulch over the last eleven months, there was still one man who had yet to be found: Randall Bowe.

Her former coworker had been on the run for months after the GGPD discovered he was tampering with evidence. His actions had led to wrongful convictions, while allowing guilty criminals to walk free. It was a mess the police were still trying to clean up, and likely would be for a while.

Still, Jillian had to admit that a small part of her was glad she no longer had to work with Randall. The man had been an insufferable know-it-all and deeply unpleasant. She'd like nothing more than to correct his sabotage and move on with her life and career. But it wasn't that simple; Bowe had been emailing and texting her lately, making it difficult for her to forget about him completely.

Which was why she now stood by her front door, gripping a baseball bat, as the pounding started up again. It was hard to imagine that Bowe was standing on her welcome mat, but she wasn't going to take any chances.

"Jillian? Are you there?"

Jillian relaxed as she recognized the voice—it was Grace Colton, one of her cousins, and a newer cop on the GGPD force.

She propped the baseball bat in the corner by the

door and unlocked it. "Grace, what's going…?" The words died in her throat as she opened the door and caught sight of the number of people standing on the other side.

Grace gave her an apologetic look, but didn't speak. Jillian's eyes darted next to the acting police chief, Brett Shea, who was sporting a worried frown. Behind them stood two uniformed officers and a third man Jillian didn't recognize.

"Ah, what's all this?" she asked. Worry made her stomach feel tight, and she glanced from Grace to Brett, searching for a clue as to why they were at her home so late. Based on their expressions, something must be horribly wrong.

"We need to come inside, Jillian," Brett said. His voice was gentle, but firm. "We have a warrant to search your condo."

"What?!" Jillian stood rooted to the spot as an icy shock spread through her body, leaving numbness in its wake. "A warrant?" she repeated, certain she had misheard. "I don't understand."

"Step aside, Ms. Colton." The stranger standing behind Brett spoke up, his tone impatient. "You're already in serious trouble. You don't want to add obstructing an investigation to the list."

Brett turned and glared at the man. "That's enough," he said shortly. Then he faced Jillian again. "It's true," he said, pulling a folded piece of paper from his back pocket. Jillian took it from him, her eyes going wide as she recognized the legal document.

She shook her head as she stared at the text on the

page, not really reading the words. "There must be some mistake. What's going on here?"

"Jillian." Grace stepped forward and placed her hands on Jillian's shoulders. Her green eyes were full of sympathy and worry, a combination that made Jillian's heart skip a beat. "You need to let us in. We have to do our jobs."

It finally sank in that she didn't have a choice. Grace, Brett and the others were here to search her place, and they would do it with or without her cooperation.

"Of course," she said dully, stepping aside as she opened the door wider.

Grace gave her shoulders a squeeze before releasing her. Brett nodded as he walked past, his lips pressed together in a thin line. The two uniformed officers slipped in without acknowledging her. Then the stranger walked inside, spearing her with a look of contempt as he entered her home.

Jillian tried to gather her thoughts as she shut the door. She turned around in time to see the two uniformed officers walk into her kitchen and heard the sounds of drawers opening as they began their search.

Brett stood in the middle of her living room, glancing around with an expression that was part misery, part embarrassment. Grace avoided her gaze, instead focusing on the bookshelves against the far wall. The stranger, whoever he was, had already started poking through her desk drawer. She narrowed her eyes as she watched his hands dig through her papers; even though there wasn't anything especially personal there, the fact that someone she didn't know was in her space was enough to jolt her out of her initial shock.

Jillian walked over to Brett. "What's this about?" She kept her voice low, hoping the stranger digging through her desk wouldn't overhear. He'd been quite eager to burst in, and she got the impression he was itching to arrest her.

Brett turned to face her, the corners of his mouth turned down. "I know it's all here," she said, lifting the warrant she still held. "But I'm not in the mood to read at the moment."

"There was a burglary early this morning," he said, his tone pained. "A rich widow living on the posh side of town."

Jillian nodded. "Ian mentioned it today," she said, referring to one of the forensic scientists she worked with. "What about it? Is there some connection to the other cases?"

Grave Gulch had seen a rash of robberies over the last few weeks, each one targeting homes in the richer, western part of the city. The thief liked jewelry, as that was the only thing missing from each home. Jillian had collected and processed evidence for all the other cases, but so far, there weren't any leads.

Brett rubbed the back of his head and frowned. "See, that's the thing, Jillian—" he began.

"I'd say there's definitely a connection."

She turned at the interruption to find the stranger standing behind her, a knowing smirk on his face.

"I'm sorry, who the hell are you?" Something about this man was rubbing her the wrong way, causing her usual good manners to fly out the window.

"Eric Wainwright. Grave Gulch IAB." He watched her closely, as though he expected her to react to his announcement that he worked for the internal affairs bureau of the police department.

Jillian wasn't about to give him the satisfaction. "Uh-huh," she said. "And you're here because?"

Wainwright stuck his hands in his pockets "The thing is, Ms. Colton, you're not only an employee of the Grave Gulch Police Department, but you're also related to several people on the force."

"I see," she said. "So you're here to insult my family members by insinuating they wouldn't follow all proper procedures while investigating someone named Colton?" On one level it made sense—she did have a lot of family members on the force. In fact, Grace herself had recently been the subject of an Internal Affairs investigation. But Camden, the IA officer in charge of that investigation and now Grace's serious boyfriend, hadn't been so rude about it.

From the corner of her eye, she saw Grace smile as she walked into Jillian's bedroom.

Eric frowned. "I wouldn't put it like that."

"Of course, you wouldn't." Jillian turned away from Brett, dismissing Eric. "What does the robbery from this morning have to do with me?"

"You'd know better than we would," Eric interrupted again.

Jillian glared at him. "What's that supposed to mean?"

Wainwright shrugged. "You tell us. Your prints were found all over the crime scene."

"What?" Jillian took a half step back as the bottom dropped out of her stomach. "That's not possible." She shook her head as she glanced at Brett's face, searching for clarification. This had to be a joke...right? There was no way Ian had found her prints at the scene of a robbery. Maybe this was some kind of ridiculous initiation for new forensic workers on the force. Even though she'd been working as a crime-scene investigator for over a year already, things had been busy. Now that Len Davison was no longer terrorizing the citizens of Grave Gulch, perhaps everyone had time to stage this practical joke.

Though, to be honest, it was going on a bit too long.

"This isn't funny," she said, hoping Brett would see the emotion in her eyes and call it off. He'd always seemed like a good guy, and she'd gotten to know him better recently now that he was with her cousin Annalise—surely he wouldn't let her suffer too much?

"I agree," Eric said. "But it does make a certain kind of sense. No wonder you didn't find any prints at the scenes of the other robberies. Since you worked those cases, I'm sure you were careful to erase any evidence of your presence there."

"I didn't rob anybody!" Panic was starting to set in, making her heart pound hard in her chest.

Brett held up a hand. "It's okay, Jillian," he said, his voice calm. "Let's just get through this and we'll figure out what to do next."

"It's got to be a mistake." Her head was spinning, her mind churning, as she tried to come up with some explanation that made sense. "Maybe the samples got switched, or cross-contaminated in the lab somehow." There had to be a reason her prints were at a robbery scene even though she'd never stolen a thing in her life!

"Like I said, let's just finish this and then we can talk." Brett ran a hand through his red hair and sighed. Jillian could tell by the lines of strain at the corners of his blue eyes that the acting police chief wasn't happy about this situation, but until the other officers had completed their search, there wasn't much he could do.

Jillian opened her mouth, but a quick glance at Eric made her close it again. The man was watching her intently, and she suddenly realized that he was filing away everything she said, likely with the intention of using it against her later.

Brett was right, she realized. Better to talk after the search was over. Once everyone concluded she didn't have any stolen jewelry in her possession, they could get down to the business of figuring out what kind of mistake had made them think she was guilty in the first place.

It shouldn't take long to wrap things up. Jillian's

condo wasn't that large—it was a basic two-bedroom unit, and while she'd been in the living room with Brett and Wainwright, the other uniformed officers had gone through her kitchen and guest bedroom. She saw them walk down the hall now, headed for the bathroom.

Brett walked around her living room, checking out the contents of her bookshelves and the pictures on her walls. But he was careful not to touch anything, and she noticed he didn't open any table drawers or make any attempt to examine anything that wasn't in plain view. It was as if the interim police chief was trying to respect Jillian's privacy, despite the search warrant. It was a small kindness, but one she noticed and appreciated nonetheless.

Wainwright, on the other hand, had no such consideration. He finished up his examination of her desk and started poking through the drawers of the small tables next to her sofa. If anything, Eric seemed to relish the opportunity to invade Jillian's space, like he was excited to find a reason to arrest her. Jillian had to bite her tongue to keep from snapping at him, because she knew it would only make the situation worse.

Unable to watch Wainwright any longer, Jillian turned away in time to see Grace emerge from her bedroom. As soon as she saw her cousin's face, Jillian knew she'd found something.

But...it's not possible, she thought.

Things seemed to move in slow motion as Grace entered the living room, holding a brown paper bag in her left hand. Jillian shook her head, unable to speak as she watched Grace walk over to Brett and nod slightly. Brett turned to face Jillian, a look of disappointment flashing across his face.

"I knew it!" Eric crowed triumphantly. Brett and Grace both glared at him, but Eric merely grinned.

"Jillian," Grace said softly. "I found the jewelry in the back of your closet."

"I don't understand!" Her throat was so tight it hurt to speak. "I didn't steal anything!"

"All evidence to the contrary," Wainwright snorted.

"It's here, Jillian," Grace continued. "The pieces are exactly as Mrs. Evans described them."

"I didn't rob her," Jillian insisted. She glanced at Brett, hoping he might believe her. "Do you really think I'm some kind of jewel thief who robs by night and works for the police during the day?"

Brett didn't say anything, so she continued, her voice growing louder as her disbelief gave way to anger. "Let's assume for one minute I'm capable of leading that double life. Would I really be so stupid as to hide the stolen goods in my closet, where anyone could find them? And if I really am some kind of master burglar, where are the other pieces I've supposedly taken off with? Why did you only find these items and not any of the others?"

"Because you've already sold them," Eric said, sounding bored. "As fun as this little intellectual exercise is, I've seen enough." He glanced at Brett. "Are you going to arrest her, or should I do it?"

A muscle in Brett's jaw drew tight, and Jillian

could swear she heard the man's teeth grind together. "I'll take care of it," he growled.

"This does seem awfully cut-and-dried," Grace said. But there was a note of doubt in her voice that gave Jillian a flicker of hope. "She has a point," Grace continued. "I mean, remember when she found that twenty-dollar bill on the stairs? She sent out a department-wide email asking if anyone was missing money. Who does that?"

Brett closed his eyes with a faint smile. "I know," he murmured.

"What if this is some kind of setup?"

Jillian seized the words like they were a lifeline. "It has to be!" She nodded vigorously, needing Brett and Grace to see the truth.

"Pretty elaborate setup," Brett said quietly.

Jillian's mind kicked into gear as she tried to figure out who might want to get her in trouble. More than that, who would have the access and ability to plant evidence and make her look guilty?

There was only one answer: Randall Bowe.

"It's Bowe," she declared. "It has to be him."

Brett nodded thoughtfully. "He does know how to manipulate evidence."

"And it's the kind of underhanded thing he'd do," Grace added.

"I can't believe what I'm hearing," Eric said. Jillian turned to find him shaking his head. "Are you two actually conspiring to let her off the hook despite the fact that her prints were found at the scene and the stolen jewelry was in her closet?" He leveled a stare at Brett. "It's a good thing I came with you tonight. I'd long suspected Coltons get special treatment, and this confirms it."

Brett put his hands on his hips. "You wait just a minute. No one is conspiring to do anything, and I don't appreciate your insinuation. We're merely having a conversation."

"What you should be doing is arresting the suspect." Eric reached for the cuffs on his belt. "But I suppose I'll have to do that for you."

"That's not necessary." Brett held up his hand and turned to Jillian. "Jillian Colton," he began, "you are under arrest for the robbery of Elsa Evans." He continued, reciting her rights as required. It was a surreal experience, one that left her feeling slightly disoriented. Even though Brett was standing next to her, his voice sounded tinny and small, and was almost drowned out by the rush of blood in her ears.

Is this really happening?

Something touched her arm, and she glanced over to see Grace's hand. "Come on," she said. "We need to go down to the station and finish the process."

Jillian nodded, too numb to speak.

She took a step forward but stopped suddenly as someone grabbed her other arm. "Not so fast," Eric said. He pulled back her arm and she felt something cold close around one wrist, then the other.

Brett's cheeks reddened. "Was that really necessary?"

"Standard procedure," Eric replied smoothly. "Unless you think she warrants special treatment?"

"Are you serious?" Jillian's throat was so tight the words came out as barely more than a whisper. "I'm not fighting you. I'm not going to try to run."

"That's what they all say," Eric replied.

Jillian's eyes stung as tears began to well. Bad enough that her friends, family and colleagues had come into her home, suspecting her of a crime. She'd thought it couldn't get any worse when they'd discovered the evidence in her closet. But the handcuffs? That was a real low point.

"I'll escort her to the car," Grace said. She stepped forward to stand next to Jillian and stared at Eric until he released her arm. Jillian blinked back tears as her cousin placed her hand between her shoulder blades.

"Come on," Grace said softly. "Let's get you to the station. The sooner we get you processed, the sooner you can post bail and come home."

"I didn't steal that jewelry," Jillian said between sniffles. "I swear I'm not involved in those thefts."

"I know that." Grace led her out the door and into the hall. One of her neighbors was just arriving home from a night out, and she stood at her door, keys in hand, staring with wide eyes.

Great, Jillian thought. *Now everyone is going to think I'm a criminal*. She dropped her eyes as they passed the woman, too embarrassed to acknowledge her.

"Brett doesn't think you did this, either," Grace continued quietly as they approached the elevator.

"We'll figure out what's going on. You just have to trust us."

Jillian nodded slightly. Her cousin's words meant a lot, as Grace had recently been through her own ordeal after being wrongfully accused of excessive use of force.

She stepped into the elevator, feeling subdued. Grace held the doors open to let Brett and Eric file in after them.

"The other officers are going to lock up your place," Brett told her. "You'll get your keys back once you post bail."

"Wow," Eric said dryly. "That's very considerate. Do you do that for all your arrests?"

No one replied. Jillian sneaked a look at Brett's face and could tell by the hard set of his jaw that he'd had just about enough of the man from Internal Affairs. At least she wasn't the only one...

Once outside, Grace helped her into the back seat of a patrol car. Her cousin climbed into the driver's seat, while Eric took the passenger seat. "Just to keep things aboveboard," he said, smirking back at Jillian. "Your last name isn't going to get you out of this."

Jillian turned away to stare out the window. It felt disorienting, seeing the world from the back of a police car. The view wasn't remarkably different; Grace didn't have the siren going or the lights flashing. If she hadn't been arrested, it would be easy to pretend this was just another night. But Jillian didn't have the energy to lie to herself.

She'd been set up. There was no other explanation. As much as Grace had assured her that she and Brett believed in her innocence, Jillian knew their faith wasn't going to get her very far. No judge would ignore the evidence that had been found in her apartment simply because her family and friends vouched for her character. No, she had to find some kind of proof, and soon.

Randall Bowe was smart, and he was devious. But he'd slipped up before. Jillian just had to figure out how he'd framed her.

Before it was too late.

SOMETHING WAS GOING on at the police station.

Baldwin Bowe decided to pause his workout and slowed his running pace to a walk as he watched a small crowd gather outside the main entrance of police headquarters. It was almost eleven at night; too late for the usual protesters to be out. Besides, now that the GGPD had caught serial killer Len Davison, the general mood of the city had improved a bit. There was still a die-hard crowd upset about the actions of Baldwin's brother, forensic scientist Randall Bowe. But for the most part, the reputation of the Grave Gulch Police Department was on the upswing.

So why was there a hum of anticipation in the air?

Trying to be unobtrusive, Baldwin made his way over to the periphery of the small group. "What's going on?" he asked when one man made eye contact with him.

The guy eyed him up and down, his gaze assessing. "News conference," he said shortly.

Baldwin scoffed. "This late?"

A woman glanced over and did a double take, her eyes glued to Baldwin's chest and the tight running shirt that fit him like a second skin. "They've arrested someone for the string of jewelry thefts." She finally looked up at his face, and in the glow of the nearby streetlight he saw her cheeks turn pink. "What's your name?" She offered her hand, and he gave it a half-hearted shake. "I haven't seen you around before. Are you new?"

"I'm Baldwin," he replied, deciding to leave his last name out of it. He was here to get information, and if these reporters knew he was related to Randall, they'd stop answering his questions and start asking their own. "And, yes, I'm new in town."

"I'm Shannon." She stepped closer, tucking a strand of blond hair behind her ear. "I'm a reporter for the *Grave Gulch Gazette*. Who do you write for?"

"I'm a freelancer," Baldwin said. It was the truth…sort of. As a ghost bounty hunter, he worked under the radar, taking on private clients who needed someone found. His job was to locate the target and deliver them to the client. He didn't ask questions about what happened next; that sort of thing didn't concern him.

The job had taken him all over the country and introduced him to people both wonderful and terrible. But despite everything he'd seen and experienced, he'd never expected that one day, he'd be hired to find his own brother.

There had always been friction between the two of them. Even though Randall was younger, he'd never looked up to Baldwin. Randall had been born with a chip on his shoulder, and his attitude meant he treated a lot of people badly. It hadn't surprised Baldwin to learn of his brother's crimes and the way he'd tampered with evidence to produce the results he had wanted. Most of his victims were understandably upset, but content to let the police handle the investigation, believing that the system would work the way it was supposed to and that Randall would eventually be brought to justice.

But Baldwin's client wasn't willing to wait that long.

Which was why Baldwin was here in Grave Gulch now, on the hunt for his fugitive brother.

Shannon edged closer. "I'd be happy to show you around," she offered. "Grave Gulch isn't a huge city, but there are some fun things to do. If you know where to look." Her voice dropped and she licked her lips suggestively.

Baldwin offered her a tight smile. "Thanks, but no thanks. I'm just here to work." Romance wasn't really his style, and he was too focused on the job to even indulge in a short-term fling, which was his usual MO. Besides, he'd grown up in Grave Gulch. He'd only been back in town for a couple of weeks, and he was already itching to leave again.

Shannon shrugged. "Your loss," she said. She tossed her hair over her shoulder and turned away from him, facing the podium that had been set up on the steps of the police building.

Baldwin took a step back, ready to resume his run. The string of robberies didn't concern him. There was no point in wasting more time here.

But as he was starting to go, he overheard a conversation.

"Do you know who the suspect is?"

"Yeah, I heard it was Jillian Colton. She works for the department in the forensics lab and in CSI."

The word *lab* made Baldwin stop in his tracks, and he turned back to the podium, suddenly interested.

Had this woman, whoever she was, known his brother?

A few seconds later, the police commissioner and the mayor approached the podium. "I have a statement to read, regarding the recent string of jewelry thefts in Grave Gulch," the commissioner said. He cleared his throat and launched into his prepared remarks, confirming the arrest of Jillian Colton and assuring the reporters that Ms. Colton would not be given special treatment despite her family connections to many of the officers in the GGPD.

Baldwin listened carefully, sorting through the details the commissioner was providing. He couldn't care less about the robberies, or Jillian's family status. What he wanted to know was if she might be able to give him information that would help Baldwin find Randall.

The commissioner finished his speech and took a step back. Before he could leave, Baldwin shouted out a question.

"How long has Jillian Colton worked for the police lab?"

The older man frowned; it was clear he hadn't intended on answering questions. But he leaned closer to the microphone to reply. "Ms. Colton has worked for the department for the past eighteen months."

A few other reporters asked questions, but Baldwin wasn't listening. A year and a half. That meant she'd definitely worked with Randall. What could she tell him about his brother?

"There she is!" someone cried out.

Baldwin glanced at the street to see a police cruiser drive by. Amid the camera flashes, he caught sight of a woman in the back of the car. Her long hair hid most of her face, but she turned briefly, giving him a view of her expression.

She was terrified. Even from this distance, he could see the fear in her large eyes.

He watched as the cruiser turned right at the corner, taking her to the back of the building. Several of the reporters started jogging in that direction, evidently hoping to nab some photos of her perp walk as she was led into the station for processing. For a brief second, Baldwin considered following them. But, no, that wouldn't answer any of his questions.

Instead, he set off down the sidewalk, resuming

his run. He couldn't talk to Jillian Colton tonight, so he might as well finish his workout and get some sleep.

There would be time for introductions tomorrow.

Chapter Two

It was close to noon by the time Jillian was released from jail.

She'd passed a restless night tossing and turning on the thin, cold mattress in the holding cell. Her body had ached for sleep, but she hadn't been able to quiet her mind long enough to relax. Her thoughts had churned in a sickening mix of questions and half-baked theories. Not even a middle of the night visit from her brother had been enough to distract her. But through it all, she remained certain of one thing:

Randall Bowe had set her up.

Jillian didn't know why he'd targeted her, or what he hoped to gain by having her arrested and charged with the thefts. They'd worked together before his crimes had come to light, and while Jillian had never considered him a friend, she'd also not seen him as an enemy. Randall had been insufferable at times, and as the newest member of the team, she'd been his favorite scapegoat whenever something went wrong. He'd even gone so far as to blame her for the issues with the Everleigh Emerson case. Everyone knew the truth now, but at the time, her confidence had taken a dive. Still, Jillian had kept her chin up and soldiered on, determined to prove she was good at her job. There was no shortage of Coltons on the GGPD payroll, and while most people didn't bat an eye at her last name, there were a few who made it clear they thought Jillian had ridden her relatives' coattails in her career.

And wouldn't Bowe be thrilled by this turn of events?

The sun was high in the sky as she stepped outside, blinking against the brightness. What she wouldn't give for her sunglasses! She had half a mind to walk back inside and drop by her desk in the lab to grab her spare pair, but since she was suspended from her job, she thought it best to steer clear. IAB would have a field day if she walked into the lab, even on such an innocent errand.

"Ms. Colton, you are not to leave town, do you understand?" The judge's words echoed in her mind, the memory of his voice loud in her head.

She'd nodded, feeling humiliated anew at having to stand in open court as the charges against her were read aloud. The only saving grace was that her mother wasn't here to see it. Her sister, Madison, had kept their mom at home, but her brother, Bryce, had insisted on being there.

Her attorney had argued that since this was a first offense and the crimes hadn't been violent, she should be released on bail until her trial. The DA had countered that the stolen jewelry was worth a lot of money, giving her the means to flee. Apparently her cousin Troy's fiancée, Evangeline, a former ADA, had been unsuccessful at talking her old boss into taking it easy on Jillian. It had taken every ounce of Jillian's self-control to keep her mouth shut as the two lawyers sparred, but she'd remained silent.

In the end, the judge had split the baby. He'd agreed to set bail, but at a steep price. Jillian's heart had sunk when she'd heard the total; it was far out of the reach of her bank account. She'd blinked back tears as she'd been led away. Bryce had shouted that he'd figure something out, but Jillian expected to spend the foreseeable future in a jail cell.

The fact that she was standing outside now was nothing short of a miracle.

"Jillian Colton?"

The unfamiliar voice made her turn. A man was standing a few feet away, booted feet planted in a wide stance on the sidewalk. Black jeans outlined his long legs, and his dark gray T-shirt strained across his broad chest. The sleeves were tight on his muscular arms, which were presently crossed. His black hair was cropped close, reminding her of a military cut. She couldn't see his eyes behind the dark lenses of his sunglasses, but she could feel his gaze on her.

"Who's asking?" she said warily. He didn't look like a reporter and there weren't any protesters on this side of the building—they were all standing out front, on Grave Gulch Boulevard.

"A friend," he replied.

Jillian narrowed her eyes as she stared at him. "A friend, huh? Then why don't I recognize you?"

He shifted, dropping his arms to shove his hands into his pockets. "I paid your bail."

She took a half step back and narrowed her eyes. No wonder her brother wasn't waiting for her. "Why did you do that?" If he was even telling the truth. "Like I said, I don't know you."

"My name's Baldwin." He took off the sunglasses, revealing intense blue eyes the color of a summer sky. "I'd like to talk to you. Maybe over a burger? Are you hungry?"

Her stomach growled at the mention of food, but Jillian wasn't ready to wander off with this guy just yet. "You're not giving me a lot to work with here, Baldwin. What's your last name? And why do you think I'd have answers for you?"

He sighed and shook his head slightly, clearly reluctant to say more. The silence stretched for several seconds, until Jillian thought he might not answer at all. When he finally spoke, his tone was resigned.

"I'm Baldwin Bowe—" he began.

"Bowe?" she repeated, cutting him off. "Any relation to Randall Bowe?" Her lip curled up in disgust as she practically spat the name out of her mouth.

Baldwin nodded. "He's my brother."

"Then we're done here." Jillian spun on her heel and started walking, determined to put distance between them. She had no idea why Randall's brother had posted her bail, or what he could possibly want with her. But she wasn't going to stick around to find out.

"Jillian, wait!" Baldwin called out behind her, but she ignored him. Footsteps pounded against the sidewalk and his hand closed around her biceps, pulling her to a stop.

She glared at his hand, then up at him. He released her immediately, holding up his palms by his shoulders in a gesture of surrender. "I'm sorry," he said. "But I really need to talk to you."

Baldwin had seemed tall before, but now that he was standing so close, Jillian was acutely aware of how much bigger he was compared to her. Not just in height—Baldwin was muscular and toned, his body solid and imposing. She got the feeling that if he planted himself in front of her, she'd have better luck trying to run through a brick wall.

She took a deep breath to quell her nerves. The stress, lack of sleep and proximity to a large, potentially dangerous man had her feeling on edge. Right now, they were on a public street, with plenty of witnesses. She could hear him out and once he was gone, she'd duck into a store to borrow a phone and call a friend for a ride home.

"All right," she said, looking up at him. "What do you want to know?"

"Let's clear the air," he said. "I haven't spoken to Randall in years. We're not friends, and I don't know where he is now."

Jillian searched his face, looking for any signs of deception. Baldwin didn't flinch from her gaze, but if he was anything like his brother, he was a practiced liar.

"I'm a fugitive-recovery agent," he continued. "I operate under the radar, and I'm good at what I do."

"Is that a fancy way of saying you're a bounty hunter?"

He nodded. "That's an older term for it. But, yeah, I find people who don't want to be found."

"Why are you in Grave Gulch?" Despite her misgivings, Jillian was curious to know more.

"I've been hired to find my brother."

She frowned. "I didn't realize the police had opted to bring in outside help." Jillian hadn't been informed of every development in the search for Randall, but she did try to keep up with the latest news.

"They didn't," Baldwin said flatly. "My client is not affiliated with the police department. But I've been working with Bryce. We've shared some leads with each other."

Interesting. She waited for him to say more, but he didn't elaborate.

It made sense that Randall had enemies. His actions had sent innocent people to jail and allowed those guilty of terrible crimes to walk free. Maybe one of his victims, or perhaps the family member of a victim, had lost faith that the GGPD could find Bowe and bring him to justice.

And now that she thought about it, she did recall Bryce mentioning that Randall's brother was helping him. It was easy enough to verify, so she doubted he was lying about that.

"So you'll…what? Find your brother and then just hand him over to your client?" That seemed awfully cold, even for a tough-looking guy like Baldwin. Surely he wouldn't leave his brother in the hands of someone who wanted revenge?

Another thought occurred to her, one that raised her already heightened suspicions. What if Baldwin wasn't really working for a client at all? Maybe he was on the search for his brother so he could warn Randall before the police closed in?

Baldwin shook his head. "As soon as I find Randall, I'm turning him over to the police."

"Uh-huh," she said skeptically.

He lifted one eyebrow. "You don't believe me." It wasn't a question; he was apparently smart enough to realize Jillian had serious doubts.

She shrugged. "For all I know, you're a double agent. You pretend to help the police on behalf of this mystery client, but really you're feeding Randall the information he needs to stay one step ahead of everyone."

Baldwin's lips twitched with a suppressed smile. "Do you question everyone's motives, or just mine?"

"I'm a crime-scene investigator," she replied. "Questioning comes with the territory."

"Nothing wrong with that," he murmured. He looked past her shoulder and nodded at something in the distance. "Look, I'm hungry. Can we continue this conversation at that diner down the street?"

Jillian didn't have to turn around to know he was talking about Mae's Diner. The place was a Grave Gulch institution, and in her opinion, home to the best pancakes in town.

She considered her options: she could leave Baldwin to his own devices, call up a ride home and scrounge around her half-empty fridge for something to eat. Or she could enjoy some decent food and hopefully get some information in return.

Baldwin said he had some questions for her. Maybe she could get him to answer a few of her own.

At the very least, she'd learn more about Baldwin's plans for his stay in Grave Gulch. Information like that might prove useful for Grace and the other cops assigned to Randall's case.

"Lunch sounds good," she said. "But I should warn you—I don't have my wallet."

"My treat," Baldwin said.

Jillian wasn't about to argue. Right now, her body needed sleep and food. If she couldn't have the former, at least she was going to get the latter.

Once she got some fuel in the tank, it would be easier to think about her next steps. She glanced over at Baldwin as they walked to the diner together. He was physically imposing, to be sure. Almost the complete opposite of his slender, fine-boned brother. And, on the surface, he seemed all business. Would he even answer her questions?

It was a good thing Jillian was used to solving puzzles. If she was lucky, Baldwin would turn out to be the missing piece she needed to prove her innocence.

BALDWIN WATCHED JILLIAN tuck into her second stack of pancakes with a combination of amazement and fascination. She wasn't a sloppy eater—far from it, as her table manners were impeccable. But after their food had arrived, she'd wasted no time digging in. He'd looked up from seasoning his meal to find she was halfway through her first stack of pancakes, with several pieces of her bacon already missing. By the time he'd eaten a few bites, she'd already ordered her second stack of the diner's all-day "limitless" special.

Where was she putting all that food? He discreetly ran his gaze over the top half of her body, verifying that she was, in fact, as slim as he'd thought when he'd met her on the street. Maybe she had a hollow leg?

"Did they forget to feed you last night?" he said, only half-joking.

She shook her head. "No," she said, between bites. "They offered. But I was too stressed to eat."

That made sense. Sympathy stirred in his chest as he imagined her pacing the confines of a cell, her mind buzzing as she tried to figure out what to do next.

"Why'd you pay my bail?"

The question interrupted his thoughts, and he refocused to find her watching him over the rim of her coffee mug.

"I told you, I have some questions for you about my brother."

"You could have visited me in jail," she pointed

out. Amusement danced in her eyes. "Would have been a cheaper option."

"Maybe so, but I need more than just a conversation."

Her shoulders stiffened, and he mentally kicked himself. *Way to sound like a creep...*

"Listen," she said, narrowing her eyes as she set down her mug with a thump, "I appreciate you posting my bail. But if you think that somehow makes me beholden to you, or that you can manipulate me out of a sense of guilt—"

Baldwin held up a hand, shaking his head. "I'm not interested in sex."

It was true, despite the fact that she was pretty. Her light brown hair hung past her shoulders and was slightly tangled from her night in jail. Her face was long, her features delicate. The dark circles under her brown eyes made her look fragile, but he could already tell that was an illusion. Based on their conversation so far, Baldwin could tell Jillian was not a precious flower that needed to be coddled.

If the circumstances had been different, he might have pursued her. But, right now, he was too focused on the job at hand to think of anything else.

She leaned back against the cracked pleather of the booth, plainly still suspicious. "Do you think I did it?"

"Did what?" He popped some eggs into his mouth, puzzled by this sudden question.

Jillian arched one eyebrow as she stared him down. "Do you think I robbed those people?"

Baldwin took a sip of water and considered his response. Unless he missed his guess, his reply would determine Jillian's cooperation. If he answered correctly, she'd stay and hear him out. But if he said the wrong thing? There'd be a Jillian-shaped hole in the door.

"I'm undecided," he said finally. "I don't know you at all. Based on our limited interactions, you don't seem like the jewel-thief type. But I've misjudged people before."

"Does it bother you? The thought that you may have freed a guilty woman to rob again?"

He shrugged. "Nope. Even if you did steal that jewelry, you didn't hurt anyone. I don't really care if some rich people get their panties in a twist."

She tilted her head to the side. "I suppose that's fair." He watched as she took another bite of pancake. "For the record," she said after she swallowed, "I didn't steal from anyone."

"Okay." Baldwin had taken one look at her and known the truth, but he'd sensed Jillian wouldn't believe him if he'd said as much. She came across as a skeptical person; she didn't seem like the type to trust a gut instinct until there was evidence to back it up. Hopefully his own admission of doubt regarding her innocence would help convince her that he was also rational and measured.

Because what he wanted to ask of her? It was going to take a lot of trust on her part.

"All right," she said slowly. "Let's assume for a minute I believe you. That you really are searching

for your brother and you'll immediately turn him
in once you find him. What do you need me for?"

Baldwin took a deep breath as his nerves sprang
to life, giving him a funny feeling in his stomach.
It was an unfamiliar sensation. He normally had no
problem asking for what he wanted or needed. But
there was a hint of vulnerability in Jillian's brown
eyes that touched him. She was putting up a good
front, but under her tough, take-no-prisoners shell,
he could tell she was frightened.

Randall had done that to her. Anger rose in Baldwin's chest as he imagined his brother's face. Randall didn't hurt people physically—he didn't have the
strength for that. Physical wounds usually healed,
though. The psychological injuries his brother preferred to inflict took much longer to repair.

"You have a history with my brother," he began. It
was important that he led up to his proposal slowly,
or she'd reject his idea outright.

Jillian frowned. "Yes. We worked together."

"And he probably wasn't nice to you."

Her short laugh held no humor. "That's an un-
derstatement. Randall found fault with everything
I did. At first, it was just criticizing little things,
like the way I held a pipette, or the way I labeled
something. But then he started finding mistakes I'd
made." Jillian shook her head. "He'd say I forgot to
put a sample in the fridge, or that I had missed a step
in a protocol." Her eyes narrowed at the memories.
"But the thing is, I *knew* I hadn't messed up. I was
always so careful, doubly so, since he seemed to be

breathing down my neck at every turn. I double-and triple-checked every step, making sure I hadn't forgotten anything."

"Let me guess," Baldwin said. "He'd move things around when you weren't looking and accuse you?"

Jillian nodded. "Yeah. It would be hours, or sometimes days later, when he would confront me. By then, I'd moved on to something else. I'd insist I hadn't done anything wrong, but he'd show me a sample out of place, or a reagent that was spoiled and I'd look like an idiot trying to argue."

"He was gaslighting you," Baldwin said softly.

"I realize that now," Jillian said. "But at the time, I was a rookie. I was fresh out of school and didn't have a ton of experience. I began to doubt myself and wonder if maybe he was right. Maybe I was making a lot of mistakes. I was so mentally exhausted from hyperfocusing on every task, trying to make sure everything I did was perfect so Randall wouldn't find fault with my work."

She took a sip of coffee, clearly bothered by the memories. Baldwin didn't blame her—it sounded like Randall had tortured her for months.

"It didn't help that my last name was Colton," she continued. "There were already some whispers that the only reason I'd gotten the job was due to my family connections. I was determined to prove myself, and Randall used that against me."

"Did you ever suspect him of manipulating evidence before everything came out?"

She nodded. "Once he'd worn me down with his

constant criticisms and fault-finding, things began to escalate. He'd suddenly find a piece of evidence he said I'd missed, or something that I had processed would mysteriously go missing and Randall would claim I had destroyed the sample with my careless handling. I was so twisted up inside and stressed that it never occurred to me to wonder why he didn't just fire me if I was so incompetent. But after his crimes came to light, I realized he needed to keep me around as a scapegoat."

"Did he ever target anyone else working in the lab?" Baldwin asked. He already suspected the answer, but he wanted her to confirm it.

"No." She shook her head. "There was a former assistant who'd worked in the lab a little before my time. He'd fired her for losing evidence, though now we know that wasn't true. Since she wasn't there anymore, I guess he picked me as his next target. He was so devious about it. He'd berate me for making a mistake, and then later that day he'd come back and apologize for losing his temper."

"That's what abusers do," Baldwin said. "He was trying to keep you close."

She smiled sadly. "I remember one day he was especially nice to me. My name had been leaked to the press in a story about evidence gone missing in a high-profile robbery case we were working. A group of protesters had shown up that next morning carrying big posters of my face, with a red *line* painted over it." She drummed her fingertips against the Formica tabletop. "I realize now that Randall must have been the one to release my name. But that morning, he seemed concerned for me and told me not to worry about it, that it would all blow over."

"He needed you to stick around," Baldwin said. It was a tactic his brother had deployed often when they were kids, but never to such an extent. Baldwin had learned early on that Randall was not to be trusted. Since Randall was never in a position of power over him, he hadn't been able to affect him that much. Nothing like the way he'd tried to wreck Jillian's career.

"Yeah," she said grimly. "When the truth came out about what Randall had been doing all along, I cried. It felt like a huge burden had been lifted and I could actually breathe again."

"I can understand that," Baldwin said. His heart did a little flip as he imagined Jillian's tear-streaked cheeks, and he was struck with the urge to pull her into his arms for a hug.

Not that she needed it. She was sitting tall and strong across from him in the booth, looking nothing like the stressed, nearly broken woman she'd once been. Jillian wasn't looking for comfort or protection.

So why did he want to provide it?

He shook off the errant desire and refocused on the conversation at hand. "Now that Randall is on the run, why do you think he's still focused on you?"

Jillian went still. "How did you know...?"

"The interim chief, Brett Shea," Baldwin said. "I stopped by a few weeks ago to officially introduce myself and let the GGPD know I'm in town, searching for my brother. Sort of a professional courtesy. The chief has given me what information he could, and he told me Randall has been calling and texting people to taunt them. Your name was on the list of targets."

Jillian relaxed. The waitress came by their table and offered to refill her coffee, but she declined politely. *Time to wrap it up*, Baldwin thought. Jillian would want to leave soon, so he'd better get to his point quickly.

"I don't know why he's still harassing me," she said. "But I'm convinced he's trying to frame me for these robberies."

Baldwin considered her theory. "That sounds like something he'd do."

"I just don't understand why he won't leave me alone," she said, sounding frustrated. "We don't work together anymore. We don't see each other. Why not leave without looking back?"

"Do you want to know what I think?" Baldwin asked. Jillian nodded, her brown eyes fixed on him. "I think Randall is obsessed with you. I think he's angry because after his crimes were revealed, you became the star of the department. That was formerly his place. It must eat him up inside to know that you, his former scapegoat, are now a big shot."

"Maybe…" She trailed off, sounding thoughtful. "He's certainly delusional enough to think that my reputation should suffer along with his."

"He must have broken into the lab to plant the new evidence," Baldwin said.

"Not necessarily," Jillian replied. "Before Randall took off, he stole a lot of files. My fingerprints and other personal information were probably part of the cache. I think he's the one behind the thefts, and he chose to plant my prints at this last scene to drag me through the mud again."

"Which is why I posted your bail," Baldwin said.

Confusion flickered across Jillian's face. "I'm not sure what one has to do with the other."

Time to lay his cards on the table. "Randall is going to be furious you're out of jail. I think he's going to escalate his behavior and come after you."

The color drained from Jillian's face as she processed his words. "So you paid my bail to use me as bait?"

Her voice was low, but not from shock. As Baldwin watched, he could practically see her anger building.

"Yes, but it's not as bad as you think," he said.

The glare she sent across the table hit him like a dagger. "Enlighten me," she said through clenched teeth.

"You don't have to worry about Randall getting to you, because you won't be alone."

"How do you figure that?" she retorted. "Am I supposed to hire a bodyguard or something?"

Baldwin leaned back and offered what he hoped was a reassuring smile. "Nope. That's what I'm for."

Chapter Three

Jillian stared at Baldwin, torn between the desires to scream and cry. "You?" she said incredulously. "Do you mean to tell me that you've appointed yourself my bodyguard?"

His smile slipped and he shifted in his seat. "I don't know if I'd call it bodyguard, per se," he said. "But I had no intention of springing you from jail and then leaving you at the mercy of my brother."

"How very chivalrous of you," she muttered. Baldwin's delusions aside, how was she going to protect herself? He was likely right, in that Randall would be angry when he discovered Jillian wasn't rotting away in a jail cell while she awaited trial. He'd have to know she would be working to prove her innocence, and it was improbable that he would sit idly by while she untangled the cocoon of lies he'd wrapped around her. But would he really come after her himself?

Randall had always been more of a behind-the-scenes kind of guy, preferring to manipulate others to his own ends. Still, he'd always had it in for her.

Now that he was on the run, he didn't have access to his usual resources. It was possible he'd take the risk of a physical confrontation to ensure she went down in flames.

But she couldn't very well rely on Baldwin to keep her safe. She didn't even know him! He talked a good game about wanting to bring in his brother, but that didn't mean she trusted him. And she certainly wasn't ready to welcome him with open arms into her home! That space had already been invaded by strangers, and the memories from last night's search washed over her, making the pancakes in her stomach turn sour.

Maybe she could hire protection? She dismissed the thought almost immediately. She might be a Colton, but she wasn't rich. Her salary covered her expenses with enough left over each month to save, but nothing like this. Normally, she'd ask her brother, Bryce, for help. As an FBI agent, he might have connections in that area. He could at least perform a background check on Baldwin for her. But as for anything else, he was still recovering from the gunshot wound he'd sustained during the final confrontation with Len Davison. He was in no position to offer her protection, and Jillian wasn't about to crash with him and his new fiancée, Olivia.

And as for the rest of her relatives on the GGPD force? She couldn't go to them. They were already under scrutiny. If any of them were seen to be helping her try to clear her name, it would spell disaster for their careers.

It looked like the man sitting across from her might very well be her best option. But that didn't mean she was going to go along with his plan without doing a little research of her own.

Baldwin had been watching her, his expression guarded as she thought things through. At least he was smart enough to give her the space and silence to mull over her choices without interruption.

"I suppose you want to move in with me?"

He nodded carefully. "You're not the only one Randall hates. If he knows the two of us are living together, it will really bother him."

Jillian ground her back teeth together. "Next you're going to tell me we have to pretend to be romantically involved."

"Nope." Baldwin's blue eyes were cool as he looked at her. "I told you, I'm not interested in sex. I just want to get my brother so I can collect the second half of my paycheck."

Heat rose up her neck, and with it, her frustration. It was a good thing Baldwin wasn't angling for a personal connection! So why was part of her the tiniest bit disappointed?

"Although," he continued dryly, "it would help if we appeared to be on somewhat friendlier terms."

Her shoulders stiffened. "What's that supposed to mean?" she asked. "I'm friendly!"

Baldwin snorted. "Okay. 'Cause right now you're looking at me as though you're trying to decide if you want to stab me with your fork or strangle me with the waitress's apron strings."

Jillian rolled her eyes and fought back a smile. "Can you blame me?" she said. "This—" she gestured to him and the diner "—wasn't exactly how I thought my day was going to go."

"I can understand that." Baldwin leaned back, his expression softening a bit. He was still a big, strong, tough-looking man, but Jillian saw a glint of sympathy in his eyes.

"So what do you think?" he asked. "I know it's short notice and it's a lot to take in at once, but are you on board with my plan?"

Part of her wanted to say yes and get it over with, but Jillian's instincts wouldn't allow her to accept his proposal. "Not yet," she admitted.

Baldwin took her refusal in stride. "What's holding you back?"

"Well…" She wasn't sure how he was going to respond to this. "You, actually."

"Me?" He sounded surprised, but not angry.

"Look at you." She lifted her hand in his general direction. "You're tall and muscular. Physically imposing. And look at me." She pointed at herself. "I'm no match for your strength."

Baldwin leaned forward. "I don't hurt women," he said gruffly. "I swear to you, I will not touch you." His voice was quiet and serious, all traces of humor gone.

"I want to believe you," Jillian said. "But I'm not in the habit of inviting men I just met into my home."

"Fair enough." Baldwin reached for a clean paper napkin, then flagged down the waitress and asked for a pen. After she gave him one, he started writing on the napkin.

"What are you doing?" Jillian asked.

"I'm giving you my personal information," he said as he wrote. After a few seconds, he set down the pen and slid over the napkin. "That's all of it. Birth date, current address, social-security number, driver's-license info. The whole nine yards."

"Why are you giving me this?" She skimmed the information, noting with some surprise that Baldwin had been born in Grave Gulch.

"Your brother is an FBI agent, right?"

She glanced up. "Yes. I'm going to ask him to run a background check on you." If Baldwin came back clean, she'd let him stay with her. If not…well, she'd come up with another idea.

Baldwin smiled and gestured to the napkin. "That'll make it easier for him."

"What's this number labeled 'DOD'?" She tapped her finger on the writing.

"That's my Department of Defense ID number."

"You're in the service?" No wonder his haircut had made her think military.

"I was," he replied. "Retired, you could say."

"Moved on to bounty hunting, I see. More interesting work?"

He tilted his head to the side. "The pay is certainly better now."

Jillian nodded, her mind made up. "All right, Baldwin. I'd like you to take me home now, please. I'm going to call my brother and give him your information. If everything checks out, I'll go along with your plan."

"You're not worried about me knowing where you live?" Baldwin asked, a teasing note to his voice.

Jillian climbed out of the booth and shrugged. "You know my brother is a federal agent. You've been working with him. I'm betting you already have my address." What else did he know about her?

"That's true." Baldwin stood, and as she watched his body unfold from the booth, she was reminded again of their relative sizes.

"Just out of curiosity," she said as they headed for the door. "What will you do if I say no?"

He shrugged. "Follow you around and wait for Randall to strike."

"So I really am just bait to you?"

Baldwin nodded. "Like I told you before, I'm after Randall. I'll do whatever it takes to bring him in so I can get the second half of my fee."

For some strange reason, that stung a little. Jillian didn't expect a stranger like Baldwin to actually care about her, but she'd never before had such a blatantly transactional experience with someone. On one level, it was kind of nice to know the truth up front. Even if he was just using her.

Her thoughts must have shown on her face. Baldwin sighed as they walked out of the diner. "Look, it's nothing personal, okay? In my line of work, it's best not to make friends. I don't get involved with people and I don't stick around once the job is done."

"I see." Honestly, it was going to be better this

way. Jillian wanted to close the book on the Randall Bowe chapter of her life—the sooner, the better.

Even if it meant working side by side with Randall's infuriating brother.

IT DIDN'T TAKE long for Baldwin to drop off Jillian at her place.

"Call me when you're ready to talk." He nodded at the napkin she was holding in one hand. "You have my number."

"Something tells me you'll be close," she replied dryly.

Baldwin merely nodded. Jillian hopped down from the passenger seat of his truck, but before shutting the door, she turned back.

"Thanks for breakfast," she said. "And for bailing me out."

Surprise flashed in Baldwin's blue eyes. "You're welcome." Apparently, he hadn't expected her gratitude. But even though he'd only gotten her out of jail to serve his own purposes, she still appreciated it.

Inside, the hallway was blessedly empty as Jillian walked to her door. Although she knew she hadn't done anything wrong, the neighbors who had seen her getting arrested last night had probably made their own assumptions about her guilt. The building's gossip mill was likely already churning...

"One thing at a time," she muttered to herself as she unlocked the door to her condo. First, she had to clear her name of these false charges. Then she'd deal with her neighbors and whatever the co-op board might send her way.

It felt strange, walking into her own home after the events of last night. She half expected to find one of the uniformed officers still there, rummaging through the rooms in search of more planted evidence.

Her cell phone was sitting on the kitchen counter. Jillian hadn't bothered to grab it last night, knowing it would only be confiscated from her. She touched the screen now and it lit up, revealing a record of missed calls and unseen texts.

She walked over to the round table at the far end of the room and sat to scroll through everything. There were dozens of messages and voice mails, mostly from Bryce and their mother, Verity. But there were also a few from Madison and her father, Wes, who had recently come back into their lives. It seemed word of her arrest had traveled fast.

She typed out a group message to her family. Home safe. Going to rest. Will call later. Then she dialed Bryce.

He picked up on the first ring. "Jillian? What the hell? Are you okay?"

"I'm fine," she assured him. She gave him a quick rundown of the situation, starting with her release from jail.

Bryce listened carefully as she spoke. When she got to the part about meeting Baldwin Bowe, he interrupted her.

"I've met him," Bryce said. "He's pretty intense."

Jillian laughed shortly. "Yeah, for sure. Here's the thing. He wants to use me as bait to draw out his brother."

Bryce sucked in a breath. "What?"

She filled him in on Baldwin's plan. "Are you actually considering this?" Bryce asked incredulously.

Jillian leaned back in the chair. "I don't have a lot of other options," she replied. "I've got to clear my name, and the only way to do that is to bring Randall in. He's been evading capture for the better part of a year. My case is going to go to trial before long, and I don't want to be sent to prison for a crime I didn't commit." Emotion welled in her chest, making her voice rise and her throat tighten. Just the thought of spending more time locked behind iron bars was enough to trigger a cold sweat.

"Okay, okay, I understand," Bryce said soothingly. "I know things look bad now, Jillian, but you have to know that everyone is working to clear your name."

"That's just it, Bryce. There's not much they can do." She reminded him of the internal-affairs case. "I don't want anyone to jeopardize their careers on my behalf. They shouldn't be punished for trying to help me."

"I'm not GGPD," Bryce said. "*I* can clear your name."

Jillian smiled and blinked back tears. "That's sweet of you. And I'll take all the help I can get. But you're still recovering from surgery. And the police might not be allowed to give you access to case files and evidence. The only way this is going to get resolved for good is to arrest Randall and get him to confess."

"I suppose you're right," Bryce said with a sigh. "But I'm not loving the idea of you putting yourself out there to draw him in. If what Baldwin says is true, and he's fixated on you, there's no telling what he might do to get back at you."

"I know," she said with a sigh. "But at this point, I'm willing to take the risk."

Bryce was quiet for a moment. She could practically feel his disapproval in the silence, but to his credit, he didn't try to lecture her.

"All right," he said finally. "But before you let this guy stay with you, I need to know more about him."

"I was hoping you'd say that." Jillian spread the napkin on the table and cleared her throat. "I have all his information so you can run a background check."

"Really?"

"Yep," she confirmed. "He wrote it all down for me."

"Huh." Bryce's tone was thoughtful. "I suppose that's a good sign. Hopefully that means he doesn't have anything to hide."

"Here's hoping," Jillian said. She rubbed her eyes, which felt gritty from lack of sleep. "Listen, I was up all night, so I'm going to send you a picture of his info and then take a nap. Will you let me know when you're done with the background check?"

"Of course," Bryce said. "Do you need anything else?"

"Just a shower," she said.

Her brother laughed. "You're on your own for that one. But I'll call Mom and Madison and let them know you're fine. I got your text just before you called, but Mom is going to want to know you're really okay." He paused. "Do you want me to talk to Wes, as well?"

Jillian considered the question. Wes had missed much of her childhood, as he'd been in witness protection since she and her siblings were kids. Bryce had had some difficulty accepting Wes once he'd returned, but Jillian knew he was working on getting to know their dad better. They all were, truth be told. "I appreciate it," Jillian said. "I think he'll probably be with Mom, though, so no need for a separate call."

"Good point."

"It's nice of you to be my secretary," she teased.

"Don't get used to it," Bryce replied. "Get some rest and I'll call you later."

"Sounds good." She ended the call and took a picture of the napkin, then texted it to Bryce. She didn't know how long it would take him to dig up information on Baldwin, but now that she'd gotten the ball rolling on the process it was time she took care of herself.

Exhaustion pulled at her, but she desperately wanted a shower first. The holding cell she'd stayed in last night hadn't been dirty, but there was something about being behind bars that made her feel gross.

The hot water streaming over her washed away the residue of fear and anger from last night. She stepped out of the steamy bathroom and headed straight for bed, not even bothering to put clothes on first. Her head hit the pillow and she had just enough energy left to draw the sheet over her body before sinking into sleep.

THE RINGING OF her cell phone woke her.

Jillian blinked several times as she reached for the phone, fumbling to find it on her bedside table. She squinted at the bright display, trying to make sense of both the time and the name on the screen.

Bryce.

"Hello?" She rubbed her eyes, trying to shake off the grogginess that still clung to her mind.

"Sorry," Bryce said. "But I figured if I didn't wake you, you wouldn't be able to sleep tonight."

"No, it's okay," Jillian responded. According to the time on her phone, she'd gotten a few decent hours of rest. "Do you have the results from the background check?"

"I do," Bryce said. "This guy is legit."

"What does that mean?" She pushed herself up on the mattress and arranged a couple of pillows behind her.

"It means he's exactly what he says he is. Born and raised in Grave Gulch. Joined the marines right after high school. Did a few tours overseas. He earned several medals for his conduct, including a Purple Heart, and a Navy and Marine Corps Achievement Medal and a Commendation Medal. He also earned several badges for marksmanship."

"Wow." That sounded impressive. She thought back to her meeting with Baldwin today; he'd given no indication of the extent of his military career or the fact that he'd been injured in combat. Talk about playing things close to the vest.

"Yeah," Bryce agreed. "He was basically a model marine. Honorably discharged, of course. Probably could have done any number of things for work, but decided to become a bounty hunter. From what I found, he started out with the conventional stuff and made a name for himself. He gradually started to go underground, and now he deals exclusively with select clients and high-profile targets."

"I figured that, based on what he told me about his current client," Jillian said. "What did you find out about his personal life?"

"Not much to find, to be honest," Bryce said. "He has excellent credit, owns his truck, rents a place. Never had as much as a parking ticket."

Jillian shifted on the bed. "What about girlfriends? Or boyfriends?" She held her breath, hoping her brother wouldn't read too much in to the question.

"He's been linked to a few women over the years, but nothing long-term," Bryce said. "Seems like the kind of guy who puts work above everything else."

"Gosh, who does that sound like?"

"Very funny," Bryce replied. "You know I'm not like that anymore."

"I do," Jillian acknowledged. "And I'm glad you have Olivia." It was true; both her siblings had found love in recent months, giving Jillian hope that her match might be out there, as well. But one thing was certain—she couldn't focus on her love life, or lack thereof, until Randall Bowe was behind bars and the charges against her had been dropped.

"Overall, I think Baldwin is a good guy," Bryce said, pulling her thoughts back to the matter at hand. "It's impossible to know everything about a person, but Bowe's records show a man who has a history of making good decisions and his military records are seriously impressive."

"So it's probably safe to have him stay with me," Jillian said.

"We definitely know more about him than some random guy you'd meet in a bar or find online," Bryce said.

"That's true." So why did the thought of Baldwin in her home make her heart pound?

"If you're determined to do this, I want you to check in with me frequently," Bryce continued. "At least once a day, so I know how things are going. Do you have any weapons in your house?"

The question sent a tingle of worry down her spine. "Just a baseball bat I keep next to my bed," Jillian replied.

"I suppose that'll have to do," Bryce said. "Just be sure to lock your bedroom door at night."

"O-o-kay…" she said slowly.

"I'm sure I'm overreacting," Bryce replied. "But Baldwin moving in with you is going to paint a very big target on your back. I just want you to be safe."

"I've been taking care of myself for years now," she pointed out. "I'm not going to suddenly become helpless just because some big, strong man has moved in with me."

"Big and strong, huh?" Bryce teased. "Do I need to get you some smelling salts?"

"Ha ha." Jillian couldn't help but roll her eyes at her brother. Even as she did, though, her stomach did a little flip at the memory of standing close to Baldwin earlier today.

"Thanks for doing the check," she said, determined to change the subject. The last person she would ever want to talk to about men was her older brother. There was only a year's difference between them, but Bryce didn't let that stop him from acting overprotective. Even their older sister was often subjected to Bryce's concerns, though Madison had confided to Jillian that Bryce had gotten better since she'd started dating Oren, a US Marshal.

"No problem," Bryce replied. "I might have to stop by later in the week, just to check on you."

Jillian sighed, knowing better than to argue. "Just call first, okay?"

"I can do that," Bryce said.

They ended the call, and Jillian climbed out of bed and dressed. She retrieved the baseball bat from the corner by the door to her place, where it had been resting since last night. As she walked to her bedroom to put it away, she punched in Baldwin's number.

He answered on the second ring. "Are you calling to say yes?"

"How did you—?" Jillian stopped and shook her head. "Never mind." Of course, he had some kind of caller ID installed on his phone. He probably even knew exactly where she was standing in her home, for crying out loud.

"It's a nice program," he said, apparently reading her mind. "I can set it up on your phone, if you'd like."

"Maybe later," she replied. "I was calling to talk to you about your plan."

"Did your brother come through with the background check?"

"He did," she confirmed. "Apparently, you're quite the hero."

"I had a job to do," he replied flatly. "I did it."

Interesting, she thought. Baldwin apparently wasn't one for sentiment or looking back. "And now you just want to finish this job?"

"Pretty much," he confirmed. "So what's it going to be? Are you ready to work with me, or am I gonna do this alone?"

It was on the tip of her tongue to tell him to go pound sand, but Jillian swallowed the impulse. She had to clear her name, and cooperating with Baldwin would hopefully put her on the fast track to do it. And if a few days passed with no results? She'd figure out another approach.

"Let's just get this over with," she said, hearing her own lack of enthusiasm in her tone.

"With an attitude like that, I'm surprised you're still single," Baldwin drawled.

Jillian's temper spiked. "My love life is not your—"

"I'll be there in ten," Baldwin interrupted.

"Bring food," she retorted. "I didn't make it to the store today, and my fridge is empty."

He hung up without acknowledging her statement, making her wonder if he'd even heard it. Normally, she wouldn't ask a guy to buy her a meal twice in one day, but after that little crack about her personal life, she felt no remorse imposing on Baldwin or his wallet.

She glanced around, fighting the urge to do a quick clean of her place. Her condo wasn't dirty but a wipe-down wouldn't hurt.

No, she told herself. If she cleaned, Baldwin would know it and probably take it as a sign she was trying to impress him.

It was the same with her clothes. She'd pulled on another T-shirt and a pair of yoga pants when she'd gotten out of bed. It wasn't fancy, but the clothes were washed and the fabric didn't have holes. That would be good enough.

With a sigh, she walked into her living room and began to straighten some of the picture frames on the bookshelves. The officers who had conducted the search had been unusually thoughtful—they hadn't left a ransacked mess in their wake. But items were still out of place, enough that it would bother her to leave them.

"This is going to work," she muttered to herself

as she moved around the room. "We're going to get Randall and then life will go back to normal."

It was the only option. The alternative was too terrifying to contemplate.

Chapter Four

Baldwin stood on Jillian's welcome mat, juggling several grocery bags while he waited for her to answer the door.

The sound of a lock echoed in the hall, and he glanced over to see Jillian's neighbor stepping out of her condo. She stopped in her tracks and stared at him, mouth agape, as though he was some kind of freak of nature.

"Evening," he said, jerking up his chin in acknowledgment.

The sound of his voice made her jump. She blinked at him, then turned and scurried away without a word.

Interesting, he thought. Apparently, Ms. Colton must not have too many visitors if the sight of him was enough to shock the neighbor.

She'd struck him as a bit of a workaholic. Nice to have his suspicions confirmed, even if only indirectly.

The door in front of him opened, Jillian on the other side.

"Hi," she said.

"Hey," he replied. He studied her face while he waited to be asked inside. Earlier in the day, she'd been tired but feisty, determined to find his brother and bring him down.

Now she looked subdued and a little resigned.

The change didn't suit her. He wanted to see that spark come back into her eyes.

Baldwin held up one of the grocery bags. "Can I—?"

"Yes, of course," she interrupted. She stepped back to allow him inside. "Sorry, let me help."

He handed her one of the bags and followed her down the short hall. The kitchen opened up off the left side, and straight ahead was a large living room. At the far end he saw another short hall, with two doors opening off it before it curved to the left. A half bath across from the kitchen completed the place.

Jillian led him into the kitchen and set the grocery bag on the counter. "What's this?"

"You said to bring food." He placed the other bags on the counter and slipped off his backpack. "I brought food."

"I didn't think you'd heard me," she said quietly. He started unpacking and she shook her head. "I thought you'd grab a pizza or something. I didn't mean for you to restock my fridge."

"Yeah, well..." He trailed off with a shrug. To be honest, he hadn't intended to stop at the grocery store. He'd meant to pick up some burgers. But then he'd realized his sarcastic remark about her love life had hurt her feelings, and he'd felt like an ass. So he'd decided to cook her dinner, as a sort of peace offering. They were going to be spending the foreseeable future together. Might as well get off on the right foot.

Jillian helped him unload. "Thank you," she said. "I didn't have a chance to stop at the store today, so I'm running a little low on supplies."

"It's not a problem," Baldwin said. "I figured I could make us something to eat and we could get to know each other a little better."

"Do you like to cook?" The surprise in her voice was evident.

Baldwin hid a smile. People were always shocked to discover he had talent in the kitchen. "I do, actually."

"Wow." Jillian didn't bother to hide her reaction. "I never would have guessed."

He turned and leaned against the counter, crossing his legs at the ankles. "Why's that? Don't I look like a guy who can make a roux or flambé some cherries jubilee?"

Jillian tilted her head. "I'm going to be honest with you, I only understood about half of what you just said. But to answer your question, no, you don't look like a chef." She eyed him up and down, her brown eyes lingering on his hips and his chest. Baldwin felt his skin prickle and warmth began to spread through his limbs. "You look like a tough guy, but I'm sure you already knew that."

"Even tough guys have to eat," he replied, willing his body's response to subside. A few minutes in, and he was already getting distracted. It was a clear sign that after he caught his brother, he needed to take some personal time before jumping into the next case. It had been a while since his last vacation; maybe he could call up one of his "friends with benefits" in Chicago or Dallas, spend a few days enjoying himself with some pleasant company. Baldwin didn't do relationships—lack of time was an issue, along with the fact that he didn't want to be tied down to any one location. His lady friends understood the score, and there were never any hard feelings. It was the perfect setup.

"Before you get started, let me show you your room," Jillian said. She nodded at his backpack on the floor. "You can get that out of your way."

"Sounds good." He bent and grabbed one of the straps of the bag and followed her out of the kitchen. He tried not to stare at her figure as she moved, but it was hard to notice anything else. She certainly wasn't dressed to impress, but even the T-shirt and stretched-out pants she wore did nothing to hide her long, lean lines. There was a grace to her walk, an intangible quality that made him wonder if she'd been a dancer at some point in her life. She seemed to carry herself with a physical awareness that he associated with athletes, like she was totally at ease in her own skin and knew exactly what her body could do. Baldwin was usually drawn to curvier women, but there was something about Jillian that made him want to touch her.

Not that he would.

He'd meant what he'd told her at the diner—he wasn't interested in sex. He was here to catch his brother and get paid.

Jillian led him into a bedroom next to the main bathroom. A glance down the hall gave him a peek into her room, but he didn't see much.

"Here you go," she said, stepping aside so he could enter.

It was on the small side, not that it mattered. A double bed was on the far wall, with a night table and lamp beside it. There was a dresser off to the side with a few books stacked on top. It was clear Jillian didn't use this space very often—there weren't any pictures or personal touches to be found. But it was clean, and he noticed a stack of folded towels on the end of the bed.

"Will this be okay?" She sounded a little uncertain, as though she was worried about his reaction.

"Oh, yeah," he assured her. "This is perfect." He set his backpack on the floor by the bed. "Is that your room down the hall?"

"Yes. The bathroom is just next door."

"Good." With the bedrooms so close, it would be easy to hear if she needed something. He glanced at the right wall. "Does your room have a window, as well?"

"Ah, yeah. Do you want to see?"

Baldwin nodded. It would be good to know the

layout of her bedroom, for security purposes. And… he was curious to know what her personal space looked like.

"Okay. It's just this way."

He followed her down the short hall into her room. It was considerably larger, with space enough for a chair and small table set in the corner. He noticed a book on the table and figured she used the chair for reading.

There were a few framed photos on top of her dresser—he spotted Bryce in one of them and guessed they were of her family. A large window ran along the left wall. He walked over and glanced out, noting it was locked; they were three stories up, and there was no fire escape. If Randall wanted to come in, he was going to have to do it through the front door.

Baldwin turned, noticing a small bathroom set off to one side of the room, next to what he supposed was her closet. He spied some crumpled fabric on the floor by the door to the bath—something light pink and small. Jillian rushed over and grabbed it, her cheeks blazing.

Her panties, he realized. He turned away, a funny feeling bubbling in his chest. It was just another item of clothing, something most people wore every day. They weren't even particularly sexy, not red lace or a black thong. So why did a glimpse of Jillian's pink cotton underwear make him uncomfortably aware of her bed just a few feet away, with its slightly rumpled sheets?

He cleared his throat. "Looks like there's only one point of entry to your condo."

Jillian nodded, the flush fading from her face. "Some of the units have a balcony, but not this one."

"That's good." He smiled faintly. "If Randall tries to get in, he's only got one option."

"I—I hadn't thought of it like that." She frowned.

"That's why I'm here," he replied. "It's my job to think of these things." He nodded at the doorway that led to the hall. "Hungry?"

"Yes." She tossed her panties into the closet and walked past him. "What's on the menu?"

He followed her, heading toward the kitchen. "I thought I'd make salmon with a dill sauce and some lemon risotto."

Jillian stopped dead in her tracks; if he hadn't been paying attention, he'd have walked right into her. She slowly turned around. "Are you serious?"

"Yes. Why? Would you prefer something else?" He knew from the way she'd inhaled the bacon at the diner that she wasn't a vegetarian. But perhaps she had a food allergy?

Jillian shook her head. "No. That sounds amazing. I just wasn't expecting something so fancy."

Baldwin laughed. "Just wait. You'll see it's not that complicated."

As soon as they reached the kitchen he started to assemble the ingredients he'd picked up at the store. Jillian hung back, giving him space to work. "Is there anything I can do to help you?"

He could tell she wasn't used to standing around

while other people worked. So he told her how to make the dill sauce while he prepped the risotto. Soon, they were standing side by side, mixing and stirring together.

Baldwin felt himself relax as they worked. Normally, he cooked alone and only for himself. But having Jillian working beside him was…nice. They didn't speak other than to talk about the recipe, or for him to ask where something was located. Still, he enjoyed having her there. She wasn't one of those people who had to talk to fill a silence. She seemed just as content as he was to remain quiet and stay focused on the task at hand.

He showed her how to drizzle the sauce over the fish. After she popped it into the oven, she leaned against the counter and watched while he added broth to the risotto.

"How did you learn how to cook?"

Baldwin shrugged. "I spend a lot of time by myself when I'm working. I don't like eating fast food and dining out gets expensive. So I started watching cooking shows online in my downtime, and I decided to start practicing."

"That's impressive," Jillian said. "I take it you stay in places with a kitchen when you travel?"

He nodded. "Yeah, I always go for the extended-stay hotels. That way I don't have to haul pots and pans around." He didn't tell her that he enjoyed cooking, as it gave him something to focus on that wasn't work-related. He had a few close friends, but due to the nature of his job he moved around a lot, so it was difficult to make connections. The kitchen was a constant for him, a place he could go and forget about the world while he made a meal.

"Sounds like you think of everything," she said softly. She nodded at the pot on the stove. "It smells delicious."

"Hopefully it'll taste just as good." He stirred the broth into the rice, waiting until it was fully absorbed before adding a bit more. He could feel her gaze as she watched him work, but he refused to let it affect him.

In a matter of minutes, the meal was ready. Jillian gathered utensils and fixed drinks while he plated the food and brought it to the table.

She sat across from him and took a bite. "Wow," she said, her mouth full. "This is wonderful."

"I'm glad you like it," Baldwin said, pleased by her reaction. It was nice to know he'd impressed her, even if that hadn't been his main goal.

They ate in silence for a few minutes. If this had been a date, he would have tried to make conversation, asked about likes and dislikes, that kind of thing. But because it was just business, he didn't feel the need to be chatty.

Apparently, Jillian didn't feel the same way. She cleared her throat, then spoke. "Can I ask you a personal question?" She sounded hesitant.

Baldwin considered the request. He didn't blame her for being curious about him. It was smart of her to have run a background check before letting him into her home. But what more could she want to know?

"Sure," he said finally.

"Was your brother always so…" She trailed off, clearly searching for the right words. "So conniving?"

Baldwin nodded, relaxing a bit since he wasn't actually the focus of her question. "Oh, yeah. Even as a kid, he would hold a grudge forever. And he was always big on getting revenge if he felt like he'd been wronged somehow."

"Were you two close at all?"

"No. We're very different, so we didn't hang with the same crowds. He completely wrote me off when I joined the marines after high school."

Jillian's features twisted in disbelief. "Really? Why is that?"

The familiar feeling of resentment began to bubble up in Baldwin's chest as he recalled Randall's hateful words just before he'd shipped out for basic training: *You're going to make great cannon fodder.*

"Randall planned on going to college. He thought anyone who chose a different path lacked intelligence and wasn't worth his time."

"What about your parents? Did they share his opinion?"

Baldwin tilted his head to the side. "In a way, yeah. None of them understood why I chose to join the military instead of go to college."

Jillian finished the last bite of salmon and leaned back in her chair. "Still, they must have been proud of you, especially after you won all those medals and commendations."

"They were, kind of," Baldwin acknowledged. "They still thought military service was beneath me, but at least I had distinguished myself, as they put it."

Jillian frowned. "Wow. I can kind of see where Randall got his attitude. How did he respond to your awards?"

Baldwin smiled. "It got under Randall's skin, to know I'd done well for myself. And when I got out and started my own business, it made him even angrier."

"So that's why you think he'll come," Jillian said.

"Exactly." Baldwin gathered Jillian's empty plate and placed it on top of his own. "He can't stand me, and he apparently has it out for you, as well. He won't be able to pass up the chance to go after us both."

He rose and took the plates to the kitchen sink, then gathered up the dishes they'd used to cook. "I'm thinking one or two days and he'll show his face. Maybe we could pose in front of the window in your bedroom—you know, make it look like we're a couple? That would really set him off."

He started the water and squirted some soap on a sponge. "Best-case scenario, he'll attack you and I can nab him while he's distracted."

Jillian appeared at his elbow. "I'll do this," she said shortly. She hip-checked him away from the sink, leaving him no choice but to step aside. He glanced down, surprised to find her face was tight with anger.

"Uh, what's going on?"

"Nothing." She practically spat the word as she attacked the risotto pot with the sponge.

Ri-i-ight. Baldwin was no expert where women were concerned, but he recognized danger when he saw it. Jillian was now a ticking time bomb, and he had no desire to stick around and wait for her to detonate.

"Okay. Well… If you're cool here, I think I'll go unpack."

"Yep. Fine." She didn't look at him, just kept her head down as she focused on the dishes in the sink.

Baldwin took a step toward the door. "Ah, good night then." It was still early in the evening, but it was clear Jillian didn't want to see him anymore. Better to retreat to the guest bedroom and get some work done on his laptop.

"Good night."

He retreated through the living room into the guest bedroom and shut the door quietly. After toeing off his boots, he lay down on the bed and stared at the ceiling fan.

Jillian was clearly upset. But for the life of him, he couldn't figure out why. She'd seemed to like the food he'd made, and she'd been interested in helping him cook. Even their conversation had been going well, at least in his opinion. Apparently, she felt differently.

He sighed, hoping this wasn't a sign of things to come. They were going to be spending a lot of time together, and it would be much easier if she wasn't so moody about it.

His phone vibrated in his pocket. Baldwin removed it and glanced at the screen. It was a message from his client, asking if there were any updates on his brother's case.

Not yet, he thought, listening to Jillian's footsteps as she moved past his door and walked to her room. *But soon.*

WHAT. AN. ASS.

Jillian clenched her jaw as she scrubbed the dishes, her anger bubbling as she processed what Baldwin had said.

Best-case scenario, he'll attack you and I can nab him while he's distracted.

That was his plan? For her to be assaulted so Baldwin could step in like some kind of savior? She knew he'd intended to use her as bait to draw out his brother, but she'd had no idea of just how far he wanted to take things.

Even the thought of Randall touching her was enough to make Jillian's skin crawl. Randall wasn't physically imposing like Baldwin; he was about her height, and if anything, he was as thin as she was. But even slight men had a deceptive strength about them, and she didn't want Randall grabbing or groping her.

And what if he had a weapon? She might be able to fend him off for a few minutes if it was just him, but if he had a knife or a gun, she wouldn't have a chance.

Where the hell did Baldwin get off? Did he honestly think that she'd sit passively and wait for Randall to attack her, then just let him do it until Baldwin deemed the time was right to intervene?

"I don't think so," she muttered, jamming the last dish into the drying rack next to the sink.

But it wasn't just Baldwin's ridiculous plan that had her seeing red. It was the fact that she thought they'd been getting along. He'd seemed a little rough around the edges earlier today, and his comment about her personal life had stung. But then he'd shown up with groceries and cooked a lovely meal. He'd even taught her some tricks in the kitchen. She'd learned a little more about his family and his relationship with his brother, and he'd started to seem like a nice guy. A little on the gruff side, but still—a decent human being.

And then he'd gone and pulled the rug out from under her.

With one careless remark, he'd shown her what he really thought of her. And while Jillian understood she wasn't going to come out of this experience with a new best friend, she hadn't expected Baldwin to be so…detached. It was almost clinical, the way he'd talked about Randall attacking her. As if he truly didn't care if she got hurt. He'd said before that he was focused on apprehending his brother so he could get the rest of his fee, but Jillian had assumed he'd act within the limits of decency. That he didn't really intend for Randall to touch her, much less assault her.

Now she knew the truth. Baldwin saw her as nothing more than a pawn, an object he could manipulate to suit his purposes. He talked a good game about keeping her safe, but really, he *wanted* Randall to try to hurt her.

Jillian stalked through the living room and down the hall to her bedroom. She had half a mind to barge into the guest room and kick Baldwin out. But as she shut her door behind her, she knew that would be a mistake.

When Randall did strike—and Baldwin was acting as though it was a matter of *when* more than *if*—having Baldwin around would prove useful. The man might not give two figs about her, but no way was he going to let his brother escape. She had no doubt he'd move heaven and earth to get his hands on Randall so he could collect the rest of his money.

And while Baldwin's apparent lack of human emotion made him a world-class jerk, it also made him predictable. Jillian could count on him to make whatever choice would lead to him getting paid.

Which meant that even though Baldwin was staying just down the hall, in effect, she was alone. There was no need for her to worry about being a good hostess or to try to keep him entertained while he lived with her. She wasn't going to ignore him—that would be rude. But she wasn't going to initiate conversation or try to get to know him. What would be the point? He'd spelled it all out for her at the diner, making his motivations and intentions very clear. She had simply been too naive to take him at his word, choosing instead to think that no one could be that coldhearted.

Now, though, Jillian knew better.

In a way, it was a good thing that Baldwin had been so transparent tonight. If he hadn't just come out and said what he'd been thinking, Jillian probably would have made the mistake of trusting him. At least this way she knew to keep her guard up when he was around.

Hopefully, he wouldn't be here for long.

Chapter Five

She woke to the smell of coffee.

Jillian glanced at the clock on her nightstand: seven on the dot. It seemed Baldwin was an early riser, too. For a moment, she considered hiding in her room until he left. But, no, that was the coward's way out. Besides, she had no idea what his plans were for the day. He might very well intend to stay in her condo 24/7, until Randall decided to make his move.

While the idea of shutting herself off from the world held some appeal, Jillian didn't have that option. She had a midmorning meeting scheduled with her attorney. Hopefully he would have good news for her on the legal front.

Jillian took a quick shower and braided her hair. Then she slipped on a green sweater dress and a pair of dark brown knee-high boots. The first time she'd met her attorney had been in jail, when she'd been sporting sweatpants and an old T-shirt. Today, she was aiming for a more professional look.

As she stepped out of her room, she recognized the scent of hot syrup mingling with the aroma of coffee. Baldwin was standing by the stove, flipping pancakes with his back to her. He was dressed in a pair of flannel pants and a long-sleeved dark gray Henley that clung to his muscles. Jillian couldn't help but stare at his butt for a few seconds before reminding herself that no matter how good he looked, Baldwin might as well be a machine for all the emotion he displayed.

"Good morning," she said as she walked into the kitchen.

"Morning," he replied. "These are almost done."

She poured herself a cup of coffee and added a little sugar. "Not one for cereal?"

When he didn't respond right away, she turned to find him staring at her, the spatula held in midair as the pancakes sizzled in the skillet, apparently forgotten.

Baldwin blinked and turned back, but not before she spied a dark flush on his cheeks. "Uh, no. I prefer a hot meal in the morning." He scraped the last pancakes free and placed them to the side of the existing pile. "I'll eat those," he muttered. "They're a little burned."

Jillian hid a smile behind her cup. Had she actually caught Baldwin checking her out? The thought of it was almost enough to make her laugh.

The table was already set with plates and silverware, so she carried over her mug and took a seat as Baldwin brought the pancakes. "These look great," she remarked as he put down the plate.

He stepped away and returned with some sliced

fruit. "Thanks," he said. "I know you had pancakes yesterday, but you don't have a waffle iron, so I couldn't make those."

"I'm not complaining," she replied. If Baldwin was going to cook every meal while he was here, she might be willing to overlook the more obnoxious facets of his jerkish demeanor.

"You look nice today," he commented. She saw his glance slide to the side, and realized he was staring at her boots.

"Thanks," she said, between bites of breakfast.

"Hot date?" His tone was deceptively casual, but she heard a note of genuine curiosity.

Why did he care? Because he was actually interested, or because he was concerned about acting like they were dating to draw Randall into the open? The latter, she decided quickly. Definitely the latter.

"Hardly," she said. "I'm meeting with my attorney to go over my case."

"Ah." His shoulders relaxed a bit, probably due to the relief of knowing she wasn't going to jeopardize this little farce. *Yes, I'm playing along*, she thought to herself. *You'll get your money soon enough.*

"What about you?" she asked between bites of pancake. Baldwin's cooking put Mae's efforts to shame, but she wasn't about to tell him that. "Any plans for the day?"

"A few errands," he said. "I have some friends in the region who are keeping an eye out for Randall. I'm going to check in with them, see if they've heard or seen anything."

Friends? Jillian nearly did a spit take with her coffee. Mr. Emotionless actually had friends?

The shock must have shown on her face because he lifted one eyebrow. "Yes, I know. Surprise, surprise, there are people out there who actually like me."

"Are they as repressed as you?"

The corners of Baldwin's mouth twitched. "You think I'm repressed?" He ran his gaze over her body, his blue eyes bright. Jillian felt a wave of heat wash over her at his frank appraisal, and she fought the urge to shiver.

He leaned forward, making her grateful for the table separating them. "Believe me," he said, his voice a low rumble, "I can be very expressive under the right circumstances."

Jillian wanted to look away, but she refused to give him the satisfaction of knowing he'd affected her. So she forced herself to shrug. "If you say so," she replied, bringing her mug to her lips to hide the flush she felt creeping up her neck.

Baldwin leaned back, the smug smile on his face making it clear he hadn't missed a thing.

"We should go out to dinner tonight."

Jillian choked on her coffee and began to cough.

Baldwin slowly got to his feet and stepped over to crouch beside her. His big hand rubbed circles on her back while she sputtered and tried to catch her breath.

"I'm sorry, what?" she squeaked out. She blinked at him, eyes watering.

"You heard me," he said, handing her a napkin. Jillian glanced down, relieved to find that although she had coffee dripping off her chin her dress was still clean.

It was hard to breathe with him standing so close. The scent of his detergent filled her nose, along with a warm, slightly spicy note that she assumed was his skin.

"Are you tired of cooking already?" She dabbed at her chin, glancing down to avoid his gaze. His eyes were practically electric at this range, almost too intense to look at. "I'm not as skilled as you are, but I do okay in the kitchen."

"That's not the issue." His hand stilled on her back and she held her breath, torn between a desire for him to keep touching her and the need for him to stop before she made a fool of herself.

Baldwin got to his feet, his fingers trailing across her shoulders as he stood. Jillian's nipples stiffened in response. She hurriedly crossed her arms as Baldwin sat across from her once again.

"Then what's the problem?"

He lifted one shoulder in a casual shrug. "We need to be seen together."

"Oh." That's right—she'd forgotten about their little public charade. If they were going to draw out Randall, he had to think they were together first.

"Any suggestions?"

Jillian considered the question. Baldwin had said they didn't have to get physical in public, so that meant no overly romantic places. But they needed to look like more than just friends, or else no one would believe Baldwin had moved in with her.

"How about Grave Gulch Grill?" she suggested. Her uncle Geoff owned the place, and the food was consistently good. "It's nice, but not too fancy."

"Sounds perfect," Baldwin replied. "Does six work for you?"

"That's fine," Jillian replied. "I'll meet you here and we can go together." She stood and began to gather up the dishes.

"I've got this." Baldwin took the plates from her hands and walked to the sink.

"You cooked," she protested. "It's only fair that I clean."

He looked her up and down, his gaze hot. "Not dressed like that," he muttered.

A tingling sensation spread through her. It had been a long time since a man had shown any kind of interest, and she was out of practice. That was the only reason she had responded to Baldwin's touch. Her hormones didn't care that he was an ass who only wanted to use her to get to his brother. Her body had its own ideas about ways he could use her, and none of them was appropriate.

I've got to start dating, she thought. Between the stress of being Randall's favorite punching bag and the long hours she'd been pulling at work as they all tried to undo the damage Randall had done, there'd been little time for a personal life. Jillian generally wasn't aware of her loneliness but being around Baldwin emphasized how long it had been since she'd made a connection with someone.

"I have a key for you," she said, desperate to change the subject. "Let me grab it."

The junk drawer was next to the stove, so fortunately she didn't have to get close to him again. The spare key was buried under several layers of crap, but she found it soon enough.

"Here you go." Jillian set it on the counter, making sure to keep distance between them.

"Thanks," he said. He shot her a glance over his shoulder. "You have my number. Be sure to call me if you need anything today."

"Ah, okay." It felt strange, this sense of needing to check in with someone. Jillian was used to being on her own, doing stuff alone and on her schedule without thinking about someone else. Knowing that she was going to come home to Baldwin was a bit unsettling. "Same to you, I guess."

He turned around and leaned against the counter, drying his hands with a dish towel. "Oh, I'll keep track of you," he said, a sly grin spreading over his face that made her stomach do a little flip. "Trust me."

BALDWIN BREATHED A sigh of relief as the door clicked shut behind Jillian.

He was used to seeing her dressed in shapeless

T-shirts and baggy pants. When she'd come into the kitchen dressed in normal clothes, he'd been stunned.

It turned out she did have curves. In all the right places.

The green dress wasn't at all revealing—it had a high neckline and long sleeves, and the hem came to her knees. But the sweater fabric clung to her breasts and hips, showing off her very feminine assets.

And those boots! There was something about knee-high leather that he found incredibly sexy. He'd had a hard time keeping his eyes off her legs, and he knew she'd caught him looking at least once.

Baldwin shook his head. Overall, it was a perfectly professional outfit, one she'd probably worn to work dozens of times.

Why, then, had it gotten to him so much?

And why was he irritated at the thought that his brother might have seen her dressed like that?

He had no claim on Jillian. She was her own woman, and they weren't involved in any way other than this temporary arrangement. It was ridiculous of him to be affected by her, or to even think about how other men might look at her.

Still, he couldn't deny that he'd felt the stirrings of attraction when they'd first met. Now that they were spending more time together, and now that he'd had a good look at what she'd been hiding under those glorified pajamas, his libido was definitely taking notice.

And unless he missed his guess, she was feeling something, too.

He'd seen the way her nipples stood at attention when he'd touched her. Oh, she'd crossed her arms to hide her response, but not fast enough. It had taken all of his self-control not to react, but he didn't want to embarrass her. He knew she thought he was a jerk, but he saw no reason to validate that opinion. After all, he had assured her that he had no romantic interest in her; he wasn't about to go back on his word now.

Better to shake off any thoughts of Jillian Colton and focus on the job at hand. The sooner he found Randall and turned him in to the police, the sooner he'd get paid and could move on to the next job.

With that in mind, he headed for the bathroom and took a quick shower, then dressed and grabbed his phone and keys. Time to check in with his associates in the region and find out if they'd had any sight of Randall. He didn't think his brother had gone far, but it was good to cast a wide net.

He headed out the door—no nosy neighbors to scandalize today—and climbed into his truck. If his hunch was correct, and Randall was still around, then Baldwin needed to make himself visible in Grave Gulch.

"Tick tock, brother," he muttered to himself. "I'm coming for you."

Chapter Six

"I'm sorry, Ms. Colton. I wish I had better news."

Jillian sat in the office of Rodney Jones, attorney at law, and tried hard not to cry. Jones had just finished going over the evidence the police had against her, and it was even worse than she'd thought.

There were several full fingerprints at the scene of the most recent robbery, along with quite a few partials. People had been convicted on less evidence. But the true nail in her coffin was the discovery of the stolen jewelry in her closet.

"I know you probably hear this all the time, but I am innocent." How many times had she said that recently? But it was important that she kept saying it, kept pushing back against the narrative that she was a thief. People would always doubt, and her reputation might never recover from this. Still, she would never stop speaking the truth.

Rodney smiled kindly. "Believe it or not, I don't actually think you did this."

Jillian blinked in surprise. "You don't?"

Rodney shook his head. "I took this case as a

favor to Evangeline," he said, referring to her cousin Troy's fiancée, the former Grave Gulch assistant district attorney. "She asked me to look after you, and I'm happy to represent you. But I have to say, as soon as I stepped in as your counsel, I heard from numerous people on the police force, everyone telling me you couldn't have committed these crimes. Not to mention, there's been a great number of people in Grave Gulch who have been framed in recent months. It's not farfetched to assume the same has happened to you."

"Really?" Her voice was barely a whisper as she struggled to contain her emotions. It meant a lot to know that the people she worked with didn't think she was a criminal, despite the forensic evidence against her.

"Yes," Jones continued. "I can call them as character witnesses if your case goes to trial. But I think the DA might be willing to cut a deal, and if so, you should consider it."

"No." Jillian started shaking her head before he'd even finished speaking. "I'm not going to jail for something I didn't do. I won't give Randall Bowe the satisfaction."

Rodney leaned back in his leather chair. "That man has caused a lot of problems in Grave Gulch," he said. "But unless we can positively link him to these crimes, I don't see how we can prove your innocence."

"Isn't it enough to show he's always had it out

for me? That we never got along and he was always picking on me?"

Rodney shook his head. "We can certainly try to create doubt and make it look like Bowe planted evidence. But that would be a tough sell for a jury, especially now that he's on the run."

"Did the police check the surveillance cameras in my building? I know there are cameras at the entrance. There's no other way for Randall to gain access to my condo, so he must be on tape!"

"They did pull the footage, and as soon as they release them I'll have my staff look over the recordings. But, Jillian, you have to know that some of the homes that were burglarized have security footage, as well. It shows a tall, slender figure dressed all in black and wearing a ski mask. Unfortunately, you match that general description."

"So does Randall," she said, a sense of desperation rising in her chest. Why couldn't anyone see? He'd planned all of this! He'd known exactly what to do to frame her, and now she was in real danger of going to prison. It was enough to drive her mad with worry!

"I know," Rodney replied. "That's a good thing—it means the surveillance footage doesn't definitively prove it was you committing the robberies."

"But that's not enough?"

"I'm afraid not," he replied. "Not at this point, anyway."

She was silent a moment, processing everything he'd told her. "So you're saying that unless I can find absolute proof that Randall Bowe is framing me, I'm going to jail?"

Rodney shifted in his chair, as though trying to dodge her question. "Nothing in life is certain," he hedged. Jillian lifted one eyebrow and he shrugged. "All right, yes. Based on how things look right at this moment, I'd say that's very possible."

Tears sprang to her eyes again and she blinked hard.

"Try not to get too discouraged," Rodney said. "We're still in the early stages of things. My team is going to examine all the evidence with a fine-tooth comb, and we'll do everything we can to exonerate you."

"I'm sure you will," Jillian said. "But I do a lot of my work in the lab. I know how powerful forensic evidence is, and how important it can be in getting a conviction. I'm sure the district attorney will have quite a lot to say about my fingerprints being found at the crime scene, and I can't imagine a jury is going to believe Randall Bowe would go to all this trouble just to frame me, despite the fact he tried to blame me for other things in the past, like the evidence he falsified in Everleigh Emerson's case. What's that saying? The simplest explanation is generally correct? Well, in this case, the simplest explanation must be that I'm guilty."

Jones nodded. "That's true. If this goes to trial, we will have a battle on our hands. But give me a little credit. I have my own rhetorical tricks, and I'm good at my job. I'm going to fight for you, Ms. Colton."

"I'm glad to hear it," she said. "I just hope it will be enough."

Jones got to his feet and extended his hand. "I'll be in touch as our investigation moves forward. Don't hesitate to call me if you have any questions, or if you find something that might help your case."

Jillian shook his hand. "I'll let you know." She debated telling him about Baldwin's plan to use her as bait to trigger an attack from his brother, but decided against it. If Baldwin's scheme worked, the case against her would disappear and Jones would be free to spend his time on his other clients. If it didn't work, well, she'd still be here, in need of an attorney.

Rodney's office was on an idyllic tree-lined street of shops, boutiques and cafés. Jillian set off down the sidewalk, feeling restless. The thought of going home held no appeal; she didn't feel like talking about the meeting with Baldwin. He'd listen to her talk all right, but he'd be about as sympathetic as a houseplant.

What she wanted was to talk about her situation with someone who cared. Grace's face popped into her mind, but no; she couldn't call her cousin, not with Internal Affairs watching her case so closely. Wainwright would assume any contact she had with her law-enforcement relatives was collusion, and she didn't want to get them in trouble.

Bryce was out, as well—he was still healing, and besides, he'd done enough by running the background check on Baldwin. And as for Madison? Her sister had already gone through so much lately; she'd found Wes, and she'd nearly been killed by the son of a man seeking revenge for his own father's death. Jillian didn't want to add to the drama.

A few of her girlfriends had called, leaving messages of support. But Jillian didn't have the energy to rehash everything with someone who wasn't already in the loop. She was just so...tired. If only she could close her eyes and wake up to find this was all just a horrible nightmare!

She was settling in for a good sulk as she walked down the street, headed in the general direction of the parking garage and her car. There had to be some way to prove Randall had planted the evidence against her, but how? He'd gone to great lengths to put her fingerprints at the scene of the last robbery, and it had probably been child's play for him to break into her condo and hide the stolen jewelry. Too bad her building didn't have security cameras on each floor... And she doubted Randall would have been careless enough to leave his fingerprints at her place. How, then, could she prove her innocence?

"I need a better lock," she muttered to herself. The idea of Randall in her home, in her private space, was distressing. He probably didn't have a reason to come back—after all, she was on the hook for these robberies, and the evidence against her was pretty air-tight. But Jillian didn't want to take any chances. Randall was the kind of man who enjoyed gloating, and she didn't want to wake up one night to find him standing over her, terrorizing her in a sick celebration of his victory.

She stepped to the side, closer to the buildings to be a little sheltered from the chilly wind, and reached into her purse for her phone. A quick search yielded a couple of numbers for locksmith services, but five minutes and two calls later, she hung up in disappointment. Neither company could come out today; she'd made an appointment for the day after tomorrow, which would have to be good enough.

"Baldwin is there," she told herself. And while he might not care about her, he was fixed on getting his brother. If Randall did show up at her place again Baldwin would stop him, if for no other reason than his paycheck.

"Jillian?"

At the sound of her name, she turned to see another of her cousins, the former police chief, Melissa Colton, walking in her direction.

"I thought that was you!" Melissa said, smiling broadly as she approached. "It's good to see you!"

Jillian couldn't help but smile at the older woman. She'd always looked up to her cousin, who'd led the GGPD for years with the kind of grace under pressure Jillian envied.

"Hey!" she said, feeling a genuine burst of happiness break through the gray clouds of her mood. "How are you?"

They hugged briefly. "I'm fine," Melissa said. "Just doing a little shopping." She held up a small bag, embossed with the label of the baby boutique just down the street. "I couldn't resist," she said sheepishly.

"Are you feeling okay?" Jillian asked. Melissa

was in her first trimester of pregnancy, and Jillian remembered their cousin Desiree having lots of morning sickness when she had been pregnant with her son, Danny.

"So far, so good," Melissa replied. "I get a little nauseated now and then, but nothing like what Dez experienced. Mostly I'm just tired."

"Then it's a good thing you turned the reins over to Brett," Jillian said.

Melissa nodded. "Yeah, he's the right guy for the job. I don't think I could have trusted anyone else. We're going to make it formal this evening. It's going to be a small ceremony, at my insistence."

Jillian touched Melissa's shoulder. "I know you don't want to make a big deal of it, but for what it's worth, I'm proud of you. You were a great chief."

Melissa smiled, but then a sudden gust of wind made them both wince. "Are you busy?" Melissa asked. "I've been craving hot chocolate, and I'd like to catch up with you."

Jillian considered her options. She could go home and wallow in self-pity, or she could spend some time chatting with her cousin.

It was a no-brainer.

"That sounds great," she said. "I could use something warm to drink."

They walked about half a block and ducked into a small coffee shop. They ordered their drinks, then snagged a table by one of the storefront windows.

"So tell me," Melissa began, after a barista delivered two big mugs, steaming with hot chocolate. "How are you really doing?"

"I'm terrified," Jillian confessed. "I don't want to go to jail."

"Do you really think that will happen?" Melissa asked.

Jillian filled her in on the meeting she'd just had with her attorney, and the fact that all the evidence was currently stacked against her. Melissa was a good listener—she didn't interrupt or try to change the subject, and she only asked a few questions while Jillian told her everything.

"I just don't know if a jury would believe I'm innocent, given the evidence." She took a sip of her hot chocolate, feeling glum.

"It does seem like the deck is stacked against you," Melissa said. "But I think you're overlooking all of Randall's behavior."

Jillian frowned. "What do you mean?"

Melissa shrugged. "This is a guy who we know fabricated evidence to interfere with the convictions of several people. He's been on the run for months, but he hasn't disappeared quietly. How many people has he contacted to taunt while he's been in hiding? How many times has he texted or called or emailed, just to gloat or antagonize?"

"A lot," Jillian admitted. Randall had even contacted her a few times, telling her she was a bad scientist and that she should quit. He'd repeated his long-standing criticism that she wasn't cut out for her job and revealed that he'd messed with more of her cases than anyone knew.

"Based on what you've told me in the past, Randall was always hypercritical of you. I'm sure your coworkers would testify to that, as well."

"He certainly wasn't quiet about his thoughts," Jillian said, shuddering at the memory of some of his tirades against her.

"All of this paints a picture of a highly disturbed egomaniac," Melissa said. "It won't be hard for your attorney to argue that Randall is vindictive and sees you as a target. Given his forensic knowledge, and the fact that he's confessed to manipulating evidence in many other cases, it's not a stretch to assume he's planted some things against you."

"Maybe you're right," Jillian mused. What Melissa was saying made a lot of sense, and Jillian appreciated her positive take on the situation. For the first time since this all began, she started to feel a bit hopeful that maybe Randall wouldn't get away with framing her after all.

Melissa smiled. "I know it doesn't seem like it now, but don't give up yet. The truth will come out. It always does."

"I just hope it comes out in time to keep me from going to jail," Jillian sighed. "I don't mean to sound so negative, but I feel like I can't talk to anyone about this." She gestured to Melissa. "Present company excluded, of course."

"Why's that?" Melissa asked.

Jillian shrugged. "I just don't want anyone to get

in trouble for talking to me. The guy from IAB who arrested me was practically salivating at the thought of implicating my family in a cover-up. I'm worried if I speak to anyone, he'll make a federal case out of it."

Melissa wrinkled her nose. "Yeah, both Grace and Brett mentioned that Wainwright got out of hand. He's new in the department. Camden wanted the case, but he was worried that given his connection to Grace, it might appear inappropriate for him to handle the investigation."

"I understand," Jillian said. "It would have been nicer to have him there the other night, but I get it."

Melissa leaned forward and lowered her voice. "Between you and me, Wainwright has been told to dial it back. A lot. Brett filed a complaint with his supervisor, so hopefully he'll calm down."

"Wow." Jillian was touched at the knowledge the police chief had stepped in like that. She had no doubt Brett would go to bat for his officers, the same way Melissa had when necessary, but as CSI, Jillian wasn't one of his direct reports. The fact that he'd stood up for her behind the scenes made her feel supported and gave her hope that the people she worked with didn't all view her as a criminal.

Melissa smiled. "We're all pulling for you, Jillian." She sipped the last of her hot chocolate. "You've been through a lot lately, what with your dad coming back into your life and the constant stress of Randall Bowe lurking over us all. Just know that a lot of people believe you're innocent and are working hard to find a way to prove it."

Jillian's eyes stung and she blinked hard to keep the tears from falling. "Thank you," she said, her voice shaking a little. "That means a lot."

"Call me if you need anything," Melissa said as she got to her feet. "My days are a lot freer now that I'm not the chief of police anymore. I'd love to meet for coffee or lunch sometime."

"That sounds nice," Jillian replied as they walked to the door. "I'll probably give you a ring soon."

Melissa pulled her in for a quick hug in front of the café. "I'm this way," she said, pointing up the street.

"And I'm this way," Jillian said, nodding in the opposite direction.

"It really was good to see you," Melissa said. She studied Jillian's face for a moment, and Jillian got the impression she was searching for something. She tried to look strong—maybe Jillian just needed to fake it until she truly felt that way?

"It's going to be all right," she said, holding Jillian's gaze intently. "I know it doesn't seem like it right now, but Randall is not going to win."

"I know," Jillian said, assuring both her cousin and herself. "I'm going to keep fighting. I'm not going to let him take me down."

BALDWIN STOPPED AT the door to Jillian's condo, taken aback by the thumping music he could hear coming from within her place. She hadn't struck him as the type to dial up the volume and disturb her neighbors. It was still daytime, though, so it wasn't like she was hosting a rave at two in the morning.

He unlocked the door and let himself in, expecting to find her relaxing on the couch or maybe working in the kitchen. As he moved into the living room, he caught a glimpse of what she was doing and it stopped him in his tracks.

She was dressed in a bright blue sports bra and black leggings, her hair pulled off her face in a braid that hung midway down her back. Sweat glistened on her skin, and in the late-afternoon light streaming in from the windows, she looked like she was practically glowing.

Baldwin swallowed hard as he tracked the movement of a droplet of sweat as it slid down her neck and into her cleavage. He tore his glance away to look at the TV screen, and realized she was watching some kind of exercise video. It looked like a combination of kickboxing and high-intensity dance. Jillian moved in time to the instructor, making him think she'd done this particular workout before.

She looked like some kind of graceful warrior, the way she planted one foot and lifted her other leg in a waist-high kick. Then she bounced on the balls of her feet, making her breasts move invitingly. Baldwin felt the stirrings of arousal and realized he needed to stop watching her or he'd wind up embarrassing himself.

Just then, Jillian pivoted to face him as she punched out. She froze in midpunch, then completed the movement and turned back to continue with her workout.

Baldwin cleared his throat. "Sorry," he said loudly, so that she could hear him over the music. "I just got here. I didn't realize you'd be home yet."

"It's fine," she said, panting as she kicked, punched and twisted in her savage ballet. "I'll be done soon. The music won't be on much longer."

"Take your time," he muttered as he walked around her to get to the guest bedroom. He couldn't very well stand there and stare at her like some kind of creep.

He shut the door behind him and took several deep breaths, trying to subdue his libido. But the sight of Jillian Colton's long, lean body clad only in a few pieces of tight fabric was going to stay with him for a while. He'd seen the hint of her curves in that dress she'd worn this morning. Now, he'd gotten enough of an eyeful that he didn't have to rely on his imagination to fill in the blanks.

The sound of her panting breaths seemed to follow him into the room, making it hard to think. If he'd known she was going to be exercising, he could have mentally prepared himself for the encounter. But walking in and seeing her skin glistening with sweat and her figure on display was making his body respond in all kinds of annoying ways.

"Not gonna happen," he muttered. He was here to do a job, that was all. Jillian was nice to look at, but looking absolutely could not lead to touching.

It wasn't that Baldwin didn't enjoy sex; he was

quite happy to sleep with a willing woman. But he never mixed business with pleasure. Sex would be a distraction that would keep him from doing his job. Not only did he have a reputation to uphold, but this case was also personal. If he let down his guard and succumbed to the temptation of seducing Jillian, Randall would have an advantage over him. And that was a thought that Baldwin simply could not tolerate.

The room seemed to vibrate with the thumping bass of her music, the walls pulsing in time to his heartbeat. He needed a distraction, and fast.

Shower. That would do it. He needed one before dinner, anyway. Might as well get it out of the way now. Perhaps the cold water would help cool his libido.

He grabbed a towel and his toiletries and opened his door. He deliberately kept his eyes focused on the floor, the wall, anything but the sight of Jillian only a few feet away, still kicking and bouncing in time to her video.

He ducked into the bathroom like a man evading enemy fire and closed the door behind him. The drone of the water soon helped muffle the lingering sounds of her workout, but he could still hear the echoes of her breathing in his head. That sexy, panting little gasp was going to haunt his dreams tonight—he just knew it.

Baldwin stepped under the cold spray of water, gritting his teeth against the chill. Focus on the job, he told himself. After he'd brought Randall into custody, he could indulge in some carnal pleasures.

Until then, he was going to embrace his inner monk.

No matter how tempting he found Jillian Colton.

Chapter Seven

"This place is nice," Baldwin remarked as they walked into the Grave Gulch Grill.

Jillian nodded. "Definitely a step up from the diner. Nothing against Mae, but she's a little too practical for tablecloths and a fireplace."

Baldwin chuckled. "I imagine syrup and ketchup leave a lot of stains."

They approached the hostess station and Baldwin said, "We have a reservation under Bowe."

Jillian gaped at him. A reservation? When had that happened? She'd assumed they'd simply show up and grab a table. But it seemed he'd put more thought into this dinner.

She eyed him as the hostess led them to their table—a small spot right next to the large bay windows facing the street. As they took their seats, Jillian couldn't help but feel like they were on display.

"Did you ask for this spot?" she said softly after the woman had walked away. "We're very visible."

Baldwin winked at her as he opened his menu. "That's the plan, remember?"

Her stomach did a funny little flip. *Get a grip*, she told herself. *The man winked. That's all.*

Still, she'd felt a kind of nervous energy ever since he'd caught her working out. She hadn't planned on him seeing her like that; when she'd arrived home to find the place empty, she'd been so restless and frustrated that she'd figured a quick exercise session would help settle her mood. And it had worked, right up until the point she'd turned and seen Baldwin standing in the doorway, his icy gaze tracking her every movement.

He'd been dark and dangerous, the gleam in his eyes making him look like some kind of predator. Jillian's body had responded accordingly, her muscles locking as she froze in shock. For a brief, unhinged second she'd considered running, hoping he would chase her. Then her brain had taken control once more and she'd forced herself to continue exercising.

Knowing he was in the shower hadn't helped things. She'd walked past the bathroom door on the way to her room, pausing slightly as she'd entertained the ridiculous fantasy of letting herself in. It wasn't hard to imagine him naked, water running over his broad shoulders and down the valley of his spine. Did he have chest hair? Or was it all smooth skin and muscles? It was a question that was probably going to keep her up tonight...

"Jillian?"

She shook herself free of the memories and focused on the present once more. "Sorry, yes?"

A small smile crossed Baldwin's face. "Where'd you go?"

"Oh, just thinking about something that happened earlier today." Heat crept up her neck and she ducked behind the menu to hide the blush that was sure to follow.

"How did the meeting with your lawyer go?" he asked.

"About as well as could be expected," she said, risking a glance. He was reading his own menu, seemingly oblivious to her reaction. "Things don't look great for me right now."

Baldwin frowned and looked up to meet her eyes. "We'll get him," he said confidently. "Randall isn't going to get away with this."

"That's what my cousin Melissa said," she replied. "I ran into her and we had a drink together. She seemed convinced the truth would come out."

"It usually does," Baldwin said, studying his menu again. "Sooner or later."

Jillian envied his certainty. Both he and Melissa had a kind of breezy confidence that everything would work out in the end. It was an attitude she herself had once held, right up until she'd been framed for robbery and now faced the prospect of prison. Since her circumstances had changed, she no longer had the luxury of embracing such platitudes.

A waitress stopped by their table and they ordered drinks. Jillian noticed the way the young woman subtly eyed Baldwin, her tongue darting out to moisten her lips when she spoke to him. Jillian couldn't exactly fault her response; he looked especially good tonight. This was the first time she'd seen him in anything other than a dark T-shirt and jeans, and the white dress shirt, slacks and sport coat gave him a classically handsome look. Not for the first time, she was glad she'd made an effort tonight, if for no other reason than to make their pairing more believable to anyone looking.

They made small talk until their drinks arrived, and then they ordered food. Once they were alone again, Jillian decided to ask a question that had been nagging her most of the day.

"You know, it's funny," she said, taking a sip of wine. "My attorney told me there's security footage from the last robbery, but the person on the tapes is dressed all in black and has a mask on. Since Randall and I have similar shapes, they can't prove it's not me."

Baldwin nodded. "But they can't prove it is you, either," he pointed out.

"I guess." She waved that way. "Don't you think it's a little odd that you and Randall look so different? I mean, he's about my height and thin, whereas you're…" She trailed off, gesturing up and down to encompass his body, which, to her eyes, was the exact opposite of his brother's.

Baldwin shrugged. "We've never resembled each other. He looks more like our father, whereas I've got our mom's coloring. For whatever reason, I put on muscle easily in high school. But then again, I worked at it. I played several sports, while Randall was more into studying. Then I joined the military, and fitness is a big part of being a marine. So while I can't help the fact that I'm taller than Randall, I think if he devoted any time to working out he'd probably bulk up a little more."

"That doesn't sound like something he'd be at all interested in doing," Jillian said with a laugh. "I got the impression he hated physical activity of any kind. Anytime we had to collect evidence from a scene, he'd complain if it involved more than simply walking into a room and getting started."

"Seems about right," Baldwin remarked with a smile. "He's always preferred to stay indoors, reading a book or watching television."

"Whereas you're the outdoorsy type?"

He tilted his head to the side. "Well, I can tell you that marines aren't known for being sedentary. And I was definitely roughing it for most of my deployments."

"I can only imagine." Jillian shook her head. "There's no way I could serve in the military."

"Why's that?" There was a note of genuine curiosity in his tone. "You're smart. You're active. You could do it."

"I like hot showers and flushing toilets and air-conditioning," Jillian retorted. "It's also nice to not have people shooting at me."

Baldwin chuckled, the low rumble sending a tingle down her spine. "Fair enough," he replied.

They chatted until their food arrived. Jillian

had opted for chicken, while Baldwin had ordered a steak.

She took a bite and moaned slightly as the flavors hit her tongue. "This is fantastic," she mumbled around the food. Baldwin watched her chew, amusement in his eyes. She swallowed and wiped her mouth. "Sorry, I was really hungry."

"I'm glad you like it," he said, cutting into his steak.

They ate in silence for a few minutes until he spoke. "I've been meaning to ask, why crime-scene investigation? It's kind of an unusual field. What made you get into it?"

Jillian leaned back a bit, surprised by the question. Up until now, Baldwin hadn't seemed all that interested in her life, outside of how she could help him get his brother. But she had asked him questions about his family and time in the military. Perhaps he was simply trying to deflect?

"I've always enjoyed science," she began, taking a sip of wine. "I had thought about going to medical school and becoming a doctor, but I really enjoyed working in a lab and at crime scenes. A lot of my family is in law enforcement, as you know. And I guess through them, I became aware of CSI and realized that it would be a good fit for me. I get to help people and still be at the bench." She shrugged. "I have to say, I do love my job. It's a lot nicer now that your brother is gone."

"I imagine so," Baldwin said. "Based on what you've told me about how he treated you."

She studied him for a second, watching his Adam's apple move in his throat as he swallowed. "You're not like him at all, you know?" she mused. "Not just physically. Your personalities are polar opposites."

Randall was cool, aloof and vindictive. Baldwin was serious and focused. And while she'd initially thought he lacked emotion, she was beginning to realize her first impression had been too harsh. Baldwin *did* feel; he just tried not to show it. But she'd caught glimpses of him when he didn't know she was looking, and in those unguarded moments, she'd seen humor, desire and compassion. Certainly more humanity than she'd ever seen Randall display.

"Like I told you from the beginning," Baldwin said quietly. "I'm not my brother."

"I know that now," Jillian replied. "And I'm sorry I keep comparing you to him. You deserve better."

Surprise flashed across his face and he blinked at her. "I..." He trailed off. Then he shook his head. "Thank you," he said simply.

They finished their meals, and the waitress brought over dessert menus. Jillian began to demur, but Baldwin caught her gaze. "We're on a date, remember?" he said softly.

"Fair enough," she said. It was strange; this morning, when he'd suggested dinner, she'd figured it would be an awkward, torturous affair. In actuality, though, she'd enjoyed spending time with Baldwin and getting to know him a little better. Her trust in him was growing, that was certain.

As was her attraction.

She focused on the menu, pushing aside that annoying realization. "What looks good to you?" she asked. "I can't decide between the crème brûlée or the cheesecake."

"Why don't you order one and I'll get the other? We can share them both," he suggested.

Jillian arched an eyebrow. "You don't strike me as the sharing type," she said teasingly.

"Let's just say I'm willing to make some sacrifices." Baldwin grinned, and for the first time, Jillian noticed the dimple in his left cheek. For a moment, she forgot he was a single-minded bounty hunter and instead saw him as a charming, handsome man. One who made her skin tingle and her stomach quaver with nervous anticipation. Once again, she reminded herself that this was just an act.

But who said she couldn't enjoy herself a bit while it lasted?

It didn't take long for their desserts to arrive. Baldwin tasted the cheesecake and made a low sound in his throat. "This is really good."

Jillian couldn't help but smile at his reaction. Before she knew what was happening, Baldwin had scooped a bite of cheesecake onto his fork and leaned over the table, offering it to her.

"Here you go," he said softly, his blue eyes warm.

Jillian held his gaze as she leaned forward and took the bite. Her lips tingled with awareness as they touched the fork, the tines still warm from his mouth. It was a quintessential date move, one she knew he was playing up for their potential audience. So why did she see desire flash across his face as he watched her eat?

Warmth spread through her, along with a hunger for an entirely different kind of dessert. *It's the wine*, she decided. She'd only had one glass, but she didn't usually drink. It had to be affecting her—that was the only reason she was responding to Baldwin so strongly. She knew this was all an act, but her body seemed to have forgotten that point.

"Well?" he asked.

"It's really good," she said, swallowing the sweet bite. "Maybe we should trade?"

He laughed, genuinely laughed, for perhaps the first time since she'd met him. It was an infectious sound, one she wouldn't mind hearing again. "You haven't even tried yours yet," he pointed out.

"So I take it that's a *no*?"

Baldwin shook his head and pushed his plate to the center of the table. "It's fine," he said, smiling indulgently. "I like to watch you eat."

Jillian swapped the cheesecake for the crème brûlée, unsure of how to react to his statement. On one hand, she was flattered that he paid that much attention to her. But now that she knew he was looking, she felt self-conscious.

"You're going to give me a complex," she muttered. "I'm not used to having an audience."

"Don't worry about it," Baldwin replied as he used his spoon to break the caramelized crust of the dessert. "Mmm," he said after the first bite. "You do what you want with the cheesecake. I'm going to stay focused on this."

Jillian watched him from under her lashes, unable to look away as pleasure flitted across his face. He closed his eyes briefly, clearly enjoying himself. It was an expression she'd never seen him wear before, and her imagination ran with it.

A dark room, Baldwin moving over her, his eyes closed as he...

"Change your mind?"

She jumped at the question and realized she hadn't eaten again since he'd given her the cheesecake. "No," she said, forking off another bite. "Just pacing myself." *And having inappropriate fantasies about you,* she added silently.

They finished their desserts in companionable silence. The waitress dropped the check at their table. Jillian reached for it, but Baldwin placed a large hand on the small leather folder, preventing her from touching it.

"My treat," he said.

"Thank you," Jillian replied, knowing there was no point in arguing with him. They were supposed to be on a date, after all, so it made sense for him to pick up the tab.

An unexpected pang of reluctance hit her as they stood to leave. This had been a surprisingly nice experience, one she didn't want to end quite yet. Even though she understood they were both playing a part, she'd enjoyed spending time with Baldwin and seeing a different side of him. Now that she knew a little more about him, it was hard to think of him as a laser-focused automaton.

They stepped out to the sidewalk just as a cold gust of wind blasted down the street. Jillian shivered, wishing she'd thought to bring a coat. She ducked her head and squared her shoulders against the wind, hoping Baldwin wouldn't mind if they double-timed it to the car.

But just as she'd taken a step, the intensity of the wind eased. A pair of shoes came into her view and she glanced up into Baldwin's eyes.

"Here," he said, shrugging out of his sports coat. "You're shivering."

"I—" She'd started to protest, knowing he'd likely now be cold. But as he draped the warm fabric around her shoulders, she sighed involuntarily. The jacket was far too big for her, but it enveloped her like a warm hug, and it smelled like Baldwin.

He leaned forward, arranging the fabric. The movement brought his face closer to hers, and she angled her head slightly to close the distance between them.

Baldwin sucked in a breath as their lips nearly touched. They stood there for a moment, breathing each other's air, hovering on the edge of a moment that could change everything between them.

Jillian felt a pull, almost as if Baldwin was tugging on the lapels of his jacket to bring her closer. She practically ached to kiss him, to feel the pressure of his mouth on hers. But she held back, unable to move that last half inch.

Time seemed to stop as they stood frozen, locked in this possibility. Baldwin's lips parted, his eyes warm as he looked down at her.

It would be so very easy to close the distance. To lift her head up, to brush her mouth across his. Her head spun with the thought of it.

She was tempted to blame her reaction on the wine, but any lingering effects from her drink had disappeared when the cold wind had hit her cheeks. No, she couldn't blame this on alcohol. She wanted Baldwin. Wanted to feel his strong body pressed against hers, wanted to run her hands along the solid warmth of his chest and arms. To know what it was like to have his arms around her.

But she just couldn't give in.

If she cast off her self-control and kissed him, she had no doubt he'd kiss her back. And kissing would lead to touching, and touching would lead straight to her bed. As tempting as that thought was, she was certain the morning after would prove awkward and uncomfortable. Who knew how much longer he'd have to live with her before Randall made his move? With everything in her life so unsettled right now, the last thing she wanted was to add more drama.

Baldwin let out a little sigh. He lifted one hand and gently brushed a strand of windswept hair off her cheek, pushing it behind her ear. "Let's go," he said softly. "Don't want you to freeze out here."

Jillian pushed down her rising disappointment and started walking alongside him. It was the right choice—she knew that. Still, a small part of her wished she'd thrown caution to the wind. At least she'd have had a nice memory to look back on later.

They made it to the end of the block when a loud bang split the air. Jillian jumped at the sound, startled. Before she could even turn her head to try to locate the source, Baldwin grabbed her arm and yanked her into the doorway of a nearby shop. He pressed her into the corner and stood in front of her, his back a solid wall shielding her from the sidewalk and the street. Her heart thumped hard in her chest as she craned her neck to see around him. She just managed to catch a glimpse of a car pulling out of a parking spot a few feet away. Its headlights passed over them as the driver took off down the road, apparently oblivious to the scene unfolding behind him.

She felt Baldwin relax as it became clear the sound they'd heard had been the vehicle backfiring. He stepped away, then turned and looked down at her. She couldn't see his face in the shadows of the alcove, but his voice was still tense.

"You okay?"

Jillian took a half step forward so her back was no longer pressed against the rough brick of the building. "Yeah," she said. Her nerves were starting to settle, now that she knew Randall wasn't shooting at them. "What about you?" He'd reacted so quickly to the noise—was that his training kicking in, or did loud noises in general bother him after his time in the military?

"I'm fine," he said shortly. "We should keep moving. I think we've been out long enough for tonight."

He took her hand, but there was nothing soft or romantic about the gesture. His grip wasn't painful, but it was the impersonal touch of someone doing a job.

Jillian walked quickly to keep up with the pace he set, each step taking them farther away from the restaurant and those enjoyable shared moments of conversation and food. Part of her was sad at the realization that their evening was at an end. She'd genuinely liked seeing Baldwin let down his hair, so to speak. It was unlikely he'd act that away around her again, not now that he was back in professional mode.

It's for the best, she told herself as Baldwin unlocked the doors to his truck and helped her climb inside. Far better to keep things the way they were now, rather than risk making a move she was guaranteed to regret later.

Her frustrated libido was just going to have to learn to live with disappointment.

BALDWIN FLIPPED HIS pillow over with a sigh, wishing his body would just relax already. But his mind was too active, thinking about this case and the woman down the hall.

Dinner with Jillian had been nice. He'd actually enjoyed himself, something he hadn't thought possible. Usually when he was working, he was totally focused on the job at hand. Anything he did was in service to finding his target. So when he'd suggested they go to a restaurant tonight to bait his brother into making a move, Baldwin had assumed it would be just another work function for him.

But it wasn't.

If he was being honest with himself, the trouble had started this morning, when Jillian had come into the kitchen wearing that sweater dress. Then, to add to his temptation, he'd seen her working out in a sports bra and leggings, with a lot more skin on display. She'd looked even better at dinner, with her hair worn down in loose waves framing her face. He could have stared at her all night and not gotten tired of the view.

Try as he might, Baldwin was finding it harder and harder to ignore Jillian.

And she wasn't as prickly as he'd first thought her to be. When they'd had breakfast together, she'd been a little sarcastic and even a bit defensive. She'd given off big leave-me-alone energy, which had been fine by him. Now, though, he realized her night in jail had rattled her more than she'd wanted to admit. His mistake had been assuming that once things calmed down, she'd keep those walls up.

But if tonight was any indication, she was warming to him. Quite a bit.

He'd seen that flash of desire in her eyes when he'd put his jacket around her shoulders. Heard her breath hitch as their mouths almost touched. She'd wanted him. If he had closed the distance and kissed her, she would have fallen into his arms, and probably into his bed.

So why hadn't he made a move?

It was the question his hormones had been asking ever since they'd arrived back at her condo and gone their separate ways for the night. It would have been so easy to lean forward and brush his lips against hers. She was beautiful—but more than that, she was smart and funny. He wanted her—he could no longer deny it. And she wanted him, too. Or at least, she had in that moment.

But something had kept him from taking the leap. He knew on a subconscious level that just one kiss with Jillian wouldn't be enough. And, as much as he enjoyed the thought of taking her to bed, sex would change things between them. So far, they'd found a kind of balance with each other. But if they slept together, the equilibrium would be destroyed. It wasn't a step he wanted to take, especially since he had no idea when Randall was going to make his move.

So as frustrating as it was, he'd made the right choice. Better to lie here alone and unsatisfied than give in to temptation and ruin the dynamic he had with Jillian.

Now if he could just scrub his memory of the images of her in that sports bra, or her dress, or somehow forget the sense of possession he'd felt as she'd worn his jacket…

He rolled onto his side, wishing his brain had an off switch. While he was in the marines, he'd had no problem dropping off to sleep whenever and wherever the opportunity presented itself. Now that he was back in the civilian world, he'd lost that particular skill.

Baldwin closed his eyes, determined to win this battle. But his attention immediately shifted as he heard a quiet scratching.

What was that?

He sat up in bed, listening hard. People generally thought the middle of the night was a time of silence, but he knew better. Was one of Jillian's neighbors doing something? Or was it the heater kicking on?

He heard the noise again, a little louder this time. Baldwin slipped out of bed and crept to the door. This wasn't one of the normal sounds Jillian's condo made at night. Something was going on in the living room, or maybe the kitchen.

Randall. It's got to be him.

It seemed their little ruse had worked.

Moving quietly, Baldwin opened the top dresser drawer and took out his gun. There was a chance Jillian was foraging for a midnight snack, but since he hadn't heard her walk past his bedroom door, he'd bet his last dollar that his brother had come to call.

Baldwin silently opened the door and slid into the hall, careful to stick to the shadows. As he moved out of the bedroom, the sounds grew louder.

Kitchen, he realized. A soft clinking of glass and the sound of drawers opening made him think whoever was in there was rummaging around.

A sense of eagerness began to rise in his chest, but he tamped down the feeling. Thanks to his time in the military, he knew how to channel his adrenaline, to keep it from interfering with his job. At least he'd retained *that* ability.

The wall that divided the kitchen from the living room was only waist-high. As Baldwin crept closer, he saw Randall, his back to the living room, reaching for something in one of the cupboards.

Taking advantage of his brother's position, Baldwin quickly crossed the living room and entered the kitchen near the small table at the far end.

"Looking for something?" he asked.

Randall jumped, dropping the glass he held. It hit the floor and shattered, shards flying everywhere.

"Let me guess," Baldwin said. "You're here for another source of prints. What are you going to frame Jillian for this time?"

Randall glared at him from across the room. "It's not her I'm after."

Realization dawned. "Oh," Baldwin said softly. "You're going to set *me* up now?" He waited to feel surprised, but the emotion didn't come. And why would it? He and Randall had never had a good relationship. Randall's attempt to frame him was just the latest in a long line of grievances between them.

He shook his head, torn between the desire to laugh and yell. "For what it's worth, you're not very good at this. I haven't touched those glasses."

Randall's eyes narrowed. "You're lying."

"Am I? It doesn't matter." Baldwin lifted his gun, pointing it at his brother. His heart squeezed a bit, but he quickly strangled any residual sense of sentimentality. Randall might be his brother, but he definitely wasn't a good guy. He'd brought this on himself.

"You're done," he said.

Randall eyed the gun distastefully. "Really? You're going to shoot me?"

"If I have to," Baldwin replied evenly. He didn't want to pull the trigger—hell, he never really wanted to shoot anybody, much less a family member. But he carried a weapon because he was prepared to use it if need be. Hopefully Randall wouldn't force the issue.

Randall leaned against the counter. "How do you think this is going to work? Do you imagine I'll just throw my hands up and surrender? That you'll shove me in the back of your truck and take me to the police station?"

"That would be the easy way," Baldwin agreed.

"Have I ever made things easy for you?" Randall taunted.

Baldwin's tightened his grip on the gun, certain his brother was going to try something. Randall had known breaking into Jillian's condo would be a risk, especially now that Baldwin was here. So he had to have some plan in place, to deal with the possibility of discovery. Baldwin just had to figure out what it was before Randall could get away.

"You're not as smart as you think you are," he said, hitting Randall where it knew it would hurt the most.

Anger flashed in his brother's eyes as the insult hit home. "And you're not as strong as you think you are," he spluttered.

"Maybe so, but at least I know when I'm beaten." Baldwin took a half step forward, keeping the gun level as he moved.

Randall laughed. "You think that's what is happening here? That you've beaten me?"

The flicker of worry grew stronger as Baldwin watched his brother. It dawned on him then that Randall's right hand was down by his side, effectively hidden from view. Did Randall have something in his pocket? Some device or weapon he thought was going to protect him? "Show me your hand," he demanded.

Randall looked simultaneously amused and bored. "What?"

"Your right hand," Baldwin insisted. "Lift it up so I can see it. Do it slowly."

Randall narrowed his eyes. "When have I ever taken orders from you?"

Baldwin opened his mouth to respond, but before he could get the words out, the situation went from bad to worse.

Jillian walked into the living room, rubbing her eyes. "Baldwin, are you hungry?" she asked.

His heart leaped into his throat at the sight of her. She had to get out of here. He could *feel* that Randall was about to make his move, and he wanted Jillian as far away as possible when his brother acted.

She looked up and saw him, then glanced over and noticed Randall. She froze, her whole body going tense as she realized who was standing in her kitchen. *"You."* The word was laced with so much venom it was a wonder Randall didn't drop dead on the spot.

Randall gave her a wave. "Nice to see you again," he said cheerily.

"Jillian," Baldwin said sternly. "Go back to bed."

Either she didn't hear him or she ignored him, because she remained rooted to the spot, glaring at Randall. "What the hell are you doing here?" she demanded.

"Just popping in for a visit," Randall said. "But don't worry, I'm leaving now."

"No, you're not." Both Baldwin and Jillian spoke at the same time. He returned his focus to Randall, taking another step forward.

Something—was it jealousy?—flashed across Randall's face. "You two make quite the pair," he said quietly.

"Jillian, go get your phone and call the police," Baldwin commanded.

Randall rolled his eyes. "Really, brother? Could you be more predictable?"

Jillian didn't move, and Baldwin risked a glance in her direction. "Jillian?"

"My phone is on the counter," she said, sounding pained.

"Right next to me," Randall disclosed, nodding at the device near him. "You know, you really should be more careful about where you leave things," he continued. "You always were sloppy, Jillian. That's why you'll never make a good CSI tech."

It was a low blow, one Baldwin hoped she wouldn't internalize. He knew how hard she'd worked to overcome the insecurities Randall had cultivated while they worked together. Hopefully, she now realized he was simply trying to gain the upper hand.

"Go to my room," Baldwin instructed her. "My phone is on the dresser." He didn't want her anywhere near Randall. If she got close to his brother, there was no telling what Randall might try to do to her.

Before she took a step, Randall spoke again. "You know what? This has been fun, but I'm bored. Time for me to go." With that, he raised his right hand, and a sense of horror washed over Baldwin as he realized his brother had drawn a gun.

Time seemed to stop as Randall aimed at Jillian. Baldwin screamed at his body to move—he needed to get to her and push her out of harm's way. But he was too slow.

Randall fired, the sound booming through the room like a thunderclap. Jillian jerked back, her mouth open in surprise. Then she started to fall.

Baldwin glanced over and saw Randall's back as he left the condo. A clinical, detached part of him knew he should pursue his brother. They might not get another chance like this, and Randall was still so close…

But he couldn't do it. All his training went out the window as he looked over in time to see Jillian land on the floor.

The instant her body hit the carpet, it was as though someone had snapped their fingers. Time started again, and Baldwin's legs responded to his brain's commands. In two steps he was by her side, tucking his gun into the waistband at the small of his back as he kneeled down to assess the damage.

She stared up at him, her face contorted with pain and confusion. The fabric of her pajama top was quickly becoming saturated with blood, making it hard for him to see exactly where she was injured. He grasped at the neckline of the shirt and ripped it apart, exposing her left shoulder. A small, neat hole marred the skin there, her blood welling up to fill the space.

Cursing at the sight, Baldwin quickly stripped off his T-shirt and hastily folded it into something approximating a bandage. Then he pressed it over her wound, pushing down hard.

Jillian's eyes went wide and he felt, more than heard, her moan. His ears were still ringing from the gunshot, and he imagined hers were, too. "It's okay," he said loudly. "You're going to be fine. I've seen worse."

It was true, but part of him was still panicking. He knew how quickly a seemingly simple injury could go south, and turn into something life-threatening. If the bullet had nicked an artery, or if she went into shock from the experience... He had to call an ambulance. The sooner she got to the hospital, the better.

Baldwin grabbed her right hand and held it on top of his T-shirt. "I have to get the phone," he said.

Tears welled in Jillian's eyes and she shook her head. "No," she said, her voice laced with pain. "Please don't leave me."

"I'll be right back," he promised. "You won't even

know I was gone." Then he pulled away, before the look on her face trapped him there.

He grabbed his phone from the dresser and returned in a matter of seconds, resuming his spot by her side. His heart thumped hard in his chest as he pressed one hand over hers to hold the makeshift bandage in place and used his other hand to dial.

How had things gotten so bad so quickly? How had he let Randall get the upper hand? As soon as he'd seen the gun, he should have fired. He was a trained marksman, much more experienced than Randall. He could have gotten off a shot and incapacitated his brother before Randall had taken his next breath.

But he'd been distracted. He'd let his worry and fear for Jillian take over, and pushed his instincts to the side.

And Randall had taken advantage of his weakness.

"Nine-one-one, what's your emergency?"

Baldwin quickly relayed the situation, his calm voice at odds with his internal chaos. If Jillian died… He shook his head, casting away the errant thought. She wasn't going to die from his mistake. She couldn't.

The operator wanted him to remain on the line until the ambulance arrived. Baldwin put the phone on Speaker and set it on the floor so he could use both hands to apply pressure to Jillian's injury.

"Baldwin." Her voice was strained, the sound

breaking his heart. Tears dripped from the corners of her eyes into her hair.

"I know it hurts," he said, trying to soothe her. He'd been grazed by bullets before, but he'd never taken a direct hit. The pain had to be nearly unbearable.

Jillian slid her hand out from under his and gripped his forearm, and he realized she wanted him to lean down. He lowered his head, his gaze locked on her eyes as he got closer.

"Go after him," she said firmly. "Get that bastard."

He nearly laughed. He was supposed to be the one worried about his job, not her. But, in this moment, their roles were reversed.

Baldwin shook his head. "I'm not leaving you," he said. "Not until the paramedics arrive." At that point, he could reassess the situation. Randall was gone, but perhaps he'd left some kind of clue as to where he was hiding.

Surprise glimmered in Jillian's eyes, a mirror of his own feelings. Since when had he let his worry for someone outweigh his sense of duty? Jillian's injury might be painful, but he could see now it wasn't lethal—the bleeding was already under control. He could have easily left her there while he searched for Randall, and he might have even caught up to his brother if he'd left after dialing 911.

So why was he still here, holding her hand and trying to reassure himself that she was going to be okay?

He gradually became aware of the operator's voice calling to him from the phone. "Sir? Sir? Are you there?"

"Yes." He picked up the phone and brought it closer to his mouth. "I'm here. What do you need?"

"The EMTs are entering the building," the woman said. "Can you make sure the door to the condo is unlocked and unobstructed?"

Jillian nodded at him, returning her hand to the shirt so she could continue to apply pressure. "Yeah," Baldwin said. "I can do that."

He got to his feet, feeling a little off balance as he walked to the door to open it. The squawk of a radio floated in the air of the hallway outside her door, and he knew the EMTs were getting close.

That was good. Baldwin needed someone to take over Jillian's care, because he was feeling so flustered, he wasn't sure how much longer he could stay focused. After propping open her door, he walked back into the living room. The sight of her lying on the ground, blood staining her carpet and her shirt, hit him anew and he started to shake, a fine tremor running through his muscles.

Fortunately, the paramedics arrived. Two men nudged past him and kneeled to assess Jillian. Baldwin hung back, giving them space to work. But as they started tending to her, Jillian started looking around, clearly searching for something.

It's me, he realized with a start. *She's looking for me.* Even though it was his fault she'd been hurt tonight, she still wanted to see him.

"I'm here," he called out. He walked over to stand a few steps behind one of the medics, making it easy for Jillian to see him.

The instant their eyes connected, he saw her body relax. And the strange thing was, his did, too.

He wasn't sure how long he stood there, holding her gaze while the medics did their thing. The police arrived and he explained what had happened, but he never moved, never looked away from Jillian. Some irrational part of him was afraid that if he stopped watching her, the EMTs would whisk her away and he'd turn back to find her gone.

"You'll need to get your crime-scene people in here," he said. "Make sure they dust for prints in the kitchen and on the door handle." Randall hadn't been wearing gloves, which was a mistake on his part. One that would prove helpful to Jillian's case. Surely her attorney could use this break-in to lend weight to the idea that Randall was framing Jillian?

"Let's go," one of the medics said. They had rolled Jillian onto a gurney, which the two men lifted to waist height as they stood. They started wheeling her out of the room and Baldwin moved to follow.

"Hey," said one of the officers he'd been talking to. "You need to stay here and finish giving your statement."

"No," he said shortly.

"Sir—" the other officer began, but Baldwin cut her off with a wave of his hand.

"I go where she goes," he declared.

At that moment, Brett Shea arrived. He stopped

at the gurney and murmured something to Jillian, then made his way toward Baldwin. "I just got the call," he said. "What happened?"

Baldwin shook his head. "Can't talk now. But it was Randall."

Brett's eyes widened in understanding as Baldwin moved past. "Keep this place secured, Chief," Baldwin called out. "He might try to come back."

"I hope so," Brett replied grimly.

Baldwin grabbed Jillian's purse from the kitchen counter and jogged after the gurney as the medics rolled Jillian down the hallway. As soon as they got into the ambulance, he was going to message a friend and ask him to watch over Jillian's condo. There was no way Randall would come back tonight, not with all the activity going on now. But the police had to leave eventually, and with Jillian in the hospital, he'd have the perfect opportunity to steal prints again for another setup.

Baldwin wasn't going to let his brother get away again. And as much as Chief Shea wanted to apprehend Randall, Baldwin wasn't going to let that happen either.

You're mine, he thought darkly, picturing Randall's face. *Now it's personal.*

Chapter Eight

"When can I go home?"

The young doctor sighed behind his surgical mask as he finished stitching the hole in her shoulder. "Ms. Colton—" he began.

"Please?" Jillian interrupted. "I'd just really like to sleep in my own bed tonight. Or what's left of it."

The hemostat and scissors made a little clinking sound as the doctor placed them on a metal tray. "I know you do," he said, reaching for the gauze squares and medical tape. "But you were shot tonight. You lost quite a bit of blood at the scene, and since you'll be getting a transfusion, we have to keep you for observation for a few hours at least."

"So maybe by lunchtime?" she asked hopefully.

"We'll see," the doctor replied evasively.

"Just rest and enjoy the pain relievers," Baldwin suggested from his spot in the corner.

He'd been standing there since they'd brought her into the emergency room, a tall, silent form watching over everything. She hadn't expected him to accompany her to the hospital—she'd assumed he'd stay behind or try to go after his brother. But he'd hopped up into the ambulance bay with the gurney, and the EMT had taken one look at Baldwin's face and swallowed any objection he might have had. It had been the same story once they'd arrived at the ER—Baldwin had silently but firmly made it known that he was staying, and Jillian had given permission for him to do so. Since he wasn't getting in the way, the staff didn't seem to mind his presence.

"I'm not going to be able to rest," she grumbled. "Not knowing that Randall is out there, waiting to break back into my condo." Just the thought of Randall lurking in the shadows of her building made her stomach cramp.

"No, he won't." Baldwin explained he'd recruited one of his friends in the area to watch her place from afar, to stop Randall if he did try to come back.

"That does make me feel better," she admitted. "You seem to think of everything."

Baldwin shrugged one shoulder.

"You're all set here," the doctor said. He pulled off his gloves and eyed her bandage appraisingly. "You'll want to see your regular doctor in a few days to get the stitches out, and in the meantime, keep the area clean and dry. The nurses will teach you how and when to change the bandage."

"Does that mean I can go? I feel fine." She sat up eagerly, hoping maybe the doctor had changed his mind.

The man shook his head. "We've been over this," he said. "You feel good now because of the drugs we've given you. Once those start to wear off, you'll be singing a different tune. Besides, your lab work shows you need blood. If I were to release you now, you'd probably pass out on the way."

Jillian knew he was right, but it didn't change the fact that she was desperate to go home. "Okay," she said.

The doctor offered her a smile. "I'll go see if the blood bank has sent up your bag yet."

"Thank you," she said as he left the room.

Baldwin's gaze was steady on her. "Why are you so eager to leave? You're safe here, and I've got someone taking care of your place."

"I know." She looked away, searching for the words to explain how she felt. "I just… I need to reclaim my home. Does that make sense?"

He tilted his head to the side. "In a way."

"Your brother…" She trailed off, then shook her head. Baldwin and Randall might share genetic ties, but she needed to stop linking the two men together beyond that. Baldwin deserved better.

"Randall broke into my home," she continued. "He touched my things. And now I'm absolutely convinced it's not the first time he's done so. I feel like my safe space has been violated, and I need to scrub the place clean of any reminder of his presence. Not to mention, a CSI investigation leaves behind a bit of a mess."

Baldwin nodded. "I'll help you." He paused, then cleared his throat. "That is, if you'll let me…?" He looked almost shy, as though he was worried that she might take offense at his offer.

She blinked, surprised at the question. "I would appreciate it," she said. "But you don't have to indulge my weird quirk."

"It's not weird," Baldwin said. "Randall destroyed your peace of mind. If cleaning your place will help restore it, then I want to help you. Besides," he added, sauntering over to the side of the bed as the corner of his mouth turned up in a grin, "you're pretty much down to one hand now. You need me."

"That's true," she acknowledged. She *did* need him, and for more than just help with the housework. She'd been on the edge of panic when Randall had shot her—between the pain and fear and shock of it all, she'd felt herself slipping into hysteria. But Baldwin's presence had kept her grounded. There was something about him that made her feel safe and protected. Even though she'd been lying there, bleeding on her rug, Baldwin's touch and voice had made her believe that she was going to come through this. She didn't understand why or how, but in the short time she'd known him, she'd come to trust him.

Maybe it was because he didn't lie to her. He'd been honest from the beginning about what he wanted from her and what he was prepared to do. While she'd initially found his honesty off-putting, she'd come to realize it was a gift. Baldwin had always told her the truth, so when he'd kneeled over her and said she was going to be okay, she'd believed him without question.

He took her hand now, his touch gentle as he stroked his thumb across her knuckles. "Jillian, there's something I need to tell you." His voice was gruff, as though the words pained him.

She could tell by the look on his face that whatever Baldwin had to say, it was going to be serious. "All right," she replied. "What's going on?"

Baldwin took a deep breath, clearly bracing himself. "It's my fault you got hurt tonight. I didn't think Randall had a weapon, and when I realized he was pointing a gun at you, I should have taken my shot." He shook his head. "I hesitated, and I'm so very sorry." He looked positively miserable, and she could practically feel the guilt coming off him in waves.

Her first instinct was to laugh—surely he didn't really think he was responsible for her injury? Except… he did. His eyes were troubled, and his lips were pressed together in a thin line. His powerful shoulders slumped, and Jillian got the impression that if she told him to go away and never return, he would.

For a man who claimed not to care about anyone, Baldwin was doing a very good impression of a guy with feelings.

"Baldwin," she said. It was important she take this seriously; she didn't want him to think she was dismissing his concerns out of hand. "I don't blame you for what happened."

"I should have acted faster," he said, apparently determined to flog himself for his perceived mistake.

"And done what?" she challenged. "Shot your brother?" Talk about a huge, life-altering decision.

He flinched at the question, so she pressed on. "Do you really think I'd blame you for not firing at your own family?"

Baldwin looked up, emotion swirling in his blue eyes. "I told you when we first met that I'd do anything to capture Randall. That I had no sense of obligation or loyalty to him."

"That doesn't mean you should be ready to shoot him," Jillian pointed out. "Even though your relationship is broken beyond repair, he's still your brother. You grew up with him. He's blood. Despite everything he's done, it's only natural you would hesitate when faced with the choice to kill him."

"I wouldn't have killed him," he grumbled.

Jillian nodded. "I know, I know. You're a marksman. I heard about your awards." She flipped her hand over so she could lace her fingers through his. "Look, I don't know anything about guns. I've never held one, much less fired one. But I imagine that shooting at someone is a big deal. And when you know the person you're aiming at, it's got to be even more complicated. I'm not going to blame you for what happened tonight. I hope you'll give yourself some grace and realize you're not at fault here." She squeezed his hand, and after a few seconds, he squeezed back.

"Thank you," he said quietly. "I'm not sure I deserve that."

"Yes, you do," she replied confidently. "Between the two of us, I'm the one in the hospital bed. That means I'm in charge."

His eyes glinted with amusement. "Are you sure? Because I don't think that doctor got the memo."

Jillian shrugged, then gasped as the movement tested the strength of the pain relievers she'd been given soon after arrival. Baldwin winced in sympathy. "Sounds like your meds are starting to wear off," he remarked.

"Maybe so," she said, breathing carefully so as not to further aggravate the situation.

"I'll see if I can find a nurse," he said, his expression worried as he watched her. "Maybe it's time for another dose."

Before she could lie and tell him that she was fine, he was out the door, a man on a mission. Once more, she was struck by the disconnect between Baldwin's gruff outer shell and his inner softie. She wasn't sure how she'd managed to get past his tough, no-nonsense exterior, but she was equal parts honored and tickled to know she'd affected him.

Not that it was all one-sided. No, he'd definitely slipped past her defenses, as well. In some twisted way, she was almost glad Randall had shown up tonight. His appearance had served to reset their focus, an adjustment she'd needed as she'd started to spend too much time fantasizing about Baldwin. Getting shot was definitely not her idea of fun, but it was a potent reminder of just what was at stake for her. She had to stop letting her hormones run the show and devote her energy to clearing her name.

In a matter of minutes, Baldwin was back. "I spoke to your nurse," he said, running a hand through his hair. "She said you can have more medication if you need it."

"I think I do," Jillian said. The ache in her shoulder was growing steadily worse, and if she wanted any chance of sleep tonight, it would help if she felt more relaxed. "You should go home. Get some rest."

Baldwin stared at her, his features twisted with disbelief. "Are you kidding me? Do you really think I'm going to leave you here alone tonight?"

A warm feeling started in Jillian's stomach and spread up into her chest. "You don't have to stay." She was touched by his offer, but didn't want him to stick around out of a sense of guilt or obligation.

"You're not getting rid of me," Baldwin replied, sinking into the chair by her bed. "But I have to say, I hope they put you in a room upstairs. I heard the chairs up there extend out into a makeshift bed." He stretched out his long legs and crossed them at the ankles, then leaned back and folded his hands over his flat stomach.

For one brief, irrational instant, Jillian considered inviting him to share her hospital bed. It wasn't terribly comfortable, but it had to be better than that stiff chair. Although, if she had Baldwin stretched out beside her, her body would be incapable of relaxing.

There was a tap at the door and a nurse entered, pushing a small cart piled with supplies. "All right," she said as she approached the bed. "Let's get you set up with this transfusion."

"If it's all the same to you," Jillian said, "I think I'll close my eyes. I'd rather not watch all of this."

"No problem, sweetie," she replied. "You just rest and I'll take care of everything."

Jillian took a deep breath and closed her eyes, trying not to think about the fact that a stranger's blood was about to be put into her veins. It was all for the best, she knew, but it was still an unsettling thought.

After a few seconds, she felt Baldwin's hand slip over her own. She sighed softly as the heat of his touch soaked into the muscles of her hand and seemed to radiate up her arm. "It's okay," he said quietly, his voice a low note in her ear. "I've got you."

"You okay, man?"

Baldwin cracked open one eye to see Bryce Colton standing in front of him, his brow furrowed.

Jillian's family had arrived soon after the nurse had set up the blood transfusion. Her mother had barged into the room first, followed closely by her sister, Bryce and her father. Baldwin had quietly slipped out the door, both to give them some time alone with Jillian and because he figured he was persona non grata to her family.

He'd found a chair in the empty waiting room and closed his eyes for lack of anything better to do. Now that Bryce was looking down on him, he wished he'd found a different spot. Like the cafeteria. Or another building.

Baldwin sat up and cleared his throat. "Yeah, I'm good." Bryce took the chair across from him, his arm in a sling. A hot sense of shame filled Baldwin as he realized that Jillian and her brother now had matching injuries, although for very different reasons.

"Look," Baldwin said, deciding to lay his cards on the table, "it's my fault Jillian was hurt tonight. I know that. I own it. I've apologized to her, and she says she doesn't blame me." He shook his head, still marveling over her quick forgiveness. "I think once the pain meds fully wear off she might come to her senses on that front."

Bryce looked a bit puzzled. "O-o-kay…" he said slowly.

Baldwin leaned forward and put his elbows on his knees. "I told Jillian I'd keep her safe, and I failed. I take that very seriously. But my brother is still on the loose, and I have to bring him in. Now more than ever."

Bryce nodded. "I think that's everyone's priority now."

Baldwin took a deep breath. "I understand that your family probably hates me right now. And I get it—I hate myself a little bit, too. But if you could just wait until I catch Randall, I'd appreciate it."

Bryce frowned. "Wait for what?"

Baldwin shrugged. "If you need to retaliate… If you or Jillian want revenge…" He shook his head, seemingly at a loss for words.

Bryce stared at him, awareness slowly dawning on his face. "Oh," he said. "You think I want to hurt you because my sister was shot tonight? That I'm going to do an eye-for-an-eye thing? Is that it?"

Baldwin shifted in his chair. "I mean, I understand if you want to. Or need to."

Bryce threw back his head and laughed, the sound echoing in the empty room. "Oh, man." He wiped the corners of his eyes with his free hand. "Baldwin, you have been hanging out for far too long with some seriously shady people."

Embarrassment rose in Baldwin's chest, making him uncomfortable. "I'm only trying to say…"

"I know what you mean," Bryce said. "And while there are a lot of Coltons running around Grave Gulch, we're not the Mafia. That's not how normal people do things, buddy."

"I know that," Baldwin replied. "It's just…" He trailed off, gathering his thoughts. "My family is very different. Randall and I were never close growing up. If he thought I slighted him in some way, he always got revenge." He shook his head as his memories and past experiences floated to the top of his consciousness. "You know I work in the shadows. A lot of the people who contact me are seeking justice, but always with an edge."

"It wears on you after a while," Bryce said.

Baldwin glanced up, a little surprised at the other man's perception. "Yeah, it does," he said.

"I can relate." Bryce leaned back in his chair. "I catch killers for a living. Part of my job is to try to get inside their heads. It can be tough to shake that off."

"Exactly." Baldwin felt himself relax as Bryce spoke. It wasn't often he talked to someone who truly knew what he was dealing with. Even Jillian didn't fully understand—she thought him cold and unfeeling, but if she'd seen even half of the things he'd experienced... If he didn't shut down his emotions and put walls up to keep from getting close to people, he wasn't sure how he'd cope.

"How do you do it?" he asked curiously. He knew from his time in Grave Gulch that Bryce and Olivia Margulies were involved and had recently gotten engaged. How did Bryce let go and trust someone like that?

Bryce considered the question for a moment, seeming to sense Baldwin's true intent. "To be honest, it's taken me a while to learn how to trust." He nodded his head in the direction of Jillian's room. "Did you meet my dad on your way out the door?"

"No." Baldwin had been so intent on escape he hadn't stopped for introductions.

Bryce tilted his head to the side. "That's okay. The thing is, Wes has been out of our lives for twenty-five years. We grew up not knowing him, because he was in the witness-protection program. Before that, he was Richard Foster. That's the name I'd always associated with him. So when he showed up again with this new name, I had a really hard time trusting him. It's taken me a lot of soul-searching to accept the reasons why my father had to leave, and to make peace with the fact that he's now called Wes."

"I can imagine," Baldwin said. "That's a lot of changes to take in at once."

Bryce nodded. "I'm not saying everything is perfect between us. But I'm working on it. And Olivia has helped me so much with that process. That's part of what I love about her. She makes me better, or at least makes me want to be better. I eventually realized I'd be a fool to walk away from that kind of support."

"Yeah," Baldwin said weakly, his thoughts turning to Jillian. There was no doubt he cared about her, but did his feelings go beyond that? More importantly, could he *afford* to let them grow deeper?

"There you are," said a male voice. Baldwin glanced over to find Jillian and Bryce's father walking toward them. "I figured I'd give the girls a few minutes to say goodbye to each other and come find you."

Baldwin and Bryce both stood as Wes drew closer. He stuck out his hand to introduce himself. "I'm Baldwin Bowe, sir."

"Wes Windham," the older man replied. "You were the one with Jillian tonight. Is that right?"

Baldwin nodded, mentally bracing himself for the vitriol that was sure to come his way. Bryce might not want to pound him into the ground, but surely Jillian's father would have something to say...

Wes clapped him on the shoulder. "I'm so glad you were there," he said, staring hard into Baldwin's eyes. "I shudder to think what might have happened if Jillian had been alone when that man broke in."

"I... Yes, sir," Baldwin stammered. Jillian's family was so *nice*, the complete opposite of the kind of people he was used to dealing with. He kept waiting for the other shoe to drop, but was starting to get the feeling that maybe it wouldn't.

He saw Bryce hide a smile at his apparent confusion. At least he was keeping Jillian's brother entertained tonight.

"Jillian said you'd stay with her until her former coworker is brought into custody?" Wes asked. It was clear he didn't like the thought of Jillian being alone right now, and Baldwin definitely couldn't blame him.

"Yes, absolutely. I plan to stay with her as long as she'll let me," Baldwin replied. Then he realized what he'd said and mentally kicked himself. He would stay with Jillian until the job was done. After that, he was going to move on. It's what he always did.

So why did the thought of leaving Jillian behind give him a pang in his heart?

"Good, that's good," Wes said, interrupting his thoughts. "I know her mother will be relieved to hear she'll have someone with her. We've been so worried about her, and after Bryce's injury—" Wes indicated Bryce with his hand "—well, Verity nearly came out of her skin when she heard that she'd been shot."

"I can only imagine how hard it is to hear your child has been hurt," Baldwin said.

"Yes, well," Wes replied. "It was bad enough when Madison was targeted by a criminal. We thought the worst was over, but when Bryce was shot it was really difficult for Verity. And then to get the news about Jillian..." Wes shook his head.

Baldwin felt a surge of pity for the man. It was clear he cared deeply for his children, even though he hadn't been there for much of their lives. He seemed like a good guy, and he was glad Jillian had her father back.

"It's okay," Bryce said, clapping his free hand on his dad's shoulder. "Madison and I are fine, and Jillian is going to make a full recovery, as well. You and Mom can stop worrying."

Wes snorted. "Sure, son. Like that's possible."

"We are all adults," Bryce said. "You don't have to fret about us all the time."

Wes chuckled. "Just wait until you and Olivia start having your own babies. I'm going to remind you of that remark, and then you'll understand. It doesn't matter how old you or your sisters get. You'll always be my kids."

"Okay, okay," Bryce replied. From the tone of his voice, it was clear they'd had this discussion before. Baldwin couldn't help but smile at the interaction, while at the same time wishing he'd had that kind of relationship with his own father. There was a real sense of affection between Bryce and Wes, a connection that had perhaps been weakened but not extinguished by the years they'd spent apart. Baldwin's own dad had never been that way with him, certainly not in any sense that he could remember.

Jillian's mother and sister joined them, and Baldwin introduced himself. He extended his hand to Verity, but before he knew what she was about she'd wrapped her arms around him and buried her face in his chest.

"Thank you," she said, her voice laden with emotion. "You saved my baby girl."

Baldwin patted her shoulders, her gratitude making him feel awkward. "I didn't do much," he said quietly.

Verity leaned back, her eyes brimming with tears. "Don't try that with me," she warned. "Jillian told us how you stopped the bleeding and called the ambulance."

"Yes, ma'am." He had done those things, but he didn't feel they were deserving of praise. "She would have done the same for me," he added.

"That's true," Verity said, sniffing delicately. "But let's hope it doesn't come to that. I think one gunshot wound is more than enough." She looked meaningfully at Bryce, who held up his free hand.

"Don't look at me," he said jokingly. "It's not my fault Jillian tried to copy me."

Verity narrowed her eyes. "At least her injury doesn't require surgery."

Bryce lifted his uninjured shoulder in a shrug. "Maybe she should have tried harder."

Baldwin bit his lower lip to keep from smiling as Madison giggled and Verity shot Bryce a mock glare. "Very funny," she said archly. Then she turned back to Baldwin. "I'm not going to try to talk you into going home tonight—I like knowing that you'll be here with my girl. The nurse said they'll be moving her soon, and I made sure to ask for a few extra pillows for you."

"Thank you," said Baldwin, touched by her gesture. He'd basically accepted the fact that he was going to spend a mostly sleepless night by Jillian's side, but if he was able to stretch out with a pillow or two, he might actually get some rest.

Verity reached up to cup the side of his face in her hand. "You come see me later, after she gets out of the hospital. I'll make us some tea and we can get to know each other better."

"I…" It was on the tip of Baldwin's tongue to protest, to explain to Jillian's mother that it wasn't like that between them. To tell her they weren't dating, that he was simply using her as part of his job. But as he looked into Verity's eyes, so full of hope, he couldn't bear to tell her the truth.

"I'd like that," he said simply. And, for a second, he let himself imagine what it would be like to accompany Jillian to her mother's house. How nice it would be to sit with them and talk, and to learn more about Jillian and her family. Verity would grill him about his own family and intentions toward her daughter, and he'd reassure her about his feelings for Jillian.

It was the normal thing to do, and the way people all over the world met the parents of their partners.

But it would never happen for him.

Because Jillian wasn't his partner. Not in the romantic sense of the word, anyway.

And wasn't that a pity?

The ache in his chest intensified, as though his heart objected to classifying Jillian as "just" a professional acquaintance. She might have started out that way, but he was well beyond emotional detachment now.

"Come on, guys," Bryce said. "Let's get out of here so Baldwin can get some rest. I know Olivia is anxious for me to let her know how Jillian is doing."

Verity leaned in for another hug, squeezing tightly before releasing him. "I hope I see you again soon," she said, smiling up at him.

Baldwin smiled back. "I think you will."

"You take care, son," Wes said, shaking his hand again. "And thank you."

Madison and Bryce said goodbye, as well, and Baldwin watched as Jillian's family headed for the exit. They walked together, Wes with his arm around Verity's shoulder, Bryce and Madison following. The very picture of a close-knit group.

Watching them, Baldwin was struck by a sense of longing. He'd never had that kind of bond with his relatives. After a while, he'd stopped wishing for it, instead convincing himself that he was better off on his own. But listening to them tease each other with no trace of underlying malice, seeing the way they'd all rallied to visit Jillian in the hospital... It made him realize he'd been fooling himself. He did need people in his life. He wanted that connection with someone, that sense of belonging. His own family would never provide support and encouragement. But perhaps he could choose his own clan.

He turned and walked back toward Jillian's room, a new possibility dancing on the edges of his mind. What if he didn't have to leave when the job was done? Why couldn't he stay in Grave Gulch, maybe make a few friends? Would it be so bad if he let himself take a break?

The door swung open silently, and he stood there for a second looking at Jillian. Her eyes were closed, her face relaxed. She didn't appear to be in any pain, a fact for which he was grateful. The sight of her tugged at his heart, and he couldn't help but wonder—what would she think about this possible change of plans? Would she be happy to see him stay, or would she want him to leave so she could move on with her life without a reminder of Randall?

They were questions he couldn't answer, not yet. And…did he really want to know? The thought that she might tell him to go made his stomach twist into knots. Maybe it was better to just ride off into the sunset, the way he'd always done.

It was certainly the safer option. Given the risk to his heart, it was probably for the best.

After all, families were overrated.

Chapter Nine

Jillian opened her eyes, blinking as she took in the unfamiliar surroundings. This room was…different, somehow. Not the same one she'd had in the ER. There was a quiet, steady beep coming from somewhere, and the faint scent of bleach in the air. They must have moved her at some point, though for the life of her, she couldn't remember when. Her last memories were of her mom and sister kissing her goodbye and walking out the door. Jillian had intended to rest for only a few minutes until the nurse came back in to check on the transfusion. Apparently, her body had decided to sleep instead.

Must have been the painkillers, she decided. They'd kicked in while her family had visited, giving her a dreamy, floaty sensation, making her feel like she was wrapped in a big cotton ball. It was a pleasant, if strange, state of being. Now her shoulder throbbed, making it clear the medication had worn off.

She shifted on the bed, debating whether she should call the nurse. What time was it? One might be coming soon, anyway, to do a check. She looked to the side, and that's when she saw him.

Baldwin was lying on the low couch against the wall, his large frame contorted into an awkward-looking position on the too-small cushions. It had to be terribly uncomfortable, but he'd managed to go to sleep. She watched the rise and fall of his broad shoulders with each breath, the way the fabric of his shirt pulled across his chest with each movement. His face was in the shadows so she had to imagine how his features must look when relaxed and peaceful. Something told her that even asleep, Baldwin probably still had a fierceness about him.

"You're awake." His voice rumbled in the otherwise quiet space, a raspy sound that made goose bumps break out along her arms.

How long had he been watching her stare at him? He must think she was some kind of weirdo. "Uh, yeah," she replied eloquently.

Baldwin sat up and stretched, unfolding his body to its normal length. He winced as he moved, confirming her suspicions about the comfort of the sofa. "I'm surprised you're still here," she said.

He tilted his head to the side. "I told you I wasn't going anywhere."

"I know. But when my family arrived, I thought maybe you figured I was okay. I saw you sneak out, but I must have been asleep when you came back."

"You were," he confirmed. "Out like a light and snoring like an asthmatic rhino."

Jillian's cheeks heated. "I don't snore!" she protested.

Baldwin leaned forward and she saw the grin on his face. "Yeah, you do," he said. "But not that bad. I've definitely heard worse."

She shifted in the bed, absorbing this new piece of information. Sleeping in the same room as Baldwin was a strange kind of intimacy, especially given these circumstances. They hadn't even kissed, so he really had no business knowing what kind of sounds she did or didn't make while unconscious.

"Are you hurting?"

"A little," she admitted. "How did you know?"

"Because you're tense," he replied. "And you're awake. If you weren't in any pain, you'd still be out."

"Maybe I'm just an early riser," Jillian said, feeling exposed. He was too damn observant, and it made her uncomfortable to be the focus of his attention while they were alone in the dark like this.

"Want me to find a nurse?" he asked.

"No," she said.

"There's no point to you staying in pain," he pointed out. "You're not going to get a prize for refusing medication."

"I know," Jillian replied. "But I'm sure they're busy. Someone will come check on me eventually. Besides," she said, "I don't really like the side effects from the drugs."

"They make you feel loopy?" he asked.

"Yeah, something like that."

"Some people would say that's the best part," Baldwin teased. "But I understand. I don't like that feeling, either."

"You've had experience with hospital-grade pain relievers before?"

He nodded, and she remembered a snippet Bryce had told her about Baldwin's record. "That's right," she said slowly. "You have a Purple Heart, don't you?"

"I do," he confirmed. "It's buried somewhere in my closet, with my other medals."

"Not one for sentimental displays?"

Baldwin shook his head. "Not really. I suppose if I ever have kids, they'll want to see them someday, but I don't need to look at a few shiny bits of metal every day."

"Your mom didn't want to frame them for you?"

He laughed. "No. I told you, my parents are not happy with the choices I've made."

Jillian shook her head. "I don't get that. You're a good man. I don't understand why they aren't proud of you. My parents are over the moon when I have a good week at work. If I actually did something that warranted a military commendation, they'd probably burst."

Baldwin shrugged. "Your family is very different," he said. He scratched the side of his cheek. "Your mom is really sweet."

"You met her?" Jillian was surprised to hear that, given the way he'd left when they'd arrived earlier.

"Yeah," Baldwin said. "I was in the waiting room while your family was here. Bryce came and found me, and he and I chatted for a bit. Then your dad came out."

"You met him, too?" Jillian couldn't help but feel a little bittersweet over this news. She would have liked to have been there when Baldwin met her family. It would have been nice to see his face and watch how her parents responded to him.

"He's a good guy," Baldwin said. "Bryce told me it's a little awkward since he's been gone so long."

Jillian nodded, feeling a pang of sadness. "It's been tough," she said. "He left when we were very young."

"What happened?" Baldwin said. "If you don't mind my asking."

Jillian shook her head. "Of course not—it's fine." She filled him in on the story, about how her father witnessed a murder on the outskirts of Grave Gulch. He'd been put into the witness-protection program and her mother had been told he'd died in combat. "Mom never really moved on," she said. "He was the only man for her, and once she thought he'd died, that was it."

"It must have been quite a shock to find out he's alive."

"Oh, yeah," Jillian said. "We have my sister to thank for that. Madison is the one who saw him first and made the connection." She told him about her sister's realization, and all the danger that had followed. "Fortunately, that part of his life is over now."

"I'm sure he's thrilled to be back with all of you," Baldwin said.

"I think so," Jillian mused. When Wes had first returned, she'd had a few doubts. She'd questioned why he hadn't tried to find them before, even after the threat that had put him into witness protection was apparently gone. But she'd come to understand Wes had been afraid. He'd been gone from their lives for so long. They'd all thought him dead and had moved on, though her mother hadn't fallen for another man. If he had shown up out of the blue, there was no telling how they might have responded. "I wish things had played out differently, of course, but I think Wes has truly always tried to do the right thing. We're still getting to know each other again, but there's no doubt in my mind that he's good for my mother, and she's good for him."

"I can see that," Baldwin said. "He had his arm around her as they were leaving."

"They're like a couple of lovebirds," Jillian said, smiling. It made her happy to see her mother head over heels, especially after all the years she'd spent alone.

"That's nice," Baldwin remarked. "My family has never been affectionate like that. I can count on one hand the number of times I've seen my parents kiss each other."

"Really?" Jillian had a hard time imagining growing up in a home that was so…cold. Though it did help explain why Randall had turned out the way he had, and why Baldwin was so reserved.

"Yep," he confirmed. "They didn't talk much. Physical affection was in even shorter supply."

"Is that why you put up a wall?" she asked. "Because they never taught you to be open with people?"

Baldwin sucked in a breath. "I suppose that's part of it," he said, crossing his arms across his chest. "I also learned in the marines not to get too attached."

"Oh." Her heart ached for him. "You lost a lot of friends?"

"One. But that was more than enough." He cleared his throat. "Anyway, in my job I can't afford to trust too many people."

"Why do you do it?" It was a question she'd been wondering from the start. Why did Baldwin want to immerse himself in the underworld of crime, to surround himself with people he couldn't trust and didn't want to get to know?

Baldwin let out a weary sigh. "Because I want to help others."

Jillian leaned back against the pillow and studied him, grateful for the shadows in the room. It was easier to talk to him in the dark, when she couldn't fully see his face or those intense blue eyes. He was less intimidating this way, and it emboldened her to ask him things she wouldn't otherwise dare to say.

"But why bounty hunting? There are other ways to help people. You'd probably make an outstanding cop, or a firefighter. Even an EMT. Why not do something like that?"

Baldwin's foot started to tap, a sure sign she was annoying him. Well, that was just too bad. He didn't have to answer her questions. But she wasn't going to stop asking them.

"Because," he said, a slight edge to his voice, "when I got out of the service, I didn't want to go through a lot of training. I'd been there, done that. I didn't have the energy or the attitude to enroll in an academy and go back to the classroom. Becoming a bounty hunter was a much simpler process."

"Do you enjoy it?"

He shifted, crossing his legs at the ankles. "It pays well. At least, the work that I do. And it's fine."

"Money isn't everything," Jillian said softly. Growing up as one of three kids with a single mother, she'd had to do without much. But she'd never lacked for the necessities or been poor in the things that really mattered. Still, the experience had taught her that she couldn't find happiness in possessions—it was the people in life that made it worthwhile.

"No, it's not," Baldwin agreed. "But money makes life a lot easier."

"Has that been true for you?" she pressed.

Baldwin went very still. "What do you mean?"

Jillian shrugged, then moaned softly as the gesture aggravated her shoulder. "I mean," she said, grinding her back teeth together as the pain subsided, "you work all the time. You talk about getting paid well for what you do, but when do you actually sit back and enjoy the benefits of having that money? Do you ever go on vacation?"

He didn't reply, so she continued to speak. "Bryce told me you rent a place and own your truck. There's nothing wrong with either of those things, but you don't act like a man who knows how to relax. Do you ever think about finding someone to share your life with? Having financial security is great, but it's not a substitute for real connection."

"I didn't realize my personal life was of such interest to you," Baldwin said. His tone was icy enough to make her shiver, but Jillian wasn't deterred. Maybe it was the residual painkillers in her system, or maybe getting shot tonight had made her realize there were things in her own life she was lacking. Either way, she felt reckless and unfiltered, and since Baldwin was here, he was the most logical target for her mood.

"You're a good guy. You deserve some happiness. I know you got into bounty hunting to help people, but at what cost to yourself? You have trouble trusting people, you don't want to put down roots, you work all the time." She shook her head. "I just don't want you to miss out."

He pushed to his feet and her heart jumped into her throat as he loomed over her. *Too far*, she thought to herself. *I said too much.*

"Baldwin, I—" she stammered. She wasn't afraid of him—she knew he would never hurt her—but she hadn't intended to make him angry or bruise his ego.

"I'm going to go find some coffee," he practically growled. "You should try to go back to sleep. It's still about an hour before the nurses change shifts."

He stalked from the room before she could respond, leaving her aching and alone in the dark.

"I'm hungry."

Baldwin glanced across the back seat of Bryce's

car and tried not to smile. "You're always hungry," he pointed out.

Jillian shot him a mock glare. "Yeah, but this time it's for real. Breakfast was a long time ago." She'd finally been released from the hospital around noon, and her brother had volunteered to drive them home.

Bryce let out a long-suffering sigh. "What do you want?" He spoke like a man who was used to catering to his sister's culinary demands.

She thought for a moment, then said, "A spinach knish, some matzo-ball soup and some of Olivia's raspberry rugelach."

Baldwin's own stomach growled in appreciation. Bryce chuckled. "Fair enough. I'll swing by the deli on the way home. But I think we should get it to go."

"Agreed," Baldwin said. "It's been a long night and I'd really like to take a shower." The nurses had given him a scrub top and he'd washed up as best as he could in the bathroom sink, but parts of his skin were still sticky with the residue of Jillian's blood.

Something flashed in Jillian's eyes, there and gone before he could identify the emotion. "I could use a nap," she said, stifling a yawn. "I didn't sleep very well in the hospital." She glanced away, avoiding his gaze.

Baldwin didn't respond. When he'd finally returned to her room, her eyes had been closed. Maybe she'd been asleep, or maybe she'd been bluffing so she didn't have to talk to him. Either way, he hadn't tried to rouse her. Instead, he'd curled up on the foldout sofa again and managed to doze a bit until a nurse had come in for shift change.

They'd fed Jillian around seven thirty, and the doctor had visited around eight. She'd done a quick exam and checked Jillian's stitches, then told her she could go home today. But it had taken a while to dot all the i's and cross all the t's, so she hadn't been released until around noon. Fortunately, Bryce had come to pick them up, since Baldwin's truck was still parked at Jillian's condo.

Bryce pulled into a parking spot in front of Bubbe's Deli. "Stay here," he instructed as he climbed out of the car. "If you come in with me, Olivia might never let us leave." With that, he shut the door, sealing them in together.

For a moment, neither spoke. The silence stretched between them, taking on an awkward, strained quality. Then Jillian sighed softly.

"I'm sorry."

He turned to look at her, certain he'd misheard. "What?"

She glanced at him, biting her bottom lip. "I'm sorry. I said some things last night that I probably shouldn't have. I didn't mean to pry in to your life, or to act like I know what's best for you."

Baldwin blinked slowly, trying to process this turn of events. "It's okay," he said. "You were tired, in pain and probably still feeling the effects of stress. People say funny things when they're upset."

Jillian nodded, relief in her eyes. "Yeah. I was feeling…unsettled from everything. Being shot kind of made me realize all the things that are missing from my life, and I lashed out at you because you were there. I shouldn't have used you as my punching bag."

Her words made his stomach do a funny little flip. Truth be told, she *had* upset him last night. But not so much because of what she'd said—he'd had the same conversation with himself countless times. No, it was the fact that she'd said anything at all. She was the only person in his life who talked to him like that. His friends occasionally made reference to his single status or joked that he should take some time off. But no one had ever come out and blasted him with the truth the way she had or interrogated him on what his actions actually meant. He'd never been asked if he was happy, never been pushed to answer for his choices.

Jillian might have been projecting a bit last night, but her words had made one thing clear: she cared.

And that scared the hell out of him.

He could handle the physical attraction. That was the easy part; sex could be a transactional affair. He touched her here, she touched him there, they both had fun and no emotions had to be involved.

But that conversation last night? It had been nothing *but* emotions; raw, unfiltered and directed at him.

The fact that she cared about him enough to say something? That made her dangerous.

Because the truth of the matter was, he was catching feelings for her, too.

And he didn't know what to do about it.

He cleared his throat, knowing he needed to say something. "Uh, what do you think is missing from your life?" Maybe if he flipped the conversation to focus on her he could get his thoughts straightened out.

Jillian ducked her head. "I…" She trailed off, her cheeks turning a faint pink. "I don't have a lot of friends," she continued. "Once I got the job at GGPD, I threw myself into work. I wanted to prove myself, to make it clear to all the naysayers that I belonged there because I'm good at what I do, not because of my last name. But then Randall put a target on my back, and things started to fall apart."

"It's hard to make connections with people when you're under constant pressure." In the marines, the shared experiences of boot camp and training and finally deployment had served to forge bonds between Baldwin and the others in his battery. In fact, some of the training exercises had been designed to be terrible, to give everyone a common enemy to unite against and help the group overcome their individual differences. But Jillian had been alone, without the benefit of any kind of support from most of her coworkers.

Jillian nodded. "Exactly. I was so stressed all the time I didn't have the emotional bandwidth to make friends or even think about dating."

He swallowed hard as he imagined Jillian with another man. Kissing him, touching him, moving over him… A possessive surge of jealousy rose in his chest and he clenched his jaw.

Don't be ridiculous, he told himself. Where did he get off being so upset over the thought of Jillian with another man? He had no claim to her. No right to expect anything from her. A sense of unease started to build as he realized what was going on. Wanting her was one thing. The troubling part was that he was moving beyond that—he wanted her all to himself.

"Anyway," she continued, apparently oblivious to the emotional storm swirling inside him. "I guess now that things are getting so complicated, I'm aware of the fact that I don't really have people in my life to share with, or to lean on. I can turn to my family, of course, but it would be nice to have more than my relatives, you know?"

"Mmm," he said in acknowledgment. Baldwin didn't trust himself to speak at the moment. He wasn't used to feeling so agitated, so internally unmoored. He was normally calm and rock-steady; even when in a tense situation, he didn't emotionally engage, but instead held himself above it all so his mind could function without distraction.

Why didn't that approach work with Jillian? What was it about this woman that kept pulling at him, making him want to break his own rules?

"Baldwin?" He looked over to find her watching him, a concerned expression on her face. "Are you okay?"

"Yeah." The word came out as a croak, so he cleared his throat and tried again. "I'm good. Just thinking."

She offered him a small smile. "I've been doing a lot of that lately. No hard feelings?"

He shook his head. "Of course not." He was quiet a moment, then added, "I appreciate your honesty. Maybe not in the heat of the moment, but I get it now. And it's okay."

Jillian nodded. "Feel free to return the favor," she said, her tone half joking. "I owe you after last night."

"No, you don't." She blinked and he realized how harsh he had sounded. "You don't owe me anything," he said, more gently this time. "I'm not a hero, Jillian. You don't need to lift me up on a pedestal because I put pressure on your shoulder and called an ambulance."

She opened her mouth, but before she could respond the driver's door opened and Bryce climbed inside. He placed two large bags onto the front passenger seat, and the air filled with the scents of warm bread, chicken and a mix of savory spices. "I hope you're hungry," Bryce muttered as he clicked his seat belt into place. "I told Olivia you just wanted a few things, but she loaded me up with challah, some fresh latkes, chicken soup and about a dozen hamantaschen." He shook his head. "She wanted me to stay until the potato kugel came out of the oven, but I told her I had to get you home."

"Oh, man," Jillian said. "Is it too late to go back inside?"

Bryce glared at her over his shoulder. "Trust me, you have enough food here to feed an army."

"Did you get the raspberry rugelach?" Jillian asked hopefully.

"Yes," Bryce confirmed. "And she threw in some chocolate ones, as well."

Jillian leaned back against the seat, humming happily to herself. Baldwin had never tried rugelach, but he could tell by the smells coming from the front of the car that he was going to enjoy this lunch very much.

Bryce pulled into the parking lot of Jillian's building a few minutes later. "Why don't you join us?" she asked.

He shook his head. "I appreciate it, but I've got to get back to work. Someone's got to pay the bills, since Olivia insists on giving away mountains of food to my mooching relatives."

Jillian stuck her tongue out at her brother. "You're just mad because she likes me better than she likes you."

Bryce laughed. Baldwin gathered the bags of food from the front seat and took a step toward the door, giving the siblings a chance to speak privately. He saw Jillian lean down and heard the murmur of voices. Then she straightened and smiled, reaching through the window to pat Bryce's shoulder. "Get out of here," she said playfully.

Bryce turned to look at Baldwin. "Thanks, man," Baldwin called out. Bryce nodded and gave him a little wave as he drove away. Together, Jillian and Baldwin walked inside.

"My friend kept an eye on your place all night," Baldwin told her. "He said Randall never came back."

"That's good," Jillian replied. They arrived at her

door and she stopped, staring at the handle as though she'd never seen it before. A strip of crime scene tape stretched across the doorway, but Bryce had passed along the message that they were okay to enter.

"Everything okay?" He figured she was mentally preparing herself to go inside, to start reclaiming her space from the memory of his brother.

She glanced up at him. "I'm glad you grabbed my purse. I never would have thought to bring my keys." She fished them out and unlocked the door but made no move to enter.

Baldwin stepped forward. "I'll go first," he said. "But like I said, no one's been here except for the evidence team. My friend Carter watched over the place for me. He's a good guy—we were in the marines together, and now he runs a security company. He's a stickler for details. He would have noticed any activity after the police left."

Baldwin walked down the entry hallway, noting the police had left the kitchen lights on. There was a faint dusting of fingerprint powder on the counters, and he noticed the larger fragments of broken glass had been collected from the floor. He set the bags of food on a small table and stepped into the living room.

The furniture had all been pushed to the side to make room for the medics and their gurney. He didn't remember doing that, so the EMTs must have moved things when he wasn't looking.

Jillian's blood stained the carpet, a dark, visceral reminder of what had happened here. Baldwin stood in place, staring at the rust-colored splotch as the sounds and scents came flooding back. The acrid stench of gunpowder. The thud of Jillian's body as she hit the ground. The metallic tang in the air. The slick warmth as he touched her shoulder, trying to assess her injury.

He felt her presence next to him and glanced over to see her staring at the same spot. "That's not gonna come out," she muttered. "Guess it's new carpet for me."

Baldwin blinked and then laughed out loud, tickled by her practical response to seeing her own blood on the floor. Most people would have been repulsed or gotten emotional at the reminder of being shot. Not Jillian. Rather than dwelling on the past, she shifted to plan for the future. It was an admirable quality—one he appreciated.

She looked up at him with a puzzled smile. He shook his head and put his arm around her shoulder, being careful not to touch her wound. "Come on," he said, leading her back to the kitchen table. "Let's eat while it's still hot."

Chapter Ten

The food was delicious—it always was. Olivia had a real gift in the kitchen. It was one of the many reasons why Jillian was glad Bryce hadn't scared her away.

Baldwin seemed to enjoy their meal, as well. "This knish is fantastic," he said around a mouthful of food. "I'm going to have to ask Olivia for her recipes."

Jillian laughed. "Good luck. She's very protective of them. A lot of them have been passed down in her family for generations. She's always happy to share what she makes, but she's quite stingy when it comes to telling others how to replicate her dishes. Except to Bryce, of course, and Chef Hernando."

Baldwin nodded. "That's only fair. I'll just have to earn her trust. Maybe I can talk her into showing me how she does it someday."

Jillian's ears caught on his last word. *Someday* implied that Baldwin might stick around after catching Randall. Was he actually considering staying in town? Did he see a future for himself here?

And if so, she thought to herself, *am I a part of it?*

It was a far-fetched idea, she knew. Baldwin had made no secret of the fact that he intended to leave Grave Gulch just as soon as this job was done. The fact that she'd developed a crush on him during their time together wasn't going to change his mind. His little comment about earning Olivia's trust and watching her make knish was simply him thinking out loud; it didn't represent an about-face in his plans for the future. As much as she might wish otherwise, she couldn't read too much into his statement. If she dared to hope, she was going to wind up disappointed.

They finished eating and Baldwin helped her wrap up the leftovers and tidy up the dishes. Jillian stood in the middle of the kitchen and looked around, making a mental list of chores she'd need to do to put things back to rights.

Baldwin stood next to her, his arms crossed. "I know you want to clean," he said. "I get why you need to erase all traces of Randall from your home. But I am desperate for a shower. So if you can wait a few minutes, I'm going to clean myself and then I'll help you tackle the bigger job."

Jillian nodded. "That sounds great. I want to wash up myself."

A wicked voice in her head urged her to suggest they save water and shower together, but Jillian refused to even jokingly mention it.

"Okay. Meet you back here in a few."

She watched him walk away, the ill-fitting scrub

top the nurses had given him at the hospital doing nothing to dampen his physical appeal. It simply wasn't fair—she'd spent a stressful night in the hospital and it showed, whereas he'd been by her side the whole time and looked like he could step onto a runway in some avant-garde European fashion show.

With a small sigh, she headed for her room and stripped off her clothes. She showered quickly, moaning slightly as the hot water washed away the blood and iodine residue and general griminess she'd accumulated overnight. It would have been so nice to linger under the spray, but Baldwin was waiting. Besides, she wouldn't be able to truly relax until she'd cleaned her place.

Jillian toweled off and replaced the bandage over her stitches, then fished out a couple of ibuprofens from the medicine cabinet and swallowed them with a handful of water from the faucet. Her shoulder ached a bit, and she knew it would only hurt worse as she used it.

She cast a longing look at her bed as she got dressed. "Soon," she muttered to herself. With Baldwin's help, it wouldn't take long to scrub her condo. Then she could collapse into bed and sleep for a week. Or at least a few hours.

The guest bathroom was quiet as she walked down the hall. Either Baldwin was getting dressed, or he was already done. As she stepped into the kitchen, she got her answer.

Baldwin was on all fours investigating the contents of the cabinet under the kitchen sink.

Jillian stopped in her tracks, unable to take her eyes off his perfect butt, so nicely displayed in the flannel pants he was currently sporting. It was rude to stare—she knew that, just as she knew that she herself hated being objectified by men. But logic and common sense were no match for her hormones. Awareness flickered to life low in her belly, and her palms itched to reach out and touch him. He would be hard and warm and, oh, God…

"Found it!"

Baldwin extracted his head and shoulders from the cabinet and sat up, holding a spray bottle of cleanser triumphantly. "I knew it had to be around here somewhere."

Jillian cleared her throat to make her presence known. "Uh, what's that?"

He glanced over his shoulder and showed her the bottle. "Most people keep cleaning supplies under the sink. You're no exception. I think this'll work for the countertops in here, but what do you want me to use to mop the floor?"

He was going to mop the floor for her? Hubba-hubba. "I, uh, I usually use a vinegar and water mix for the mop," she stammered, trying to reconcile her physical attraction for Baldwin with her growing mental attraction, as well. She'd assumed that she would have to ask him to do specific chores for her as they cleaned, but it seemed Baldwin was perfectly happy to take the initiative and get to work without making her assume command of Project Restoration.

Baldwin nodded. "All right. Here's what I'm

planning. I'm going to wipe everything down in the kitchen, then sweep and mop the floors. I'm going to wipe off the door handles, the cabinet pulls and anything else Randall may have touched. Then I'm going to dust and vacuum the living room and wipe down the guest bathroom."

"Wait a minute," Jillian protested. "You can't do everything! What am I supposed to do—just sit on my hands and watch you work?"

Baldwin shrugged. "Why not? Maybe you can find something to watch on television."

"Absolutely not," Jillian said. She was touched that he was so willing to take on all the jobs, but it simply wasn't fair. She couldn't stand back and do nothing while he worked, especially since she knew he was doing it all as a favor to her.

"Of the two of us, I'm not the one who got shot last night." A shadow crossed his face at the memory, and unless she missed her guess, Jillian thought he might be feeling some residual guilt. Even though she'd made it clear he wasn't to blame, she knew he still felt at least partially responsible for her injuries. Scrubbing her condo was likely his way of trying to make amends.

"I'm fine," she said. "I just took some ibuprofen."

"You need to rest and let your body heal. If you do too much now, it'll make things worse."

Jillian sighed, recognizing that all-too familiar stubborn note in his voice. Not only had she been hearing it from Baldwin lately, but Bryce also had an identical tone he often deployed. "I'm going to try to clean the carpet in the living room," she said. "And I'll keep going until I get tired."

Baldwin opened his mouth, but wisely shut it again without argument. "Promise me you won't overdo it?" There was real concern in his voice, and she couldn't help but smile.

"I promise."

About an hour and a half later, Jillian sank her aching body onto the couch.

As it turned out, falling to the floor after being shot last night had left her with some bruises. And lying in an uncomfortable hospital bed hadn't helped the situation.

Neither had her determination to keep up with Baldwin.

She'd spent some time on all fours, scrubbing at the bloodstains on the carpet with hydrogen peroxide and dish soap. It looked much better, though the area was still discolored. But more in a people-live-here kind of way as opposed to a haunted-house-murder-scene vibe.

Satisfied that she'd done all she could do for the carpet, she'd set out to dust everything. Her desk against the far wall, the bookshelves, the end tables—everything. Even though Randall hadn't made it as far as her closet on his last visit, she was more convinced than ever he'd planted the evidence there. Which meant at some point, he had gone through her entire condo to invade her most personal space. Just the thought of him standing in her closet, possibly touching her clothes, was enough to turn her stomach.

She tackled her bedroom next, dusting and wiping and vacuuming until she felt like she'd erased his presence from every surface in her bedroom, closet and bathroom. Then she'd gathered up most of her clothes and sorted them into piles for laundry. The logical part of her knew this was bordering on overkill, but her peace of mind demanded she continue. She was determined to reclaim her space and take back her feeling of security.

Eventually, though, her shoulder insisted she take a break. Her spirit was all too willing to continue sanitizing, but her flesh was weak. So she allowed herself to rest, with the understanding that she was going to start up again after a few minutes. Right after she rested her eyes for a spell…

JILLIAN OPENED HER eyes to discover she was lying flat on her stomach, her head turned to the side. She was warm and secure, and as she gradually woke, she realized the cushions she was pressed against were slowly moving up and down in a soothing rhythm.

No, scratch that. *Not* the cushions. Baldwin's chest was moving under her.

She sucked in a breath as she appreciated the full magnitude of her situation. Jillian was stretched out on top of Baldwin, her torso pressed flat against his chest, her cheek on his breastbone, their legs tangled. His muscular arms encircled her, with one of his big hands splayed on her back to anchor her in place while the other cupped her butt in a gesture of masculine possession. He was warm under her, and though his body was hard and solid, he made a surprisingly comfortable mattress.

Her head spun as she tried to figure out how, exactly, this had happened. The last thing she remembered was sitting down on the couch—alone—to rest for a few minutes. She'd clearly fallen asleep, and Baldwin had apparently joined her at some point. But surely he hadn't pulled her on top of him? She dismissed the thought almost immediately. That kind of move wasn't his style, and besides, Jillian would have woken up if she'd felt herself being repositioned like that.

The only conclusion was that *she* had moved in her sleep. But had she curled up to him after he'd drifted off, or had he been aware of her somnolent activities?

Her face warmed at the thought that Baldwin had been awake when she'd flung herself on top of him. If that was the case, the poor man must have felt trapped. He acted like a tough guy, but she knew that a soft heart lurked underneath that hard shell. If he'd seen her moving, he would have tolerated her embrace so as not to disturb her rest. Especially since she'd been shot and he blamed himself.

If she had any luck at all, they'd both fallen asleep and moved together afterward. That meant she could extract herself, and Baldwin would wake up none the wiser about the fact that she now knew exactly how good it felt to be pressed up against him.

It was going to be tricky, though. If they were in a bed… Her mind started to drift at the possibility, conjuring up fantasies about all the *other* things they could do in a bed.

Focus, she told herself sternly. Now was not the time to get distracted!

She returned her attention to the dilemma at hand. Since they were on the couch, she couldn't simply roll off him, because she'd land on the floor. Their legs were entwined, which meant it was going to be difficult to plant a foot on the floor. And she couldn't very well slide up his body or she'd wind up crawling over his face, which was a surefire way to wake him up.

No, it seemed her best bet would be to shimmy toward his feet. The problem was, Baldwin's big frame covered up all of the seat cushions, leaving her no place to put her hands to support herself while she tried to move. She was just going to have to slide against him until she got to his hips, where there should be space for her to plant her hands and take her weight off him.

She slowly drew in a breath, closing her eyes briefly to enjoy her last few seconds pressed against Baldwin's muscular form. It had been a long time since she'd had full-body contact with a man, and she knew that any future guy was unlikely to live up to Baldwin's build.

Still, she couldn't stay like this forever. It was time to get off him.

Slowly, carefully, she started to shift down. His

hands slid along her back as she moved, triggering a wave of goose bumps along her skin. The fabric of her shirt remained trapped between their bodies, exposing a growing strip of her skin as she continued her journey south. This was turning out to be more complicated than she'd thought, but she couldn't stop now.

Her shoulders were even with his hips when Baldwin shifted under her. She froze in place, holding her breath and silently pleading with the universe for him to stay asleep. If he woke up and found her like this, her breasts lined up with his crotch, her cheek at the level of his belly button…well, she'd have a lot of explaining to do.

Fortunately, his eyes remained closed. She exhaled quietly and braced herself to move again.

"I can tell you have a plan," he drawled, his voice deep and slightly rough from sleep. "Mind filling me in on it?"

Startled, Jillian let out an undignified squeak and nearly jumped out of her skin. Before she knew what was happening, Baldwin's large hands wrapped around her biceps and he carefully pulled her up his body as he sat up. She wound up facing him, nearly plastered to his chest as they shifted to untangle their legs.

"I will admit," he continued as Jillian leaned back to sit on her bottom, "I didn't mind the direction you were headed, but I could tell you didn't have seduction in mind."

Jillian's eyes locked onto his mouth, which was

presently turned up at the corners in a faint smile. "Uh, no," she admitted. "No, I was trying to move without waking you."

Baldwin snorted. "Let me give you a little tip for next time. If you want a man to stay asleep, don't drag your breasts across his chest and down his stomach."

Her cheeks burned so hot she imagined she looked like a tomato. "Good to know," she muttered. "Sorry about that."

"Don't be," he replied. "I'm not."

Jillian glanced up and discovered his eyes were locked on her face, the blue of his irises practically electric at this distance. A shiver ran down the valley of her spine and she realized he was still holding on to her arms.

His gaze dropped to her mouth. Reflexively, her tongue darted out to swipe across her bottom lip. Baldwin made a low noise that was more vibration than sound as he stared at her. Jillian's tenuous grip on her arousal began to slip. Her nipples hardened, as though begging for his attention. The expression on his face was captivating; he was normally so cool and composed, but right now he was staring at her with such blatant desire that it made her a little dizzy. It was a heady thing, knowing Baldwin wanted her.

She leaned forward, wanting to get closer, needing to see how much she affected his self-control. Would he draw back and deny this pull between them? Or would he accept it and give in to the temptation that had been plaguing them both?

The muscles of his jaw tightened as she moved. "Jillian," he said, his voice deadly calm. "I'm going to count to three and then I'm going to kiss you. If you have any misgivings, now is the time to stop me."

Jillian bit her bottom lip to hide a smile. Baldwin made a strained noise. "One," he said, sounding like a man on the edge. "Two."

Before he could say another word, she closed the distance between them and pressed her mouth to his.

He moved like a striking snake. Between one breath and the next, his arms banded around her, pulling her flush against his chest. There was a hunger to his kiss, a hint of desperation in the way he gripped her. It was almost as if he couldn't believe this was happening and he didn't want to risk letting her go.

Jillian felt her own sense of urgency as their lips and tongues connected. Kissing Baldwin was like trying to bottle the wind; he was thrilling and unpredictable and intoxicating. But despite the intensity of their embrace, she could tell he was holding himself back. Even as his hands roamed over her he was careful to avoid her injured shoulder. He broke free from her mouth to trail his lips down her neck, but he made sure to hold her so she didn't fall against the arm of the sofa. Even now, Baldwin was still fully in control of himself. Jillian was touched by his consideration, but part of her wanted to see him let go, to give in and just *feel*. She wanted to be the one to drive him wild, to cause Mr. Professional to totally lose it. She wanted to watch that composure melt, to see his powerful body respond to her touch.

So much of this year had been about things happening to her. Randall targeting her at work. Protesters going after her because they thought she'd played a part in guilty people going free. Randall framing her for the robberies. Hell, even Randall breaking into her home and shooting her. She'd been at the mercy of other people's actions for long enough, and she was tired of it. She wasn't about to simply lie back and let Baldwin have his way with her. It was her turn to be in charge, her turn to call the shots.

He just didn't know it yet.

One of his hands cupped her breast, his thumb stroking over her nipple as his licked his way down her neck. Jillian leaned her head back, giving him full access to her skin. For a few seconds she reveled in the sensation of his breath on her, his hands on her curves. The scent of him filled her nose, her entire awareness shrinking down until all she saw, all she knew, was the man in front of her.

More. She needed to see more of him, feel more of him. The couch was too small; it was time to graduate.

Jillian stood and tugged Baldwin to his feet. He gave her a questioning look, his hands on her hips as he leaned in for another kiss. "My room," she murmured against his lips.

He made a sound of agreement as she started to lead him down the hall. When they stepped into her room, she turned around and rose to her tiptoes to kiss him. She joined her hands at the back of his neck and gently guided him until the back of his thighs hit her mattress. Then she pushed him down, climbing onto the bed to straddle his hips.

Baldwin kept his arms around her torso, holding her against him as they explored each other's mouths. The thin fabric of his flannel pants did nothing to hide his body's response, and she felt his hard length between her legs. He released his grip on her waist to tug up the hem of her shirt, and she obliged by slipping it off. But before he could touch her skin, she slid down his legs, hooking her thumbs into the waistband of his pants to draw them down as she moved.

"That was efficient," he said as she pulled the pants free from his ankles. He yanked his shirt over his head, leaving him fully naked now.

Jillian tried not to gape at the sight of his long, lean body draped across her bed. Even her wildest fantasies hadn't come close to matching the reality. He was muscled and hard and broad, and just so overtly masculine that she didn't know where to look first. Should she trace the tattoos on his chest with her tongue, or run her fingertips along the ridges of his stomach? Should she lick his nipples, or wrap her hand around his length? So many choices, and none of them bad…

Apparently, Baldwin wasn't in the mood to pose. "Hey," he said, reaching for her. "You're still wearing pants."

Jillian looked down to discover he was right. She

was mildly surprised to find they hadn't melted off her at the sight of him. He tried to draw her close, but she evaded his touch. If he got his hands on her, she'd be totally at his mercy. And she wasn't ready for that. Not yet.

"Is everything okay?" Concern danced across his features, and Jillian realized she was giving him the wrong impression. The last thing she wanted was for him to think she was having second thoughts when she wasn't.

"Oh, yes," she said, smiling as she stepped between his legs. "Everything is definitely okay."

She placed her hands on his chest and lightly raked her fingernails across his skin, moving down his stomach to his hips. Baldwin shuddered out a sigh of pleasure, then sucked in a breath as she bent her head and licked along his length.

"Jillian." His voice sounded broken as she used her hands and lips and tongue to take control of the situation. His muscles tensed, building with leashed power as she pleasured him. The knowledge that she affected this strong, solid man filled her with a sense of feminine satisfaction. She hummed as she moved, enjoying his response to her every touch.

A thin sheen of sweat glistened against his skin and he seemed to grow hotter against her. His scent intensified, taking on a new, slightly darker note that heightened her own arousal. His hips began to move in small, almost restless thrusts that told her he was getting close.

One minute, Jillian was gripping Baldwin, focused entirely on him. The next thing she knew, he pulled her up his body and rolled so that she was flat on her back. She blinked up at him, startled by the look of intensity on his face.

"You need to catch up." His voice was practically a growl as he bent his head to give her a fierce, possessive kiss. Then in one smooth motion, he pulled her pants and panties down her legs. She dimly heard the thump of the fabric as it hit the floor and felt a rush of cool air against her skin, but suddenly Baldwin was there, his hands and mouth radiating heat. The stubble on his chin rasped against her inner thighs, setting off sparks of sensation throughout her body. She threaded her fingers through his hair, wishing the strands were longer. Tension built, her muscles feeling like tightly coiled ropes.

"Baldwin." Jillian moved against him in an instinctive rhythm, seeking release. He had to stop teasing her—she couldn't stand this buildup much longer.

"Hmm?" The lazy sound made her groan in frustration. The man was torturing her on purpose.

Her body demanded she beg, though her pride wouldn't allow it. So she tugged lightly on his hair and said his name again.

He began to work his way up her stomach, pausing to cup and fondle her breasts before lightly dragging his teeth along the length of her neck. She stretched an arm toward the bedside table and he followed the motion.

"Condoms?" he asked.

Jillian nodded, and he breathed out a sigh of relief. "Thank God. Mine are all the way in the other room."

She laughed as he retrieved a foil square from the drawer. "Afraid I wouldn't wait for you?"

Baldwin shook his head as he donned protection. "I'd hate to keep you waiting."

"You might be worth it," she teased as he settled over her again.

"Only *might*?" he whispered. She gasped as he slipped inside, stretching and filling her in the best ways.

Jillian wrapped her legs around his hips as he began to move. "I take it back," she gasped as he settled into a rhythm that made her eyes roll back in her head. "You're definitely worth it."

Chapter Eleven

Baldwin woke slowly, finding his way to the surface of consciousness like a man driving through dense fog. It wasn't yet morning, but he could tell by the hint of light coming in through the window that it would be soon.

He turned his head to look at Jillian, lying next to him. She slept on her stomach, her face turned toward him and her hand resting flat on his chest, right over his heart. It was as though she didn't want to lose their connection, even for a moment. A sense of tenderness filled him as he watched her breathe, and wondered what she might be dreaming about.

Last night had been...incredible. *Amazing* was too small of a word to encompass what had happened between them. It wasn't just the sex, though that had been among the best he'd ever had. No, it was the connection they'd made that had shocked him. Baldwin was used to enjoying himself in bed, and he made sure the women he was with had fun, too. But the pleasure had always been physical. He'd never made an emotional link with someone, and in truth, had never really wanted to.

Jillian had changed all that. He didn't fully understand it and couldn't really articulate what was happening between them. But he wanted her. His desire…no, his need for her went beyond sexual. He cared about her in a way that went beyond friendship.

When had that happened? How had she become so important to him, so quickly? He'd come here to do a job and bring in his brother. He wasn't looking for a relationship of any kind. It was a distraction he didn't need.

And yet here he was, smiling like a lovesick fool as he watched Jillian sleep next to him.

What was it about this woman that had gotten under his skin?

There was something about her mix of qualities— she was beautiful, approachably intelligent, tough but vulnerable—that pulled him in. Some strange alchemy between them was at play, and Baldwin was helpless to understand it or fight it. He'd have better luck arguing with a thunderstorm.

So what was he going to do about it?

That was the crux of the issue, the question that was going to plague him for the foreseeable future. This link he felt to Jillian was special—he knew that. He just wasn't sure where to go from here.

For years, Baldwin had been focused on his career. After everything he'd experienced in the military—the good and the bad—he'd decided the safest thing to do was to invest in himself. He was sick of witnessing loss and suffering, tired of the paralyzing bureaucratic red tape that permeated every facet of an organization. By becoming his own boss, he could do what he wanted, when he wanted, on his own terms.

And if the nights got a little lonely? Well, at least he didn't have to contend with a broken heart.

Even in his hazy plans for the future, those "maybe someday thoughts" he had from time to time, he hadn't considered a relationship. Given his lifestyle, it had never seemed like a realistic possibility. He had a few close friends, a few friends with benefits and complete control over his life. The thought of adding a partner to the mix had seemed… unappealing.

Now, though? Maybe it wouldn't be so bad after all.

Except… Grave Gulch *was* his past. He'd left years ago, and apart from the occasional, awkward visit to his parents, he hadn't been back. But Jillian's whole family was here, along with her job and friends. He couldn't imagine she would want to go anywhere else.

He frowned at the direction of his thoughts. Why was he even worrying about this stuff? Who said Jillian even wanted to be with him in the first place? Sure, they'd slept together. But they were both adults. Sex didn't have to mean promises of forever. It was foolish of him to spend time thinking about a future with her, when he didn't even know how she was going to react when she woke and found him still in her bed.

On that note, his stomach began to rumble. As much as he would rather spend the day naked with Jillian, he was going to have to get up eventually.

Moving carefully, he put his marine training to good use and rose stealthily from the bed. Then he slipped out the door and walked down the hall to the guest room.

A few minutes later, he stood in the kitchen making coffee. Maybe he was taking the coward's way out, crawling out of bed before Jillian got up. He could have returned to her after a quick trip to the bathroom. But he thought it was best to give her a little space, a bit of privacy to process what had happened between them. At least this way if she regretted last night, he didn't have to see the look of disappointment cross her face.

He was checking out the contents of the fridge when he heard the shower turn on. Omelets, he decided. Quick, easy to prepare and, most important of all, he had the necessary ingredients.

He pulled out the eggs and butter, then grabbed the mushrooms and cheese. A quick search of the pantry turned up a can of diced tomatoes. Baldwin set to work, humming tunelessly to himself as he chopped the mushrooms and grated cheese.

Twenty minutes later, Jillian walked in as he folded the omelets in the pan. She stopped, eyes widening as she watched him expertly flip their breakfast. "Wow," she said, sounding impressed. "This is a nice surprise."

He shot her a grin, pleased by her reaction. "Good morning."

"Good morning to you, too," she said, heading for the coffeepot. He watched her from the corner of his eyes, searching for any indication as to what she was thinking. Was she happy about the development between them? Or did she wish they'd kept things professional?

Baldwin mentally shook his head. Since when did he get so twisted up about the morning after?

Since you care about her, came the immediate answer.

It was the truth. Baldwin always felt affection for the women he slept with, but Jillian was different. He was attached to her now and no matter what happened between them, she'd always have a space in his heart. He sat with that realization for a moment, expecting to feel nervous or uncomfortable. But instead it just seemed right.

Jillian walked over to stand next to him as he plated their food. "I should have guessed I'd find you here."

He glanced at her, but since she was watching his hands he couldn't see her face. "Did you think I'd run away?"

She lifted her uninjured shoulder in a shrug, still not looking at him. "I did wonder for a second," she said softly.

"No way," he said firmly. He placed the empty

pan in the sink and turned to face her, then put his finger under her chin to tilt her head up slightly. A flash of insecurity danced across her face, making his heart squeeze hard. "You're not getting rid of me that easily."

She smiled faintly at that, warmth entering her gaze. "Good," she said, pushing herself onto her tiptoes. "Because I'm not done with you yet." She brushed her lips across his as her hands landed on his shoulders.

He knew she'd meant to keep the kiss light, but the second their mouths touched, sparks seemed to arc through his body. He pulled her in until her breasts flattened against his chest and he slid one hand down to the small of her back, anchoring her in place. She moaned as he teased her lips apart with his tongue, delving inside to taste her. Would he ever get enough of her unique flavor?

Jillian ran her hands up his neck, threading them through his hair. Wanting to change the angle between them, he locked his hands on her hips and lifted her onto the counter, then stepped between her legs. He grabbed the hem of her shirt and started tugging upward.

"What about breakfast?" she asked between kisses, a hint of laughter in her voice.

"Later," he said, nipping gently at her bottom lip. "We have more important things to do right now."

THE FOOD HAD long gone cold by the time they turned their attention to breakfast. Baldwin offered to make fresh omelets, but Jillian insisted a quick spin in the microwave would make them edible again. They weren't the greatest, but he'd certainly had worse.

They were just finishing up the dishes when the doorbell rang. Jillian frowned as she hung the dish towel on the refrigerator door.

"Expecting anyone?" Baldwin asked.

"No," she said, shaking her head. She started for the door but he put his hand on her arm to stop her.

"Let me get it." It was probably nothing—maybe a neighbor, or one of her relatives checking in. But after the events of the last couple of days, he didn't want to take any chances.

Jillian hung back in the hallway as he approached the door.

"Who is it?" he called loudly. She really needed a peephole; he made a mental note to get one installed.

"Greg's Locks," a voice on the other side of the door said. "You made an appointment to change the locks?"

Jillian came up alongside him and nodded. "I scheduled it two days ago," she said. "After the meeting with my attorney."

"Okay." Baldwin opened the door to reveal a thin young man wearing a blue work shirt and a baseball cap with the company name embroidered on the fabric. He held a large canvas duffel bag and a clipboard.

His eyes went wide when he saw Baldwin cross his arms. "Uh, hi. I'm here to change the locks?"

Jillian moved around him and the young man visibly relaxed. "Yes, that's right. Come on in."

Baldwin took a step back to give them room, but he kept his guard up. Jillian explained what she needed and pulled Baldwin down the hall to the living room.

"You don't have to glare at him the whole time," she muttered.

"I'm not glaring," he protested. "Just keeping a watchful eye. He's a stranger."

"He's a kid doing his job," Jillian said. "Not one of your brother's henchmen."

"We hope," he said darkly. Randall generally had too much contempt for other people to want to work with them, but he might be getting desperate. Still, the idea that he'd somehow recruited a random employee from the locksmith on the off chance Jillian would get her locks changed was a bit far-fetched...

"What made you call them?" he asked, curious about the timing of it all. "Randall broke in the night before last, but you'd already set up the appointment."

"I knew someone had been in my home," she replied. "I wasn't certain who had planted the evidence, but someone had broken in to set me up. I figured changing the locks was a good idea, and if they'd come out sooner, it might have stopped Randall from getting in the other night."

"If it makes you feel any better, I don't think he had a key," Baldwin said. "When we were kids, Randall used to enjoy cracking safes and picking locks. I'm almost positive that's how he got inside."

"Let's hope this new lock will put up more of a fight," she said, a shadow crossing her face.

"We won't be caught off guard again," Baldwin said softly, drawing Jillian into his arms. He hated that she felt afraid in her own home. Hated more the fact that they were on the defensive, waiting for his brother to make another move. There had to be something he could do to knock Randall off his game. His brother was smart, but he wasn't a fighter. Baldwin needed to surprise Randall. If he could shake up his brother's world, it would give him the upper hand.

But how, exactly, to do it?

Jillian's phone rang and she stepped back. "That's probably my attorney," she said. "He was supposed to call this morning."

"Good," Baldwin replied. The fact that Randall had been caught in the act of breaking into her place to steal additional sources of fingerprints strengthened the case for Jillian's innocence in the robberies. Now that the police had concrete proof Randall was targeting Jillian, he hoped the DA would drop the charges against her.

He listened with half an ear as the locksmith worked, his mind churning as he planned and dismissed various scenarios to find Randall. But no matter what he imagined, he kept circling back to one conclusion:

He was going to have to talk to his parents.

Chapter Twelve

"I don't understand." Jillian paced the length of the kitchen, frustration building as she listened to her attorney talk. "The man broke into my home and shot me! What more evidence does the DA need to accept that he's framing me and I didn't commit the robberies?"

"I know it's hard," Rodney said soothingly. "But it's not as bad as it sounds."

"Are you sure about that?"

"I am," he said, sounding more confident than she felt. "The DA doesn't disagree that you're a victim here. But until we can conclusively link Bowe to the robberies, there's still the matter of your fingerprints at the last crime scene."

"So nothing has changed," Jillian said flatly. She wanted to scream at the unfairness of it all. It seemed that unless Randall put out a billboard confessing to the jewel thefts, she was still going to be blamed for them.

"Actually, this has been a positive development." Rodney sounded almost gleeful. "I am sorry you got shot, of course," he hastily added. "But I have to say, this will make you incredibly sympathetic to a jury. Remember, we don't have to prove you're innocent. We just have to create reasonable doubt in the minds of the jurors. Randall's recent actions certainly help with that."

"I suppose," Jillian grumbled. It didn't seem right that she'd had to get shot to make a jury believe she wasn't a thief, but there was nothing to be done about it now.

"Try not to get discouraged," Rodney said. "I know things are stressful now. Just keep your chin up and let me do my job."

"Thank you," Jillian replied. She did trust the man, even if her faith in the system was being tested.

An incoming call beeped, so she said goodbye to Rodney and switched over.

"Jillian? It's Grace. How are you doing?"

Her mood brightened at the sound of her cousin's voice. "I'm hanging in there," she said honestly.

"I heard about the shooting," Grace said, her voice full of concern. "I'm so sorry I didn't come to the hospital. I was working a double shift and couldn't get away."

"It's okay," Jillian assured her. "You didn't miss much. Besides, with Mom and Wes and Bryce and Madison and Baldwin all there, the place was pretty crowded."

"Baldwin was there?"

Jillian didn't miss the note of curiosity in her cousin's seemingly innocent question. "Yeah," she said, warmth rising in her chest as she recalled how he'd spent the night by her side, despite the uncomfortable conditions for him. "He was there the whole time."

"Wow." Grace sounded impressed. "I'm glad you weren't alone."

"No chance," Jillian confirmed.

They chatted for a few minutes and then Grace said, "Listen, I don't know if this makes you feel any better, but Ian is working almost around the clock trying to find some evidence that Randall was at those robbery scenes."

"He is?" Jillian was surprised to hear that. Ian Elward was one of her coworkers in the lab. They had a decent working relationship, but he wasn't what she'd consider a friend. Ian was a nice enough guy, but he was a bit of a know-it-all and came across as arrogant at times. He wasn't very personable and didn't go in for friendly chitchat, which she knew through the grapevine rubbed some people the wrong way.

"Yeah," Grace confirmed. "He told me that he felt bad about the way he'd treated you when Randall was still there. Something about how he'd thought you were bad at your job, but he now realizes that was all Randall's doing. I guess he's trying to make up for his assumptions?"

"I'm glad to hear it," Jillian said. She and Ian had argued from time to time, and she'd occasionally gotten the impression he didn't think she knew what she was doing. It was nice to know Ian realized she'd been targeted by Randall. She was even more impressed that he seemed to be doing something about it.

"I was shocked," Grace said. "He's normally so standoffish I couldn't believe he was talking to me, much less admitting he'd been wrong about you."

"I have to confess I don't know what to think anymore," Jillian said. "With everything that's been going on, it feels like my life has turned upside down and I don't know what normal is anymore."

"I know," Grace said sympathetically. "Things are definitely unsettled right now, but everyone here is rooting for you. Chief Shea has even brought in an outside CSI team to examine all the evidence and search for any links to Randall."

"Wow," Jillian said. The knowledge that the department really did have her back brought tears to her eyes and made her feel a little less alone. "I don't know what to say."

"You don't have to say anything," Grace responded. "We all know how devious Randall is. We're not going to stand by while he targets you."

"Just don't put your own jobs at risk," Jillian said. "I don't want anyone to get in trouble with IAB on my behalf."

"Not to worry," Grace said confidently. "Things have cooled off on that front, especially since Randall broke into your condo and attacked you."

"My attorney said it helped my case," Jillian said. "I guess it's good to know I didn't get shot for nothing."

"Gotta find that silver lining," Grace teased.

"Look, I'm going to spend the rest of my day catching up on paperwork, but I'm off tomorrow, too. Want to grab a bite?"

"That would be great," Jillian said. "Are you sure Camden won't mind being left out?"

"Of course not! He knows I need my regular dose of girl-time. It won't bother him at all. The real question," Grace said, a sly note entering her voice, "is will Baldwin mind?"

At the mention of his name, Jillian automatically glanced across the room to where he was sitting in one of the recliners. He was faced toward the locksmith, but she could tell by the look on his face that he was lost in thought. "Why would he mind?" Jillian said, trying to sound nonchalant.

Grace simply laughed. "Oh, my," she said. "It's more serious than I thought."

"What do you mean—?"

"I'll text you later," Grace interrupted. "We'll figure out a time and a place for tomorrow. 'Bye!"

Her cousin hung up before Jillian could reply. She shook her head and pocketed the phone, then walked over to Baldwin.

"Everything okay in here?"

He nodded absently, making her wonder if he'd even heard her question.

"I was thinking we could hop on a plane and get out of town," she said, testing him.

"Sounds good," he replied.

"But first you should sell your truck."

"Uh-huh."

"And adopt a dog."

"Yep. Wait, what?" He turned to look at her, eyebrows drawn together in confusion.

"Hi, there," she said, smiling down at him. "I take it you're back now?"

"Back from where?"

"You were clearly lost in thought," she informed him. "I'm just giving you a hard time."

"Sorry about that," he said, reaching for her. She let him pull her into his lap, enjoying the contact. Every time he touched her, a spark of energy traveled through her body. It was probably because this thing between them—however they were going to define it—was so new.

But would it last? They hadn't had a chance to talk about the physical turn their relationship had taken. Baldwin had been clear from the start that he had no plans to stay in Grave Gulch. Jillian doubted one night together had changed his mind, but a small part of her heart hoped that maybe he was having second thoughts about leaving. He clearly liked her, and based on his actions before they'd slept together, she was fairly confident his attraction to her went beyond sex. She was probably jumping the gun to even wonder at his future plans and her potential place in them. But Grace wasn't the only one who was curious to know what was going on between them.

"What did your lawyer have to say?"

His question pulled her from her wandering thoughts. She filled him in on the conversation with

Rodney, mentioning his positive outlook on the situation. "I just wish I shared his optimism," she sighed.

Baldwin pushed a strand of hair behind her ear. "I know it's not easy," he said softly. "But we will bring Randall to justice."

Jillian leaned down until their foreheads touched. "I believe you," she said simply.

His eyes warmed and he smiled. "Good," he replied.

"I just wish I knew why Randall was so fixated on me." She leaned back and shook her head. "I mean, he's targeted people before. But it seems like he has a vendetta against me or something."

Baldwin frowned. "I noticed that, as well. I've been reviewing some of the cases he tampered with, to see if you have anything in common with the people affected."

Jillian sat up straight. "That's a good idea." She didn't try to hide the admiration in her voice.

Baldwin rolled his eyes. "I may not be a forensic scientist, but I can hold my own in an investigation."

She ran her fingers through his short hair, mussing up the strands as much as possible. "I never doubted you."

"Uh-huh," he said doubtfully. "Anyway, from what I can tell, Randall is obsessed with cheaters. It seems like every case he mishandled had something to do with cheating of some kind, be it in a romantic or business relationship."

"Hmm." Baldwin's observation made something

stir in the back of her mind, but she wasn't sure what it was yet…

"Did he ever accuse you of misconduct at work?"

Jillian started to shake her head, then stopped with a gasp as a memory pushed to the front of her mind.

"I take it that's a yes?"

She turned to Baldwin, her eyes wide as she nodded. "Once. Not long after I started working in the lab. He asked me if I wanted to grab a bite to eat with him after work one day. I wasn't sure if he was asking me on a date, or just wanted some company while he ate. Either way, I turned him down." The idea of spending more time with Randall had made her want to gag. "I told him I had a boyfriend and he'd get upset if we went out together just the two of us."

"And did you?" Baldwin asked, his eyes steady on her face.

"Did I what?"

"Have a boyfriend?"

Jillian shook her head. "That's what you want to focus on here?" When he merely arched one eyebrow, she sighed. "No, okay? I wasn't seeing anyone at the time. But Randall didn't know that. He made a big deal of the fact that I was being faithful to my boyfriend. Said I was doing the right thing, stuff like that. I found out later he was married, so I don't even know why he asked me to dinner in the first place."

"She cheated on him," Baldwin said.

Jillian felt her mouth drop open. "She did?"

Baldwin nodded. "Yeah. I'm not supposed to know about it, but our mom let it slip once."

"No wonder he's been going after the cheaters." It all made a sick kind of sense now. But that still didn't explain why he was focused on her. Jillian had never been unfaithful in a relationship.

"Why me, though?" she asked. "I'm more confused now than I was before."

"So am I, to be honest," Baldwin said. "I don't know why Randall is trying to hurt you. Maybe he's lost his grip on reality and for some reason sees you as a threat. After all, you're part of the team who uncovered his crimes."

"I'm not the only one, though," Jillian pointed out. "Several people work in the lab with me. He's not going after Ian or any of the other techs."

"You're special," Baldwin said with a lopsided smile.

"Thanks," Jillian said dryly. "That's very reassuring."

Baldwin kissed the tip of her nose. "Listen, I've been thinking."

Jillian straightened. "I noticed," she said. "You were miles away earlier. Are you going to fill me in now?"

Baldwin nodded. "I'm tired of waiting for Randall to come to us. I think he got spooked the other night, and there's no telling when he'll make another move."

"That makes sense," Jillian said. "He's probably

going to lay low for a while, until he comes up with another plan."

"Exactly," Baldwin said. "I don't want to give him the chance to regroup. I want to go after him, put him on the defensive for a change."

"Okay. How are we going to do that?"

"Well, that's the thing." Baldwin glanced away and shifted a bit, looking uncomfortable. "I think we're going to have to talk to the people who know him best."

Jillian frowned. "I don't think your brother has any friends," she said. "And his wife insists she doesn't know where he is."

"I'm not talking about his wife," Baldwin said, sounding resigned. "I think it's time we visited my parents."

"ARE YOU SURE you want to do this?"

Baldwin put the truck in Park and glanced over to find Jillian looking at him with an expression of concern on her face. He reached over and placed his hand on top of hers. "I'm fine," he told her.

"We don't have to go inside."

"What makes you think I don't want to go inside?"

She flipped her hand over to lace her fingers through his. "Because the closer we got to the house, the less you spoke and the more tense your shoulders became."

Baldwin deliberately relaxed his muscles and took a deep breath. She was too perceptive for her own good. "I'm fine," he repeated. "We need to talk to my parents. They might know something that will lead me to Randall."

"Don't you think they would have gone to the police?"

Baldwin considered the question. His parents weren't bad people, but they had always been protective of Randall. "I think if they knew something obvious, they would share it with the police. But I'm wondering if they might have insight into where Randall could be hiding and just not realize it."

Jillian studied him for a moment, her gaze warm. "I don't want you to hurt yourself for my sake," she said quietly. "I want to get your brother as much as anyone, but not if it means causing you pain."

Baldwin clenched his jaw to push back the sudden sting of tears. What had he done in this life to deserve Jillian's concern? His brother had spent the better part of a year psychologically torturing her, he'd broken into her home and shot her and Baldwin himself had started out their time together acting like a jerk. And yet she still cared about him and worried at how he would be affected by seeing his parents.

"Jillian," he said, his voice rough. "I would crawl through broken glass if it meant putting an end to this nightmare for you."

Her eyes widened and she sucked in a breath. "Baldwin—"

"Let's go," he interrupted. He didn't want her gratitude, didn't want to hear her thank him for doing the bare minimum. He had promised her he would keep her safe and find his brother. It was time he did just that.

He climbed out of the truck and walked to the passenger side to help her down. She took his hand and gave it a squeeze in a silent gesture of support.

His parents' home was at the end of a quiet, tree-lined street. The lawn was trimmed and although the front flower beds were currently bare, he had no doubt his mother planted something pretty every spring.

It wasn't the house he'd grown up in; he had no memories of riding his bike down the sidewalk or playing hide-and-seek with the neighbor kids. In fact, he'd only been here a handful of times over the years, always for short, painfully awkward visits that he'd completed more out of a sense of obligation than any real desire to see the people inside.

Jillian's shoulder brushed against his arm as they stood on the porch. In some ways, he was glad to have her with him. She was certainly the first woman he'd ever brought home to Mom and Dad. It was the kind of thing couples did when they were getting serious about each other, and not for the first time, he wished he had a normal family.

But maybe this was for the best. He certainly didn't know what was going to happen between them, and at least Jillian wouldn't mistake meeting his parents as a sign of his intentions for their relationship.

The door opened to reveal his father, who blinked in surprise.

"Baldwin," Dave Bowe said, clearly taken aback. "We weren't expecting you."

"Sorry about that," Baldwin replied. "I'll call next time."

His dad nodded, then turned his attention to Jillian. "And who is this?" The question was more of an accusation, as though he couldn't believe Baldwin had showed up without warning and dared to bring a stranger with him.

"This is Jillian Colton."

"Nice to meet you." Jillian extended her hand, but his father didn't shake it.

"Is she pregnant?" his father asked bluntly.

Baldwin's temper went from zero to full boil in the space between heartbeats. He opened his mouth to reply, but before he could tell his father to go to hell, Jillian laughed.

"You're right, he is funny," she said, clapping a hand on Baldwin's shoulder. She turned to the older man and offered him a tight smile. "Baldwin and I work together. I'm going to assume he got his charm from his mother."

Baldwin's father had the grace to look contrite. "Dave Bowe," he said gruffly. "Please come in."

Baldwin placed his hand on Jillian's lower back as they walked into the house together. "I am so sorry," he murmured.

Jillian shook her head. "Don't worry," she whispered back. "I've dealt with worse."

His father led them into the living room and gestured to the sofa against the wall. "Have a seat," he said. "I'll tell your mother you're here." He walked away, leaving them alone.

Baldwin turned to Jillian. Before he could say anything, she held up a hand. "I'm fine," she assured him. "Let's just get this over with."

"My thoughts exactly."

After a moment his father returned, his mother trailing behind. "Oh!" she exclaimed. "We weren't expecting you!"

Jillian slid him a look of disbelief. "I'm sorry, Mom," Baldwin replied dutifully. "I didn't have a chance to let you know we were coming."

"Lost your phone?" his father grumbled.

His mother brushed aside his apology. "Well, that's all right. You're here now." She made no move to hug him, and Baldwin didn't try to force any affection on her. Linda Bowe turned to look at Jillian. "And who is this?" she asked, echoing his father's earlier question.

"I'm Jillian Colton." This time, Jillian's attempted handshake was accepted.

"Nice to meet you," his mother replied. "I'm Linda. Please, have a seat. Can I get you something to drink?"

"No, thank you." He and Jillian spoke at the same time, and he smiled mentally. Neither one of them wanted to stay any longer than necessary.

They sank onto the sofa while his parents took the chairs seated across the coffee table. The fabric of the couch was stiff and the cushions well-stuffed. It was clear no one sat on this furniture regularly, and a small part of Baldwin was insulted that his father had left them in the formal living room rather than the den, where his parents spent most of their time. It further underscored the distance between them and drove home the point that they considered him a guest and not family.

"Well, what brings you out here?" his mother said. "We haven't seen you in ages, Baldwin."

"Work has been keeping me busy," he replied.

"That's good," Dave interjected. "Keeps you out of trouble."

Baldwin ignored the jab and focused on his mother. "I'm actually here because of a job."

"Oh," Linda replied. She glanced at Jillian. "Are you his client?"

Jillian shook her head. "No. I'm more of a co-worker."

His mother frowned faintly. "I see," she said, though it was clear from her tone she didn't.

"My case is connected to Randall," Baldwin said.

His father raised his hands above his head in a gesture of irritation. "Oh, here we go!" he exclaimed. "I knew there had to be some reason for you to come here. There's no way he's here to visit, I told myself. Of course it has something to do with your brother." He fixed Baldwin with an angry, almost challenging stare, as if daring Baldwin to argue with him.

Linda pursed her lips and shook her head. "I'm afraid we can't help you. We spoke with the police a few months ago and told them everything we know, which isn't much." She studied him for a few seconds, a look of disappointment crossing her face. "Did you really have to take a case involving your own family?"

Baldwin took a deep breath to tamp down his rising temper. "Randall has hurt a lot of people. He needs to answer for what he's done."

His mother looked away. "Randall has always been...complicated," she said. "If he truly did those things, I'm sure he had his reasons."

Baldwin felt Jillian's body go tense beside him and he reached over to take her hand. "I'm not here to argue about Randall's motivations, or to debate the question of his guilt with you."

"Then why did you come?" his father asked angrily.

Baldwin leveled his gaze on the older man. "Everyone is searching for Randall. The police, the FBI. Even me. At some point, we're going to find him. It's not a matter of *if*, it's a matter of *when*. Do you want some trigger-happy rookie looking to make a name for himself to be the one to bring him in?"

His mother looked away, biting her lower lip. His father's anger receded somewhat. "No," he said quietly. "Whatever your brother has done, he doesn't deserve to die for it."

Depends on who you ask, Baldwin thought wryly. His client would happily choke the life out of Randall and not blink an eye. And now that his brother had shot Jillian, Baldwin shared that sentiment.

"Who are you working for?" his father asked.

For a split second, Baldwin debated lying to them.

They still clearly thought Randall hung the moon, and they likely felt the whole investigation was an overreaction to what they believed were some honest mistakes their golden child had made at work.

But they needed to hear the truth. They needed to know how Randall had ruined lives, even if they refused to accept it.

"My client's name isn't important," Baldwin said. "But because of Randall's deliberate mishandling of evidence, that man's son was falsely imprisoned. When his son refused to join one of the prison gangs it was treated as a sign of disrespect and he was murdered."

The color drained from his mother's face, and his father squeezed his eyes shut.

"Two nights ago, Randall broke into Jillian's condo and shot her," Baldwin continued, keeping his voice even. "Randall and Jillian used to work together at the police department. He's now framing her for a series of robberies."

Tears began to track down Linda's cheeks, but Baldwin felt no sympathy for her. She needed to understand that Randall was not the good guy. He wasn't some misunderstood genius, or a man who was being unfairly persecuted. He was deliberately and methodically hurting people, and he had to be stopped.

"Why are you here?" His father's voice was quiet, but Baldwin heard the anguish in his tone.

"I want to know where you think Randall might be hiding. What are some places he might think to

go? Places that are specific to our family, maybe?"
Baldwin had been wracking his brain trying to come
up with a list, but he hadn't had much luck. They'd
never gone camping as kids, never really had a favorite place to stay nearby. The police had already
checked all the hotels and motels in the surrounding
area and were doing regular spot-checks of nearby
campgrounds. Everyone knew he had to be close,
but where?

His mother was shaking her head. "We don't
know anything!" she insisted. She was openly crying now, her voice thick with emotion. "We haven't
spoken to your brother in months, ever since all of
this started. I've been worried sick about him, thinking of him alone and scared, wondering if he's okay."

Baldwin felt a surge of disgust at her words. Even
after learning about the horrible things his brother
had done, his mother was still more concerned for
Randall than his victims.

"If we knew something we would tell the police,"
his father chimed in.

Baldwin looked at the carpet and shook his head.
"See, that's the thing," he said, almost to himself.
"I'm not so sure you would."

His mother gasped but Baldwin didn't acknowledge her reaction. He stood, tugging gently on Jillian's hand to bring her to her feet. "This was a waste
of time," he declared. He started for the door, Jillian
trailing behind him.

"Now you wait just a minute," his father yelled
after them. But Baldwin didn't stop. This wasn't a

both-sides issue, where he could understand how he and his parents might think differently. Randall had blood on his hands. And while he knew that his parents would always love their son, they also needed to accept that Randall had done some bad things and deserved to face consequences for his actions.

But if their reactions today signified anything, it was that his family was never going to embrace the reality that their perfect son was guilty.

Baldwin walked out the door and headed directly to his truck, not wanting to give his father a chance to catch up to them. This was it, the last straw. He couldn't even pretend that his parents cared about him anymore. They hadn't been happy to see him at all, had been more annoyed that he hadn't warned them ahead of time that he was coming. And the way his dad had treated Jillian? Even if she had been just a coworker and not the woman he was falling in love with, his father's actions had been inexcusable.

Love? Did that word really apply here? He glanced down at Jillian as she walked alongside him. Despite his anger and frustration, her presence made him feel grounded. Like she was the eye of the storm swirling inside his heart.

He could fight it. Try to deny the truth. But what would be the point? He was falling in love with Jillian Colton. It was a heck of a time to realize it, but since when had he ever taken the conventional path?

He unlocked the doors and helped Jillian inside, then rounded the hood and climbed behind the wheel. He glanced up as he put the engine in Reverse to see

Dave Bowe standing on the porch, arms crossed as he watched them with a frown.

Probably wants to make sure I leave, Baldwin thought bitterly. Well, the older man needn't worry. Baldwin was going, all right. And he was going to stay gone.

Jillian waited until they were on the main road before speaking. "Are you…?" She trailed off, then tried again. "How are you?"

"Fine," Baldwin muttered, ignoring the ache in his chest. "Just fine."

He'd been such a fool to think that a visit to his parents might have been helpful! The distance between them had only grown larger over the years, and now the gap was insurmountable. He wasn't surprised, but part of him was still hurt to know that he would never have a meaningful relationship with his parents. He'd long ago given up on Randall, but he'd still held out a small glimmer of hope that things with his parents might improve.

Now he knew better. Apparently, in their minds, Randall's sins paled in comparison to Baldwin's desire to live his life on his own terms.

Jillian didn't say anything. She was smart enough to know he wasn't capable of talking right now. But after a moment, he felt her hand on his leg.

It was a simple gesture. Just a light touch, one that he could either acknowledge or pretend to ignore. A reassurance that she was here if he needed her.

As it turned out, he did.

Baldwin had spent most of his adult life alone.

Not physically speaking; he was always around people, especially in the military. That wasn't the same as forming real connections with others, though. He mostly kept to himself, content with his own thoughts. An island in the great sea of humanity.

Except now that he'd met Jillian, he didn't want to be an island anymore.

He took one hand off the steering wheel and placed it over hers. He still felt too raw to try to talk about anything, but there were other ways to tell her that he needed her.

"I have an idea," she said quietly.

"What's that?"

"I'd like to take you somewhere, if you're willing."

Baldwin didn't hesitate. "Sure." He didn't know where Jillian wanted to go, but it didn't matter. As long as she was with him, he didn't care.

She gave him directions and he nodded. "The forest?" It was an unexpected destination, but Jillian must have something in mind. "Isn't that where Len Davison was killed?"

He glanced over as she shook her head. "It's a different place. You'll see."

Chapter Thirteen

"It's just a little farther."

Baldwin grunted but didn't say anything. Jillian trudged along the snow-dusted path, grateful she'd chosen to wear sneakers today. She hadn't imagined they would go hiking, but after the visit with Baldwin's parents, she'd sensed he needed to get away for a bit.

The forest was quiet this time of year; it was the off-season for tourists, and most of the campgrounds were closed until the spring thaw. Fortunately, they hadn't had much snow yet, so the trail was still passable.

Jillian led Baldwin another fifty yards, taking one more curve that led them out of the trees. They stepped up to the shoreline of a small lake, a hidden gem tucked away in the forest. Usually during the summer it was filled with hikers and swimmers and campers. But right now, the water was so still, it looked like a mirror reflecting the gray sky overhead.

She took Baldwin's hand and together they walked to a large log set several feet from the water's edge.

The gravel crunched under their feet as they walked and overhead she saw a hawk riding the thermal drafts in search of its next meal.

The log was cold when she sat on it, but the view was worth the chill. Baldwin sank down next to her with a small sigh and stared out across the expanse of water. "I had no idea this was here," he said finally.

"It used to be a bit of a secret," she told him. "But as the years have gone by, more and more people have discovered it."

"It can't be more than what, a hundred and fifty yards across?"

"Two hundred," she corrected.

Baldwin glanced at her. "You seem very certain of that."

Jillian shrugged. "I may have swum across it on a dare before."

He chuckled. "Is it deep?"

"Deep enough," she confirmed. She'd never been an especially strong swimmer, but one summer Bryce had taunted her so much that she'd jumped in the water just to shut him up. She'd made it a quarter of the way across before realizing she'd made a mistake, but her pride wouldn't let her turn around. So she'd pushed ahead, barely making it to the other side. She could still recall the rubbery feel of her limbs when she'd crawled out of the water on the opposite shore. Bryce had been there waiting for her, his face as white as a ghost. They'd gone home without another word, and to this day, neither one of them had told their mother about her stunt.

"It's beautiful," he said quietly. He turned his head up to the sky and watched the hawk circle for a few minutes. Jillian reached for his hand, squeezing gently. There were so many things she wanted to say, so many questions she wanted to ask. But she knew that in this moment, he needed silence. If she tried to talk to him, it would only drive him further into his shell.

After a while, he spoke. "They weren't always like that."

Jillian didn't need to ask who he was talking about. "Were you ever close?"

"I don't know." He laughed, but there was no humor in it. "I know that's a strange thing to say. Things weren't as bad as they are now. I guess if you'd asked me a few days ago if we used to be close, I would have said yes. But after seeing the way your family is around each other, I realize that we've never had something like that."

"Every family is different."

He tilted his head to the side. "Yeah, but you and your siblings and your parents seem to have this unspoken connection that ties you together. You might annoy each other sometimes, but I don't think you've ever really doubted that you guys love each other."

Jillian nodded. It was true—despite any differences they may have had over the years, she'd never worried that she'd lose the love of her relatives. And even though her father had been gone for most of her life to date, they were still strengthening their bond with every passing day.

"With us," he continued, "it was like we tiptoed

around each other. My parents made no secret of the fact they thought Randall walked on water. He was the smart one, the clever one, the one destined for success. Whereas I..." He trailed off, shaking his head. "My interests were more pedestrian. More middle-class."

Jillian frowned. "Your parents didn't strike me as being snobby about wealth." Their home had been nice, but not overly so. If they had money, they certainly hadn't spent it on furnishings or decor.

"They're not," Baldwin replied. "But my dad was a college professor, which he thought made him the smartest person in any room. He and my mother still think of themselves as part of an intellectual upper class. Randall fit in nicely with their idea of success. I did not."

"You told me a bit about that before," she said, recalling what he'd said about their reactions to his joining the marines after high school.

"I embarrassed them when I chose the military instead of college. Then, when I got out, I embarrassed them again when I went into bounty hunting rather than use my GI bill to pursue higher education."

"But you don't need a college degree to be successful," Jillian protested. "Lots of people do very well for themselves without one. It's not a measure of intelligence."

Baldwin smiled faintly. "It is in my father's eyes," he said quietly.

"Well, he's wrong," she said firmly.

Baldwin smiled at her this time, a hint of warmth

entering his eyes. "I'd almost like to see you go toe-to-toe with him over that subject," he said. "He'll never change his mind, but it would be entertaining as hell to watch you smack him down."

"Take me there," Jillian said. "I'll do it right now." Anything to chase the sadness from Baldwin's gaze.

"It doesn't matter," he said. "I realized today that they're never going to accept me. They'd rather make excuses for Randall than believe the truth about him, and despite everything he's done, they'd rather claim him as a son than me."

Jillian scooted closer to him, until their hips were touching. "That's their loss," she said, putting an arm around his back to hug him. "You are an amazing man. The fact that they choose not to see it means there's something wrong with them, not you."

Baldwin didn't reply. He simply stared at the water, his mind clearly a million miles away. Jillian didn't speak. She wanted to give him time to process what she'd said. Because it was the truth. And she needed him to believe it.

His parents were fools to toss him away. And even though Baldwin was putting on a brave face, she knew he was hurting inside. It broke her heart to see this strong, confident man questioning his worth after spending a few moments with the people who were supposed to love him unconditionally. There was no excuse for their behavior; no justification for the way they'd treated him.

They sat in silence for several minutes. The wind started to pick up and the clouds took on a darker hue, but they didn't move. The truck wasn't too far away, and a little rain never hurt anyone.

Jillian wasn't sure how much time passed. She was content to sit next to Baldwin, her arm around his back, holding him as best as she could.

"Why here?"

She took a deep breath. "I wanted to bring you somewhere different. Some place you maybe hadn't been before. One that wasn't at all connected to your parents or your brother."

"Why?"

She leaned her head against his biceps. "I thought it might be easier for you to work through everything if we went somewhere that didn't have any past associations for you."

"A blank slate," he said quietly.

"Yeah," she replied.

He turned and kissed the top of her head. "You really are amazing, you know?"

Jillian smiled, warmed by his compliment. "What makes you say that?" She leaned back to see him look down at their feet.

"You're the only person in my life who cares enough about my feelings to do something like this." He gestured to the log and the lake before them. "If one of my friends had been with me during that visit, they would have asked if I was okay and then left me alone when I lied and said yes. But you..." He shook his head. "You brought me here so I could think in peace, and then you didn't pester me to talk."

"Would that have worked?"

"Nope," he confirmed. "It would have annoyed me."

"So you're saying I made the right choice," she teased. "Sounds like I know you pretty well."

"You do." There was a somber note in his tone that made her glance up, and she found him watching her, his expression serious. "You see me. Probably better than anyone ever has. I know we haven't known each other very long, but you seem to get me." He paused, swallowing hard. "I… I think I…" He shook his head, unable to continue.

Jillian's heart beat so hard in her chest, it was a wonder it didn't break through her rib cage and fly away. Was he saying what she thought he was saying? Was Baldwin Bowe professing his feelings for her?

"I know," she said, reaching up to cup his cheek with her hand. "I feel it, too," she assured him.

It was the damnedest thing. A few days ago, she'd thought him heartless. Now she realized the depth of his emotions and wanted to pull him close to help ease the ache of his parents' rejection. There hadn't been a magic moment when she'd suddenly realized Baldwin cared more than he tried to let on. But somewhere along the way, he'd gotten under her skin and Jillian knew she'd never be the same.

The only question was, where did they go from here? After Randall was no longer a threat, Baldwin would have to move on to the next case, wherever that might take him. Her job was here, in Grave Gulch. So were her family and the few friends she had. Did they even have a chance of making it work between them? Or was this destined to be a short-term connection, one that she'd remember for the rest of her life?

It was on the tip of her tongue to ask, but she didn't want to add to Baldwin's stress. He was already tied up in knots about finding his brother, and the meeting with his parents had only added to his burden. If Jillian was to press him about where they stood, he'd probably run away and never look back.

As much as she might like to plan for the future, she was going to have to live in the present. That meant enjoying the time they had now, for as long as they had it.

Baldwin turned his face into her palm and kissed her hand. Then he leaned down and brushed his lips against hers.

The heat of his mouth chased away the chill of the wind. Jillian leaned against him, determined to set aside all her questions and worries. She turned down the volume in her mind and focused on savoring the taste of Baldwin, the delicate pressure he put on her lips and the feel of his hand on her back.

There was something different about this kiss. Before, she'd felt the need driving him, the energy he was containing lest he lose control. But this was soft, tender. It wasn't about desire or sex. It was a connection, a communion between them.

It was love.

Jillian wasn't going to say it. To acknowledge it aloud would only further complicate an already complex situation.

But her heart knew the truth. And later, when things settled down, she could figure out what it all meant.

Baldwin drew back and rested his forehead against hers. Then he chuckled softly. "Your nose is like an ice cube," he said.

"Really?" She hadn't noticed. She'd been too caught up in the moment to register anything else, but now that he'd mentioned it, she realized how cold she was.

"Come on," he said. He stood and tugged her up, as well. "We need to get you someplace warm."

They set off down the path together, walking arm in arm. "Thank you for showing me this," he said.

"You're welcome." Jillian smiled up at him. "We used to ride our bikes here a lot as kids during the summer. Our house was pretty small and Mom worked all the time, so we were on our own for entertainment."

"I bet you had fun," Baldwin said.

"Oh, yeah," Jillian confirmed. "Did you do anything like that as a kid? Go off exploring?"

Baldwin shook his head. "Not really. Closest we ever got was my aunt's house the next town over. She had a big backyard that jutted up to a creek. We'd go there a few times a year and I loved catching tadpoles and stuff. Not Randall, though. He always stayed inside to read."

Suddenly, Baldwin stopped walking. The muscles under her hand tensed, as though an electrical current was passing through his arm. Jillian glanced up, worried.

His eyes were wide, his mouth slightly agape. He looked like he'd just been hit over the head with a log, and Jillian glanced around to see if he'd walked into a tree branch. But the path around his head was clear.

"Baldwin? What's going on?"

He sucked in a breath as a gleam entered his eyes. "I think I know where my brother is hiding."

HE DROVE LIKE a man possessed.

Baldwin kept his foot on the accelerator and one hand on the wheel as he talked to Carter, his buddy from the marines who had since started a private security company. Carter had been the one to watch Jillian's apartment that night she'd been shot, and he trusted him completely. Jillian sat quietly in the passenger seat, her curiosity so intense he could practically feel it.

"No, I don't need you to come with me," he said. "You've got to stake out the condo in case Randall doubles back."

"You shouldn't go alone," Carter protested. "You know that goes against all our training."

"I'll be fine," Baldwin said shortly. Carter had a point, but there wasn't anyone Baldwin trusted enough to accompany him.

"Look, man—"

"Will you do this for me?" Baldwin interrupted. He had additional arrangements to make and didn't want to spend more time than necessary on the phone.

Carter sighed, his displeasure coming through loud and clear. "Yeah, I will. But I'm about two hours away."

"That's fine," Baldwin replied. "Just get here as soon as you can."

He ended the call before Carter could argue further. A small part of him recognized he was being rude, but now was not the time to worry about manners.

"Is it my turn to talk now?" Jillian asked quietly.

The tires screeched in protest as he took a turn a little faster than advisable. "Yeah," he said. "I'm sorry."

"Where do you think Randall is hiding?"

"My aunt's house," he said. "She lived on the outskirts of Lakeside on a big plot of land that backed up to a creek."

"Would she help Randall?"

Baldwin shook his head. "She died about five years ago. She never had children of her own, so her house and everything in it was left to my parents. They decided to rent the home." He turned into the parking lot of Jillian's building and pulled into a spot near the entrance.

"As far as I know, the house is still being rented. But there was a large shed at the edge of the property, almost like a barn, and my parents used it to store some of her things. They kept it locked so the tenants couldn't access it."

"But Randall has a key?"

"I'm guessing so. Even if he doesn't, it wouldn't be hard for him to pick the lock."

They walked into the building together and headed for the elevator. He was so full of adrenaline that he could have happily raced up the stairs, but Jillian looked tired and she was still recovering from her injury.

Why had it taken so long for him to think of Aunt Ginny's house? The old shed was the perfect place for Randall to lay low and was close enough that his brother would still be aware of everything going on in Grave Gulch.

Jillian unlocked her door and they walked inside. "So what's your plan?" she asked, tossing her keys on the kitchen counter. "I'm assuming that you're going after him?"

"Absolutely," Baldwin said. No way was he going to let Randall spend another night as a free man.

Jillian spun around and leaned against the counter, then crossed her arms. "Alone?" There was a strange note in her voice that he'd never heard before, one that made the fine hairs on the back of his neck stand on end.

"Yes," he said carefully. He could tell she was tense, though he wasn't yet certain why. Was the thought of apprehending Randall making her emotional?

"You're an idiot," she said flatly.

Baldwin reared back slightly. Of all the things she could have said, he hadn't expected that.

"Excuse me?"

"You heard me." Now he recognized her tone—she was angry. Furious, even.

"Jillian, I—"

"Going off after your brother alone is not smart," she interrupted. "You should call the police, call your friend, take someone with you."

"I can't."

"You won't," she stormed. "You're determined to be the one to take down your brother. Your ego won't let you ask for help, because you want all the credit."

"That's not true," Baldwin said, his temper starting to build. This had nothing to do with his pride and everything to do with trying to keep Jillian safe. Why couldn't she see that!

"The sooner I bring him in, the sooner your life can go back to normal. Isn't that what you want?" She glanced away, so he pressed on. "Besides," he said, stepping closer, "I can't risk the chance that if someone goes with me, they'll end up hurt or worse. He's already shot you—I won't put someone else in danger."

"The police are trained to arrest people!"

Baldwin shook his head. "And if he resists? What then? They'll just shoot him?" He couldn't let that happen. "I know he's a bastard, but I want him to stay alive so he can answer for what he's done. He deserves to rot in prison."

"But what about you?" Tears brimmed in her eyes and her voice wavered. "What if he hurts you? Or…" She trailed off, shaking her head. "If something happens to you, Randall isn't going to stop to help you. He'll leave you there, all by yourself."

Baldwin took another step closer, touched by her concern. "Nothing is going to happen," he said quietly.

"How can you be so certain?" She looked so vulnerable, staring up at him. He wanted to pull her close and hold her, to promise her that he would come back whole and unharmed.

But he couldn't say that for sure. No matter how confident he was, no matter the fact that he had experience and training for this kind of situation, there was always an element of chance that couldn't be discounted.

Still, it would be easy to lie to her. To play up his past as a marine, to emphasize his medals and awards, as if they were some kind of proof that he was untouchable. At one point in his life, he *had* felt bulletproof. It wouldn't be hard for him to pretend that he truly was.

Except…now he had something to lose. He had no idea what the future would look like for the two of them, but he couldn't deny he cared about Jillian. If he was being truly honest, he was falling in love with her. If the worst happened, he didn't want to lie to her in their last moments together. Better to leave her with the truth, no matter how unpleasant.

"Nothing is ever certain," he began. "But I have experience on my side. Not to mention the element of surprise. Randall doesn't know I'm coming. I'm betting he's gotten comfortable, having spent so much time out there with no one ever thinking to check the storage shed. The police have been looking for him for most of the year with no luck—you know from the messages he's sent people that he's getting even cockier, if that's possible."

She was quiet a moment, clearly thinking. "I get that you don't want anyone to hurt your brother. And I know you're a big, bad ex-soldier."

"Marine," he interrupted with a smile.

She rolled her eyes. "Ex-marine," she corrected. "But didn't you always have at least one partner when you went on a mission?"

Her words echoed Carter's earlier objections. Baldwin recognized they both had a point, but he couldn't afford to waste time. If he called in the cops, they'd insist on taking control of the situation and he wouldn't be able to act. Despite everything, he still held a sliver of hope that he could talk Randall into coming in peacefully. Surely his brother was smart enough to know when he'd been beaten? But if Baldwin turned up with the Grave Gulch Police Department, Randall would panic.

Panicked people got themselves killed.

"Maybe I should come with you," she suggested. "I can wait in the truck. Just in case—"

"Absolutely not." Baldwin started speaking before she even finished. "There is no way I'm bringing you close to Randall. If it was up to me, you'd never see him again."

The ghost of a smile flitted across her face. "Am I not allowed to worry about you?"

He hooked a finger through one of her belt loops and tugged her close, until they were only a couple of inches apart. She hesitated a few seconds, then leaned against his chest.

Baldwin wrapped his arms around her, dipping his head until his nose touched her hair. He took a deep breath, drawing in the scent of her.

"I won't be gone long," he said. "I'll be back before you know it."

Her arms came around him as she rested her cheek against his sternum. "Am I just supposed to sit here twiddling my thumbs until that happens?"

"No." He rubbed a hand down her back, hoping she would agree to this next part without much fuss. "You're going to call your brother and hang out with him."

She tensed in his arms. "Why would I do that?"

"I'm just being cautious."

Jillian leaned back to look up at him. "You can't have it both ways," she said. "You can't tell me this is going to be a walk in the park, and then insist that I spend the evening with my brother while you're gone."

He should have known she would argue. Nothing about this woman was ever simple.

"If it's safe for you to go after Randall by yourself, then it should be safe for me to stay here alone. Besides, didn't you call your friend? Charles, is that his name?"

"Carter," Baldwin grumbled.

"Yeah, him," she continued. "You asked him to

do something for you. Is he coming back to watch my place again?"

"He is," Baldwin admitted.

Jillian nodded. "Right. So even though everything is perfectly fine, you've asked someone to guard my condo while you're gone."

Baldwin closed his eyes. "Please don't make this harder for me," he said.

"Oh, yes," she said, dropping her arms to end their connection. "Wouldn't want to inconvenience *you*."

"Jillian—" This wasn't how things were supposed to go. Why couldn't she understand he had to do this alone? That he couldn't handle it if his brother hurt anyone else?

"You should go," she said shortly. "I know how important your job is to you. Don't let me hold you back."

There were so many things he wanted to say to her. It was clear he hadn't explained his strategy very well, and he hated that Jillian was upset. But she was too angry to talk to at this point. Even if he tried to tell her that she wasn't holding him back— that she was more important to him than his job— she wouldn't believe him.

He sighed, a sense of resignation creeping over him. This conversation was effectively over, at least for the moment. Hopefully, once he returned from successfully capturing Randall, she'd be so happy that the threat from his brother was gone that her anger would disappear and they could move forward.

"I'll wait until Bryce gets here," he said quietly. "I don't want you to be alone."

"I'm not calling him," she said. "If he knows what you're doing, he'll insist on going along. And since he's already been shot once…"

"Who, then?" Baldwin asked, ignoring the jab. "I don't want you here alone. Carter is two hours away."

"Grace," Jillian replied. "Maybe she can come over."

Baldwin nodded. "Will you call her, please?"

Jillian stared at him a moment, emotions swirling in her eyes. Then she nodded once and stepped away with her phone.

It was on the tip of his tongue to call after her, to warn her not to tell her cousin about his plans. But he knew if he said anything, her simmering temper would likely boil over. He was already on shaky ground here; he didn't want to make things worse between them.

After a few minutes, Jillian returned. "She'll be here in ten," she said, her tone flat.

"That's good," Baldwin said quietly. "Thank you."

She nodded, but didn't look at him. "Go on," she said. "Wouldn't want you to miss your shot."

Baldwin was torn. On the one hand, she was right; the longer he stayed here, the greater the chance he'd miss finding Randall. He was fairly certain his brother was at their aunt's old storage shed, but what if he wasn't? Better to find out quickly so he could come up with another plan if needed.

But on the other hand…he didn't want to leave Jillian. Not just because it was risky to leave her alone. Because he cared about her and enjoyed spending time with her. She made him laugh, and she lightened his mood. And when things were stressful, like now, her presence helped keep him grounded. Even though she was angry with him, he still didn't want to walk away from her. Part of him was worried that if they didn't resolve this issue before he left, they might never be able to do it. It made him feel unsettled, as though he was walking blindfolded through a field of land mines. One wrong step, and things between them would explode, never to be repaired.

It was clear Jillian was upset. She'd told him to leave twice already; he wasn't going to make her ask a third time. Despite his worries, it was probably best to give her some space. They could talk about this later, when they were both calmer.

"I'll go," he said. He walked over to where she was standing and leaned down to kiss her forehead. He would have liked to have kissed her lips instead, but he wasn't going to press his luck. "I'll be back later. And then we can finish talking."

Jillian looked up at him, her expression worried. "You'd better come back," she muttered. "If you wind up hurt, I'll kill you myself."

He chuckled, happy to see she seemed to be moving from anger to irritation. "Yes, ma'am." He turned and took a step toward the door, then stopped as Jillian grabbed his arm and tugged hard.

She spun him back around and in one fluid motion she stood on her toes, cupped his face in her hands and pulled him down for a kiss. Baldwin started to put his arms around her, but she stepped back, evading his touch.

"You'll get the rest when you return," she said, touching her fingertips to her mouth as if to prolong the feel of his lips against hers.

Baldwin smiled, desire flickering to life inside his chest. "Then you'd better wait up for me."

Chapter Fourteen

At Baldwin's insistence, Jillian followed him to the exit. He waited until he heard the lock click into place before walking away. She turned and leaned against the door, listening to the fading sound of his footsteps and trying not to cry.

Stubborn, infuriating man!

Why was she surprised? Baldwin was bound and determined to catch his brother. She should have known there was no way he would entertain the possibility of waiting for help, not once he'd figured out Randall's likely hiding place. The man was like a dog with a bone, refusing to give up his precious, hastily put together plan. No amount of talking was going to change his mind; she would've had better luck trying to argue with a brick wall.

Not even her worry for him had mattered. Baldwin was so convinced of his tactical skill that he hadn't stopped to think about the fact that what his brother lacked in physicality, he made up for in deviousness. Randall was no match for Baldwin in a fair fight, but since when had Randall ever fought fair?

But Baldwin didn't appear to consider the possibility that he might be outmaneuvered. His ego wouldn't allow him to acknowledge it. In that way, the two brothers were alike—both supremely confident of their own abilities.

So why was she sitting here, almost crying over a man who had made it clear he didn't need her tears?

"You idiot," she muttered, not sure if she was talking to herself or to Baldwin. Things had been so much easier when he'd just been the jerk who was using her to get to his brother. If they'd stayed impersonal, she could have waved him off without a second thought. But now that she'd gone and fallen for him, it was different. All she saw were the risks he was taking, all she could think about were the ways he might get hurt, or maybe even killed. Her chest grew tight as her mind worked, as if someone was cinching a belt around her rib cage. She'd never forgive him if he died. She'd spend the rest of her life angry with him for leaving before they knew what was going on between them.

"Stop it," she told herself. This line of thinking was only making things worse. Baldwin was a decorated marine veteran—he didn't get that way by sitting in the barracks while everyone else went out to fight. He knew what he was doing, and she had to trust that he wouldn't take any unnecessary risks. He'd practically promised her he was going to come back. She should believe him—after all, he'd never lied to her before.

Jillian pushed off the door and wiped her eyes. Grace would be here in a few minutes, and Jillian didn't want her to think anything was wrong. She'd told her cousin that Baldwin was meeting with some friends in the area to see if they had any leads on Randall's whereabouts. She felt a little guilty about the white lie, but Baldwin had been insistent that he didn't want the police involved. Even though she wanted him to have backup, she understood his desire to do this alone. Baldwin had a lot of complicated feelings about his family and she knew he'd never forgive himself if Randall was killed, even though his brother was guilty of so many crimes.

She walked to the bathroom and splashed cold water on her face, then went back to the kitchen and poured herself a glass of iced tea. Part of her was glad Grace would be joining her shortly—she would be a good distraction. If left to her own devices, Jillian would spend the evening pacing the condo and clutching her phone, desperate for some kind of update from Baldwin. At least if Grace was here she'd have company, should the news be bad.

A knock on the door interrupted her maudlin thoughts. "It's me," Grace called from the other side.

Jillian opened the door and tried to smile, but it must not have worked very well. "Oh, no," Grace said. "What's wrong?"

"It's nothing," Jillian said, waving her cousin inside. "I'm fine."

Grace gave her a doubtful look. "Uh-huh. I can

see that." She lifted one hand to emphasize the bottle she held. "Good thing I brought this. Now let's get some glasses and you can tell me what's going on."

Jillian led her to the kitchen, debating what to say. She had to tell Grace something, but she didn't want to betray Baldwin. How to thread this needle?

"Baldwin and I had an argument," she said finally. It was the truth…mostly. She retrieved two wineglasses and set them on the counter.

Grace had already found the corkscrew and was busy peeling the label off the top of the bottle. "I see. What were you fighting about?"

"He thinks he needs to go after Randall alone," Jillian said carefully, keeping her eyes on Grace's hands. "I told him he should have backup, in case something goes wrong."

Grace nodded as she twisted the corkscrew. "That's the smart thing to do," she said. A *thunk* punctuated her words as she pulled the cork free from the bottle.

"Yeah, well, he's worried that Randall's actions have made things personal between him and a lot of people on the force. He thinks Randall might provoke someone into shooting him, so that he wouldn't be taken alive."

"Suicide by cop?" Grace poured wine into each glass, then set the bottle on the counter. "It's possible," she said. "It definitely happens sometimes. And with Randall's outsized ego, he might try that approach."

"What do you mean?" Jillian picked up her glass

and took a small sip. The red wine had a woodsy flavor that burned a little going down.

Grace shrugged. "I'm just saying, Randall prides himself on his intellect. He thinks he's outsmarted us all. Can you imagine what it would do to him to be arrested and forced to answer for what he's done? He thinks he's above normal people. It wouldn't surprise me at all if he'd rather die than be judged by us."

A chill skittered down Jillian's spine as she realized Grace was likely correct. She hadn't thought of it like that before, but it made a lot of sense. No wonder Baldwin didn't want the cops involved.

But…what if Randall tried to get Baldwin to kill him? It was the ultimate act of revenge between the two siblings, as Randall had to know his brother would carry the guilt for the rest of his life. Baldwin wouldn't hurt anyone except to defend himself. What if Randall didn't give him a choice?

Was Baldwin even now walking into a trap?

Jillian's heart jumped into her throat and she fought the urge to run out the door to try to find him. *Don't be silly*, she told herself. Not only was she clueless as to the location of the storage shed, but she was also almost certain Baldwin had thought of this exact possibility.

Right?

"Are you okay?" Grace eyed her over the rim of her wineglass. "You look like you've seen a ghost."

Jillian forced herself to take a deep breath. "Just hungry," she said. "Should we order a pizza?"

"O-o-oh, yes please," Grace said. "That sounds delicious."

"Any preference?"

"Veggie supreme with sausage, please," Grace said. She walked into the living room and glanced around. "You don't seem to be in the winter spirit."

"Can you blame me?" Jillian picked up her wineglass and followed her cousin. "I haven't exactly been thinking about cocoa or ice skating, what with everything else going on."

"Maybe putting up some cozy decor would help cheer you up?" Grace asked. "Should we give it a try?"

Jillian considered the suggestion. She didn't automatically hate it, which meant it was probably worth doing. "Yeah," she mused. "I think we should." At the very least, that would help keep her mind off Baldwin and the risks he was taking. "I'll call in for the pizza and then start pulling stuff out of the closet."

"Perfect!" Grace walked over to the television and picked up the remote. "I'll find us a cheesy movie to watch while we work."

Jillian dialed the number for Paola's Pizza and placed their order. A few minutes later she hung up and joined Grace on the couch. "They said it'll be about an hour."

"They must be busy tonight," Grace remarked.

"That just gives us more time to get stuff done. Let's get started!"

Grace's enthusiasm was infectious, and soon Jillian found herself smiling and even laughing as they worked to retrieve her wintry decorations from the depths of her closet. In no time at all, they had everything spread out in the living room.

"Where did you get all of this?" Grace asked.

Jillian shrugged. "Some of it I bought because it caught my eye. I always have big decorating plans, but they never seem to materialize because I get so busy with other things. A lot of it came from my mom—she's always buying me little things, and eventually, it adds up to this." She lifted her arms to encompass the room. "We definitely don't need to put everything out."

"I don't think we could even if you wanted to," Grace remarked. "You still need to live here, after all."

"That's true."

"What's in this box?" Grace gestured to the corner of the room."

"Fairy lights," Jillian said. "I put some up last year but haven't gotten around to it yet."

"We'll start there," Grace decided. "Once we get the lights up and some of the other wintry decorations out, we can figure out what the rest of the room needs."

Jillian was happy to let her cousin take the lead. Normally, she enjoyed decorating her space with the changing seasons. But there was nothing normal about this year.

Together, they maneuvered the tangled ball of lights out of the box.

Grace stood back and eyed it critically. "This looks complicated."

"It'll just take a bit of time," Jillian said. "At least we'll have something to do while we wait for our dinner."

Grace shook her head. "I can see I'm going to need to help you take everything down later."

"What makes you say that?"

Her cousin sighed. "Your storage strategy leaves a lot to be desired. For someone who is so organized in her job, I'm surprised you don't apply a similar philosophy at home."

"Not everything can be perfect," Jillian said absently as she worked to untangle the strands of lights.

It took a few minutes, but soon she and Grace were hanging the lights between sips of wine, the light from the television screen adding a warm glow to the room.

He's okay, Jillian told herself for what had to be the millionth time. Baldwin would be back soon, filled with triumph over finally catching his brother. They'd spend the rest of the night holding each other, celebrating the fact that Randall was finally going to face justice. And, most importantly, Baldwin would be safe and whole and in her arms.

It was a nice thought, one she was going to cling to until Baldwin walked through her door again.

It's going to be fine. It's all going to work out.

Maybe if she said it enough times, it would turn out to be true.

The alternative was too upsetting to contemplate.

BALDWIN SPENT THE drive to his aunt's place thinking about Jillian, worried about how he'd left things. She'd seemed okay when he'd walked out the door, but what if she was only pretending? What if that kiss was her way of telling him goodbye, and he'd been too distracted to notice? So many questions, but no obvious answers.

As he pulled into his aunt's old neighborhood, he forced his mind to focus on the job at hand. If he allowed himself to be distracted, he'd make a mistake. Possibly the last one of his life.

Aunt Ginny's house was set about twenty feet off the street, shaded by two large oak trees that had been there since his youth. They were much bigger now, obscuring most of the front of the house. This area was mostly ranchettes, so the nearest neighbor was at least fifty yards away. Hopefully the distance meant he wouldn't have to deal with any bystanders.

Baldwin coasted to a stop about ten yards up the road and cut the engine. He sat in the dark for several minutes, studying the house and the surrounding area. The windows were dark, betraying no hint of light within the home. That was good; if he was lucky, the renters wouldn't be home to catch him prowling around the backyard.

Satisfied that no one was around, Baldwin reached

into the glove compartment and retrieved a flashlight and his gun. The textured grip of the Glock was a familiar extension of his hand, but he felt a flicker of reluctance as he held the weapon. Randall had surprised him in Jillian's condo. He couldn't let that happen again.

Even if that meant shooting his own brother.

Baldwin quietly shut the door of the truck and walked toward the house, sticking to the shadows as much as possible. He crept along the side until he came to the gate that led to the large backyard. Fortunately, the gate was partially open and he was able to squeeze through the gap without making any noise. Once inside the yard, he paused, listening hard for the sound of a dog, or any indication someone was aware of his presence. But all he heard was the hum of the heater as it kicked on inside the house.

Moving carefully, he approached the large storage shed in the far corner of the yard. There were no lights back here, and at this distance, it was unlikely anyone would see him from the house. Still, he didn't rush. If Randall was inside, Baldwin didn't want to give him any warning of what was about to go down.

The mini barn loomed up before him, still solid and strong after all these years. Baldwin crept cautiously around the perimeter of the structure, looking for any signs of life within. No light escaped the cracks around the windows and the night was still and calm. He sniffed quietly, hoping to detect some hint of cologne or food that would give away his brother's presence. But the cold air held no clues for him.

Time to go inside.

Baldwin approached the door and flicked on his flashlight, angling his body to hide the light from the house as much as possible. The silver handle was dull where the plate joined to the door, but the knob itself was shiny, indicating recent use. A latch was bolted to the door a few inches above the handle, and a padlock hung open through the hook.

Baldwin's heart sank. Since the padlock was there, Randall couldn't be inside. There was no way for him to enter the shed, close the door behind him and replace the lock. So where was he?

His thoughts immediately turned to Jillian, and he was tempted to run back to the truck and head to her place. But he forced himself to stay put. She wasn't alone; Grace was with her, and Carter would be watching the condo soon. Much as he hated to be away from her with Randall at large, he needed to see this through to the end. Maybe there were clues inside the building. If Randall had been hiding here all along, he must have left something behind. Baldwin might even be able to figure out what his brother was going to do next. Spending a little more time here might yield big dividends in this case.

He holstered his gun in the waistband of his pants and used his now free hand to carefully remove the lock from the latch, pocketing it so he could put it back when he was done. Then he pulled the flat metal piece away and placed his hand on the doorknob.

Just before he turned the knob, a thought occurred to him. What if his brother had set up booby traps? It was the kind of thing he'd do, to ensure anyone looking for him would receive a nasty surprise. A quick glance around the frame of the door betrayed no wires or signs of explosives, and Baldwin didn't see any tape or other markers commonly used to determine if a site had been disturbed. Still, he didn't trust Randall. His brother was too clever by half, and Baldwin wasn't about to walk into one of his snares.

Instead of standing in front of the door, Baldwin changed position so he was pressed against the wall of the barn, with only his hand on the knob. His body was no longer in the line of fire, decreasing his chances of being the victim of a booby trap. He turned off his flashlight, then slowly turned the knob and pushed open the door.

It swung inside the building on silent hinges. Baldwin remained still for a moment, waiting to see if something was going to happen. But nothing did. No sounds came from inside the structure, not even the squeak of a startled mouse.

Interesting.

He angled his head to the side slightly, chancing a quick glance at the door and the dark interior it had revealed. It was pitch-black inside the barn, too dark for even shadows.

Time to go inside.

Baldwin clicked on his flashlight and aimed the beam through the door. It landed on the far wall, which was plastered with what looked like photographs and newspaper clippings. Off to the right side, at the edges of the light, he saw a cot with a pillow and blanket strewn on top.

"Gotcha," he whispered.

He swept the floor with the light but saw no traps. He took a step into the storage shed, and immediately realized his mistake.

A blur of movement came from the left. As Baldwin turned to react, a burst of foul, oily liquid coated his face.

His eyes and mouth began to burn, and his chest constricted as he fought to breathe. Almost instantly, he was back in training, when he'd been forced to stand in line with his fellow marines while they endured pepper spray directly to the face.

Baldwin staggered back, reaching for his gun. But before he could grab it, something hit him hard in the knees and he went down.

"Hello, brother."

He would have known that smug voice anywhere. Randall. But how—?

"The window, you idiot," Randall said, apparently sensing Baldwin's question. "I put the lock back into place and climbed in through the window."

Baldwin coughed, then gagged as he fought to breathe. He couldn't see a thing, but he sensed a light had been turned on in the barn. Randall would want to watch him suffer.

"I figured you were coming," his brother continued. "I've been keeping tabs on you."

"How?" he choked out. He didn't try to get up

yet—given the intense pain in his left knee, he didn't think his legs would support his weight.

"Her phone," Randall said, as if it should be obvious. "I noticed it on the counter when I was there the other night. Saved me having to search for it. I installed a little program before you interrupted me. Lets me track where she's going. And as a bonus, I can see who she's calling or texting."

"You've been listening?" He was wheezing now, but he knew from experience it wouldn't last forever. Still, that was cold comfort at the moment.

"No, it's not that good," Randall said ruefully. "It just tells me the number she's contacting."

"Why?" Just the one word triggered a bout of coughing so intense he thought he might break a rib. Tears streamed from his swollen eyes but they did nothing to wash away the acrid, burning chemicals.

"How are Mom and Dad?" Randall asked, ignoring his question. "Were they surprised to see you?"

Baldwin refused to waste a breath answering him.

"Doesn't matter," he said. "I don't have time for this, anyway. I have a date with Jillian."

"No!" Baldwin lunged in the direction of Randall's voice. If he could just get his hands on him, he could overpower his brother...

Randall dodged and laughed. Baldwin felt the air move and then something hit him on the back of the head. He fell, temporarily dazed by the blow.

"I think it's cute you have a crush on her." Randall grunted and Baldwin realized he was being pulled across the floor. "Stand up," Randall instructed.

When Baldwin didn't respond right away, Randall pulled the gun from his waist and pushed the muzzle into his side. "Now."

Baldwin managed to get his feet under him and he stood, biting back a scream as his knee protested his weight.

"Good boy," Randall said. He clicked a handcuff around Baldwin's left wrist, then pulled his right arm behind him to finish the job. "You're going to stay here until I get back."

Baldwin moved his arms and felt a tremor as the cuffs made contact with something metallic. It seemed Randall had circled his arms around a pole of some kind.

"That's right," his brother said. "You're stuck here. But don't worry. I won't be gone long. I might even bring Jillian back to join us."

"Leave her alone," Baldwin choked out. "This is between us." Some of his vision was starting to come back now, and he saw Randall's blurry figure standing several feet away.

"It was," Randall agreed. "But the more, the merrier." He moved out of Baldwin's field of view, then returned a second later holding something in his hands. He reached out and Baldwin jerked as he felt his brother's hands on his head.

Randall fit the gag over his mouth, positioning it between Baldwin's teeth. "There, that's better," he said, standing back once more. "You should know the people who rent the house are out of town for the holidays, and the neighbors are too far away to

hear you scream. Besides," he said, a note of anticipation entering his voice, "you might want to save
your strength for what's to come."

His words sent a chill down Baldwin's spine,
but he refused to show any reaction in front of his
brother. Truth be told, he wasn't worried for himself. He was terrified of what Randall was going to
do to Jillian.

Randall reached for him again, shoving his hand
into Baldwin's front pocket and withdrawing his cell
phone. He held it in front of Baldwin's face, wiggling
it back and forth to taunt him. "You won't be needing this anymore."

Baldwin glared at him. He considered provok-
ing Randall into staying here and attacking him,
but under the current circumstances, there was no
guarantee he'd be able to get free and overpower his
brother. If Randall started beating him, Jillian would
be unprotected once his brother was done. As much
as he hated to do it, Baldwin had to feign helpless-
ness now so Randall would leave.

"See you soon," Randall called as he walked
through the door. A few seconds later Baldwin heard
it shut and the latch click into place. Randall cursed
when he noticed the lock was missing, but apparently
he thought Baldwin was secured enough without it,
because he didn't come back inside.

Good. Randall's cockiness was going to be his
downfall. He just didn't know it yet.

Baldwin waited until he no longer heard the sound
of his brother's footsteps outside. He took the op-

portunity to try to control his breathing, overriding the intense urge to cough and gasp. His eyes still burned, but they were getting better. His main problem was going to be his knee, which was throbbing in time to the beat of his heart. Still, all things considered, he'd been in worse situations. Granted, he was older now and not quite as fit. But his determination to save Jillian more than made up for any softening of his skills.

Randall had taken his gun. But if he'd done a thorough search of Baldwin's pockets, he would have found the multitool Baldwin always carried. He fumbled for it now, twisting and contorting his body so he could get one of his bound hands into his pocket. It took longer than he liked, but his fingers finally brushed over the metal. Once he extracted the tool from his pocket, it didn't take long to pick the lock of the cuffs. They opened with a click, and Baldwin felt a burst of gratitude toward his younger self for absorbing all the training the marines had offered him. He'd never be an academic like his parents or his brother, but he'd taken his time in the military seriously and had focused his efforts on learning everything he could. The lessons had saved his life on more than one occasion while in the service, and they were still paying off now.

He ripped off the gag and tested his knee, gritting his teeth as a fresh burst of pain radiated up and down his leg. It hurt like hell, but it still supported his weight. As long as he could walk, he'd be fine.

He moved toward the door, his foot hitting something on the floor. Based on the rolling sound it made, he figured it was his flashlight. Baldwin kneeled and managed to find it nearby. The beam wouldn't help his vision much, but he felt better holding the solid, heavy weight. He missed his gun, but he was never truly unarmed.

The journey back to his truck was slow and painful. He wanted to run, his desperation to get to Jillian driving him to go as fast as possible. But there was only so much his knee could take, and if he pushed it now, he wouldn't be able to help her later. So he plodded along until he reached his truck.

The steering wheel was cold against his hands. There was an unopened bottle of water in the passenger seat; he grabbed it and unscrewed the cap, then opened his eyes as wide as he could and poured the water over them. The cool liquid temporarily soothed the still-burning tissues, but the feeling didn't last long enough. His shirt was saturated with both water and pepper spray, so he carefully peeled it off and tossed it in the bed of the truck. Then he reached into the glove compartment and retrieved his backup gun.

"Hold on, Jillian," he muttered as he started the truck and pulled onto the road.

"I'm coming."

Chapter Fifteen

The place didn't look half-bad.

Jillian took a step back and eyed it up and down as she held her wineglass. She and Grace had wrapped the strands around the room, giving it a soft, cozy glow, and now it twinkled in a multicolored display that reminded her of the storefront windows along Grave Gulch Boulevard.

Grace picked up a plaid throw pillow. "Ready to start adding accents?"

Jillian nodded. "Absolutely. That will clear up some space for the pizza."

A new romantic movie was starting on the television. Grace glanced at the screen for a minute, watching the opening scenes. "She's going to get stranded in a small town and fall in love with the local vet. Or maybe the mechanic?"

Jillian chuckled. "Have you seen this one before?"

Grace shook her head. "No. But the signs are there."

"The signs?"

"Yeah. High-powered job, small dog. She's traveling for the holiday but has to take a car. The car is going to break down and because of the storm or the holiday, the part she needs won't be in for a few days. So she'll be stuck in town and she'll start to get to know the locals."

Jillian laughed. "Sounds like you've seen a few of these."

Grace grinned. "Oh, yeah. They're my kryptonite. I watch as many as I can."

"Does Camden like them, too?" Jillian had a hard time imagining the straitlaced Internal Affairs officer curled up on the couch in front of a romantic movie.

"He tolerates them for my sake. Honestly, I think they're growing on him. They can be a little cheesy, but there's something really nice about watching a story that has a happy ending."

"Especially in your line of work," Jillian remarked.

Grace nodded as she glanced around the room. "I think that's why I like them so much. It's like the best version of real life, you know? Even if something bad happens in the movie, you know it will all turn out okay in the end."

"Yeah." Lately, Jillian had been wishing for that kind of guarantee in her own life. Everyone around her seemed so certain that the charges against her would be dropped and Randall would be brought to justice, but unless that happened soon, she was on the hook for these robberies.

Her thoughts circled back to Baldwin and her anxiety ratcheted up another notch. Was he okay? Had he found his brother? Was he even now bringing him to the police station?

Or was he out there alone and injured, subject to Randall's unlikely mercy?

Grace touched her shoulder and she jumped, startled. She glanced over to find Grace standing next to her. When had she moved?

"Do you want to tell me what's really going on now?" her cousin asked quietly.

Jillian's eyes stung as tears built. She should have known she couldn't fool Grace for long. She so badly wanted to talk to her, but Baldwin had insisted on going alone. If she talked to Grace, it would be a betrayal of the trust he'd placed in her.

Except…she didn't know where he was. Not exactly. So even if Grace wanted to call for backup on his behalf, she wouldn't know where to send them. The stubborn man had made sure of that.

"Baldwin has gone after Randall," she said in a rush. It felt good to get the words out, even though it didn't change anything.

Grace's eyes went wide. "Alone? I thought you said he was meeting with friends."

Jillian shook her head. Damn that man, and damn her twisted sense of loyalty to him! It was one thing to support him emotionally and connect with him physically. But there was nothing healthy about keeping a secret that might cost him his life. She should have told Grace from the start.

"He thinks his brother is hiding in a storage barn

on his dead aunt's property," she said. "His parents are renting the house but the barn has always been locked. He thinks Randall might be holed up there."

"And so he went to investigate by himself," Grace muttered.

"Yeah," Jillian confirmed. "I told you earlier why he didn't want to take anyone."

"Idiot," Grace said under her breath. She glanced up at Jillian. "Sorry. I know you two have a thing."

Jillian shook her head. "Don't apologize. I agree with you. I would have told you earlier, but I don't know where he's gone."

"We can find out," Grace said. She pulled her phone from her pocket and dialed. "This is Grace Colton," she said. She rattled off her badge number. "I need a records search. We're looking for the address of Randall Bowe's dead aunt." She glanced at Jillian. "Do you know her name?"

Jillian shook her head, feeling powerless to help. "His parents are Dave and Linda Bowe. But I don't know the aunt's name."

Grace relayed the information. "Call me back when you get an address, please," she said. She ended the call, then dialed another number.

"Chief? It's Grace."

Jillian listened to Grace talk, her chest growing tighter with every passing second. Baldwin would be furious if the police showed up to his aunt's home, but Jillian wouldn't be able to live with herself if something happened to him, knowing she could have acted to stop it.

Her biggest worry now was would they get there in time to help him?

Grace hung up and looked at Jillian. "Okay. As soon as we get an address, he's going to send some officers out there to check things out. Chief Shea is excited about this new information, but he doesn't want to go in guns blazing unless we have more evidence that Randall is really there."

Jillian nodded, biting her bottom lip. "That's understandable." It was a neighborhood, after all. And Baldwin wasn't certain his brother was present.

The doorbell rang, signaling the arrival of their dinner. "I'll grab it," Grace said, still holding her phone. "Why don't you pour us some more wine? You look like you could use it."

Grace headed for the door, and Jillian took the moment alone to pick up her phone. She held it for a few seconds, debating. Should she text Baldwin to check in? Or would that distract him at a crucial moment?

She heard the door open and the sound of Grace's voice as she spoke to the delivery guy. But then Grace screamed her name.

"Jillian!"

There was a dull *thwack*, as if a baseball bat had struck a bag of rice. Then a thud sounded.

Jillian's heart pounded hard as adrenaline flooded her system. Something was terribly wrong.

"Grace?" She started for the hallway to the front door, intent on helping her cousin. Grace might be the trained police officer, but if she was being attacked Jillian wasn't going to stand by and do nothing.

She reached the entrance to the hallway to see Grace curled up on the floor, a man standing over her. He looked up and Jillian caught sight of his face.

Randall.

Her stomach knotted as he smiled at her. "Hi, Jillian. Good to see you again."

She turned and dashed back into the living room, frantically looking for anything she could use as a weapon. Randall was blocking her only exit, but surely she could find something to use to defend herself.

His footsteps grew louder as he approached, his pace measured and deliberate, like every villain in a bad horror movie. It was almost enough to make her laugh, but this was real life. And her cousin was lying unconscious on the floor.

Desperate, she moved to stand by the tree. Before Randall walked into the room, she hid her phone behind her back, careful to stay near the branches so he couldn't see her arm. She located the button on the side of her phone and pressed it five times in rapid succession, activating the safety feature that automatically dialed 911.

Randall stood in the doorway to the room, glancing around. "Getting ready for winter, I see." He sounded so casual, as if he was a friend dropping by for a visit and not a man trying to make her life hell.

A small voice from her phone spoke as the dispatcher answered her call. Jillian began to talk, hoping Randall wouldn't notice.

"What do you want, Randall? Where is Baldwin?"

Randall shrugged as he stepped into the room. He was holding a tire iron, and a wave of nausea swept over her as he lifted it to rest on one shoulder. If he'd hit Grace in the head with that, she might very well be dead.

"Baldwin is fine. He sends his regards." Randall began a slow tour of the room, stopping every few steps to examine her things. Jillian began to move, as well, trying to keep as much distance between them.

"Did you kill Grace Colton?" She spoke loudly, hoping the dispatcher would catch her words.

Randall paused and frowned. "Why did you do that?"

"Do what?"

"Say her full name. Grace Colton. Why not just say Grace?"

Jillian tried to shrug but panic clawed up her throat as she watched Randall connect the dots. "Who are you speaking to, Jillian?" His voice was harsh now, and a dangerous gleam entered his eyes.

"N-no one," she stammered, but Randall began to walk toward her.

Knowing her time was short, Jillian yelled out her address as she tried to dodge him. "Randall Bowe is here!" she screamed. "Officer Grace Colton is down!"

Randall grabbed her arm and pried the phone from her hand, then threw it to the ground and stomped on it. The glass of the screen cracked, and plastic pieces shot out in all directions from under his boot.

He wrenched her arm behind her back in a painful twist, pulling her up against his chest. "That wasn't very nice," he snarled. "I only came here to talk."

"You're lying." Her voice trembled but she held his gaze, refusing to show weakness. "If all you wanted was a conversation, you wouldn't have hurt Grace."

"She was in my way," Randall replied. "I needed her to move."

"So you killed her?" A pang of guilt and grief stabbed her like a knife in the heart. Her cousin was dead, all because she'd asked her to come over tonight.

"She's not dead," Randall said dismissively. "At least, I don't think she is."

"And I'm supposed to trust your assessment?" Jillian shook her head. "No way."

"It doesn't matter." He tugged on her arm, forcing her to take a step or fall. "We're leaving."

"No." Jillian planted her feet, determined not to move. "I'm not going with you."

"I thought you might say that," Randall replied. "But you should know, I have your precious boyfriend bound and gagged and totally at my mercy. If you ever want to see him alive again, you'll come with me now."

Anguish washed over her as her imagination painted a picture from Randall's words. It was possible he was lying to her, preying on her emotions to get her to cooperate with him. That was definitely the kind of thing he would do.

But what if he wasn't? What if he really did have Baldwin tied up somewhere? If she antagonized Randall, she was risking his life. And with Grace already seriously hurt, Jillian didn't want another victim on her conscience.

"Why are you doing this?" she asked. She was trying to buy herself some time, but she also needed to know the truth.

"You know very well why," Randall said, his voice low and tight.

Jillian shook her head. "No, I don't. I've never understood why you targeted me. After your crimes were exposed, I figured you were trying to plant doubt about my abilities so that any irregularities would be dismissed, and if anyone ever suspected you, you could simply point the finger at me. But now that the truth is out and people know what you did, why are you still focused on me?"

She spied a flicker of movement over Randall's shoulder, coming from the direction of the hall to the door. Her breath caught in her throat—was that Grace?

No. It was Baldwin!

Jillian nearly sobbed with relief. He was here! And even though she could tell he'd been hurt, he was still alive.

He lifted his forefinger to his lips, telling her to

keep quiet. Jillian blinked in acknowledgment, resisting the urge to say his name.

Randall noticed her change in expression. He started to turn his head, so Jillian jerked against his grip to hold his attention. "Tell me!" she demanded.

"You lied to me," Randall barked. "I couldn't let you get away with it."

"What are you talking about?" She squirmed, trying to put distance between their bodies. Randall responded by wrenching her right arm up behind her back until she cried out in pain.

"I never lied to you," she spluttered, trying to find a position that would relieve the stress on her arm. If Randall moved it again, her bones would break.

"Yes, you did," he insisted. "I asked you out to dinner once, do you remember?"

He punctuated the question with a squeeze of her wrist. Jillian bit her bottom lip and nodded. "Yes," she said, her voice thick with tears.

"You turned me down."

Another squeeze, and this time he added a little tug to her already strained arm.

"I remember."

"You told me you had a boyfriend and that he was the jealous type. But that wasn't true, was it? You weren't dating anyone." He waited, and Jillian realized he expected her to respond.

"No," she said. "I wasn't."

"You cheated me, Jillian. You cheated me of the opportunity for us to spend time together, to get to know each other."

Jillian saw movement in her peripheral vision, but from this angle, she couldn't tell what was happening. All she knew was that the longer she kept Randall talking, the harder it would be for him to escape the police.

"So you decided to frame me for the robberies?" Since he was in a chatty mood, maybe she could get him to confess. Surely her lawyer could do something with that, even if Baldwin was the only witness.

Randall laughed, his breath hot on her cheek. "You made it so simple," he said. "It wasn't hard to break in here and lift some of your prints. Easier still to return and leave the jewelry. You work all the time, so it's not like you were ever home to catch me."

"So now what?" she asked. "Did you decide the courts weren't moving fast enough for you? Is that why you're here—to punish me for lying to you?"

"Something like that," he said. "Now move."

He swung her roughly around, apparently determined to shove her down the hall and out the door. But as soon as Randall turned around, he froze.

"Let her go."

Baldwin stood just inside the living room, feet planted in a shooter's stance, his gun pointed directly at Randall. Jillian noticed an officer standing a step to the side of him, also aiming a weapon at Randall.

He wrapped his arm around her neck in a loose choke hold, keeping her body between him and the guns. She heard a thud as the tire iron hit the floor, and then something small and hard was pressed into her ribs.

"Let's not be so hasty," Randall said. His muscles trembled against her, betraying his nerves. He was caught, but he wasn't ready to admit it just yet.

"Drop your weapon," the officer commanded.

"You must be new here," Randall sneered. "That's not how a hostage negotiation goes."

"What do you want?" Baldwin asked. His eyes were swollen and his face was red, but Jillian could tell he was looking at her, trying to determine if she was okay.

"I'm going to leave," Randall replied. "And you're going to let me."

He pushed her forward a step, testing them. When no one fired, he pushed her forward again. And again.

She stared at Baldwin as they drew closer, saw the uncertainty on his face. She could see he wanted to act, but he feared doing so would cause her to get hurt. So he waited, clearly hoping to find an opening.

The other officer adjusted his stance as they approached, obviously trying to find a better angle. But Randall maneuvered to keep her body in the line of fire as they haltingly made their way across the room.

Jillian's heart pounded as they walked closer to the hallway. She wasn't going to let Randall take her out of here tonight. If she struggled, he would shoot her, but at this point, she was willing to take her chances.

She just had to time it right.

Her eyes caught on the decorations on one of the end tables. Most of them were too flimsy to use as a weapon, but one candlestick stood tall and proud above the rest. It was solid wood, hand-carved by her great-grandfather on her mother's side and passed down through the generations.

It would have to do.

Jillian held her breath as they got closer to the table. If she moved too soon, Randall would see what she was trying to do and shoot her. If she waited too long, the opportunity would pass. She was only going to get one shot at this.

She stared hard at Baldwin, trying to communicate with him. But his eyes were so bloodshot she wasn't sure he could even see her. Still, she dropped her gaze to the table, then back to him. He nodded almost imperceptibly.

Message received.

They were coming up alongside the table. It was now or never.

Jillian grabbed the candlestick with her left hand, quickly drew it up as high as she could and then brought it down against Randall's knee. He shrieked in pain, temporarily loosening his grip on her neck. She jerked free of him, stumbling forward.

As soon as she was clear, a thunderous boom split the air and Randall screamed again. Jillian turned in time to see him fall to the floor, his hand clutching his shoulder as blood welled around his fingers.

An officer rushed forward to retrieve Randall's

gun, then he ran his hands over Randall's body to ensure he wasn't hiding another weapon.

Baldwin stood in place, his gun still pointed at his brother. Jillian walked over to him and put her hand on his arm.

"It's over," she said, watching his face.

A storm of emotions swirled in those pale blue eyes. Pain, disappointment, betrayal. Maybe even a hint of guilt. Baldwin was clearly distraught, but Jillian couldn't help him just yet. She had to check on Grace first.

"Grace?" She stepped into the hallway to find another officer at Grace's side. Her cousin was sitting up, holding her head with her hand and wincing in pain.

"Are you okay?" Jillian dropped to her knees next to the other woman, relief making her want to cry.

"I will be," Grace replied. "I'm sorry he got past me. As soon as I recognized him he hit me with something and I went down."

"Don't apologize," Jillian said. She wrapped her arms around Grace in a gentle hug. "I was so afraid he'd killed you," she whispered, tears stinging her eyes.

"A Colton head is far too hard for that," Grace teased. "Now go to your man," she said. "He needs you."

EMTs and additional police arrived at her door. Jillian stood and walked back to the living room. Baldwin still hadn't moved. She took his arm and led him to the side of the room, making space for the medics and police to do their jobs. She dimly heard someone reciting Randall's rights and felt a huge weight lift off her shoulders as she realized he was being arrested.

It was all over. Randall was in custody.

"Hey." Jillian searched Baldwin's face, looking for some hint of his thoughts.

Baldwin glanced at her. "Are you okay?" His voice was thick with emotion and probably a little shock.

"I'm fine," she assured him. "More importantly, how are you?" He looked terrible, his eyes puffy and red, his lips a little swollen. She looked down the length of him and realized with a small shock that he wasn't wearing a shirt. "Where are your clothes?"

"Pepper spray," he said, as though that explained everything. "Randall ambushed me with it. Had to take off my shirt or it would keep affecting me."

"I see," she said. She didn't ask about what had happened after the pepper spray. There would be time for that later. Right now, all she wanted to do was hold him tightly until she no longer felt like falling apart. But as she studied him, she realized she had to keep it together a little bit longer. Baldwin's body was so tense she thought his muscles might snap. He was clearly on the edge, and it was up to her to bring him back.

"You shot him." It wasn't a question; he'd barely looked away from his brother since Randall had fallen to the floor.

"Had to," he said shortly. His voice was flat, but Jillian heard all the things he wasn't saying. By shooting his brother, he'd effectively ended any hope of a reconciliation with his parents. Baldwin was now a man without a family.

Jillian's heart ached for him, as she realized that he'd made the choice to save her life even though it had cost him dearly. He talked a good game about not needing his family, but she could tell that deep down, he still wished that things could be different between them. After seeing the way his parents had reacted to seeing him, and hearing their defense of Randall, Jillian knew they would never forgive Baldwin for what he'd done.

"You saved my life," she said, touching his shoulder. He didn't respond. Worry began to bubble in her stomach, growing more intense with each passing second. Baldwin was withdrawing before her eyes. If she couldn't reach him now, she'd lose him forever.

"And you saved his, too."

He turned to look at her then, his eyes glassy with unshed tears. "What did you say?" he asked.

"I said you saved your brother's life."

He blinked at her, clearly not believing her. She started speaking before he looked away again.

"You did, Baldwin. Anyone else would have shot Randall when they had the chance. He was armed and had taken me as a hostage. Police are trained to neutralize a threat in that kind of situation. But you pulled the trigger first, before the officer acted. And you made certain not to hit him in a vital area."

He pressed his lips together but didn't deny her words.

"I know you feel guilty about hurting your brother," she said, lowering her voice so that the other people in the room wouldn't overhear their conversation. "But better for you to hurt him than for him to wind up dead."

He looked away then, his eyes finding his brother. The medics had placed him on the gurney now and were preparing to wheel him out of the room. "Maybe," he muttered.

Just then, two uniformed officers approached. "Ms. Colton? Mr. Bowe? We need to take your statements, please."

Jillian went in one direction, Baldwin the other. It took a while, but she described everything that had happened and answered all of the officer's questions. While she talked, her condo slowly drained of people as Grace was loaded up by the medics and the other responding officers wrapped up their business.

Finally, the officer she was talking to finished questioning her. "Thanks for your time," he said, getting to his feet. "I'll be in touch over the next few days with some follow-up questions."

"That's fine," Jillian said automatically. She glanced around the room, expecting to find Baldwin still talking to the other officer.

He wasn't there.

He wasn't in the guest room, either. Or the bathroom, or the kitchen.

She was alone.

One week later

BALDWIN PULLED INTO a parking spot along Grave Gulch Boulevard and climbed out of his truck, then started walking across the street. The courthouse loomed large in front of him, the domed structure a tangible symbol of justice and the rule of law.

Today, at least, he knew justice would be served.

Jillian was inside right now, attending a hearing in which the DA was going to formally drop the charges against her. After Randall had been arrested, both Baldwin and the other officers at the scene had given statements about Randall's confession of framing Jillian. With so much evidence pointing at his brother, the case against Jillian had fallen apart. Bryce had called to let Baldwin know that today was the big day.

He found a spot outside the entrance to the courthouse, his stomach aflutter with nerves. Would Jillian be happy to see him? Or would she be angry with him for walking away without saying goodbye first?

He glanced around, taking note of the decorations hanging on the light poles up and down the street. The mayor had scheduled a celebratory parade to tout the hard work of the police department. Hopefully, the move would help restore relations between the

GGPD and the community. He'd seen on the news that the protests had stopped after Randall had been brought into custody. With his brother due to stand trial in the New Year, confidence in the police department was at an all-time high.

Part of him felt proud to have been involved in bringing his brother in. Shooting Randall had been one of the hardest things he'd ever done, but at the same time, it was a bit cathartic. In that split second, he'd realized that his family and their issues were all part of his past. They were never going to be close, never going to have a loving, supportive relationship. If Baldwin kept clinging to that misguided hope, it would sink him emotionally. He had to let them go.

He'd pulled the trigger, drawing a line under that part of his life so he could move forward, into the future.

With Jillian.

If she'd still have him.

He shifted, scuffing at the ground with the toe of his boot. He hadn't meant to leave without saying goodbye. But he'd been so twisted up inside he'd had to get away from everyone, get some air. Clear his mind of the shock of the moment and take stock of what he wanted in his life. So he'd laid low for a few days, figuring it all out. He was tired of working underground. His bank balance reflected his client's satisfaction for a job well done, but Baldwin wanted more. He craved legitimacy, to work out in the open again.

To be with Jillian. He knew through the grapevine that she'd been reinstated as a CSI for the Grave Gulch Police Department. Her life was getting back to normal, which was what she'd wanted.

And as for him? He could keep working in the shadows. Maintain his underworld contacts, his growing roster of anonymous clients. But if he did that, he'd be subject to the rules of that lifestyle. In certain circles, he would be a target. Along with anyone he loved.

After everything that had happened here, it wasn't a risk he was willing to take.

Jillian had already been through too much. Baldwin couldn't ask her to be with him if he had painted a target on her back.

The front doors to the courthouse opened, and a small group of people started walking down the steps. He picked her out of the group immediately, his eyes drawn to her as if she was some magnetic force.

She walked alongside an older man—her attorney, most likely. Her sister, brother and parents trailed a few steps behind. They were all smiling, and he could tell even from this distance that a weight had been lifted off their shoulders.

They stopped at the bottom of the steps, and Jillian hugged the older man. He walked away, while she and her family turned and started moving in Baldwin's direction.

He didn't move from his spot by the tree until she'd walked past him.

"Jillian Colton," he called out.

She froze, then slowly turned around to face him. Her family stopped, but when Bryce saw him, he gestured to his sister and parents to keep walking. Baldwin nodded at him in a silent expression of gratitude.

Jillian eyed him up and down. "You came back." Her tone was neutral, betraying no hint of her emotions.

Baldwin's anxiety made his hands shake. He could face down a lethal sniper, lead a squad into battle and perform first aid on a wounded buddy while under heavy fire, but standing in front of this slender woman in broad daylight on a public street was enough to make him crack.

"I shouldn't have left like that."

She tilted her head to the side. "No," she agreed. "I deserved better than that."

It was the truth. He thought about making excuses, wondered how he could explain what had been going through his mind at the time. Instead, he opted for the simpler answer.

"You're right," he said. "I'm so sorry. I had to figure some things out, and I needed to be alone to do it."

"And did you?" she asked, sounding a little curious. "Figure it out, I mean?"

He took a step closer, hoping she'd tolerate his presence. "I think so," he said quietly.

Jillian nodded. "That's good." She looked down and swallowed hard, then glanced back up at him. "What are you doing in Grave Gulch again?"

"I have unfinished business here." He risked another step, wanting so badly to touch her. But, no, he had to earn that privilege again.

"I see." She discreetly swiped at her eye and he realized she was trying hard not to cry. "Then I imagine you'll be off again, going to work for another client in search of a bad guy?"

"No."

Her head jerked up at his response. "What?"

"I said no."

Confusion danced across her face, along with something else: hope.

"I...don't understand," she said slowly. "I thought you loved your job. Are you taking a break or something?"

"Not exactly," he said, taking another step. "I found another job."

"Really? Doing what?" She was genuinely curious now and he resisted the temptation to smile.

"I'm going to be a private investigator," he said. "I start after the holidays."

Jillian nodded. "Good for you." A quick, sad smile flashed across her face. "I'm glad you're doing something different. I know you were good at being a bounty hunter, but now I don't have to worry about you living in the shadows."

He did smile then, touched by her admission that she worried about him still. "I haven't told you the best part," he said.

She lifted an eyebrow. "Oh? Well, don't keep me in suspense."

Baldwin took the final step, bringing him directly

in front of her. They were now only a few inches apart, close enough that he could see the amber flecks in her brown eyes. "I'll be working with the Grave Gulch Police Department."

Jillian sucked in a breath, her eyes going wide. "Are you serious?"

Baldwin nodded. "Have I ever lied to you?"

She shook her head, her gaze warming as she looked at him. "No. You haven't."

His hands itched to touch her but he held himself back. She had to make the first move. He needed to be sure she really wanted this.

Wanted him.

"So that means…" She trailed off.

"I'll be living here. Working here."

"No taking off for parts unknown," she said.

"Not anymore," he replied.

"And that unfinished business?"

"It's you," he said. "It's us."

"So there's an 'us'?" she asked.

The question made his heart skip a beat. This was it, the moment he was going to put it all on the line. He was about to take the biggest risk of his life, with no guarantee of success.

"There is if you want it," he replied quietly.

Jillian studied him for a moment, clearly thinking it over. Just when he thought she'd decided to let him down, she nodded and a smile spread across her face.

"Yes," she said. "I'd like that very much."

She jumped into his arms, wrapping hers around his neck. He dipped his head to kiss her, joy spreading through him as he held her against him once more. He wasn't sure what he'd done to deserve this woman, but now that he had her, he was never going to let her go again.

Epilogue

End of January

"Are you sure you like it? Because we can always exchange it for a different one."

Jillian smiled at Baldwin, then looked down at the ring on her left hand. He'd proposed that morning as they'd sipped coffee together. She'd said yes before he could even finish the question, and they'd spent the morning making love and planning their future.

"Baldwin, it's perfect. I love it and I love you."

It was the truth. He'd chosen a beautiful ring, a square-shaped diamond solitaire channel set in white gold. The ring was smooth all over, with no protruding prongs to catch on her gloves while she worked. Practical and romantic—a perfect reflection of the man himself.

"You won't hurt my feelings," he continued. "If you have something else in mind—"

She leaned over and kissed him, interrupting his ramblings. "No," she said firmly. "I have no intention of taking this ring off my finger. Now, are you ready to go inside?"

They were parked in the driveway of her mother's house—no, her parents' home, she reminded herself. Wes and her mother had been living together for some time now, but Jillian still slipped on occasion. She was doing better, though. They all were, especially Bryce. His relationship with Wes had deepened over the past few months. They could never regain the time they'd all lost, but at least they could move forward together.

"I'm ready," Baldwin said. "Let's go inside."

Her mother was hosting a family reunion of sorts, a party to celebrate the capture of Randall Bowe, and all the weddings, engagements and pregnancies that had happened over the past year.

She led Baldwin up to the house and walked in without bothering to knock. As soon as the door opened, she was hit with the soft buzz of conversation and the smell of her mother's sugar cookies. Her stomach growled loudly.

Baldwin suppressed a laugh. "No wonder you wanted to come inside," he teased her.

She took his hand. "Come on," she said. "Let's get some food and I'll introduce you to everyone."

It wasn't that simple, of course. As soon as they were spotted, a cheer of greeting went up in the room. They stopped to talk to everyone on the way to the kitchen, starting with Melissa. She pulled Jillian in for a hug as Baldwin shook hands with Antonio, Melissa's husband.

"I told you it would all work out," Melissa whispered.

"You were right," Jillian said softly. "You always are."

Melissa released her with a smile. "Go get some food and then come back and say that louder so my husband can hear you."

Jillian laughed and moved down the line to greet Grace and Camden. "Doing okay?" she asked as she hugged her cousin.

"Never better," Grace replied. "Looks like I could say the same for you." She touched Jillian's left hand with a smile.

"You're the first one to notice," Jillian said quietly.

"I'll let you break the news," Grace said. "Your mother will be thrilled. She hasn't stopped talking about that nice young man from the hospital since you got shot."

Jillian laughed. "Where is she?" She glanced around but didn't see Verity in the mix.

Grace nodded her head toward the kitchen. "Hard at work, as usual. We've all offered to help, but only Soledad and Olivia are allowed in there right now."

"At least she's letting them assist her," Jillian replied. Verity was infamous for driving everyone out of her kitchen and insisting on preparing everything herself. Apparently, she'd decided the baker and restaurateur of the family were skilled enough to contribute.

She and Baldwin made their way through the room, stopping here and there as they went. She introduced him to the relatives he hadn't met before, and their significant others. He and her cousin Clarke immediately hit it off; no surprise, as Clarke was also a PI working with the GGPD.

She left them talking and slipped away to find her mother. She poked her head into the warm kitchen to find the older woman arranging cookies on a plate while Soledad and Olivia chatted as they placed hors d'oeuvres on a platter.

Verity glanced up as she walked in. "Jillian! You made it!"

She walked over to hug her mother, then greeted the other women. "Sorry we're late."

"Not at all. I'm just happy you're here now." She took Jillian's hands in her own and her eyes widened. "Honey, do I feel a ring?" She lifted Jillian's left hand and let out a whoop. "It is! Oh, my goodness, it's gorgeous! Where is that man?"

She dropped Jillian's hand and barged into the other room, loudly calling Baldwin's name. A hush fell over the group and Jillian stepped into the room to see her mother reach for Baldwin, pulling him down for a hug. He embraced Verity, looking around for her, clearly hoping for some kind of explanation for this rather public display of affection.

Verity released him and wiped her eyes. "I am so happy," she said, reaching up to touch his cheek. Then she seemed to realize everyone was watching them. She glanced around and laughed. "Jillian, come here, honey."

Jillian walked forward to stand next to Baldwin, slipping her hand into his.

"They're engaged!" Verity announced, beaming with happiness and pride. "Isn't that wonderful! My baby is getting married!"

Everyone let out a cheer, and Wes, Bryce and Madison closed in to congratulate them.

As soon as her siblings stepped away, another round of family approached. The next few minutes were a blur of smiling faces, handshakes and hugs. After they'd spoken to everyone, Jillian took the opportunity to tug Baldwin into a quieter corner of the room.

"Doing okay?" she asked softly.

He nodded, looking a little shell-shocked. "I had no idea your family was this large," he confessed.

"It can be a lot to take in," she said. "Especially now that everyone has a partner. We've grown a lot in the past year."

"I don't know if I remember everyone's name." He sounded worried, as though he feared there might be some kind of test.

Jillian laughed. "Don't sweat it. You have the rest of your life to learn them all."

He leaned down to kiss her softly on the mouth. "I can't wait to get started."

Jillian wrapped her arms around him and rested her cheek against his chest, loving the solid feel of him. She could stand like this forever, holding Baldwin and basking in the glow of her family's happiness. They'd been through some dark times this year, but they'd all come through intact and together. In some ways, they were all better than ever.

She watched Antonio place his hand on Melissa's growing bump, smiled as Danny weaved through the crowd and felt a tug of longing as she saw her cousins Palmer with baby Lyra and Travis holding his newborn daughter.

"Someday," Baldwin said quietly, apparently reading her mind.

She looked up at him, needing to see his face. "Really?"

He nodded. "Yes. I want them. Do you?"

"Yes." Her smile grew until she feared her face would break. She did want to be a mother. But not right now. Still, knowing that she and Baldwin were on the same page gave her a sense of peace and reinforced her belief that they were meant to be together.

The sound of a fork hitting a glass rang through the room. Everyone focused on the center once more, where Wes and Verity stood together.

"Thank you all for coming today," Wes said. "It means a lot to have us all together again."

"We've lost some things over the past year," Verity said. "But as I look around, I see that this family has gained so much."

"Hear! Hear!" Geoff remarked, raising his glass.

Wes nodded at the older man. "With that in mind, we have one more announcement to make."

Verity smiled up at him. "We're going to be gaining another family member," she said. "Wes and I are getting married!"

"About time," shouted Frank, Verity's oldest brother.

Everyone laughed, and a new round of congratulations began.

Jillian and Baldwin were among the last to reach the happy couple. "Congratulations, Mom and Dad."

Wes teared up and pulled her in for a hug. "Thanks, baby," he said softly.

Verity wiped her eyes. "Who's hungry?" she called out. "I think it's time to eat." An affirmative noise rose up from the group and people started making their way into the dining room, where Verity had set up a table full of food.

Jillian and Baldwin hung back, letting the group move ahead. He glanced down at her. "I thought you were hungry?"

"I am," she said, smiling up at him. "But I'd rather be with you."

"You don't have to choose," he said, sliding his arm around her shoulders. "You're stuck with me forever now."

Her heart seemed to swell as they headed for the dining room. She was so happy in this moment it was a wonder she didn't burst with it.

"I'm counting on it," she said, slipping her arm around his waist. "Forever is exactly what I had in mind."

* * * * *

LET'S TALK

Romance

For exclusive extracts, competitions
and special offers, find us online:

f facebook.com/millsandboon

y @MillsandBoon

⬚ @MillsandBoonUK

Get in touch on 01413 063232

For all the latest titles coming soon, visit

millsandboon.co.uk/nextmonth

JOIN US ON SOCIAL MEDIA!

Stay up to date with our latest releases, author
news and gossip, special offers and discounts, and
all the behind-the-scenes action
from Mills & Boon...

 millsandboon

 millsandboonuk

 millsandboon

t might just be true love...

MILLS & BOON

Desire

Indulge in secrets and scandal, intense drama and plenty of sizzling hot action with powerful and passionate heroes who have it all: wealth, status, good looks…everything but the right woman.

MILLS & BOON

MODERN

Power and Passion

Prepare to be swept off your feet by sophisticated, sexy and seductive heroes, in some of the world's most glamourous and romantic locations, where power and passion collide.